A PARISIAN AFFAIR
AND OTHER STORIES

GUY DE MAUPASSANT (1850–1893), internationally acknowledged master of the short story, spent childhood alternately at the homes of his separated parents in Paris and the Normandy coastal resort of Etretat. As an adolescent, he was taken under the wing of Flaubert, a family friend who encouraged him in his efforts to become a writer. After a brief period in the army during the Franco-Prussian war, he became a minor civil servant at various ministries. He developed a variety of sporting skills to a high standard; rowing, sailing, fencing, etc. and became a crack shot. As a result of his many amorous affairs and of an inherited predisposition, he also developed syphilis. After the publication of 'Boule de Suif', the story which made his name overnight, he became hugely popular as a writer and his work was translated into many languages. He led a hectic social life, using his observations as copy for the over three hundred short stories and six novels he produced. He refused, however, the accolades which society was anxious to bestow upon him. His physical and mental health deteriorated until in 1891, after an attempted suicide, he was admitted into psychiatric care and died two years later.

SIÂN MILES was born and brought up in the bi-cultural atmosphere of Wales and educated there and in France where she lived for many years. She has taught at a number of universities both at home and abroad, including Tufts University in Massachusetts, Dakar University in Sénégal and York University in Toronto. She now teaches at Warwick University in England. Her publications include: *Simone Weil: An Anthology*, now in its third edition, *George Sand: Marianne*, a translation of Violet Trefusis' *Echo* and, in collaboration, Paul Valéry's *Cahiers/Notebooks*.

GUY DE MAUPASSANT

A Parisian Affair
and Other Stories

Translated with an Introduction and Notes by
SIÂN MILES

PENGUIN BOOKS

PENGUIN BOOKS

Published by the Penguin Group
Penguin Books Ltd, 80 Strand, London WC2R ORL, England
Penguin Putnam Inc., 375 Hudson Street, New York, New York 10014, USA
Penguin Books Australia Ltd, 250 Camberwell Road, Camberwell, Victoria 3124, Australia
Penguin Books Canada Ltd, 10 Alcorn Avenue, Toronto, Ontario, Canada M4V 3B2
Penguin Books India (P) Ltd, 11 Community Centre, Panchsheel Park, New Delhi – 110 017, India
Penguin Group (NZ), cnr Airborne and Rosedale Roads, Albany, Auckland 1310, New Zealand
Penguin Books (South Africa) (Pty) Ltd, 24 Sturdee Avenue, Rosebank 2196, South Africa

Penguin Books Ltd, Registered Offices: 80 Strand, London WC2R ORL, England

www.penguin.com

First published 2004

024

Copyright © Siân Miles, 2004
All rights reserved

Set in 10.25/12.25 pt PostScript Adobe Sabon
Typeset by Rowland Phototypesetting Ltd, Bury St Edmunds, Suffolk
Printed and bound in Great Britain by Clays Ltd, Elcograf S.p.A.

ISBN-13: 978-0-140-44812-2

www.greenpenguin.co.uk

Contents

Acknowledgements

I should like to acknowledge with gratitude permission by Editions Gallimard to use their Bibliothèque de la Pléiade edition of Maupassant: *Contes et Nouvelles* published in 1974.

I am very grateful to both Hilary Laurie, whose idea it was to produce a new selection of Maupassant short stories, and to Mark Treharne whose work is both an example and an inspiration, for guiding me into this hugely enjoyable project.

I have been helped throughout its development by a number of friends and colleagues without whom I would be lost, and who include: Marie-Thérèse and Tony Allen, Cara Chase, Catherine Hoskyns, Elsbeth Lindner, Shirin Rai, Sue Shaw, Helen Siebenmann and Jasper Snyder.

Others who have generously provided both practical and moral support and whom I warmly thank are Kate Astbury, Laura Barber, Paula Bartley, Hilary Bourdillon, Saskia Brown, Charlotte Brunsdon, David Carpanini, Jo Crozier, Jonathan Dudley, Fergus Durant, Janet Goodfellow, Barrie Hinksman, Jill Irving, Maryanne Izzard, Peter Larkin, Pauline Matarasso, Lajpat Rai, Douglas Smith, Jo Smithies, Ann Swarbrick, Alan Teuton and Raya Trofimowa.

Any errors of commission and omission remain my own.

Chronology

1850 Birth of Henry René Albert Guy de Maupassant on 5 August at Fécamp in Normandy.

1851 Coup d'état of Louis-Napoléon Bonaparte who proclaims himself Napoléon III the following year. Beginning of Second Empire, background to many of Maupassant's stories.

1856 Birth of Hervé, Maupassant's brother.

1857 Publication of Flaubert's *Madame Bovary* and Baudelaire's *Les Fleurs du mal*, as a result of which each author is subject of prosecution for offences against public morals.

1859–60 Maupassant a pupil at the Lycée Impérial Napoléon in Paris. After effective separation of parents, he moves with mother and brother to Etretat, on the Channel coast.

1863 Legal separation of Maupassant's parents. Salon des refusés in Paris shows work of Manet, Pisarro, Cézanne, et al. Maupassant attends Yvetot seminary.

1868 Expelled from hated Yvetot seminary. Enters lycée at Rouen. Flaubert and his friend the poet Louis Bouilhet take him under their wing.

1869 Moves to Paris to read law. Lives in same building as father at 2, rue Moncey.

1870 Outbreak of Franco-Prussian war. Called up and posted to Rouen. Defeat of the French at Sedan. Napoléon III taken prisoner. Fall of the Empire and proclamation of the Third Republic.

1871 Bombardment of Paris followed by Franco-Prussian armistice. Popular uprising of Paris Commune repressed with great savagery by Thiers government. Leaves army.

1872 Begins career as a clerk in various government ministries, beginning in Naval Administration.

1873 Appointed to Ministère de la Marine or French Admiralty. Acquires boat and sleeps at room near Argenteuil, on the river, twice a week. Becomes part of roistering river set. Develops fencing and shooting skills.

1874-5 First Impressionists exhibition *chez* the photographer Nadar. Meets influential Edmond de Goncourt at Flaubert's apartment in the rue Murillo. Also meets his polar opposite in character, the poet Mallarmé, and is invited to join the latter's select Thursday gatherings. Regular meetings with Huysmans, Zola and other writers. Spends Sundays with Flaubert. Confides to friend he has contracted the pox from which François I died, i.e. syphilis. Begins to place the articles and short stories he has begun to write. His first *conte*, 'La main d'écorché' ('The Shrivelled Hand') is published under the pseudonym Joseph Prunier in *L'Almanach lorrain de Pont-à-Mousson* in February 1875.

1878 Zola effects a meeting between Sarah Bernhardt and Maupassant to discuss a play he is writing. Works on his first novel. Through Flaubert, is appointed to Ministry of Education and resigns from Naval Administration.

1880 Publication in April of the short story 'Boule de Suif' which is to make his name. Heart trouble begins. Suffers from alopecia and increasingly poor vision. Throughout his life from now on his health is in constant decline. Death of Flaubert on 8 May and Maupassant becomes his literary executor. Begins to ease out of Ministry work, securing a succession of variously paid leaves of absence. Attempts to get Hervé a position with newly formed Panama Company. Begins affair with Gisèle d'Estoc.

1883 Publication of his first novel *Une Vie*, at first usefully banned from the Hachette chain of station bookshops. There now follows a ceaseless flow of short stories as Maupassant's name becomes well known and his writing is much in demand.

1884 Begins relationship with the Comtesse Potocka as well as a correspondence with Marie Bashkirtseff. Has house built on mother's land at Etretat and rents suite of rooms with cousin at a Paris hotel. Spends much time from now on in the south of France.

1885 Publication of his best-known novel, *Bel-Ami*, in serial form. With the proceeds buys a higher tonnage boat at Antibes to replace his *Louisette*. Helps Hervé set up horticultural business.

1886 Last exhibition of Impressionists in Paris. Narrowly misses having to fight a duel. Honour satisfied in time. Ever more prolific output of stories.

1887 Publication of *Mont-Oriol*, set in the Auvergne and reflecting life at a spa town. Signs petition protesting against construction of the Eiffel Tower. Work on *La Guillette*, his Normandy house. Balloon trip to Belgium generates publicity. Further travels in Italy and North Africa. Hervé begins to show signs of mental instability. Mother's chronic ill-health begins to deteriorate still further.

1888 Publication of *Pierre et Jean*, a study of jealousy, accounted by some to be his finest novel. Purchase of new boat, the *Zingara*, which becomes *Bel-Ami II*. Publication of a series of travel sketches, *Sur l'Eau*.

1889 Begins to oversee anthologizing and translation (into English, Russian, Spanish, German, etc.) of his now large number of short stories. Arranges with *Compagnie des Chemins de Fer de L'Ouest* for Zola to travel on engine of locomotive to research material for the latter's *La Bête humaine*. Opening of the International Exhibition in Paris. Publication of novel *Fort comme la mort*. Hervé sectioned at Lyon and dies on 13 November.

1890 Next collection of travel sketches, *La Vie errante*, published in serial form. Maupassant spends increasingly more time in south of France. Purchases bachelor flat in Paris. Publication of his last novel, *Notre Coeur*. Makes friends with Dr Henry Cazalis who, with colleague Dr Blanche, will attend him to the end of his life. Maupassant's illness reaches its apotheosis. The number of short stories he is able to write decreases.

1891 Maupassant's intellectual powers are now seriously on

the wane and he suffers from loss of memory and confusion. General paralysis of body begins to affect his mind.

1892 Attempts to slit his throat. Is admitted to clinic of Dr Blanche at Passy.

1893 Dies on 6 July.

Introduction

The circumstances surrounding the birth on 5 August 1850 of Guy de Maupassant are prophetically tinged with the fiction for which he was later to become so widely renowned. Although reliable evidence suggests he was born in the modest summer apartment of his grandmother in Fécamp, on the Normandy coast, his birth certificate gives as place of birth the imposing eighteenth-century Château de Miromesnil some ten miles inland and rented shortly before by his parents to ensure that their first-born should enter the world from as good an address as they could possibly afford.

The twenty-eight-year-old couple were an ill-assorted pair. Gustave de Maupassant, Guy's father, who on the same document describes his occupation as 'living on a private income', came from an upper-bourgeois, not to say aristocratic family and spent his time as a dandy and man about town. His wife Laure, née Le Poittevin, was the daughter of a traditional and prosperous Rouen businessman, owner of two important spinning-mills and with roots deep in the city's ship-building industry. Her family was linked through friendship with another eminent Rouennais family, that of Dr Flaubert, father of a very different Gustave, the future author of *Madame Bovary*. Laure's brother Alfred was, until his sudden and early death, one of the young Flaubert's closest friends and admirers. Each young man was a strong and formative influence upon the other, and the atmosphere prevailing throughout Laure's childhood and youth was conspicuously bookish. Given that Laure's grandmother was a highly witty eighteenth-century woman of letters and that Laure's own ambitions as a writer were thwarted, it is unsurprising that those she harboured for her elder son should also come to privilege the literary over all else.

The Maupassants spent just over three years at Miromesnil after Guy's birth, and when he was four, they moved out to less grand accommodation near Le Havre where, in 1856, his brother Hervé was born. The delights and freedoms associated with childhood spent at the seaside were tempered by less than idyllic scenes at home. The frequent fierce disagreements, quarrels and physical fights between their parents were a heavy and lasting influence upon the boys' future views of love and marriage and upon Guy's basic understanding of the relation between the two sexes.

When Guy was thirteen, Gustave and Laure de Maupassant drew up a private formal contract of separation, there being no legal divorce in France. Under its terms, Gustave was bound to support his family, which he did with a relatively generous allowance of 1,600 francs a year, at today's equivalent some £6,000. It also stipulated that both parents should be responsible for the care and education of the children. In this matter, the father was less scrupulous. He quickly withdrew to Paris, seeing his sons on occasional visits only, while Laure set up a home for them at Etretat and brought them up there alone.

Etretat was a small fishing village with a large beach surrounded by spectacular cliffs. Already a popular bathing spot, when Laure and the boys settled there it was becoming an increasingly fashionable resort, with a casino frequented by the many artists and celebrities now beginning to buy or rent summer cottages and elegant villas in its vicinity. The composer Offenbach was one such, and Monet, Courbet and Corot used the many local beauty spots as the subjects of their land- and seascapes.

For the next twelve years, apart from some brief spells visiting his father in Paris, and two terms at school in the capital, Guy and his brother were brought up by Laure with what has been described as a surfeit of maternal affection, pride and hope. Many years later, after his son had achieved widespread recognition, Maupassant *père* joked, 'Guy owes to me his sexual potency. To his mother he owes what is worst in him, that is to say, all his other so-called development.' The tensions between the two parents had clearly not diminished with the passage of time, but it is equally clear from Guy's own accounts that these years were for him some of the happiest of his entire existence.

It was here that he became familiar with the Norman peasant life so often portrayed in his short stories and here that he began to develop the passion for boats and the water which was to become such an important part of his own life. He mixed easily with the local fishermen and their sons as well as with the sons of the farms and smallholdings surrounding the town. He also mixed with the smart summer set of Etretat and came to know the characteristics of both populations, moving without difficulty from one to the other and developing both the social and the physical skills associated with each.

If his practical education *en plein air* was wide and comprehensive, his intellectual and literary development under the supervision of his mother was no less rigorous. After a brief, unhappy spell at the Lycée Impérial Napoléon in Paris, he returned to Normandy where a local priest taught him his catechism, his mother read him Shakespeare and another cleric gave him instruction in French grammar, maths and Latin.

Laure was by all accounts a neurotic and controlling mother to whom Guy was always closely, some would say unhealthily attached. Under the circumstances, his sexual development might have been for those days problematic. In the event, it was both rapid and precocious. At the age of thirteen, his first sexual experience – with a country girl one year his senior – was the prelude to an adolescence and manhood in which love affairs would feature prominently, both in his life and his work. His own sexual appetite, athleticism and stamina became his trademark as a young man. In combination with an inherited susceptibility, these led him to contract the venereal disease which was ultimately to be the cause of his death.

In this same fourteenth year, an equally important event took place. He was sent off to board at the seminary of Yvetot, which he hated. Particularly loathsome to him were the discipline and bigotry of the establishment and the curtailment of the freedom he had by now come to take for granted. He rebelled, misbehaved and, finally, was expelled when an allegedly obscene poem, written on the occasion of a pretty girl cousin's marriage, was discovered by the authorities.

It was during the hiatus between his ignominious but welcome dismissal from the seminary and his enrolment at the Lycée of Rouen that his first and unexpected meeting with a literary figure took place. One morning, on the beach at Etretat, he heard cries for help coming from the direction of the Petite Porte, one of the rocky points off the coast. Guy quickly became involved in the rescue of the stranger who was then pulled from the water to safety on board one of the local fishing boats. Grateful and touched by the boy's gesture, the swimmer, one Charles Algernon Swinburne, invited him to lunch the next day. Also resident at the remote little cottage the homosexual Swinburne had rented was an intimate of his, a Welshman by the name of Powell, as well as a somewhat anti-social pet monkey called Nip. The place, which Swinburne had named Chaumière Dolmancé after the protagonist of de Sade's *La philosophie dans le boudoir*, was unusually furnished and decorated. The boy was shown grotesque objects as well as male nude photographs and various bones or *ossements* scattered about. The wraith-like Swinburne reminded Guy of Edgar Allan Poe who, since the time of Baudelaire, had been regarded by the French literary world as the embodiment of Anglo-Saxon sophistication. On a subsequent visit he was given a shrivelled hand as a souvenir and based several of his more macabre stories on this grisly relic of an encounter he was never to forget. The monkey later came to a bad end at the hands of a valet and was buried under a tombstone marked, with gallows humour, NIP.

During the time Maupassant spent as a boarder at the Lycée in Rouen, he was fortunate enough to be taken under the wing of two very different men of letters. One was Louis Bouilhet, a well-established poet, and the other, after a series of carefully worded letters from his mother, the great Flaubert himself. Maupassant was schooled rigorously by them in the art of writing. Masters of their respective crafts, they were also sympathetic and friendly towards the boy's development as a poet and encouraged him in his efforts. The two bachelor artists' mixture of serious arguments about literary matters and bawdy humour over sexual affairs was an irresistible one to the fatherless young man and their influence upon him was both incalculable and enduring.

Bouilhet died the year Maupassant passed his *baccalauréat* and from then on it was Flaubert who became his permanent mentor. After being cleared of the charges of offending public morals with the publication of *Madame Bovary* in 1857, Flaubert became a well-established literary figure. Laure had taken care to remind him, in the unlikely event he should have forgotten it, of the great friendship which had existed between him and her late brother and played mercilessly on his feelings, suggesting he might take some responsibility for the fate of their dear Alfred's nephew. In particular, she was anxious to secure his support in continuing to instruct and encourage her son in his literary ambition. Flaubert responded with generosity and managed to instil into his protégé, whose initial efforts were clumsy and banal, the belief that the most important aspect of writing was to learn to see with his own eyes. The images produced must be those of his own vision and based on careful, attentive, idiosyncratic and possibly unique observation of the particular.

This precept, as well as many others, he carried with him to Paris where he was now to join his father and read law. His life as a student, however, was neither an exciting nor a long one. He did not experience the bohemian existence for which university life in Paris is well known, but at his father's side saw rather more of the sophisticated social life of the capital. His stay there was cut short in any case by political events and his student days abruptly curtailed by the outbreak of the Franco-Prussian War.

On 19 July 1870, France declared war on Prussia and Maupassant joined the army. Once enlisted, he was posted to the second division of the commissariat at Le Havre from where he was sent as a messenger to Rouen. He spent the short-lived but disastrous war going between that city and Paris where, after the terrible siege and weeks of suffering and starvation, the equally traumatic and brutal suppression of the Commune took place. The war had a profound effect on him, as it did on the whole of France, which was obliged to acknowledge a crushing defeat and endure occupation. Many of his most successful stories, including his best-known work, the *nouvelle* or long short story 'Boule de Suif', are based on his experience of that period and its effect upon ordinary people of both sides. The complacency and petty-mindedness of the bourgeoisie, who were more interested in the continued running of their businesses than in the defence of their country, is a theme to which he often returns in his writing.

Once the war and the Prussian occupation were over, he felt it was time to look for a job. His experiences as a soldier had given him both confidence and resourcefulness and he now decided to try to embark on a life of independence. He applied for, and was appointed to, a post in the Naval Administration, from which he moved to the Central Administration and subsequently the Department for the Colonies. Guy remained at the Colonial Office until 1877 when he joined the Ministry of Education. His knowledge and experience of the ministries, the world of the civil servant and in particular that of its myriad clerks and functionaries provided rich material for the stories he would later write. His years as a minor bureaucrat were for him, however, the most devastatingly miserable of his life and despite the fact that they provided him with valuable experience on which to draw in his writing, they also took their toll upon his spirit. That he managed to rise above the pettiness of such an existence, surrounded as he was by those whom he considered philistines, is a tribute both to Flaubert's constant care and interest and to his own tenacity in continuing to work at writing at night after a mind-numbing day totting up figures at the office. His letters home during this period make sad reading, and his longing for the open air and the water were satisfied only by considerable physical effort.

He acquired a boat and rented a small room in a house at Argenteuil on the banks of the Seine downstream from the centre of Paris. After work, he would take the train out to this idyllic spot and go sailing or rowing before dawn and his return to work. He became part of a gang of pleasure-seeking young men who loved the social activity of the landing-stages immortalized in the contemporary paintings of Renoir. The orgiastic character of his riverside life, though hugely enjoyable, resulted in his contracting syphilis and he now began to suffer from the ill-health that was to dog him for the rest of his days.

Eventually Maupassant managed to obtain tenure and thereby relative security at his hated job. More importantly, through Flaubert, he also gained entrée into the literary world of Paris. He began to meet on a regular basis such well-established writers as Turgenev, Alphonse Daudet, Emile Zola, Huysmans, Edmond de Goncourt and a host of others, as well as an extremely powerful group of publishers and editors who were also habitués of the writers' circle.

Through this network he was able to place the work he was now beginning to produce with increasing ease and fluency, and in 1875 his first *conte*, a ghost story called 'La main d'écorché' ('The Shrivelled Hand'), was published. From then on, he contributed poems, reviews and literary chronicles to various newspapers and journals including *La République des Lettres*, *La Nation*, and *La Nouvelliste de Rouen*. Two years later, he had become an accredited member of a group of young Naturalists under the leadership of Zola, and in 1880 published in the latter's collection *Les soirées de Médan*, the key work 'Boule de Suif', which was to make his name overnight.

The life of Maupassant, whose fame now began to spread not only in France but also abroad, was changed radically. Hugely in demand and increasingly certain of an income from his writing, he was able to resign from the Ministry, travel a little in Italy, North Africa and England, and begin to prepare himself for the writing of novels as well as short stories. His subjects, hitherto predominantly peasants, clerks and prostitutes, now became more exclusive to include the property-owning and professional classes. His material circumstances improved still further as his popularity increased. He had a house built at Etretat, bought better and better boats, and finally was able to spend more time on the Riviera at Cannes, Nice and Antibes. It also enabled him to form associations of varying intimacy with a series of wealthy, well-placed and influential society women.

Success and fame now propelled Maupassant into the sparkling, hedonistic world founded on booming industry, finance

and colonial development. His rise up the social ladder is par-
tially imitated by the hero of his second novel, *Bel-Ami*, published in 1885, in which the machinations of the journalistic
world and the hidden adulteries controlling politics and finance
are exposed. Observing from within, Maupassant presents a
harshly realistic account of the double standards at play in
society during the Third Republic.

He continued to publish short stories and a further four novels
but, despite the respect and prestige he now commanded, there
was a marked and growing worry in his mind. His health was
beginning to deteriorate mentally as well as physically. He began
hallucinating, imagining he had a doppelganger on his tracks,
and wrote increasingly on the subject of derangement and madness. Symptoms of megalomania began to manifest themselves,
and his younger brother's madness and then death exacerbated
his already fragile condition. The eye trouble from which he
had for long suffered became increasingly serious and he began
to entertain thoughts of suicide. Numerous doctors, including
his friends Dr Blanche and Dr Cazalis, were consulted as he
shuttled between the place he now owned in Cannes, and Nice
where he had installed his sick and ageing mother. Eventually,
the balance of his mind became so disturbed that he attempted
to kill himself by cutting his throat. In January 1892 he was
voluntarily admitted to a *maison de santé* in Passy, near Paris,
where he died on 6 July of the following year at the age of
forty-three.

Of the roughly 330 stories Maupassant wrote during his life,
most were produced during his *decennium mirabile* 1880–90,
that is to say the decade between the death of Flaubert and
the beginning of the *belle époque*. This selection represents,
therefore, approximately one-tenth of his total output and contains some of the most familiar as well as the finest of his oeuvre.
It differs from previous anthologies in English in two important
respects. First, although a good, representative proportion of
the best-known stories set in Normandy is included (such as
'Boule de Suif', 'Hautot & Son', 'The Christening'), many of
the stories here show Maupassant writing about the lives of

those earning their living in the increasingly important urban settings of the time, notably Paris. In 'The Jewels', for example, Monsieur Lantin's future wife and her mother have moved from the provinces to the capital in order to better themselves. The two peace-loving anglers caught up in the war in 'Two Friends' earn their livings as a Parisian watchmaker and haberdasher respectively. The collection also includes accounts of the *demi-monde* vacationing at Riviera resorts such as Nice and Biarritz (as in 'Rose'), as well as those travelling to other similar destinations, using the relatively recently established railway system beginning to link French citizens in ways hitherto undreamt of ('Train Story', 'Idyll' and 'Encounter').

Furthermore, many previous English-language collections, both British and American, include a preponderance of stories (with the exception of 'Boule de Suif') showing Maupassant as, if not misogynistic, at least deeply cynical in his portrayal of women. His reputation in Victorian and, even more so, Edwardian Great Britain has been perpetuated by successive generations of editors who present stories emphasizing a cavalier or superior attitude to the opposite sex, cautionary tales, possibly, for the use of unsuspecting milords up against the perceived *rouerie feminine* or wiles of French minxes under the Entente Cordiale. This collection seeks to redress that previous imbalance by attempting to show the great struggle the writer engages in to resist the commonly held view that it was both necessary and laudable in a man to adopt such an attitude. In reality, there exists in Maupassant deep sympathy for the often ignominious position of women in the society in which he lived, and his portrayal of the female characters in 'Mother of Invention' and 'Minor Tragedy' for example, is untypical of his times. That women often feature in his tales as devious, fickle, mendacious and greedy there is no doubt. Stories such as 'Laid to Rest' and 'The Million' amply illustrate this. But so too do the male figures, who, like the females, also frequently exhibit other equally unattractive characteristics. We need look no further than the stupid and brutal count in 'A Woman's Confession' or the insufferably chauvinistic doctor in 'Madame Husson's Rose King' to note Maupassant's even hand.

In the Normandy farm and peasant life of his time, harsh conditions bred equally harsh and unforgiving social attitudes. But even with increasing education and urbanization, Maupassant witnessed in the capital and at the fashionable resorts frequented by the wealthy an equally brutish ethos which he exposes with both frankness and humour. Under a façade of opulence and sophistication, his characters operate on a level no higher, as Henry James put it, than the gratification of an instinct. That instinct was to follow blindly and unquestioningly the exhortation made earlier in the century by Guizot but frequently attributed to Napoleon III: '*Enrichissez-vous*!' ('Get rich!').

Although Maupassant earned his living through the observation and exposure of the society in which he mixed, he refused all of the many honours which it was keen to award him. Behaving as the polar opposite of Flaubert's Lheureux, that embodiment of Second Empire values in *Madame Bovary*, he turned down the *Légion d'honneur* as well as the offer of membership into the highest ranks of French 'grands hommes', the Académie Française.

Similarly, he refused to write literature which was 'sympathique et consolant', calling it 'tarte à la crème!' Of the themes underlying these stories, which are both many and varied, it is not surprising, given Maupassant's history, to find those of filial and parental relations ('Monsieur Jocaste'), childlessness and surrogacy ('Duchoux'), regret and betrayal ('Regret' and 'Femme Fatale'). There is often conflict within them (as in 'A Bit of the Other') between the idealism of love and the reality of lived experience. Some of the tales express violent emotions and no writer better presents the dish of revenge stone cold. No story illustrates this more clearly than 'Mother of Invention', in which a wife refuses for six long years to tell her husband which of their children is not his, then finally turns the whole situation on its head.

Maupassant's attitude towards retribution in the form of war was for many years untypical of serving soldiers. While he had little love for the strutting, spike-helmeted Prussians under whose heel the French squirmed when he was a young man,

and about whom he had recurring nightmares long after
their departure, he is able to present their blue-uniformed hussars as no worse in their attitude towards the civilian population than the Light Infantry of the French army. Such views
as he expressed were considered highly unpatriotic but Maupassant stuck to his literary guns with courage and steadfast-
ness, emphasizing in his masterly and lengthy 'Boule de Suif',
as well as in 'Mother Sauvage', both the futility and barbarity
of war.

A comparable tension between the primitive and the civilized
is brought out in the several stories connected, in one way or
another, with hunting, shooting and fishing. A first-class all-
round sportsman, Maupassant is incomparable in conveying
the thrill of the chase as well as the sights, sounds and particularly the smells of a variety of natural surroundings under dif-
fering climates and weathers, as in 'Cockcrow' and 'Love'. He
is wonderfully sensual, as in 'Moonlight', in his descriptions of
night and the river, when all the human perceptions, including
the olfactory, are heightened. Indeed, as Henry James writes in
Partial Portraits 'Human life in his pages appears for the most
part as a concert of odours.' Some might argue that not for
nothing have the French, of all European nations, come to
dominate the culture of perfume. In the areas of both taste and
smell and their influence on the mind, on the faculty of memory,
and on the emotions, the contributions of Maupassant, Colette
and of course others such as Proust, are important to the study
of a field still to this day in its infancy.

When Maupassant met the schoolboy Proust in 1885, it was,
of course, in Paris. During Maupassant's lifetime the capital was
enjoying what might be described as its defining moment. His
parents' generation, and he as a young man under the Second
Empire, had witnessed the virtually wholesale destruction of the
old, medieval Paris and its transformation under the Baron
Haussmann into the architecturally elegant and logically
planned city we know today. Accompanying industrialization,
radical changes in its social life were well under way, with the
nineteenth-century equivalent of shopping malls established in
the glassed-in arcades, department stores opening for the first

time and, on the wide new boulevards, large terrace cafés to replace the earlier, smaller and more private *cercles*.

The newly laid out city parks and *buttes* or escarpments were happy hunting grounds for both the *flâneur* and the pick-up. Shops, which hitherto had been smaller, more intimate venues for negotiation became places of display, often with pretty women at the counters acting as attraction. A new, and to him suspect, spirit of exhibitionism was beginning to manifest itself, culminating in what he regarded as the ultimate monstrosity of the Eiffel Tower, built for the Paris Exhibition of 1889. In 'A Parisian Affair', a story in which the wife of a country solicitor daringly seeks in Paris the excitement missing in her home life, he is quick to note the proliferation of objects and *bibelots* with which the crowded, cluttered, overstuffed and overdecorated interiors of home are filled. He speculates, again before his time, on the meaning behind these emblems of acquisition and collection. Stories such as 'Encounter' and 'New Year's Gift' hint at the reification and commodification of girls and women as he gives telling glimpses of the fake princesses, the mock marquises and, of course, their moneyed manipulators. The time is ripe for managers such as Svengali and Professor Higgins, types whose names, associated with baser motives, are legion under the Third Republic.

Mesmerism, hypnotism, magnetism, spiritualism and even vampirism are buzzwords of the day, and Maupassant in these stories provides examples of his belief that the instruments of perception possessed by humankind are wholly unreliable. His forays into the world of the supernatural in stories such as 'The Horla' and 'Who Knows?' are linked to the new theories of evolution being explored by the scientific and literary naturalists of the time. To a writer like Maupassant, these tentative explorations into human psychology often lurch away from the scientific to the horrific. Uncertainty and doubt concerning the unknown and the unconscious assume the terrifying aspect of hallucination and madness. Though his aim is to tear off the mask which obscures and distorts, stories reveal the mortal fear engendered by the prospect of seeing what lies beneath. In most of the tales, however, a strong sense of fun and vitality is conveyed and an intoxicating *joie de vivre* leaps off the page. Vigour, energy and raunchiness characterize his richly comic vision of the human condition.

His preferred medium, the *conte*, is ideally suited to a writer whose vision of the world is fragmented, disjointed or partial, and where abiding constants are conspicuous by their absence. Maupassant often frames the stories by placing them in the context of either the beginning or the final stages of some social gathering or other: men telling stories after supper at the club (as in 'Laid to Rest' and 'The *Lull-a-Bye*') or, as in 'Happiness', a mixed group chatting in crepuscular light before the lamps are brought in. Often the narrator is established from the start as some kind of authority, a doctor, say, as in 'Train Story', or a famous faded beauty as in 'A Woman's Confession'. Though this device has fallen somewhat out of fashion, it has two distinct advantages, one peculiar to Maupassant's time and one applicable today.

First, since the stories mostly appeared initially in the newspaper, sometimes in *feuilleton* or serial form and often on the front page, the frame acted as a means of clearly signalling a piece of fiction, in contrast to the many news items with which it had to compete for attention. Second, it provides a sense of continuity with strong links to the oral tradition of story-telling, a kind of once-upon-a-time which evokes the magic of being read to before bed as a child and sets up a pleasurable sense of anticipation mixed with a willing suspension of disbelief.

Rarely do the stories exceed 2,000–3,000 words in length. Maupassant is working under what Baudelaire describes as 'les bénéfices éternels de la contrainte' ('the infinitely beneficial influence of constraint') in which less means more. His style is therefore highly economical, with sentences sometimes as brief as two words. The strokes are swift, spare and deliberate in an effort to achieve concentration and distillation. He is often concerned with recording one single, sometimes life-changing instant. Like the best of the Impressionist painters who were his contemporaries, and following Japanese wisdom in the concept of *utsuroi*, or point of change, he manages to convey the timeless fragility of the moment as well as the flux in which it occurs.

When Maupassant himself takes the stage as narrator, he often appears as a type: Maupassant the sailor ('At Sea'), the Norman ('Hautot & Son'), the civil servant ('The Jewels'), the sportsman ('Coward'), or the traveller ('Minor Tragedy'). Looking for the drama concealed beneath the surface of everyday life, he finds undercurrents which go unnoticed by others and concludes that chance rules all. Contrary to popular belief, the trick endings often associated with his stories are comparatively rare, though a sting in the tail is a characteristic feature. No morals are drawn and the irony which informs his work shows him anticipating our own times.

For many writers, including the austere James in his *Partial Portraits*, they are 'a collection of masterpieces'. He conveys no disrespect in adding that 'as a commentator, Monsieur de Maupassant is slightly common while as an artist he is wonderfully rare'. In the eyes of his friend Turgenev, through whom his name became well known in Czarist Russia, he is an admired and esteemed colleague. Later, Joseph Conrad in his *Notes on Life and Letters* was to join the ranks of the many who acknowledge him as the master of the short story and see the consummate simplicity of his technique as stemming from moral courage. Like Elizabeth Bowen, who translated him and recognized him as a quintessentially French writer, Conrad notes that he 'neglects to qualify his truth with the drop of facile sweetness' and 'forgets to strew paper roses over the tombs'. Later writers still, like Maugham and Hemingway, acknowledge with gratitude their debt to him. Ultimately, however, his reputation at the beginning of the twenty-first century depends, Gentle Readers, on those like yourselves in whose hands this book now lies.

Further Reading

On Maupassant's life and work

Chaplin, Peggy, *Guy de Maupassant: Boule de Suif* (Durham: University of Durham Press, 1988)

Conrad, Joseph, *Notes on Life and Letters* (London: Dent, 1921)

Galsworthy, John, *Castles in Spain and Other Screeds* (New York: Scribner's, 1921)

Ignotus, Paul, *The Paradox of Maupassant* (London: University of London Press, 1966)

James, Henry, *Partial Portraits* (London: Macmillan, 1888)

Lerner, M. G., *Maupassant* (London: George Allen and Unwin, 1975)

Steegmuller, F., *Maupassant* (London: Collins, 1950)

Sullivan, E. D., *Maupassant: The Short Stories* (London: Edward Arnold, 1962)

On contemporary French literature, culture and history

Magraw, Roger, *France 1815–1914: The Bourgeois Century* (London: Fontana, 1983)

Moretti, Franco, *Atlas of the European Novel* (London and New York: Verso, 1998)

Rigby, Brian (ed.), *French Literature, Thought and Culture in the Nineteenth Century* (London: Macmillan, 1993)

Watson, Janell, *Literature and Material Culture from Balzac to Proust* (Cambridge: Cambridge University Press, 1999)

Zeldin, Theodore, *France 1848–1945* (Oxford and New York: Oxford University Press, 1973)

On nineteenth-century Paris

Benjamin, Walter, *Charles Baudelaire: A lyric poet in the era of high capitalism* (London: Verso, 1983)
—— *The Arcades Project* (Cambridge, MA, and London: Belknap, 1999)
Burton, Richard, *The* Flâneur *and his City* (Durham: University of Durham Press, 1994)
Prendergast, C., *Paris in the Nineteenth Century* (Oxford: Blackwell, 1992)
Seigel, Jerrold, *Bohemian Paris* (London: Penguin Books, 1987)

Translator's Note

The stories are taken from the text of the standard two-volume *Bibliothèque de la Pléiade* edition of Maupassant *Contes et Nouvelles* edited by Louis Forestier and published by Gallimard in 1974.

BOULE DE SUIF[1]

For several days in succession remnants of the routed army[2] had been passing through the town. Formerly disciplined units had now turned into a disorganized rabble and separated from their regiments and colours, men with dirty, unkempt beards and uniforms in tatters now dragged their feet listlessly on. All the men looked crushed and exhausted, incapable of thought or resolve, marching out of sheer habit and collapsing with fatigue whenever they came to a halt. Bent under the weight of their rifles, they consisted mostly of reservists who until call-up were easy-going men used to minding their own business. These were combined with fit young conscripts, easily excited, easily scared and prone in equal measure to fight or flight. Mixed in with the latter and quickly identifiable by their red breeches were a few regulars, the remains of some division pulverized in battle, some sombrely uniformed gunners and a sprinkling of infantrymen of various sorts. The occasional glint of a helmet flashed as a dragoon lumbered clumsily in the steps of lighter soldiers of the line. Detachments of *francs-tireurs*[3] also passed through, their bandit-like appearance contrasting vividly with their grandiose names: 'Avengers of Defeat', 'Citizens of the Tomb', 'Brothers to the Death'. Their leaders were former drapers, corn-merchants, soap- and tallow-dealers, turned soldiers by force of circumstance and officers on the strength of a fat wallet or a long moustache. Armed to the teeth and covered in gold-braided flannel, in loud, boastful voices they discussed plans of campaign as if the burden of the dying homeland rested on their broad shoulders alone. In fact, however, they often went in fear of their own men who, though brave in the extreme, were often criminal characters to whom rape and pillage were second nature.

Rumour had it that the Prussians were on the point of entering Rouen. The National Guard[4] who for the previous two months had been carefully reconnoitring the nearby woods, sometimes shooting their own sentries in the process and preparing for action whenever a rabbit stirred in the bushes, had now returned to their firesides. With them, the arms, the uniforms and the entire military apparatus which had made them the terror of the highroads for miles around, had all suddenly disappeared for good.

The last remaining French soldiers had finally crossed the Seine to reach Pont-Audemer via Saint-Sever and Bourg-Achard. In the rear, flanked by two staff-officers, their despairing general walked. Incapable of commanding this undisciplined mob, he was bewildered by the disarray in which his normally victorious nation now found itself and, despite the legendary courage shown, by the disastrous scale of its defeat.

A deep quiet, an atmosphere of silent, terrified foreboding hung over the city. Many of its inhabitants, fat and flabby businessmen waiting anxiously for the conquerors to come, trembled with fear lest the roasting spits and long kitchen knives of their comfortable homes be taken for weapons. Life seemed to have ground to a halt. Shops were closed and streets deserted. From time to time a stealthy figure slithered by, frightened by the silence, and keeping close to the shadows of the walls.

The strain of waiting made everyone long for the enemy to arrive.

On the afternoon following the departure of the French troops, a few Uhlans[5] appeared out of the blue and galloped through the town. A short while later, a dark mass of troops swept down the hill of Sainte-Catherine as two further waves of invasion flooded the approaches from Darnetal and Boisguillaume. The advance guard of the three corps, arriving simultaneously, linked up on the Place de l'Hôtel de Ville. Along all the neighbouring streets, German troops poured, making the cobblestones ring with the heavy, measured stamp of their battalions.

Orders shouted in a foreign, guttural tongue echoed between

the walls of the houses, which appeared dead and deserted. Behind closed shutters many eyes watched the victors. The latter, according to the rules of war, were now masters both of the city and of the lives and fortunes of its denizens. These, in their darkened rooms, had fallen victim to the panic engendered by natural disasters, those devastating upheavals of the earth against which neither wisdom nor strength is of any avail. For the same feeling re-emerges each time the established order of things is upset, when security is destroyed and when everything protected by the laws of man or of nature finds itself at the mercy of some brutal, unreasoning force. The earthquake which crushes an entire population under the rubble of its houses; the river in swollen spate sweeping away the corpses of drowned peasants along with the bodies of their cattle and the rafters torn from their roofs; the glorious army which slaughters all who resist, takes others prisoner, pillaging by right of the sword, praising God to the roar of cannon; all of these are so many terrifying scourges which destroy our belief in eternal justice and any trust we may have been taught to place in divine protection or the power of human reason.

Small detachments of men were soon knocking on the door of every house and disappearing within. The time had come for the vanquished to show courtesy to the conquerors. After a short while, once their initial terror had loosened its grip, a new sort of calm descended. In many homes, a Prussian officer ate with the family. Sometimes he was sufficiently civil as to express polite sympathy with France, and distaste for his own part in the war. This sentiment was gratefully accepted by his hosts and, besides, who knew when they would be glad of his protection? If they handled matters diplomatically with him, perhaps not so many men would be billeted on them. Why offend someone who had complete power over you? Such an attitude would smack more of temerity than courage, and temerity was no longer one of the failings of the burghers of Rouen as it had been in the days when the heroic defence of their town had brought them both honour and glory.[6] Lastly, they found their greatest justification in traditional French urbanity: it was perfectly permissible to act politely to the foreign soldier in your

own home provided you demonstrated little friendliness toward
him in public. Outside they were strangers, but in the house you
and he could chat away together as long as you liked. The
German would stay on with the family a little longer each
evening, basking in the warmth of his new home from home.

The town itself gradually began to reassume its normal
appearance. Though the French were slow to re-emerge, the
streets swarmed with Prussian soldiers. And indeed, it had to be
said, these Blue Hussars arrogantly trailing their instruments of
death along the pavements were no more contemptuous of
ordinary civilians than the French Light Infantry who had sat
drinking in exactly the same cafés no more than a year before.

Nevertheless, there was something in the air, some strange-
ness hard to pin down, an unbearably alien atmosphere which
hung about like a smell. It was the feel of Occupation. It per-
meated homes as well as public places, altered the taste of things
and made people feel they were living in some foreign land
surrounded by dangerous tribes of barbarians.

The conquerors demanded money and lots of it at that. The
rich inhabitants kept paying up as of course they could afford
to do. But the more a Norman businessman's wealth grows, the
more keenly does he feel any sacrifice of it, and the more he
suffers to see his fortune pass into the hands of another.

Meanwhile, five or six miles downstream, towards Croisset,[7]
Dieppedalle or Biessart, bargees and fishermen often hauled up
the bodies of German soldiers bloated under their uniforms,
stabbed or kicked to death, thrown over a parapet into the
water, their heads smashed in with a stone. All the secret acts of
vengeance, the brutal yet understandable deeds of quiet heroism,
the silent attacks more dangerous than pitched battle and less
glorious in consequence, all slid downwards into the bed of the
river. For hatred of the Stranger will always arm the intrepid
few ready to give up their lives for their principles.

At length, since the invaders, while imposing a rule of iron
upon the town, had not committed any of the atrocities which
rumour had attributed to them throughout the course of their
triumphal progress, confidence began to return to the populace
and the desire to conduct business stirred again in the hearts

of the local tradesmen. Some of them had major commercial interests in Le Havre, still in the hands of the French. They were keen therefore to try and reach that port overland via Dieppe and thence by ship. Using the influence of the German officers whom they had come to know, they managed to secure a transport permit from the general in command.

Accordingly, a large, four-horse coach was hired for the journey. Ten people reserved places on board and it was decided to meet one Tuesday morning before daybreak so as not to attract attention. For some time now the ground had been frozen hard, and on the Monday, at about three in the afternoon, great dark clouds from the north brought snow which fell continuously all that evening and throughout the night.

At half past four in the morning, the travellers met in the courtyard of the Hôtel de Normandie where they were to board the coach. They were still half-asleep and shivering with cold under their wraps. It was hard for them to make each other out in the dark, and with so much heavy winter clothing on they all looked like portly priests in long cassocks. Two of the men, however, recognized each other; a third joined them and the trio stood chatting.

'I'm taking my wife out of this,' said one.

'So am I.'

'Me too.'

The first man added: 'We won't be coming back to Rouen in a hurry, and if the Prussians advance on Le Havre, we'll be taking off for England.'

Being like-minded fellows, all three had made similar plans for the future. Still there was no sign of the horses. Every so often a small lantern carried by an ostler appeared in one dark doorway only to disappear into another. The sound came occasionally of horses' hooves stamping on the ground, muffled by the dung in the stalls. From the far end of the building the voice of a man swearing at the animals could also be heard. A faint tinkling of bells indicated that the harness was being put on and this sound was soon transformed into a continuous jingle, changing rhythm with the horse's movements, stopping occasionally and then starting up again with a sudden jerk and the dull thud of an iron-shod hoof hitting the ground. Suddenly the door closed. Silence fell. The frozen townsfolk stopped talking and stood there, stiff and motionless.

A curtain of white flakes swirled ceaselessly to the ground, blurring outlines and powdering every object with a dusting of ice. In the deep silence of the town buried in wintry stillness nothing could be heard save the vague, mysterious rustling whisper, more sensation than sound, of the falling snow, a mingling of weightless particles which seemed to be filling the sky and covering the world.

The man reappeared with his lantern, leading at the end of a rope a miserable and unwilling horse. He tethered it to the hitching post and fastened the traces, spending a long time fixing the harness with one hand while the other held the lantern. As he was about to fetch the second horse, he noticed the travellers standing motionless and already white with snow from head to toe.

'Why don't you get on board?' he said. 'At least you'll be under cover.'

This thought had apparently not occurred to them before and they rushed to the coach. The three men settled their wives at the far end then got in beside them. The other indistinct, muffled figures took the remaining places in silence.

Their feet sank into the straw covering the floor. The ladies at the far end, having brought little copper foot-warmers which ran on chemical fuel, now began lighting these contraptions. For some time they could be heard quietly extolling the virtues of them and exchanging civilities.

At last the coach was ready, with six rather than four horses harnessed because of the heavy weather. A voice from outside called: 'Everybody in?' They set off.

The coach lumbered slowly and laboriously forward. The wheels sank into the snow, the whole vehicle creaked and groaned, the horses slipped and panted and steamed and the driver's huge whip cracked ceaselessly. It darted in every direction, knotting then uncoiling itself like a thin snake to give a sudden sting to a firm rump which then tensed into greater effort.

Imperceptibly it grew lighter. The feathery snowflakes, likened by one of the passengers – a Rouen man born and bred – to a fall of cotton-wool,[8] had stopped. A murky light filtered through vast, lowering clouds whose leaden tints set off the dazzling whiteness of the countryside. Against it stood out here a row of tall trees covered with frost, there a cottage in a cowl of snow. Inside the coach, by the melancholy light of dawn, the travellers began to cast inquisitive glances at each other. At the far end, in the best places, Monsieur and Madame Loiseau, wholesale wine merchants of the rue Grand Point sat dozing opposite each other. Once clerk to another wine merchant, he had bought his master's business when the latter went bankrupt, and made a fortune. He sold at a very low price very poor wine to small country retailers and was considered by his friends and acquaintances to be a wily old rascal with the typical Norman mixture of heartiness and guile in his blood. His reputation as a crook was so well established that one evening, at the Prefecture, Monsieur Tournel, a songwriter and raconteur of locally legendary dry and caustic wit, had suggested to the ladies, who were looking, as he thought, a little drowsy, that they should get up a game of *l'oiseau vole*.[9] The joke spread like wildfire through the Prefect's drawing rooms and from there to others of the town, having the whole province in stitches for a good month.

Loiseau himself had a reputation moreover for practical jokes in both good and dubious taste and whenever his name came up in conversation, someone would be sure to say, 'Priceless, old Loiseau.' He was a small man with a large paunch and a ruddy face framed by grizzled sidewhiskers. His wife, tall, stout and determined looking, had a shrill voice and a brisk manner. It was she who ran the shop and did the book-keeping while he kept business bubbling with his lively bonhomie.

Next to them, more dignified, as might be expected from a member of a superior class, sat Monsieur Carré-Lamadon, a man of considerable substance, well established in the cotton trade, proprietor of three spinning-mills, officer of the *Légion d'honneur* and member of the General Council. Throughout the Empire[10] he had remained leader of the loyal opposition solely in order to obtain a higher price for his support of a policy he had opposed with what he termed the weapons of a gentleman. Madame Carré-Lamadon, who was much younger than her husband, had been a source of constant comfort to all officers of good families who found themselves stationed at Rouen. This dainty, demure, pretty little thing sat swathed in furs opposite her husband and looked disconsolately round at the miserable interior of the coach.

Her neighbours, the Comte and the Comtesse Hubert de Bréville, were descended from one of the most ancient and noble families of Normandy. The Comte, an elderly gentleman of distinguished countenance and bearing, tried as hard as possible to accentuate through dress the resemblance he bore to Henri IV. The latter, according to proud family legend, had fathered a child on a Madame de Bréville whose husband had been rewarded with the title of Comte and the governorship of a province. A colleague of Monsieur Carré-Lamadon on the General Council, Comte Hubert was the Departmental representative of the Orleanists.[11] The story of his marriage to the daughter of a small Nantes shipowner remained shrouded in mystery. But since the Comtesse was possessed of a distinguished manner and was said to have been the mistress of one of Louis-Philippe's sons, she was celebrated by the local aristocracy and her salon, the only one in which the spirit of genuine French chivalry still survived, was considered the most exclusive of the region. The Bréville's fortune, all in landed property, was said to produce an annual income of half a million francs.[12]

These six people occupied the far end of the coach and represented the wealthy, highly self-confident and stable element of society; respectable and morally upright men and women with a proper respect for both religion and principles. By strange coincidence, all the ladies happened to be seated on the same side. Next to the Comtesse were two nuns, telling their rosaries and muttering paternosters and aves. One was elderly with a face as pockmarked as if it had received a charge of grapeshot at point-blank range. The other, puny and sickly-looking about the face, had the narrow chest of the consumptive but appeared eaten up instead by the all-devouring faith of the visionary or martyr.

All eyes were now upon the man and woman sitting opposite the two nuns.

The man, Cornudet, was a well-known local democrat and the terror of all respectable people. For the previous twenty years he had been dipping his red whiskers into the tankards of every pro-democrat café around and with the help of friends and comrades had squandered the sizeable fortune left to him by his father, a retired confectioner. He waited impatiently for the coming of the Republic which would put him at last in the official position so many revolutionary libations had surely earned him. On the fabled Fourth of September,[13] possibly as the result of a practical joke, he had been appointed Prefect. However, when he attempted to take up his duties, the Prefecture office boys left in sole charge of the place refused to acknowledge his authority and he had had to beat a retreat. He was a good-natured sort, harmless and willing, and had applied himself with commendable enthusiasm to the organization of the town's defences. He had had pits dug in the open country, all the saplings of the neighbouring forests felled and all the roads booby-trapped. Satisfied that he had done all he could, as the enemy advanced ever closer he had quickly retreated into town. Now, he thought, he could make himself so much more useful at Le Havre where defensive positions would also have to be put into place.

The woman, one of those usually known as a good-time girl, was famous for the premature portliness which had earned her the nickname Boule de Suif. Small, round as a barrel, fat as butter and with fingers tightly jointed like strings of small sausages, her glowing skin and the enormous bosom which strained under the constraints of her dress – as well as her freshness, which was a delight to the eye – made her hugely desirable and much sought after. She had a rosy apple of a face, a peony bud about to burst into bloom. Out of it looked two magnificent dark eyes shaded by thick black lashes. Further down was a charming little mouth complete with invitingly moist lips and tiny, gleaming pearly-white teeth. She was said to possess a variety of other inestimable qualities.

As soon as she was recognized there was frantic whispering

among the respectable women, and the words 'prostitute' and 'public disgrace' were whispered loudly enough for her to raise her eyes. Her gaze as she met those of her neighbours was so direct and challenging that they all immediately fell silent. Everyone looked down again apart from Loiseau who watched her with a lecherous eye. Soon, however, conversation resumed between the three ladies whom the presence of this prostitute had made friends, and close ones at that. It seemed to them it was their duty to present a united front of marital dignity in the face of this shameless harlot. Institutionalized love always looks down on her more liberal sister.

The three men were also drawn together by the presence of Cornudet. Speaking in disparaging tones about the ever-present poor, they began to discuss money. Comte Hubert mentioned both the damage the Prussians had caused him and his losses as a result of stolen cattle and ruined crops, but in the confident tones of a great landowner, a millionaire ten times over who would recoup these losses within a year at most. Monsieur Carré-Lamadon, whose cotton business had been hard hit, had taken the precaution of sending 600,000 francs to England so as to have, as usual, something stored away for a rainy day. As for Loiseau, he had managed to sell the French Commissariat all the *vin ordinaire* he had left in his cellars so that it now owed him a large sum of money which he was expecting to collect at Le Havre. All three exchanged quick, friendly glances. Differences in social class notwithstanding, they were all conscious of belonging to a wealthy fraternity, the great freemasonry of the well-heeled who always have gold to jingle in their pockets.

The coach was moving so slowly that by ten o'clock that morning they had travelled less than ten miles. Three times the men got out to lighten the burden on the hills. They were beginning to worry again for they had hoped to stop for lunch at Tôtes[14] and there seemed little chance now of their reaching it before nightfall. Everyone was keeping an eye out for a wayside inn when the coach sank into a snowdrift from which two hours were needed to free it once more.

Increasing hunger had begun to dampen the company's spirits. The Prussian advance, preceded as it had been by the passing of French troops on the verge of starvation, had scared away all trade and not a single eating-house or bar, however basic, was to be found anywhere en route. The gentlemen even went off hunting for food in the nearby farms but not a crumb was to be found. The wary locals had hidden away all their stores lest ravenous soldiers should rob them of all they could find.

At about one o'clock in the afternoon Loiseau declared that there was no getting away from it, he had an aching void in his stomach. Everyone had been suffering similarly for some considerable time and the craving for food, growing steadily more acute, had killed all conversation. From time to time someone would yawn, another would follow suit and each person in turn, according to character, degree of sophistication and social standing, would open his or her mouth noisily or put a polite hand over the gaping, vaporous hole.

Several times Boule de Suif leaned down and made as if to draw something out from under her petticoats. She would hesitate for a second, look over at her neighbours and then straighten up again. Every face was pale and drawn. Loiseau announced that he would give 1,000 francs for a knuckle of ham. His wife began a gesture of protest which quickly subsided. It hurt her to hear of money being wasted, even as a joke.

'I must say, I don't feel at all well,' said the Comte. 'Why on earth didn't it occur to me to bring along some provisions?' Each of the passengers was regretting precisely the same lack of foresight.

Cornudet, as it happened, had on him a flask of rum which he offered round. It was coldly refused by all except Loiseau, who, having accepted a drop, returned the flask with thanks: 'Good stuff, that. Warms your cockles. Takes the edge off.'

The alcohol cheered him up and he suggested they do like the sailors in the shanty about the little ship where the fattest passengers were gobbled up. This oblique reference to Boule de Suif shocked his more refined companions. No one took it up and only Cornudet managed a smile. The two nuns having stopped mumbling over their rosaries now sat motionless with their hands stuffed deep into their long sleeves, eyes cast resolutely down, offering up to Heaven no doubt all the suffering now sent to test them.

At last, at three o'clock, as they were bowling along in the middle of a great plain with not a village in sight, Boule de Suif bent down quickly and drew out from under her seat a large basket covered with a white napkin. From it she took first a small china plate and a dainty little silver goblet, then an enormous terrine containing two whole chickens jointed and set in their own aspic. More goodies could be seen wrapped up in the basket; pâtés, fruit and other delicacies still. She had brought along enough provisions for three days so as not to have to depend on the unreliable cuisine of wayside inns. The necks of four bottles protruded from among the packed food. She picked up a wing of chicken and began daintily to eat it accompanied by what in Normandy is known as a Regency roll.

Every eye was fixed upon her. Then the smell of the food spread through the coach causing nostrils to distend, mouths to water and jaw muscles to contract painfully just under the ears. The ladies' contempt for this harlot turned into a fierce longing either to kill her or to throw her, with her goblet, her basket and all her provisions out into the snow. But Loiseau was devouring the terrine of chicken with his eyes.

'Well I must say,' he said. 'Madame here has had a lot more foresight than all the rest of us put together. Some people manage to think of everything.'

She turned her face towards him.

'Perhaps, Monsieur, you would care for a little something? It's awful to have had nothing to eat since morning.'

He bowed.

'I wouldn't say no, indeed. I can't hold out another minute. Wartime conditions, eh, Madame?' And glancing round at everyone, he added: 'At times like this, one is only too glad of the kindness of strangers.'

He had a newspaper which he spread on his knees so as not to get grease on his trousers and, with the point of his handy pocket-knife, speared a leg of chicken thickly coated with jelly. He tore at it with his teeth then sat munching with such obvious relish that a great sigh of distress went up from his companions.

At this, Boule de Suif in a gentle, respectful voice invited the two nuns to share her refreshments. Immediately they both accepted and, after stammering their thanks, lowered their heads and began to eat as fast as they could. Nor was Cornudet a man to reject a neighbourly gesture and the four made a sort of table by spreading newspaper over their knees.

Mouths opened and shut without pause, chewing, swallowing and gulping ravenously. Loiseau, munching solidly away in his corner urged his wife, *sotto voce*, to accept as he had. For a long time she held out but finally, after a pang of hunger pierced through to her vitals, agreed. Whereupon her husband, choosing his words carefully, asked their 'charming companion' if he might offer a small portion to Madame Loiseau. 'But of course, Monsieur,' she replied, smiling sweetly and passing him the dish. A slight difficulty arose when they opened the first bottle of claret. There was only one goblet. They passed it around with each person giving it a wipe before drinking. Only Cornudet, from gallantry it must be assumed, put it straight to his lips while it was still moist from those of his neighbour.

Surrounded by people eating and drinking, and half suffocated with the smell of food, the Comte and Comtesse de Bréville and Monsieur and Madame Carré-Lamadon were suffering the hideous torment associated with the name of Tantalus. Suddenly, the manufacturer's young wife heaved a sigh which made everyone turn and look. She was as white as the snow outside. Her eyes closed, her head fell forward and she lost consciousness. Her distraught husband appealed for help from everyone. Nobody knew what to do except for the elder of the two nuns who, lifting her patient's head, forced Boule de Suif's goblet between her lips and made her swallow a few drops of wine. The pretty lady stirred, opened her eyes, smiled and said in a faint voice that she felt perfectly well again. To prevent a recurrence of the incident, however, the nun made her drink a whole cupful of claret, saying as she did: 'It's lack of nourishment, that's all.'

Boule de Suif, blushing with embarrassment and looking at the four travellers still without food, stammered: 'If only ... goodness me ... if only I might make so bold as to offer you ladies and gentlemen . . .' She broke off, fearing it might be deemed insulting.

Loiseau took up where she had left off:

'Times like this, dammit . . . all in the same boat. Help each other out. Come along ladies please, no silly nonsense now . . . For God's sake, eat up! Who knows, we may not even have a roof over our heads tonight. Way we're going . . . won't be in Tôtes before noon tomorrow . . .'

Still they hesitated. No one wanted to be the first to accept. Finally it was the Comte who settled things once and for all. Turning to the plump, shy girl with his most seigneurial air, he said: 'Madame, we are all most grateful to you.'

That was all it took. Once the Rubicon was crossed, they fell on the food like wolves. The basket was emptied and found still to contain a pâté de foie gras, a lark pâté, a piece of smoked tongue, some Crassane pears, a slab of Pont l'Evêque cheese, some petits fours and finally a jar of mixed pickled onions and gherkins since, like every other woman, Boule de Suif liked to include something raw.

They could hardly eat this girl's food without including her too in the conversation. So include her they did, albeit with a certain initial reserve which, as she turned out to have perfect manners, was soon broken down. Mesdames de Bréville and Carré-Lamadon, both ladies of great sophistication, were diplomatically gracious towards her. The Comtesse in particular, showing the kindly condescension of one whose nobility of character can be sullied by no human contact, was especially charming. Stout old Madame Loiseau, who had the soul of a sergeant-major, remained her usual surly self throughout, eating heartily and speaking little.

Naturally, they discussed the war, the terrible things done by the Prussians and the brave deeds of the heroic French. All these people running away as fast as possible from the scene of the action paid tribute to the bravery of those who stayed behind. They soon moved on to personal experiences and Boule de Suif, with the genuine passion girls have when expressing their instinctive feelings, told how she had come to leave Rouen:

'I thought to begin with that I'd stay,' she said. 'My house

was well stocked-up and I thought I'd prefer to put up a few
soldiers than uproot myself to goodness knows where. But when
I clapped eyes on those Prussians something came over me! It
just made my blood boil. I wept from shame every minute of
the day. Oh, I thought, if only I was a man! I used to look at
them from my window, the fat pigs, in those spiked helmets!
My maid had to hold my hands down to stop me chucking
furniture at them! Then some of them were sent to take up their
billets with me. First one in, I went for his throat. I thought,
they're no harder to strangle than any other man. I'd have
finished him off, too, if they hadn't dragged me off him by the
hair. After that, of course, I had to go into hiding. So, when I
got the chance, I upped sticks and here I am.'

She was much praised and rose in the esteem of her fellow-
travellers, none of whom had shown as much guts. Like a priest
hearing one of his flock praise God, Cornudet, listening to her,
smiled the benevolent and approving smile reserved for true
apostles. For just as men of the cloth have a monopoly on
religion, so democrats with long beards have a monopoly on
patriotism. He too spoke, but in the stuffy, pompous style he
had picked up from the proclamations posted daily on the walls
of the city. He wound up his speech with a scathing diatribe
against 'that scum of a Badinguet'.[15]

At this, Boule de Suif, a Bonapartist as it turned out, flew into
a rage. As red as a beetroot and stammering with indignation,
she cried: 'I'd like to see you do any better! A right mess *you*'d
have made of things! You're the very people who let him down!
If France had people like you in charge we might as well all
emigrate, I'm telling you!'

Although Cornudet still smiled his superior, disdainful smile,
it was obvious that pretty soon the tone would be lowered, and
the Comte intervened. Managing not without difficulty to calm
down the furious young woman, he declared that all opinions
sincerely held were worthy of respect. Nevertheless, the Comtesse and the manufacturer's wife, who harboured in their
breasts the irrational hatred all respectable people have for the
Republic, as well as the instinctive warmth of attachment all
women feel towards strong, not to say despotic, governments,

were drawn despite themselves to this dignified prostitute whose convictions so exactly mirrored their own.

The basket was now empty. Between the ten of them they had made short work of its contents and only wished it had been larger. Conversation continued for a while but languished a little after they had all finished their meal. Night was falling and with it a deepening darkness. The cold, felt all the more keenly during digestion, made Boule de Suif shiver despite her chubbiness. Seeing this, Madame de Bréville offered her the little foot-warmer which had already been refuelled several times since the morning. Boule de Suif, whose feet were freezing, accepted with alacrity. Following suit, Madame Carré-Lamadon and Madame Loiseau offered theirs to the nuns.

The coachman had lit the lanterns. They cast a vivid glare on the steaming rumps of the two horses nearest the wheels and, at each side of the road, on the snow which appeared to be unrolling under the shifting beams of light. Within the coach nothing could be made out clearly now. Suddenly, however, there was some kind of movement between Cornudet and Boule de Suif. Loiseau, his sharp eye piercing the darkness, thought he saw the long-bearded man recoil abruptly as if from some silent, well-aimed blow. Little points of light began to appear some way ahead. It was Tôtes. They had been travelling for eleven hours which, with the two hours made up by four rest periods for the horses to eat their oats, amounted to thirteen in total. They entered the town and drew up in front of the Hôtel du Commerce.

The door was opened. Then a familiar sound made all the travellers quake. It was the grating of a sword sheath against the ground. Instantly a voice cried out something in German. Although the coach had come to a complete standstill no one alighted, as if to do so were to invite massacre. The driver appeared, carrying in his hand one of the lanterns which suddenly lit up the entire interior of the carriage. Two rows of terrified faces stared out open-mouthed and wide-eyed with shock and fright.

Standing beside the driver in the full glare of the lantern was a German officer. He was a tall, fair and extremely slim young man wearing a uniform as tightly fitting as a woman's corset and, at a rakish angle on his head, a shiny pill-box of a hat which made him look like a pageboy in an English hotel. His massive moustache, with its long straight bristles tapering off on either side into a single hair so fine as to appear infinite, seemed to weigh down both the corners of his mouth and his cheeks in such a way as to make his lips droop. In a heavy Alsatian accent he invited the passengers to alight, saying curtly: 'Ladies end chentlemen get out please.'

The two nuns were the first to obey, with the meekness of holy sisters accustomed to total submission. The Comte and Comtesse appeared next, followed by the manufacturer and his wife, then by Loiseau using his better half as a shield. As soon as his feet touched the ground he said, 'Good evening Monsieur', more from prudence than politeness. The officer, with the insolence of absolute power, looked at him without replying.

Boule de Suif and Cornudet, although closest to the door, were the last to get out, grave and haughty in the presence of the enemy. The plump young girl was trying to keep some degree of self-control and remain calm. With a slightly tremulous hand the democrat tugged histrionically at his long red beard. Each wished to remain dignified, conscious that in such circumstances each person is in some respect a representative of the nation. Disgusted by her fellow citizens' easy compliance, Boule de Suif for her part was trying to muster greater self-respect than the respectable women with whom she had been travelling. Cornudet, also, feeling that it was his duty to do so, showed in his whole attitude the resistance he had begun by blocking the roads.

They entered the inn's vast kitchen where the German, having been shown the transport permit signed by the general in command, looked carefully at the travellers, checking each one against the written details. Then: 'It's good,' he said brusquely and disappeared.

They breathed once more. And since they were now hungry again, supper was ordered. It would take half an hour to prepare. While two servants busied themselves with what was obviously its preparation, they went to inspect their rooms. These were all off one long corridor, at the end of which was a glazed door

marked '1oo'. Just as they were about to sit down at the table
the innkeeper himself appeared. He was a former horse-dealer,
a fat, wheezy man from whom emanated a series of bronchial
whistles and gurgles. Like his father before him apparently, his
name was Follenvie.

'Mademoiselle Elisabeth Rousset?' he inquired.

Boule de Suif gave a start and turned round.

'That's me, yes.'

'Mademoiselle, the Prussian officer would like a word with
you immediately.'

'With me?'

'If you are Mademoiselle Elisabeth Rousset, yes.'

Disconcerted, she thought for a moment then said flatly: 'I
don't care. I'm not going.'

There was a stir behind her as everyone speculated on the
reason behind this summons.

The Comte approached her.

'That would be a great mistake, Madame. A refusal on your
part could have disastrous consequences not only for yourself
but for all your companions. You should never resist those who
are stronger than you are. I'm certain there's absolutely no
danger in complying with this request. It's probably just some
formality that has to be cleared up.'

Everyone agreed with the Comte. She was urged and implored
and lectured until in the end she was convinced. Everyone was
afraid of what might happen if she followed her own fanciful
impulse.

'Well as long as you know I'm only going for your sakes,' she
said at last.

The Comtesse took her hand:

'And we're *so* grateful to you, really.'

She left the room and everyone waited for her to come back
before sitting down at the table. Each wished it had been one of
themselves who had been called rather than this violent and
quick-tempered girl. They rehearsed the platitudes they would
mouth should it be their turn next. In ten minutes however she
was back, breathless, red in the face and choking with furious
rage: 'The swine!' she stammered, 'the filthy swine!'

Everyone was longing to know, but she would reveal nothing of what had taken place.

When the Comte pressed her, she replied with great dignity, 'No! It's nothing to do with you! I don't wish to discuss it!'

They all took their places at the table around a large soup tureen from which rose the smell of cabbage. Despite the earlier setback supper was a jolly affair. The cider was good and Monsieur and Madame Loiseau, as well as the two nuns, drank it for the sake of economy. All the others ordered wine, apart from Cornudet who called for beer. He had a particular way of opening the bottle, giving the contents a good head and examining the colour in the glass which he held tilted against the light. When he drank, his large beard – which in colour took after his favourite drink – seemed to quiver with emotion. As he kept a constant, surreptitious watch on his glass, his demeanour was that of a man fulfilling the one function for which he had been put on earth. There was an undoubted affinity in his mind between the two great passions of his life: revolution and good brew. The taste of one immediately brought to mind the other.

Monsieur and Madame Follenvie were eating their supper at the far end of the table. The husband, wheezing like a broken-down locomotive, had too tight a chest to speak as well as eat, but his wife never stopped talking. She gave a comprehensive account of the Prussians' arrival, what they had done and what they had said, and cursed them first for costing her money and second because she had two sons in the army. Flattered to be in conversation with a lady of quality, she directed most of her comments to the Comtesse. Lowering her voice to broach the more delicate matters involved, she was from time to time interrupted by her husband:

'You'd better just be quiet there, Madame Follenvie.'

She took not the slightest notice and continued: 'Oh yes, Madame, let me tell you. All they eat, this lot, is pork and potatoes. Then after that more pork and potatoes. And talk about dirty! They do their . . . begging your pardon, Madame . . . their business . . . just anywhere. And the drilling! Hours at a time they do. Days! There they all are out in the field . . . forward march, to the left . . . *and* . . . forward march again. If

only they was working on the land or mending the roads back
where they belong. But not on your life, Madame, that's soldiers
for you not a scrap of good to the world. And there's us poor
people having to fatten them up for what? More killing. I'm just
an old woman I know . . . no schooling and that, but when I see
them turning themselves inside out tramping up and down from
morning to night I say to myself, when you think . . . how much
other people are doing to discover things and then there's this
lot doing as much harm as they possibly can, really . . . I mean
it's just horrible, isn't it, all this killing? Prussians, English,
French, Polish, the lot! Say you want to get your own back on
somebody who's done you harm, the law's on you, right? But
when all our lads get shot down like animals, well that's fine,
you get medals for that. I'm telling you, I'll never get my head
round it, never.'

Cornudet raised his voice to say: 'War is barbaric when it's
an attack on a peaceful neighbour, but in defence of one's
country it is a sacred duty.'

The old woman bowed her head.

'In defence of the country I agree. But wouldn't it make more
sense to polish off all the kings instead? They're the ones who
get all the pleasure from it.'

Cornudet's eyes flashed.

'Bravo, citizen!' he said.

Monsieur Carré-Lamadon was deep in thought. Though he
had the keenest admiration for great soldiers, this captain of
industry was struck by the old peasant woman's common sense.
It made him think of all the wealth that could be created for the
country if so many idle and therefore costly hands and so much
unproductive manpower were diverted into the great industrial
enterprises it would otherwise take centuries to complete.

Loiseau, getting up from his seat, went over to join the innkeeper and started whispering to him. The fat fellow coughed
and spluttered and spat as he burst out laughing and his great
belly heaved at his neighbour's jokes. He ordered six casks of
claret to be delivered in the spring, after the Prussians had left.

As soon as supper was over, the exhausted travellers went
straight up to bed.

Loiseau, however, who had been taking everything in all the while, got his wife settled into bed before putting first his ear then his eye to the keyhole so as to learn 'the secrets of the corridor' as he put it. After about an hour, hearing a slight rustle, he went quickly to look and saw Boule de Suif, looking more Rubenesque than ever in a blue cashmere dressing-gown edged with white lace. She was carrying a candle and making for the door with the number on at the end of the corridor. Yet another door, this one to the side, opened a little way, and when she returned a few minutes later Cornudet in his shirt sleeves was following her. There was a whispered conversation, then silence. It looked as though Boule de Suif was doing all she could to stop him from coming into her room. Unfortunately, to begin with Loiseau could not make out what was being said but eventually as their voices rose he managed to catch the odd phrase. Cornudet was putting on considerable pressure.

'Oh come on now, don't be silly. Why d'you make such a song and dance?'

Indignantly, she replied: 'No! Listen! There are times when you just don't do that sort of thing. Especially here. It would be disgraceful.'

It was clear that he simply did not understand. He asked her why not and at this she lost her temper. Raising her voice still further she said: 'Why not? You mean you don't *know*? When there's a *Prussian* under the same roof as you? In the next *room* maybe?'

He said no more. The patriotic propriety of this prostitute who banned sex in the presence of the enemy revived something of his own flagging sense of decency. He kissed her chastely and tiptoed quietly back to his room.

Loiseau in a state of high excitement skipped away from the keyhole, put on his nightcap and lifted the sheet beneath which lay the sturdy frame of his life's companion. Waking her with a kiss, he murmured: 'Do you love me, darling?'

After that the whole house fell silent. In a short while, however, from some indeterminate place which might have been anywhere from the cellar and the attic, rose the sound of a powerful, monotonous and regular snore; a low, prolonged rumbling with the vibrations of a boiler under pressure. Monsieur Follenvie had fallen asleep.

It had been agreed to make a start at eight and accordingly the following morning they all gathered again in the kitchen. The coach, however, its roof covered with snow stood alone in the middle of the yard with no sign of either horses or driver. They looked in vain for the latter in the stables, in the haylofts and in the coach-house. The men of the party then decided to leave the hotel and search the town for him. They found themselves in the main square with a church at one end and on either side a row of low-roofed houses in which Prussian soldiers could be seen. The first they came across was peeling potatoes. Further on, a second was scrubbing out the barbershop. Yet another, this one heavily bearded up to the eyes, was holding a crying baby on his knee and trying to rock it to sleep. Buxom peasant women whose men were 'gone for soldiers' mimed to their obedient victors what jobs needed to be done: chopping wood, ladling out soup, grinding coffee beans. One was even doing the washing for the person with whom he was billeted, who happened to be a frail old lady.

The Comte, amazed by what he saw, questioned the verger who was coming out of the presbytery.

'Oh they're all right, these lads,' said the old church mouse. 'Apparently they're not really Prussians at all. Come from further on, I'm not sure where. Every one of them's got a wife and children back home. The war's no picnic for them either, you know. I'm sure there's many a tear shed for them as well. And it'll knock them back economically, just like us. It's not so bad here for the moment. They're pretty harmless and they work just as they would at home. You see, Monsieur, we poor people, we've got to give each other a helping hand where we can. It's always the people in power that start these things.'

Cornudet, shocked by the friendly relations existing between victors and vanquished, went off, preferring to withdraw to the inn. Loiseau had to see the funny side of it: 'Repopulation, I call it.'

'Reparation, you mean,' Monsieur Carré-Lamadon gravely replied.

Still the coachman was nowhere to be seen. Eventually he was discovered in the village café sitting at the same table as the officer's orderly. The Comte hailed him: 'Weren't you told to have the horses ready by eight o'clock?'

'I was. But then I got another order.'

'What was that?'

'Not to.'

'And who gave you that order?'

'Prussian officer of course!'

'Why?'

'No idea. Go and ask him yourself. I'm told not to harness, I don't harness. Simple as that.'

'He told you himself?'

'No, monsieur. The innkeeper. On his behalf.'

'When?'

'Last night. Just when I was going to bed.'

The three men, now seriously worried, retraced their steps. They asked to see Monsieur Follenvie but were told by the maid that on account of his asthma Monsieur never got up before ten. They had strict orders not to wake him earlier unless there was a fire. They asked to see the officer but were told this was out of the question, despite the fact that his headquarters were at the inn itself. Monsieur Follenvie alone was allowed to address him on civilian matters. So they had to wait. The women went up to their rooms again and did little odds and ends of jobs to while away the time.

Cornudet settled down in the inglenook of the kitchen where a huge fire was blazing. He called for one of the little tables from the café, ordered a beer and drew out his pipe which, in local democratic circles, enjoyed almost as much prestige as he himself did, as if in serving Cornudet it too was serving its country. It was a superb meerschaum, beautifully seasoned and as black as its owner's teeth, but fragrant and gleaming. Its graceful curve fitted beautifully into his hand and rounded off the features of his face. He sat motionless, his eyes gazing now at the flames, now at the head of foam which crowned his beer. After each draught he ran his long, thin fingers through his long, greasy hair in a gesture of satisfaction and sucked through his froth-flecked moustache.

Loiseau, under the pretext of wanting to stretch his legs, went round the local retailers, taking orders for wine. The Comte and the manufacturer began to talk politics and speculated on the future of France. One was an Orleanist, the other believed in the existence of some as yet unknown saviour who would appear only when all seemed lost – another du Guesclin[16] or another Joan of Arc, maybe? Or another Napoleon! Oh if only the Imperial Prince[17] were not so young! Listening to them Cornudet smiled like a man from whom Fate has no secrets. The smell of his pipe pervaded the kitchen.

On the stroke of ten Monsieur Follenvie appeared. They tackled him immediately but all he did was repeat over and over the same words: 'The officer says to me, he says, Monsieur Follenvie you will give orders that the coach is not to be got ready in the morning I do not wish them to leave without my express permission, is that clear, carry on.'

They then asked to see the officer. The Comte sent in his card, to which Monsieur Carré-Lamadon had added his name and all his titles. The Prussian sent a reply saying he would hear what the two gentlemen had to say after he had had his lunch, in other words at about one o'clock.

The ladies reappeared and they all ate a little despite their anxiety. Boule de Suif looked unwell and extremely worried. They were finishing their coffee when the orderly came to fetch the gentlemen. Loiseau joined the first two, but when they attempted to rope in Cornudet so as to add more weight to the deputation he declared proudly that he had no intention of ever negotiating with the Germans. Returning to the fireside he ordered another beer.

The three men went upstairs and were admitted into the inn's best room. The officer received them, stretched out in an armchair with his feet up on the mantelpiece. He was smoking a long porcelain pipe and wearing a hideously loud dressing-gown looted no doubt from the abandoned residence of some rich man with no taste. He did not rise, did not greet nor even deign to look at them. Here was a prize example of the boorishness which is second nature to the soldier in occupation. Finally, after a while, he spoke: 'Vot is it you vant?'

The Comte acted as spokesman: 'We would like to proceed, Monsieur.'

'No.'

'And may I make so bold as to inquire the reason for this refusal?'

'Because I do not vish you to.'

'I would respectfully point out, Monsieur, that the transport permit allowing us to travel to Dieppe is signed by your own commanding officer. I cannot see what we may have done to incur this prohibition.'

'I do not vish it. Zet is all. You may go.'

The three men bowed and withdrew. A miserable afternoon ensued. No one could understand what was behind this German's whim and the strangest ideas were entertained. Everyone remained in the kitchen debating endlessly and imagining the most unlikely scenarios. Perhaps they were going to be held hostage. But then what for? Or taken prisoner? Or held up to a hefty ransom? This thought struck terror in the hearts of all. The richest were the most terrified. They saw themselves having to hand over sacks full of gold to this arrogant soldier in order to save their skins. They racked their brains for convincing lies, strategies to conceal their wealth and pass for the poorest of the poor. Loiseau took off his watch-chain and hid it in his pocket. The evening shadows fell, deepening their gloom. The lamp was lit, and since it was another two hours before dinner Madame Loiseau suggested a game of *trente-et-un*.[18] It would take their minds off things. Everyone agreed, even Cornudet, who politely put his pipe in his pocket.

The Comte shuffled the cards and dealt. Boule de Suif got thirty-one straight away and, in the excitement of the game, the fear which was haunting their minds faded. Cornudet noticed that the Loiseau couple had a little system going which allowed them to cheat in tandem.

As they were about to sit down at the table Monsieur Follenvie reappeared.

'The Prussian officer wishes to know if Mademoiselle Elisabeth Rousset has changed her mind yet.'

Boule de Suif remained standing. At first very pale, she

suddenly turned crimson, choking so much with rage that she was unable to speak. Finally she burst out: 'Tell that bastard, that sod of a Prussian, that I never will, d'you hear? Never, never, never!'

The fat innkeeper left the room. Immediately, Boule de Suif was surrounded, questioned, and implored to reveal the secret of her visit. At first she refused but very soon was carried away by her own fury.

'Want? What does he want? He wants me to sleep with him, that's what!' she cried.

Such was the general indignation that her frankness shocked no one. Cornudet slammed his glass down on the table so hard that it smashed into smithereens. There was a chorus of angry protest against the designs of this uncouth soldier, a wave of anger and as much solidarity with her as though each one had been required to share in the sacrifice demanded of her. The Comte declared with disgust that these people were behaving like barbarians. The women especially lavished intense and affectionate sympathy on Boule de Suif. The nuns, who appeared at mealtimes only, kept silent and bowed their heads. Although they all sat down to dinner after the initial furious reaction, there was little talk and much reflection.

The ladies retired early. The men, whom they left to smoke, got up a game of *écarté*[19] to which they invited Monsieur Follenvie in the hope that some subtle questioning might reveal a way of getting round the officer's refusal. He was so absorbed in his hand, however, that he scarcely heard them, offering no reply save his oft-repeated 'Play, gentlemen, play!' So deep was his concentration on the game that he forgot to spit, a lapse which produced a few organ notes from his chest. His wheezing lungs played up and down the whole scale from deep bass to the squawking treble of the young cock's first crow. He refused to go upstairs to bed even when his wife, dropping with tiredness, came to fetch him. So she retired alone; an early bird up with the lark, as she said, she always rose at dawn while her night-owl husband was always glad to stay up with his friends till all hours. He called out to her: 'Put my egg-nog by the fire, will you?' and continued with his game.

When they realized they would get nothing out of him they decided it was time for bed themselves and retired for the night.

They rose quite early again the following morning with vague hope in their hearts and an even stronger desire to get away. The thought of yet another day in that dreary little inn filled them with horror. Alas, the horses remained in the stables and again the coachman was nowhere to be seen. For want of anything better to do they hung around the coach. Lunch was a miserable affair. There was chilliness in the general attitude towards Boule de Suif, since, having slept on the problem, her companions' views had slightly changed. Now, there was even a touch of animosity towards the prostitute. Could she not have gone on the quiet to the Prussian and given them all a lovely surprise in the morning? What could have been simpler? And who would have known? She could have saved face by telling the officer she was doing it out of pity for her companions in their plight. For her, after all, it would have been such a little thing to do. No one of course yet put these thoughts into words.

In the afternoon, since they were all bored out of their minds, the Comte suggested a walk round the village. Everyone wrapped up warmly and the little party set off, with the exception of Cornudet who preferred to stay by the fire, and the two nuns who were spending most of the day either in the church or at the priest's house. The cold which was becoming more intense every day nipped their noses and ears painfully; their feet hurt so badly that every step was torture, and when the countryside came into view it looked so appallingly bleak under its endless shroud of snow that they all turned back immediately, their spirits chilled and their hearts turned to ice. The four women walked in front while the three men followed a little way behind.

Loiseau, who had a perfect grasp of the situation, wondered aloud how long 'that whore' was going to keep them stranded in this godforsaken hole. The Comte, gallant as ever, said no woman should be asked to make such a painful sacrifice and that the answer would have to come from her herself. Monsieur Carré-Lamadon observed that if, as was likely, the French launched a counter-offensive by way of Dieppe, the place where

the two armies would converge was Tôtes. This remark worried
the other two.

'What if we tried to get away on foot?' said Loiseau.

The Comte shrugged his shoulders.

'In this snow? With our wives in tow? They'd be after us
straight away, catch us up in ten minutes, then bring us back
prisoners. At the mercy of their soldiers.'

It was all too true. Nothing more was said.

The women were talking about clothes but a certain distance
was beginning to creep into their conversation. Suddenly, who
should come into view at the end of the street but the officer
himself. His tall figure in its wasp-waisted uniform stood out
sharply against the all-encompassing snow. Knees wide apart,
he was walking as soldiers do to preserve the shine on highly
polished boots. He bowed as he passed the ladies and looked
disdainfully at the men, who in turn maintained enough self-
respect not to raise their hats, though Loiseau did make as if to
do so.

Boule de Suif blushed to the roots of her hair and the three
married ladies felt deeply humiliated at being seen by an officer
in the company of the prostitute treated by him in such a cavalier
way. They began to talk about him, commenting on his looks
and general appearance. Madame Carré-Lamadon, who had
known a great many officers in her time and considered herself
a connoisseur, found him not bad at all. A pity he wasn't French
– he'd have made a very handsome hussar and all the women
would have fallen for him.

Back at the inn, they no longer knew what to do with themselves. Harsh words were exchanged over mere trifles. Dinner
was a brief and silent occasion and everyone went up to bed
hoping to kill time by sleeping.

They came down the next morning with tired faces and frayed
tempers. The men hardly spoke to Boule de Suif. A church bell
began to ring. It was for a christening. The plump young woman
had a child, it turned out, who was being looked after by a
peasant family in Yvetot. From one year's end to the next, she
neither saw it nor gave it a thought. But the thought of this one
now filled her heart with a sudden overwhelming feeling of love

for her own. She decided she simply had to attend the ceremony.

No sooner had she left than they all looked at each other and drew together their chairs. It was high time they came to some sort of a decision. Loiseau had an idea. What about suggesting the officer keep Boule de Suif alone and allow the others to go? Monsieur Follenvie once more agreed to act as go-between but returned almost immediately. The German, wise in the ways of the world, had shown him the door. Everyone must remain until his wishes were carried out.

At this, Madame Loiseau's vulgar instincts broke out.

'We're surely not going to sit here for the rest of our days, are we? It's that slut's job to do it with any man. She's got no right to pick and choose. I mean, I ask you! She takes any man in the whole of Rouen, even coachmen! Yes, Madame, even the Prefect's coachman! I happen to know because he buys his wine from us. And now, when it comes to getting us out of this pickle, that tart starts to get sniffy! As a matter of fact, I think the officer's behaved pretty well. Who knows how long he's been without? And there's the three of us he'd probably much prefer really. But there you are, he makes do with a common prostitute. He respects married women. Just think! He's in charge. He'd only have to give his soldiers the word and have us taken by force!'

The two other women gave a little shudder. Madame Carré-Lamadon's eyes flashed and her face paled as if already in the clutches of the officer. The men, who had been conferring privately, returned to the ladies. Loiseau, beside himself with anger, wanted the wretched girl bound hand and foot and handed over to the officer. But the Comte, the product of three generations of ambassadors, and himself the soul of diplomacy, advocated a subtler approach.

'We must make her see the sense of it herself,' he said.

They began to hatch a plot. The women huddled closer together, voices were lowered, and in the general discussion which ensued each had something to contribute. The ladies in particular found delicate turns of phrase, charming euphemisms to convey the crudest ideas. So carefully worded were their proposals that a stranger to the whole business would never guess

what exactly it was they were suggesting. The veneer of modesty
in every worldly woman is skin deep only, and they therefore
relished the naughtiness of it all, savouring every salacious detail
like greedy chefs preparing with loving care the supper others
are to eat.

The whole thing was so richly amusing that the mood of the
party eventually lifted. The Comte made a few slightly risqué
quips that were so cleverly turned you had to smile. Loiseau in
turn added some coarser ones to which no one really objected.
The general consensus, somewhat crudely expressed by his wife,
was that since it's a prostitute's job to take on all and sundry,
this one had no more right to refuse him than to debar any other
man. Dear little Madame Carré-Lamadon went so far as to say
that were she in Boule de Suif's place she would find the officer
rather more acceptable than most. Detailed plans were made
for the siege ahead. Each was allotted a part in the action and
given an argument to use or a particular manoeuvre to deploy.
A plan of attack was laid, complete with stratagems which
included surprise assaults to force this human citadel to yield
publicly to the authority of the enemy. Cornudet, however, kept
aloof and refused to have anything at all to do with it.

So deeply were they absorbed that no one heard Boule de Suif
return. The Comte's whispered 'shush' made everyone look up.
There she was. Everyone stopped talking at once and, at first, a
feeling of embarrassment prevented them from speaking to her.
At last, the Comtesse, more practised than the others in the art
of salon politics, asked: 'And did you enjoy the christening?'

The plump young woman, still moved by the ceremony, gave
them all the details of it, describing people's faces, their expressions, their demeanour and even the church itself, adding:
'Does you good, doesn't it, to say a little prayer every once in a
while?'

Until it was time for lunch the ladies contented themselves
with being agreeable to her, thereby lulling her into a false sense
of security which might make her more amenable to their advice
later on. As soon as they sat down to eat, however, the first
approaches were made. There was an initially general discussion
on the subject of self-sacrifice. Historical examples were quoted:

Judith and Holophernes; then, irrelevantly, Lucretia and Sextus;[20] and Cleopatra, who took all her enemy generals into her bed and reduced them to slavish obedience to her will. This was followed by a wholly fictitious tale cobbled together from the imagination of these moneyed ignoramuses in which the women of ancient Rome travelled to Capua where they lulled to sleep in their arms not only Hannibal but all his lieutenants, as well as his phalanxes of mercenaries. They cited examples of all sorts of women who had halted invading hordes in their tracks by turning their own bodies into a battlefield, and won over with their heroic caresses hideous and hated oppressors, thereby sacrificing their chastity on the altar of devotion and revenge.

There was even a veiled reference to the English aristocrat who had herself injected with a fatal and contagious disease so as to transmit it to Bonaparte, who was miraculously saved by a last-minute indisposition that prevented his meeting both the lady and his own death. All these stories were told in a sober, matter-of-fact manner with occasional bursts of enthusiasm calculated to inspire emulation. To hear them talk, one might have thought that a woman's sole duty on earth was the perpetual sacrifice of her person as she became the bawd of all barrack-room boys.

The two nuns, deep in meditation throughout, appeared to hear nothing. Boule de Suif remained silent. All afternoon they left her to her own thoughts. However, instead of addressing her as 'Madame' as had hitherto been their practice, without knowing why they now used mere 'Mademoiselle' as if wishing to shift her down from the heights of respectability she had scaled and make her feel the shamefulness of her position.

As soon as soup was served, Monsieur Follenvie appeared, repeating the previous day's formula: 'The Prussian officer wishes to know whether Mademoiselle Elisabeth Rousset has still not changed her mind.'

Boule de Suif replied curtly: 'No, monsieur.'

Over dinner, the coalition weakened. Loiseau made three somewhat unfortunate remarks. Everyone was racking their brains to think of yet more role-models, when the Comtesse, possibly without premeditation beyond a vague desire to give a little nod to religion, questioned the elder of the nuns on the great events in the lives of the saints. Apparently many had committed what we would call crimes, but which the Church had forgiven since they were done for the glory of God or out of neighbourly love. This was a powerful argument and the Comtesse made the most of it. Then, whether by a tacit understanding or a veiled complicity in which men and women of the cloth excel, or whether through blissful ignorance and fortuitous stupidity, the old nun contributed hugely to the conspiracy. While they had considered her timid, she now showed herself bold, forceful and articulate. Not for her the groping hesitancies of casuistry in grasping the truth. Her doctrine was as solid as a bar of iron, her faith equally unshakeable and her conscience unclouded by a single doubt. Abraham's sacrifice of his son Isaac seemed to her the most natural phenomenon in the world. She would have dispatched unhesitatingly both mother and father if the order had come from above. In her view, nothing could fail to please God if it stemmed from laudable intentions. The Comtesse, taking advantage of the sacred authority vested in her unsuspected ally, made her construct an edifying paraphrase of the precept that the end justifies the means. She pressed her: 'So . . . Sister . . . you mean . . . all means are acceptable to God and that he pardons any action whose motive is pure?'

'Who could doubt it, Madame? A reprehensible action in itself is often meritorious by virtue of the idea which inspires it.'

And so they went on, interpreting the will of God, predicting his decisions and making him allegedly interested in things that were hardly any of his concern. All this was couched in allusive, veiled and discreet language. Yet every word emanating from under the holy wimple took its toll on the indignant resistance of the prostitute. Then the conversation took a different turn as our lady of the rosary talked about the different houses of her order, about her Mother Superior, about herself and her sweet companion, dear Sister Nicéphore. They were being sent to Le Havre to nurse the hundreds of soldiers there suffering from smallpox. She described these poor wretches and their disease in detail. To think that while they were being held up on the whim of this Prussian, so many French lives which could otherwise be saved were going to be lost! Military nursing was her field; she had been out in the Crimea, in Italy and in Austria, and as she recounted all the campaigns she had experienced, she was revealed as a real banner-carrying Sister Hannah bearing the wounded off the field and quelling with a single glance the toughest of undisciplined other ranks. She was a seasoned old warhorse whose ravaged, pockmarked face symbolized perfectly the devastation of war.

After her excellent contribution, there was no need for anyone to add a single word. As soon as the meal was over, everyone went straight up to their rooms and did not appear till late the following morning. There followed a quiet lunch during which the seed planted the previous day was given time to germinate and bear fruit.

In the afternoon, the Comtesse suggested a walk. As planned, the Comte offered his arm to Boule de Suif and lingered with her a little way behind the others. He spoke to her in the familiar, paternal, slightly patronizing way certain mature men of the world use with women of her sort, calling her 'my child' and talking down to her from the heights of his well-established respectability and infinitely superior social rank.

'So . . . you would prefer to make us languish here, exposed like yourself to all the outrages which would ensue if the Prussians were to suffer a reversal, rather than perform another one of the many services necessary to your way of life?'

Boule de Suif made no reply. He tried all sorts of means on her, including gentle persuasion and an appeal to both her reason and her finer feelings in turn. He maintained the dignity required of his social position, while simultaneously playing the flattering and gallant ladies' man when necessary. He stressed what a huge favour she would be doing them all, and how enormously grateful they would all be. Then suddenly, addressing her as an intimate, he said: 'And I'll tell you something, my dear, he'll be able to brag he's had a prettier girl than any back where he comes from!'

Boule de Suif made no response and moved to join the rest of the party.

Immediately upon her return, she went up to her room and

did not reappear. The suspense mounted. What was she going to do? How awful if she continued to hold out! The hour struck for dinner. They waited for her in vain. Then Monsieur Follenvie came in, announcing that Mademoiselle Rousset was indisposed and that they should begin without her. Everyone pricked up their ears. The Comte went over to the innkeeper and whispered: 'Everything going all right then?'

'Yes.'

Out of propriety he conveyed none of this verbally to his companions but gave them a very slight nod. At this a huge sigh of relief went up and every face brightened. Loiseau cried: 'Well I'll be . . . ! Champagne! On me! If there *is* any in this establishment.'

To his wife's obvious dismay the landlord returned with four bottles. Suddenly everyone became very noisy and voluble and the party was full of ribald merriment. The Comte appeared to notice for the first time Madame Carré-Lamadon's charms. The manufacturer in turn began paying flattering compliments to the Comtesse. The conversation became gay and lively, not to say racy.

Suddenly Loiseau with a concerned expression on his face raised his arms and cried: 'Quiet!'

Surprised and even a little scared again, everyone stopped talking. Cocking his ear and holding up his hands for silence, he raised his eyes ceilingwards, listened again then continued in a normal voice: 'Nothing to worry about. Everything's fine.'

A quarter of an hour later he went through the same performance, repeating it several times throughout the evening. From time to time he would hold an imaginary conversation with someone on the floor above, dredging up every lewd innuendo and double entendre with which his dirty little mind was stocked. At times he would put on a pained expression and breathe, 'Oh the poor girl!' Or again, muttering angrily between clenched teeth, 'Oh you swine of a Prussian, you!' Often, when the conversation had moved on he would repeat in a voice quivering with emotion: 'Stop it will you! That's enough!' adding, as if to himself, 'Let's hope she lives to tell us the tale! That he's not the death of her, the bastard!'

Though the jokes were in the most deplorable taste, everyone, far from being shocked, was in fits of laughter. Indignation, like everything else is the product of environment and the atmosphere gradually created around them was by now frankly bawdy. By dessert, even the women were making risqué little remarks. Eyes were sparkling and much wine had been drunk. The Comte, who even in his cups maintained a façade of great seriousness, made a much enjoyed comparison between their present situation and that of shipwrecked sailors at the Pole when winter ends and an escape route to the south opens up.

Loiseau, by now well away, stood up with a glass of champagne in his hand, crying, 'I drink to our deliverance!' Everyone rose to their feet and applauded him. Even the two nuns, urged by the ladies, agreed to take the tiniest sip of the sparkling wine never tasted by them before. They concluded it was just like fizzy lemonade, only more delicate of course. Loiseau caught the general mood when he said, 'Pity there isn't a piano. We could have had a bit of a prance.'

Cornudet throughout had not uttered a single word nor made a single gesture. On the contrary, he appeared plunged in serious thought, tugging angrily at his beard from time to time as if to lengthen it still further. Finally, around midnight just as the party was breaking up, Loiseau staggered over to him, dug him in the ribs and slurred: 'Barrel of laughs you are, tonight, I must say. S'madder with you?'

Cornudet simply raised his head sharply, threw a fierce glare round the entire company and said, 'The way you've all behaved tonight's disgraceful!'

He got up and, reaching the door, added: 'Absolutely disgraceful!'

At first this cast something of a pall. Loiseau, a little stunned, stood gawping and then, recovering his wits, he doubled up with laughter.

'Sour grapes, my friend! That's what it is . . . sour grapes!'

Since no one got the joke he explained the 'secrets of the corridor'. At this, there was a great burst of renewed mirth. The ladies were in hysterics. The Comte and Madame Carré-Lamadon laughed till they cried. They could not believe it.

'You mean . . . ? You're sure. . . .? He wanted to . . . ?'

'I tell you I *saw* him!'

'And she wouldn't . . .'

'Because the Prussian was in the next room.'

'Never!'

'I swear to God.'

The Comte was choking with laughter. The industrialist was holding his sides. Loiseau went on: 'So you see why he doesn't see the funny side of it tonight! Not funny at all, *oh* no!'

And they were off again, coughing and choking and making themselves sick with laughter. At this point the party split up. Madame Loiseau commented in her waspish way, as she and her husband were getting into bed, that 'that little minx' Madame Carré-Lamadon had had a touch of the green-eyed monster in her eyes all evening. 'Some women'll go for anything in uniform. They don't give a hoot what sort. French, Prussian, you name it. Honest to God, it makes you weep!'

All night long from the darkness of the corridor all sorts of soft, barely audible sounds could be heard – faint rustles and creaks and the patter of bare feet on boards. From the narrow strips of light showing under the doorways it was clear that no one got to sleep until very late. Champagne is like that, it has the effect of a stimulant, apparently.

The following day, the winter sun shone brightly on the dazzling snow. Hitched up at last, the coach stood waiting at the front door while an army of white pigeons with black-centred pink eyes preened themselves as they strutted importantly between the legs of the six horses and pecked for food in the steaming dung.

The coachman, wrapped up in his sheepskin on the box, was puffing at his pipe as the ecstatic travellers all hurriedly packed in provisions for the remainder of the journey. Only Boule de Suif was missing. At last she appeared. She looked anxious and shamefaced. As she timidly approached her companions they turned, as one, away from her as if she were invisible. The Comte offered a dignified arm to his wife and led her away from possibly degrading contact. The plump young woman, shocked, stopped in her tracks. Then, summoning all her courage, she

went up to the manufacturer's wife and murmured politely:
'Good morning, Madame.'

The other woman in reply gave the curtest of contemptuous
nods, accompanied by a glare of outraged virtue. Affecting
to be very busy, everyone kept their distance as though she
were carrying some infection in her skirts. Rushing to the coach
they left her to arrive last and alone to take the seat she had
previously occupied during the first part of the journey. They
appeared neither to see nor to recognize her. Madame Loiseau,
however, looking indignantly over in her direction, muttered to
her husband: 'Thank goodness I'm not sitting next to *her*.'

The heavy carriage jerked into motion and they set off once
more on their journey. At first no one spoke. Boule de Suif dared
not look up. She felt simultaneously angry with her neighbours,
humiliated by having given in to them, and defiled by the caresses
of the Prussian into whose arms they had so hypocritically
thrown her.

The Comtesse, however, turning towards Madame Carré-
Lamadon, soon broke the awkward silence.

'I believe you know Madame d'Etrelles?'

'Oh yes, she's a great friend of mine.'

'What a delightful woman!'

'Charming. Very special indeed. Well-educated too and an
artist to the tips of her fingers. She has a wonderful voice and
she draws like a dream, did you know?'

The manufacturer was talking to the Comte and above
the rattle of the window panes the occasional word or phrase
could be heard: 'Dividends ... maturity date ... option ...
mature ...'

Loiseau who had stolen the ancient pack of cards belonging to the inn and greasy with five years' contact with sticky
table-tops, embarked on a game of bezique with his wife.

The two nuns, taking up the long rosaries that hung from
their belts, made a simultaneous sign of the cross. Suddenly their
lips began to move at an ever-increasing speed as if competing
in some *salve regina* steeplechase. From time to time they would
kiss a medal, cross themselves again, then once more take up
the mumbling at a rate of knots. Cornudet sat motionless, lost

in thought. After three hours' travelling Loiseau gathered up his cards. 'Time to eat,' he said.

At this his wife reached for a packet tied up with string from which she extracted a joint of cold veal. She cut it into neat, thin slices and the two began to tuck in.

'Perhaps we should follow your example,' said the Comtesse.

A chorus of approval rose and she set about unpacking the provisions which had been prepared for the two couples. In one of those long, oval vessels with a china hare for a lid indicating that within there lay a *lièvre en paté*, a succulent piece of charcuterie in which the hare's dark flesh mixed together with other finely chopped meats was streaked with white rivulets of bacon fat. There was also a fine slab of Gruyère, wrapped in newspaper and now carrying the words 'NEWS IN BRIEF' on its satiny surface. The two nuns unwrapped a hunk of garlicky *saucisson* and Cornudet, plunging his hands into the gigantic patch pockets of his greatcoat, brought out from one of them four hard-boiled eggs, and from the other the crusty end of a loaf. The shells of the eggs he threw into the straw at his feet, and as he munched each in turn a constellation of bright yellow flecks was scattered into the dark firmament of his beard.

When she rose that morning Boule de Suif had been in such haste and trepidation that she had had no time to think of anything. Choking with rage, she now looked on as around her all these people carried on calmly eating. A wave of anger surged over her and she opened her mouth to release the torrent of abuse she felt rising within her. It was so deep, however, that she was unable to utter a word. No one looked at her. No one gave her a thought. She felt overwhelmed by the contempt of these respectable swine who, having used her as a scapegoat, now rejected her as something unclean. She thought then about her great big basket full of the goodies they had greedily devoured – her two glistening chickens in aspic, her pears and her four bottles of claret. Suddenly, like a piece of string stretched to breaking-point, her anger collapsed and left her on the verge of tears. She tried desperately to control her feelings, bracing herself and swallowing back her sobs like a child. The tears welled up regardless, glistening at the tips of her eyelids.

Soon two great drops, brimming over, fell and rolled slowly down her cheeks. Others followed, flowing faster. Like drops of water trickling from a rock they fell in steady succession on to the rounded curve of her bosom. She sat erect, staring directly ahead with a set expression. She hoped no one would notice.

The Comtesse, however, did, and nudged her husband. He shrugged his shoulders as if to say, 'Well? It's nothing to do with me.' Madame Loiseau gave a quiet snigger of triumph and muttered, 'She's crying from shame, that's all.' The two nuns, having rewrapped the remainder of their *saucisson*, returned to their prayers.

Then Cornudet still digesting his eggs stretched out his long legs under the seat opposite, leaned back, folded his arms and smiled. He had just thought of a great joke: softly, he began to whistle the *Marseillaise*.

Across every face a shadow fell. The song of the Republic was obviously not a favourite of his neighbours. They shifted about uncomfortably in their seats and looked ready to howl like dogs at a barrel-organ. Well aware of its effect he continued with the song regardless. From time to time he even mouthed some of the words:

> *Amour sacré de la patrie,*
> *Conduis, soutiens, nos bras vengeurs,*
> *Liberté, liberté chérie,*
> *Combats avec tes défenseurs!*

> (O sacred love of Fatherland,
> Guide and support our venging hands,
> Dear freedom, dearest Liberty,
> Staunch guardians with us ever be!)

They were gathering speed since the snow was harder now. All the way to Dieppe, throughout the long, tedious hours of the journey along the bumpy roads, as twilight turned to night inside the coach, he kept up his monotonous, vengeful whistling, dinning into his weary and exasperated companions every word and every note.

Boule de Suif wept on, and, from time to time, in the pause between verses, a sob she was helpless to stifle escaped into the darkness.

A PARISIAN AFFAIR

Is there any keener sense known to man than woman's curiosity? There is nothing in the world she would not do in order to satisfy it, to know for certain, to grasp and possess what has hitherto remained in her imagination. What would she not do to achieve that? When her impatient curiosity is at its height, she will shrink from nothing, and there is no folly to which she will not stoop, no obstacle she will not overcome. I refer, of course, to the really feminine woman, the sort who on the surface may appear quite reasonable and objective, but whose three secret weapons are always in a high state of readiness. The first is a kind of watchful, womanly concern for what is happening around her; the second, even more deadly in its effect, is guile disguised as common decency; and the third is the exquisite capacity for deception and infinite variety which drives some men to throw themselves at her feet, and others off the parapets of bridges.

The one whose story I want to tell you about was a little provincial woman who had led until then a boringly blameless life. Her outwardly calm existence was spent looking after her family, a very busy husband and two children whose upbringing, in her hands, was exemplary in every way. But her heart was ravaged by an all-consuming, indefinable desire. She thought constantly about Paris and avidly read all the society pages in the papers. Their accounts of receptions, celebrations, the clothes worn, and all the accompanying delights enjoyed, whetted her appetite still further. Above all, however, she was fascinated by what these reports merely hinted at. The cleverly phrased allusions half-lifted a veil beyond which could be glimpsed devastatingly attractive horizons promising a whole new world of wicked pleasure.

From where she lived, she looked on Paris as representing the height of all magnificent luxury as well as licentiousness. Throughout the long, dream-filled night, lulled by the regular snoring of her husband sleeping next to her on his back with a scarf wrapped round his head, she conjured up the images of all the famous men who made the headlines and shone like brilliant comets in the darkness of her sombre sky. She pictured the madly exciting lives they must lead, moving from one den of vice to the next, indulging in never-ending and extraordinarily voluptuous orgies, and practising such complex and sophisticated sex as to defy the imagination. It seemed to her that hidden behind the façades of the houses lining the canyon-like boulevards of the city, some amazing erotic secret must lie.

And she herself was growing old. She was growing old, never having known a thing about life beyond the hideously banal monotony of regularly performed duties which, by all accounts, was what happily married life consisted of. She was still pretty. The uneventful life she lived had preserved her like a winter apple in an attic. Yet she was consumed from within by unspoken and obsessive desires. She wondered if she would die without ever having tasted the wicked delights which life had to offer, without ever, not even once, having plunged into the ocean of voluptuous pleasure which, to her, was Paris.

After long and careful preparation, she decided to put into action a plan to get there. She invented a pretext, got herself invited by some relatives and, since her husband was unable to accompany her, left for the city alone. The alleged discovery of some long-lost friends living in one of its leafy suburbs enabled her as soon as she arrived to prolong her stay by a couple of days or rather nights, if necessary. Her search began. Up and down the boulevards she walked, seeing nothing particularly wicked or sinful.

She cast her eye inside all the well-known cafés, and each morning her avid reading of the *Figaro*'s lonely hearts' column was a fresh reminder to her of the call of love. But she found nothing that might lead her to the great orgies she imagined actresses and artists enjoyed all the time. Nowhere could she discover the dens of iniquity about which she had dreamed. Without the necessary 'Open Sesame' she remained debarred from Ali Baba's cave. Uninitiated, she stood on the threshold of the catacombs where the secret rites of a forbidden religion were performed. Her petty bourgeois relatives could offer her an introduction to none of the fashionable men whose names buzzed in her ears. In despair, she had almost decided to give up when, finally, happy chance intervened.

One day, as she was walking down the Chaussée d'Antin,[1] she stopped to look at the window of a shop selling Japanese *bibelots*[2] in such gay, cheerful colours as to delight the eye. She was looking thoughtfully at its amusing little ivories, its huge oriental vases of vivid enamelwork and its strange bronzes, when she heard from within the voice of the proprietor. With low, reverential bows, he was showing a fat, bald-headed little man with grizzled stubble the figure of a pot-bellied Buddha, the only one of its kind, or so he claimed.

With each of the merchant's utterances, the famous name of his customer sounded like a clarion call in her ears. The other browsers, young ladies and elegant gentlemen, cast oblique, highly respectful glances in the direction of the well-known author who was absorbed in his examination of the figure. One was as ugly as the other. The pair might have been taken for brothers.

'To you, Monsieur Jean Varin,' the shopkeeper was saying, 'I'll let it go for 1,000. Cost, in other words. To anyone else, it would be 1,500. My artist customers mean a lot to me. I like to offer them a special price. Oh yes, they all come to me you know, Monsieur Jean Varin . . . Yesterday, for example, Monsieur Bus-nach[3] bought an antique goblet from me . . . and the other day . . . you see those candlesticks over there, aren't they lovely? Sold a pair like them to Monsieur Alexandre Dumas[4] . . . and I mean . . . that piece you've got there . . . if Monsieur Zola[5] saw that, it'd be gone in five minutes, I can assure you, Monsieur Varin . . .'

The writer hesitated, undecided. He was obviously attracted to the figure but not the price. Had he been standing quite alone in the middle of a desert, he could not have been more oblivious of the interest he was arousing. Trembling, she went in. Young, handsome, elegant or not, it was nevertheless Jean Varin himself and on Jean Varin alone she now fixed a bold gaze. Still struggling with himself, he finally replaced the figure on the table.

'No,' he said, 'it's too expensive.'

The merchant redoubled his efforts.

'Too expensive, Monsieur Jean Varin? But you know it's worth two thousand if it's worth a franc!'

Sadly, as he continued to gaze into the enamelled eyes of the figure, the man of letters replied, 'I'm sure it is. But it's too expensive for me.'

At this, wildly daring, she stepped forward and said: 'Supposing I were to ask. What would it be to me?'

Surprised, the merchant replied: 'Fifteen hundred, Madame.'

'I'll take it.'

The writer, who until then had been totally unaware of her presence, turned round quickly and at first somewhat coldly looked her up and down. Then he cast more of a connoisseur's eye over her. She was charming, vibrant and suddenly lit up by the flame which had till this second been dormant within her. After all, a woman who snaps up a curio at 1,500 is not exactly run-of-the-mill.

With exquisite delicacy in her movement, she turned to face him now and said in a trembling voice, 'I'm so sorry, Monsieur. I'm afraid I rather rushed in. Perhaps you had not yet decided.'

He bowed. 'I had indeed, Madame.'

In a voice shaking with emotion she said: 'If you should ever change your mind, either today or at some later time, it shall be yours. I bought it solely because you liked it.'

Visibly flattered, he smiled. 'But how on earth do you know who I am?' he inquired. She listed his works and expressed with some eloquence her admiration of them. Leaning his elbows on a piece of furniture he settled down to a conversation, weighing her up all the while with his penetrating gaze.

New customers had come into the shop and from time to time the merchant, delighted with such living testimony to the excellence of his stock, called from one end of the shop to the other: 'There you are, you see, Monsieur Jean Varin! What about that then?' Everyone looked over and she felt a thrill of pleasure at being seen chatting on such intimate terms with one of the great and the good.

Dizzy with success, she felt like a general about to make one supremely daring attack. 'Monsieur,' she said, 'would you do me a great, a very great favour? Will you let me give you this figure as a keepsake from a woman of ten minutes' acquaintance who has the most ardent admiration for you?'

He refused. She insisted. Laughing happily, he resisted yet again, but she was determined.

'In that case, I shall take it to your home straight away. Where do you live?'

He refused to give his address but having acquired it from the merchant as she paid, she rushed off to find a fiacre.[6] The writer ran to catch her up, unwilling to expose himself by accepting this gift from a total stranger, and, with it, who knew what sort of obligation. Reaching her just as she was jumping into the cab, he flung himself in and nearly fell on top of her as it jolted into motion. He sat down beside her, more than a little embarrassed.

She was quite intractable. His protests and pleas fell on deaf ears. As they arrived at the door, she set out her conditions.

'I shall agree not to leave it with you if, throughout the whole of today, you will carry out all my wishes.'

The whole thing sounded so extraordinarily amusing that he accepted.

'Now,' she said. 'What would you normally be doing at this time of day?'

After a little hesitation, he said: 'I'd be going for a walk.'

In a firm tone she ordered, 'To the Bois!'[7]

And off they went. After this, he had to tell her the names of all the women people were talking about, especially the flighty ones, and give her every intimate detail he could about where they lived, how they spent their days, and all their wicked little ways.

It was now getting towards evening time.

'What do you usually do at this sort of time?' she asked.

Laughing, he replied, 'I go for a glass of absinthe.'[8]

They went into a large boulevard café where he was a regular and met all his colleagues. He introduced them to her. She was wild with joy. And in her head, there echoed ceaselessly the words 'At last! At last!'

Time passed. 'Is this when you normally dine?' she asked.

'Yes, Madame,' he replied.

'Then, Monsieur, let's go and dine,' she said.

Emerging from the Café Bignon,[9] she asked, 'What do you normally do in the evening?'

He looked at her steadily.

'It depends. Sometimes I go to the theatre.'

'Well then, Monsieur, let's go to the theatre.'

He was recognized by the management at the Vaudeville[10] who found seats for them straight away. To crown it all, she was seen by the entire audience, sitting by his side in the first row of the balcony.

After the show, he kissed her hand gallantly and said, 'It only remains, Madame, for me to thank you for a delightful . . .'

She interrupted. 'What is it you do at this time of night?'

'What do I do? You mean what do I . . . ? Well I go home, of course.'

'In that case, Monsieur, let us go to your home,' she said, laughing shakily.

Not a word more was spoken. From time to time a shiver ran through her, half of terror, half of delight. She was in an exquisite agony, torn between the desire to run away and her determination, in her heart of hearts, to stay and see it through.

As they mounted the stairs, her feelings nearly overcame her and she leaned heavily on the banister while he wheezed on ahead, carrying a taper.

As soon as she was in the bedroom, she undressed quickly, slid wordlessly into bed and, huddling up against the wall, waited.

She was as unsophisticated, however, as only the lawful wife of a country solicitor can be, while he was as demanding as a pasha with three tails. They did not get on at all well. Not at all.

Afterwards, he fell asleep. The night hours passed silently

save for the ticking of the clock as, motionless, she thought of her conjugal nights at home.

By the yellow light of a Chinese lantern, she looked in dismay at the tubby little man beside her, lying on his back with the sheet draped over his hot-air balloon of a belly.

While he snored like a pipe-organ, with comic interludes of lengthy, strangulated snorts, the few hairs he possessed, exhausted by the onerous responsibility of masking the ravages of time on his balding skull during the day, now stood perkily on end. A dribble of saliva flowed from the corner of his half-open mouth.

When dawn finally broke, light fell through a gap in the drawn curtains. She got up, dressed noiselessly and had just managed to ease the door open when the latch grated. He woke up and rubbed his eyes. It took a few seconds for him to recover his senses, when the whole affair came flooding back into his mind.

'Oh . . . so . . . you're leaving then, are you?' he asked.

'Well . . . yes,' she stammered, 'it's morning.'

He sat up in bed.

'Look . . .', he said, 'let *me* ask something for once, will you?'

As she made no reply, he went on, 'I don't understand what you've been up to all this time . . . since yesterday. Come on . . . tell me what you're up to . . . I can't work it out . . .'

Gently, she drew closer, blushing like a young girl.

'I always wanted to know what it was like to be . . . wicked . . . and actually . . . it turns out to be not all that much fun . . .'

She ran from the room, flew down the staircase and flung herself out into the street.

Down it an army of sweepers was sweeping. They swept the pavements and the cobblestones, driving all the litter and filth into the stream of the gutter. With the same regular movement, like reapers in the field, they swept up all in a wide semi-circle ahead. And as she ran through street after street, still they came to meet her, moving like puppets on a string with the same, mechanical, mowing movement. She felt as though something inside her, too, had now been swept away. Through the mud, down to the gutter and finally into the sewer had gone all the refuse of her over-excited imagination.

Returning home, the image of Paris swept inexorably clean by the cold light of day filled her exhausted mind, and as she reached her room, sobs broke from her now quite frozen heart.

A WOMAN'S CONFESSION

My friend, you asked me to tell you what is the most vivid memory I have of my life. Well, since I am now extremely old and have neither children nor any remaining relatives I feel I can quite freely confess something to you. All I ask is that you never reveal my name.

I was often in love and over the years had many admirers. Now that there is no trace of it left I can tell you I was once considered quite a beauty. And it was love that put life into me. It became the air I breathed. I would have sooner died than not be in the heart and mind of someone else every minute of the day. Although some women claim there is never more than one serious love in life, for me it was different. I have often loved someone with such intensity that I thought it would last till the end of time. But these affairs, too, petered out quite naturally, like a fire with no fuel to sustain it.

I shall tell you about the very first of my adventures. I was very much the innocent party in this and it had a strong influence on all my other affairs.

It was that dreadful story in the papers about the revenge taken on that chemist[1] which reminded me of an appalling business I was once reluctantly involved in myself.

I had been married for a year to a very rich man, the Comte Hervé de Ker—— a Breton aristocrat with whom I was of course not in love. True love in my view can only flourish in conditions where there is a mixture of freedom and constraint. An imposed love, sanctioned by law and blessed by a priest does not really seem the same thing at all. One stolen kiss is worth a thousand of the other kind, don't you think?

My husband was tall, elegant, every inch a gentleman but a bit short on intelligence. He used to bark out the most ill-considered opinions and it was clear that his mind was full of received ideas handed down to him from his mother and father, who in turn had inherited them from theirs. He never mulled a thing over but came up with an immediate and naturally inadequate response. He was not in the least aware of this limitation or that there might be more than one way of looking at things. His was a closed mind in which nothing much was really going on. There was no ventilation of ideas, no renewal of the spirit. It was like a house all the doors and windows of which are firmly shut.

The manor house in which we ourselves lived was in the back of beyond. It was a great gloomy place surrounded by enormous trees whose trunks were covered with moss and looked like bearded old men. The parkland in which it was set was heavily wooded and itself surrounded by a deep trench or ha-ha.

At the furthest boundary of the property, giving on to moorland, were two small lakes full of reeds and water plants. Between them, at the edge of a small stream, my husband had had constructed a small shelter or blind for duck-shooting.

In addition to the usual servants, we had a watchman, a brute of a fellow totally devoted to my husband for whom he would have happily laid down his life; and, for myself, a personal maid who by this time had become almost a friend and who was equally attached to me. She was a foundling I had brought back from Spain five years previously. With her deep olive skin and her dark eyes she could easily have been taken for a gipsy. She had thick, black hair always a little dishevelled around the forehead, and looked about twenty years of age though in fact she was only sixteen.

It was the beginning of autumn and a great deal of hunting was under way either on our property or that of our neighbours in the area. A young man, the Baron de C—— began calling at the manor rather more often than was normal until his visits quite abruptly stopped. I thought no more about it but noticed that my husband's attitude towards me was much changed.

He seemed preoccupied, spoke little and never kissed me. Despite the fact that we had separate rooms so that I could have a little privacy, often at night I would hear furtive footsteps come as far as my door and after a few minutes retreat.

Since my window was on the ground floor I often used to fancy that I also heard someone wandering around outside the manor itself. I said as much to my husband, who stared fixedly at me for a few seconds before saying: 'Nothing to worry about. It must be the nightwatchman.'

One night as we were finishing dinner, at which Hervé had been in unusually and therefore suspiciously good spirits, he asked me: 'How would you like to spend a couple of hours with me down at the duck blind? There's a fox who's started helping himself to my chickens every night. I want to get him.'

I was surprised and hesitated a little before replying: 'Certainly, my dear, if that's what you would like.'

I should add that I myself was a keen huntswoman and would go after both wolf and boar with the best of them. So it was not unnatural for him to suggest what he did. But suddenly he started to look very nervous. It was most peculiar. All evening long he was restless. No sooner had he sat down than he got up again and so it went on. He was obviously in a state of very great agitation.

Then at about ten o'clock he asked if I was ready and I rose. He brought me my gun himself and I asked if we were using bullets or shot. At this he looked surprised and said, 'Oh, shot will do the trick, you can be sure of that!'

Then after a few seconds he turned round and said, again in this peculiar sort of tone: 'Well I have to hand it to you. You're a very cool customer indeed!'

I started to laugh.

'Why on earth do you say that? It doesn't take much to go and pick off an old fox! What on earth's got into you, my dear?'

We then set off across the grounds in silence. The full moon cast a yellow sheen on the dark old building and its gleaming slate roof. A patch of light could be seen at the summits of the two towers flanking the house. No sound disturbed the melancholy silence of the clear night air and the heavy, subdued atmosphere in which we walked seemed lifeless. Not a breath of air moved, not a frog croaked, and in the deep gloom which weighed upon the world not even the hoot of an owl could be heard.

When we reached the parkland trees, however, the smell of fallen leaves brought a freshness to the air. My husband remained silent. He was obviously listening and watching for something. With his huntsman's instinct now fully aroused he seemed almost to be sniffing the shadows for a scent.

Soon we reached the edge of the lakes. Here again not a breath of air ruffled their tresses of reeds. But barely perceptible movements could be seen in the water itself. A point would appear on the surface and from it would spread, like luminous furrows on a brow, a series of gently widening ripples.

When we reached the blind where we were to lie in ambush my husband ushered me in first then slowly loaded his gun. The click of the flintlock produced a strange effect on me. Sensing my alarm, my husband said, 'Perhaps you have seen enough by now. If so, do feel free to leave.'

His words surprised me and I said, 'Certainly not. Why should I leave now, for goodness' sake? You *are* in a strange mood tonight.'

'Just as you wish,' he murmured.

We remained there motionless until, after half an hour or so when still nothing had come to disturb the deep tranquillity of the clear night, I whispered: 'Are you absolutely certain this is the way he comes?'

Hervé started as if I had suddenly bitten him.

'Absolutely sure! Get that straight!' he hissed, close to my ear.

Once again, silence fell. I was just beginning to nod off when my husband gripped my arm. In a changed voice he whispered urgently again, 'There! Can you see him? Over by the trees!'

I looked but could make out nothing. Slowly and without taking his eyes off me he put his gun to his shoulder. I too was about to fire when suddenly, no more than thirty paces away, a man came out into the moonlight. He was moving quickly, his body hunched, as if running away from something. I was so stupefied that I cried out loudly. Before I could turn round I saw a flash and heard a deafening report. I watched as the man rolled on the ground like a wolf struck by a bullet.

I started to scream with fright when suddenly Hervé grabbed me furiously round the throat with his hand. I was thrown to the ground, then picked up bodily and carried aloft by him towards the figure stretched out on the ground. He hurled me hard on top of it as if he wanted to crack open my skull. I thought my last moment had come. He was about to kill me. Already his heel was poised over my forehead.

Suddenly, before I could see what was happening, it was his turn to be grabbed and thrown to the ground. I got up quickly and saw Pepita, my maid, kneeling on top of him. She was clinging to him like a furious wildcat, frenziedly tearing out his hair and clawing the skin of his face. Then, as if suddenly overwhelmed by another instinct, she got up and threw herself now on the other man's dead body. She clasped it to her bosom, kissed the eyes and the mouth, searching desperately for some breath of life beyond her lover's precious lips.

My husband, now on his feet again, stood and watched. As understanding dawned upon him, he flung himself at my feet.

'My darling! Forgive me! I thought *you* were being unfaithful to me. It's this poor girl's lover I have killed . . . my watchman!'

But I was watching the terrible sight of the living girl, her distracted kisses raining on the dead man and her pitiful starts of despair as she sobbed.

It was then that I decided to give my husband real grounds for suspicion.

COCKCROW

Madame Berthe d'Avancelles had rejected the advances of her admirer Baron Joseph de Croissard to such an extent that he was now in despair. He had pursued her relentlessly throughout the winter in Paris, and now at his château at Carville in Normandy he was holding a series of hunting parties in her honour.

The husband, Monsieur d'Avancelles, turned a blind eye to all this. It was rumoured that they lived separate lives on account of a physical shortcoming of his which Madame could not overlook. He was a fat little man with short arms, short legs, a short neck, short nose, short everything in fact.

Madame d'Avancelles, in contrast, was a tall, chestnut-haired, determined-looking young woman. She laughed openly at old Pipe and Slippers as she called him to his face but looked with tender indulgence on her admirer, the titled Baron Joseph de Croissard, with his broad shoulders, his sturdy neck and his fair, drooping moustache.

Until now, however, she had granted him no favours despite the fact that he was spending a fortune on her, throwing a constant round of receptions, hunting parties, and all kinds of celebrations to which he invited the local aristocracy.

All day long the woods rang to the sound of hounds in full cry after a fox or a wild boar and every night a dazzling display of fireworks spiralled upwards to join the sparkling stars. A tracery of light from the drawing-room windows shone on the huge lawns where shadowy figures occasionally passed.

It was the russet season of autumn when leaves swirled over the gardens like flocks of birds. Wafting on the air came the tang of damp, bare earth, caught as the smell of a woman's naked flesh as her gown slips down to the floor after the ball.

On an evening during a reception held the previous spring, Madame d'Avancelles had replied to an imploring Monsieur de Croissard with the words: 'If I am to fall at all, my friend, it will certainly not be before the leaves do likewise. I've far too many things to do this summer to give it a thought.' He had remembered those daring words of hers spoken so provocatively and was now pressing his advantage. Each day he crept closer, gaining more and more of the bold beauty's heart until by this point her resistance seemed hardly more than symbolic.

Soon there was to be a great hunting party. The night before, Madame Berthe had said laughingly to the Baron: 'Tomorrow, Baron, if you manage to kill the beast I shall have something to give you.'

He was up at dawn reconnoitring where the wild boar was wallowing. He accompanied his whips, setting out the order of the hunt in such a way that he should return from the field in triumph. When the horns sounded for the meet, he appeared in a well-cut hunting costume of scarlet and gold. With his upright, broad-chested figure and flashing eyes he glowed with good health and manly vigour.

The hunt moved off. The boar was raised and ran, followed by the baying hounds rushing through the undergrowth. The horses broke into a gallop, hurtling with their riders along the narrow forest paths while far behind the following carriages drove noiselessly over the softer verges.

Teasingly, Madame d'Avancelles kept the Baron at her side, slowing down to walking pace in an interminably long, straight avenue along which four rows of oaks arched vaultlike towards each other. Trembling with both desire and frustration he listened with one ear to the young woman's light badinage, the other pricked for the hunting horns and the sound of the hounds growing fainter by the minute.

'So you love me no longer,' she was saying.

'How can you say such a thing?' he replied.

'You do seem to be more interested in the hunt than in me,'

she went on.   He groaned. 'You do remember your own orders don't you? To kill the beast myself.'

'Indeed I do,' she added with great seriousness. 'Before my very eyes.' At this he quivered impatiently in the saddle, spurred on his eager horse and finally lost his patience.

'For God's sake, Madame, not if we stay here a minute longer.'

'That is how it has to be nevertheless,' she cried laughingly. 'Otherwise, you're out of luck.'

Then she spoke to him gently, leaning her hand on his arm and, as if absentmindedly, stroking his horse's mane. They had turned right on to a narrow path overhung with trees when, suddenly swerving to avoid one of their low branches, she leaned against him so closely that he felt her hair tickling his neck. He threw his arms around her and pressing his thick moustache to her forehead planted upon it a passionate kiss.

At first she was motionless, stunned by his ardour, then with a start she turned her head and, either by chance or design, her own delicate lips met his beneath their blond cascade. Then, out of either embarrassment or regret for the incident she spurred her horse on the flank and galloped swiftly away. For a long while they rode straight on together, without so much as exchanging a glance.

The hunt in full cry was close and the thickets seemed to shake, when suddenly, covered in blood and shaking off the hounds that clung to him, the boar went rushing past through the bushes. The Baron gave a triumphant laugh, cried 'Let him who loves me follow me!' and disappeared, swallowed up by the forest. When Madame d'Avancelles reached an open glade a few minutes later he was just getting up, covered with mud, his jacket torn and his hands bloody, while the animal lay full length on the ground with the Baron's knife plunged up to the hilt in its shoulder.

The quarry was cut by torchlight on that mild and melancholy night. The moon gilded the red flames of the torches which filled the air with pine smoke. The dogs, yelping and snapping, devoured the stinking innards of the boar while the beaters and the gentlemen, standing in a circle around the spoil, blew their horns with all their might. The flourish of the hunting horns

rose into the night air above the woods. Its echoes fell and were
lost in the distant valleys beyond, alarming nervous stags, a
barking fox and small grey rabbits at play on the edge of the
glades. Terrified night birds fluttered above the crazed pack
while the women, excited a little by the violence and vulner-
ability surrounding these events, leaned a little heavily on the
men's arms and, without waiting for the hounds to finish, drifted
off with their partners down the many forest paths. Feeling
languid after all the exhausting emotion of the day Madame
d'Avancelles said to the Baron: 'Would you care for a turn in
the park, my friend?'

He gave no answer, but trembling and unsteady with desire
pulled her to him. Instantly they kissed and as they walked very
slowly under the almost leafless trees through which moonlight
filtered, their love, their desire and their need for each other was
so intense that they almost sank down at the foot of a tree.

The horns had fallen silent and the exhausted hounds were
sleeping by now in their kennels.

'Let us go back,' the young woman said. They returned.

Just as they reached the château and were about to enter, she
murmured in a faint voice: 'I'm so tired, my friend, I'm going
straight to bed.' As he opened his arms for one last kiss she fled,
with the parting words: 'No . . . to sleep . . . but . . . let him who
loves me follow me!'

An hour later when the whole sleeping château seemed dead
to the world the Baron crept on tiptoe out of his room and
scratched at the door of his friend. Receiving no reply he made
to open it and found it unbolted.

She was leaning dreamily with her elbows on the window
ledge. He threw himself at her knees which he showered with
mad kisses through her nightdress. She said nothing, but ran her
dainty fingers caressingly through the Baron's hair. Suddenly, as
if coming to a momentous decision, she disengaged herself and
whispered provocatively: 'Wait for me. I shall be back.' Her
finger raised in shadow pointed to the far end of the room where
loomed the vague white shape of her bed.

With wildly trembling hands he undressed quickly by feel and
slipped between the cool sheets. He stretched out in bliss and

almost forgot his friend as his weary body yielded to the linen's caress. Doubtless enjoying the strain on his patience, still she did not return. He closed his eyes in exquisitely pleasurable anticipation. His most cherished dream was about to come true. Little by little his limbs relaxed, as did his mind, where thoughts drifted, vague and indistinct. He succumbed at last to the power of great fatigue and finally fell asleep.

He slept the heavy, impenetrable sleep of the exhausted huntsman. He slept indeed till dawn. Then from a nearby tree through the still half-open window came the ringing cry of a cock. Startled awake, the Baron's eyes flew open. Finding himself, to his great surprise, in a strange bed and with a woman's body lying against his he remembered nothing and stammered as he struggled into consciousness: 'What? Where am I? What is it?'

At this, she, who had not slept a wink, looked at the puffy, red-eyed and dishevelled man at her side. She answered in the same dismissive tone she took with her husband. 'Nothing,' she said, 'it's a cock. Go back to sleep, Monsieur. It's nothing to do with you.'

MOONLIGHT

The abbé Marignan lived up to his illustrious name.[1] His un-wavering faith was as solid as a rock and he believed he under-stood God, as well as his every wish, intention and design. As he walked on the path leading to his little country presbytery he would sometimes ask himself why God had done a certain thing. He would think very carefully, and after putting himself in God's position he nearly always discovered a reason. Far be it from him to murmur in a moment of pious humility, 'O Lord, how mysterious are thy ways . . .' Instead, he would say, 'I am God's servant on earth. Therefore it is right that I should know the reason for his actions and, if I don't, to hazard a pretty good guess what it might be.'

Everything in nature seemed to him to have been created with impeccable and admirable logic. Every great 'Why?' could always be answered by some great 'Because'. Dawns were made so that the world should be glad to rise; daylight so that the crops should ripen; rain for irrigation; evening to prepare for sleep and dark night for slumber itself.

The four seasons similarly met all the needs of agriculture, and never would it have occurred to the priest that nature might have no purpose or that all life might be the product of blind temporal, geographical and physical necessity.

Women, however, were another matter altogether. He loathed them. It was an unconscious loathing based on instinctive mis-trust. Often he would quote the words of Christ: 'Woman, what have I to do with thee?'[2] adding, 'It's as if God himself were not happy with that particular work of his.' Woman for him was most certainly the 'twelve times impure' of whom the poet speaks.[3] She was the temptress who had first led man astray and continued to this day her execrable work. She was a weak, dangerous and mysteriously disturbing creature. Even more than her fatal body, he hated her loving soul.

Often he had felt a certain tenderness directed towards himself by women and, though impervious to it, he was irritated by the constant need for love which throbbed within them. In his view God had created woman solely in order to tempt man and thereby to test him. She was to be approached with infinite caution and wariness, as a snare. With her parted lips and arms outstretched towards man she was in fact exactly like a trap. The only exception he made was in the case of nuns, whose vows made them harmless. However he was sometimes harsh towards even them, sensing within their captive and contrite hearts that same eternal tenderness which, priest or not, got under his skin. He sensed it in their gaze, more tearful and pious than that of monks; he sensed it in the ecstasy which, in their case of course, was mixed up with sex; their surges of love for Christ infuriated him for being, when all was said and done, purely carnal and female. He could feel this wretched tenderness in their docility, in the gentleness of their voices when they addressed him, in their lowered eyes, in their mournful resignation to his rough reprimands. At the door of the convent when he left, he shook out the skirts of his cassock and lengthened his stride as if fleeing from some danger.

Despite all this, he was determined that his niece, who lived with her mother in a little house nearby, should become a nun. She was a pretty, fun-loving young scatterbrain. Whenever the priest pontificated to her she laughed in his face, and when he was cross she hugged him tight and showered him with kisses. He would automatically try to extricate himself from this embrace which, he had to admit, he found absolutely delightful, awakening within him as it did the paternal instinct lying dormant in every living man.

Often as he walked beside her on the meadow paths he would speak to her of God. She scarcely listened and the joy with which she contemplated instead the sky, the grass, and the flowers was reflected in her eyes. Sometimes she would rush off to try and

catch some winged creature, crying as she brought it back,
'Look, uncle! Isn't it sweet. Don't you want to give it a little
kiss?' This need of hers to kiss butterflies and lilac buds made
the priest sick. He was both worried and irritated to find even
in her that ineradicable tenderness that lurked always in the
heart of woman.

Then one day his sacristan's wife, who did the Abbé Marignan's housework, informed him, choosing her words very carefully, that his niece had a lover. He was appalled when he heard
this news as he was shaving, and stood there speechless, with
lather all over his face. When he had gathered his wits and could
put his thoughts into words again he spluttered: 'It's not true!
You're making it up, Mélanie!'

But the simple woman put her hand on her heart.

'As God is my witness, Father, as soon as your sister's gone
to bed, off she goes. Along the river they meet. See for yourself
between ten and midnight.'

He stopped scratching his chin and, as was his wont when he
wanted to think something through, started pacing briskly up
and down. Taking up his razor again later, he managed to cut
himself three times between the nose and the ear. All day long
he remained silent, suppressing his growing anger and indignation. As a priest he was furious at losing a future nun to
earthly love. As her moral tutor also he was exasperated. He
was like a father to her, after all, the guardian of her soul. And
to think that he had been deceived, tricked and cheated by this
slip of a girl! He felt all the selfish shock of parents confronted
with the news that their daughter has chosen her own husband
without or despite their advice.

After dinner he tried to read for a while but failed. His
exasperation increased. When the clock struck ten he took up
his stick, a formidable oak staff which he always took with him
on night visits to the sick. He smiled down at the great cudgel
he now twirled menacingly in his horny hand. Suddenly he
raised it and, gnashing his teeth as he did so, brought it down
on a chair with such force that the back split and it crashed to
the floor.

He opened his door and was about to leave when suddenly

he stopped in amazement on the threshold of the house. He had rarely in his life seen such magnificent moonlight as now. Like some of the early Christian Fathers, he was blessed with a soul open to rapture and with a poetic disposition. He was suddenly moved, not to say overwhelmed, by the great serenity and beauty of the pale night before him. In his little garden bathed in soft light his rows of fruit trees threw in shadow the shapes of their branches barely in bud; the breath of the huge honeysuckle spreading over the wall of the house wafted its sweet perfume like the soul of fragrance upon the clear and balmy air. He began to breathe deeply himself, drinking it in greedily and slowing down his pace. He was entranced by the scene, so lost in wonder that the thought of his niece all but faded away.

As soon as he reached the open country he stopped in order to contemplate the whole plain which was suffused with this caressing glow and basking serenely in the tender, languid charm of the night. The brief, metallic croak of frogs filled the air on which the notes of a distant nightingale fell one by one. Its clear and delicate song was made more for reverie than reflection and its music to accompany kisses in the magic of the moonlight. As the priest took up his walk again he felt something within him, he knew not what, begin to falter. He felt suddenly tired and weak. He needed to sit down and look, to admire the work of God.

In the distance a long line of poplars snaked along the winding river's edge. A fine, vaporous white mist through which gleaming silver moonbeams shone hovered over and around the banks and enveloped in a transparent cocoon every twist and turn of the waters.

The priest stopped once more, touched to the depths of his soul as he felt growing within him a mounting and irresistible tenderness. He could feel a worrying doubt creep into his thoughts: a question was beginning to grow once more in his mind. Why had God created this? Since night was obviously made for sleep and unconsciousness, rest and all-embracing oblivion, why make it even more lovely than the day and sweeter than any twilight or dawn? Why did this slow and stately star, more beautiful than the sun itself, banish all shadow and illumine things too delicate and mysterious for the light of day? Why did the finest of nature's songbirds not rest like her fellows but sing alone in the darkness of night? Why this veil cast over the world? Why the wild beating of his heart? This yearning of his soul? Why this languor of the body? Why this panoply of loveliness which no one sees if asleep in bed? For whom was this sublime spectacle created, this poetry beamed down from heaven to earth?

The priest could find no answer.

Suddenly in the distance at the meadow's edge, under the arch of trees resplendent in the glistening haze, two shadowy figures walking side by side came into view. The man, the taller of the two, had his arm around the shoulders of his partner and from time to time, drawing her closer to him, he kissed her forehead. The couple gave life to this still landscape which surrounded them like some divine frame. They seemed as one, the single being for whom this calm and silent night was made. They came towards the priest as a living response sent to him by his Maker.

As he stood there stunned and with his heart pounding, the sight before him seemed almost Biblical, like the love of Ruth and Boaz, an expression of God's will set in one of the great scenes of holy writ.[4] Words from the 'Song of Songs' began to form in his mind and the cries of passion, the yearning of the flesh, the fierce, burning ardour of that most tender of poems returned to him.

And he said to himself, 'Perhaps God has created this sort of night in order to imbue the love of man with something of the ideal.' He retreated as the two, entwined, approached ever closer. And though she was his niece he now wondered whether he could disobey the will of God. How could God disapprove of love since he surrounded it with such obvious splendour? Distraught and almost ashamed, he disappeared quickly from sight, as if trespassing in a temple where he had no right to be.

AT SEA

The following lines appeared in several recent newspaper reports:

Boulogne-sur-Mer, 22 January.
We are informed that:
A further tragedy has been added to the many trials already suffered over the past two years by our coastal population. A fishing vessel under the command of skipper Javel, while attempting to reach port, was blown westward on to the breakwater rocks of the jetty and wrecked. Despite efforts on the part of lifeboatmen, and the use of projectile life-lines, four men and one boy lost their lives. Foul weather persists and further incidents are expected.

I wonder who this man Javel is and if he could perhaps be the brother of a one-armed man I know. If he's the man I think he is, this poor fellow crushed by the waves and battered to death by the shattered remains of his own ship was involved eighteen years ago in another of those stark, terrifying dramas which happen so often at sea.

At that time, Javel the elder was skipper of a trawler, which is the best kind of fishing boat in the world. Built to withstand all kinds of weather, her round hull bobs up and down on the waves like a cork. Out winter and summer and whipped this way and that by the stiff, salt winds of the Channel, she works the sea tirelessly. Under sail, she carries on one side of the hull an enormous net which rakes the bottom of the ocean and gathers up, among other things, all kinds of creatures asleep on the rocks of the deep – enormous hook-clawed crabs, moustachioed lobsters, and flatfish lying peacefully on the surface of the sand.

The boat sets out to fish in a fresh breeze and a choppy sea. Her net is fixed to a long, iron-clad spar of wood which is lowered by means of two cables running off two rollers fore and aft. Drifting in the wind and the current, she pulls this juggernaut of a dragnet along the seabed, scooping up all in its path.

Javel had on board his younger brother, four men and a ship's boy. He had set off on the trawl from Boulogne in beautiful, clear weather. Soon, however, the wind rose and a sudden squall forced the trawler to tack out of its way. She reached the coast of England, but here a raging sea was hurling itself against the cliffs and beating so hard upon the coast that it was impossible to put in at any harbour. The trawler put out again into the open sea and made for the French coast. The storm was raging still. It was impossible to put in: every approach to safety was barred by perilous, roaring white water.

The trawler set out yet again, running over the back of the sea, buffeted and battered by streaming banks of water. Despite the conditions, the crew were undaunted. The ship was built for the sort of weather which could keep her drifting between the two countries and unable to make landfall on either for five or six days at a time. At last, when she was way out in the open sea, the storm subsided. Despite a heavy swell, the skipper ordered the net to be cast.

Accordingly, the great apparatus was set in motion. Two men, one fore and one aft, controlled the cables on the rollers holding it in place. Suddenly, the net touched bottom. But just at that same moment the boat was pitched sideways by a huge wave and young Javel, up in the bow, stumbled, only to find his arm pinned behind the cable as the tension momentarily slackened. With his free hand, he made a desperate effort to shift the cable, but the weight of the net pulling it downwards meant it would not give an inch.

Doubled up in agony, the man called for help. Everyone ran up. His brother left the helm, and the entire crew now hurled themselves on the cable in an effort to disengage the limb in process of being crushed. It was no good.

'Got to cut it!' said one of the sailors, drawing out of his pocket a large knife which in two strokes would have saved young Javel's arm. But that meant losing the net, which was worth a vast amount of money – fifteen hundred francs. The net belonged to Javel the elder who valued his property highly.

His heart in torment, he shouted, 'No! Don't cut yet! See what happens if I bring her into the wind.'

He ran to the tiller and brought it right over. The boat scarcely moved, paralysed now by the net, in conjunction with the force of the current and the wind.

Young Javel had sunk to his knees, his teeth clenched and his face haggard. His brother returned to see no one used the knife.

'Wait! wait!' he said. 'Lower the anchor first!'

The anchor was released and the whole chain extended to the full. They then began to heave at the capstans to loosen the trawler lines. Finally these slackened and from them the crew disengaged the arm, now inert inside its bloodied woollen sleeve.

Young Javel was near senseless. His pea-jacket removed, a terrible sight was revealed. The flesh was crushed to a pulp from which blood was spurting as if from a pump. The man looked at his arm and murmured, 'Finished.'

As he continued to haemorrhage a pool of blood on to the deck, one of the sailors cried: 'He'll bleed to death! Quick! Tie the vein!'

Using thick brown tarred thread, they laced the limb over the wound as tightly as they could. The bleeding diminished and finally stopped altogether. Young Javel got up. His arm dangled at his side. Grasping it with the other hand, he turned it over and shook it. Everything was broken. The flesh was hanging on by the muscles alone. He looked at it with a sad, reflective gaze, then sat down on a furled sail while his mates advised him to keep the wound wet so as to avoid gangrene.

They put a bucket beside him so that he could keep dipping a glass into it and bathe the horrible wound with a constant trickle of clear water.

'You'd be better off below, mate,' said his brother.

Young Javel went down but returned after an hour, wanting

company. Besides, he preferred to be out in the fresh air. He sat down again on his sail and continued to bathe his arm.

It was a good catch. Wide, white-bellied fish thrashed next to him in spasms of death, while he went on soaking his own pulverized flesh.

Just as they were about to reach Boulogne, the wind began to buffet them once more, and the little ship ran wildly before it, every lurch and crash a fresh torture for the injured man. Night fell and the storm still raged till daybreak. As the sun rose, England was in sight, but since the sea was less rough now, they turned into the wind and headed for home.

Towards evening, young Javel called his mates and showed them threads of black where the part of his limb no longer attached to him was beginning to develop a nasty, putrid look.

The sailors looked and gave advice.

'Looks like the black to me,'[1] was one opinion.

'Needs salt water putting on it,' declared another.

Salt water was brought and poured over the wound. The patient blenched, gritted his teeth and writhed in silent torment. When the pain had subsided, he said to his brother: 'Give us your knife.' Javel the elder handed it to him.

'Hold the arm up, straight. Stretch it up.'

They did as he asked. He then began to cut himself. Gently and thoughtfully at first, he sliced back the last few tendons with the razor-sharp blade until finally only a stump remained. He gave a deep sigh, and declared: 'Had to be done. It'd had it.'

Breathing heavily now, he seemed relieved, and carried on pouring water on what was left of his limb. It was a foul night again, with no hope of landing. When day broke, young Javel picked up his severed arm and examined it for a long time. It was definitely putrefying. His mates came and looked also, passing it around, feeling it, turning it over and sniffing it.

His brother said: 'Better chuck it overboard, smartish.'

At this, young Javel got annoyed. 'Not on your life, mate! Not having that! Whose arm is it anyway?'

He took it back and tucked it between his knees.

'It'll rot, you watch,' said the elder brother.

Suddenly, an idea came to the wounded man. To keep fish

fresh on board a ship likely to be at sea for some time, they were piled into barrels of salt.

'What about pickling it?' he asked.

'That'll do it,' the others declared. They then emptied one of the barrels full of the latest catch and placed the arm at the bottom. Having poured salt all over it, they replaced the fish, one by one.

One of the sailors joked: 'As long as we don't put it in the auction.'

Everyone apart from the two Javel brothers laughed.

The wind was still gusting, and just off Boulogne they sailed close-hauled till ten the next morning. The wounded man continued to pour water on the injury, walking from time to time from one end of the boat to the other. His brother, watching him from the helm, shook his head. Finally they reached port.

The doctor examined the wound and declared it to be in satisfactory condition. Having bandaged it all up, he prescribed rest. Javel, however, would not go to bed before retrieving his arm. He hurried back to the harbour to find the barrel he had marked with a cross. It was emptied for him and he picked up the limb which had kept well in the brine and looked fresh and puckered. He wrapped it in the towel he had brought with him, and returned home.

His wife and children studied this relic of the father, touching the fingers and picking off grains of salt stuck under the nails. They then called for a carpenter to come and measure it for a small coffin.

The following day, the entire crew of the trawler came to bury the severed arm. Side by side, the two brothers headed the procession. The parish sacristan carried the coffin tucked under his arm.

Young Javel left the sea and found light work in the harbour. Later, whenever he told the tale, he would confide quietly to his audience: 'If my brother had been willing to cut the net, I'd still have my arm today, that's for sure. But he was what you might call a careful owner.'

A MILLION

There was once a modest little civil servant and his wife. The husband, who worked at one of the Ministries, was a stickler for propriety and worked meticulously at his job. His name was Léopold Bonnin. Though a very correct and orthodox young man brought up in the Church, he had become slightly less of a believer since the Republic's recent tendency to separate the Church from the State.[1] He could be heard openly declaring in the corridors of the Ministry, 'I *am* a religious man, in fact very much so, but I believe in God and not priests.' He was above all, as he proclaimed striking his breast, a man of honour. And indeed he was a man of honour in the most pedestrian sense of the word. He arrived at work punctually, left it punctually, hardly ever wasted time once he got there and was conspicuously honourable in what he called 'matters pecuniary'.

He had married the daughter of a poor colleague. The latter had a sister who, by contrast, having married for love, was now a millionairess. This sister, to her lasting sorrow, had never had children of her own and was therefore obliged to pass on her wealth to her only niece. This inheritance was all the family thought of. Its presence floated around the house and over the entire Ministry where everyone knew that the Bonnins would one day 'come into a million'.

The young couple too were childless but this was no problem to them as they carried on calmly in their honourable, straight, not to say narrow little ways. The apartment was neat and clean and had a slightly soporific effect on them. Their watchword was moderation in all things. A child, they thought, would only disturb their life together, their home, and their tranquillity. They would have gone to no special lengths to remain without issue, but since Heaven had sent them none, so much the better.

The millionairess aunt, however, was dismayed by their childlessness and advised them how to reverse it. She herself had tried out, with obvious lack of success, thousands of tips offered by friends and fortune-tellers alike and now, past childbearing age, she had heard thousands more, all allegedly infallible. She grieved over their present uselessness to her and redoubled her efforts to have her family put them into practice. 'Well?' she would incessantly ask, 'Have you tried what I was recommending to you the other day?'

She died. In the hearts of the young couple a joy was born, concealed from both themselves and from others by mourning. The deep black veil of conscience hid eyes that sparkled with delight. They were advised that the will was deposited with a certain notary, to whom they rushed directly after the funeral service.

The aunt, true to her apparently lifelong intent, had left her million to their first-born with the usufruct to the parents during their lifetime. If, after three years, the young couple still had no heir the fortune was to go to charity.

They were stunned, prostrated. The husband became ill and stayed off work for a whole week. Then, when he had recovered, he swore he would become a father.

For six months he tried so hard that he became a mere shadow of his former self. He recalled all his aunt's helpful hints and conscientiously put them into practice but to absolutely no avail. His unflagging determination gave him a kind of artificial energy which proved nearly fatal. He was consumed by anaemia. Tuberculosis was suspected. The prognosis of a doctor he consulted frightened him so much that he reverted to the comfortable routine of his former life and returned to even greater peace and quiet than before.

At the Ministry there was much hilarity and mirth. The contents of the disappointing will were public knowledge and in every department there were sniggers about the 'missed million'.

Bonnin was given some dubiously helpful suggestions and some offers to fulfil the conditions of the will on his behalf. One young bachelor in particular, allegedly a great ladies' man, whose exploits were office legend, kept making crude digs at him and saying he could make him inherit in twenty minutes. One day Léopold Bonnin lost his temper and, rising suddenly, pen behind the ear, flung at him: 'Monsieur, you are disgusting! If I hadn't more respect for myself I'd spit in your eye!'

Witnesses and seconds were called and there ensued a great to-do at the Ministry lasting three entire days. The corridors were full of people sending affidavits and opinions back and forth about the whole affair. Finally an agreement was reached by the four delegates involved and accepted by the two interested parties who, in the presence of the department head, bowed gravely to each other, murmured mutual apologies and formally shook hands.

For the following month they continued to greet each other with studied formality like enemies meeting face to face. Then one day when they bumped into each other coming round a corner Monsieur Bonnin said, 'I do hope I haven't hurt you, Monsieur.'

'Not in the least, Monsieur,' the other replied.

From that moment on they began to exchange a few words whenever they met. Gradually they became more and more informal with each other. They got used to each other's ways and began to get on well together. They came eventually to respect each other and forget their former misunderstandings to such an extent that they became inseparable.

But Léopold was unhappy at home. His wife kept up a stream of hideous, hurtful allusions and hidden barbs. And time was passing. It was already a year since the aunt's death. The inheritance seemed lost forever. Madame Bonnin sitting down to a meal would remark: 'We've not got much for dinner. Of course it would be different if we were rich.'

When Léopold left for the office Madame Bonnin would hand him his cane, saying: 'If we had an income of 50,000 a year you wouldn't have to go and slave the day away at that place, you stupid little hack.'

When Madame Bonnin was leaving to go out in the rain she would mutter: 'If we had a carriage, we wouldn't have to get ourselves filthy on days like this.'

In other words, every minute of the day and in every circumstance it was as if she blamed her husband for something shameful that he alone was guilty of and for which he alone was responsible, namely, the loss of that fortune. Driven beyond endurance, he took her to a famous doctor who, after a lengthy consultation, could diagnose nothing. He said he could see nothing wrong, that such cases were by no means rare, that the body was like the mind, and that he had seen as many couples riven by physical incompatibility as by its temperamental counterpart. The cost would be forty francs please.

Another year passed. It was open warfare now and an unrelenting, bitter hatred raged between husband and wife. Still Madame Bonnin continued: 'How tragic to lose a fortune through being married to an idiot!'

Or alternatively:

'To think that if you'd been any other sort of man I'd have 50,000 a year by now!'

Or again:

'Some people are a misery in life. They manage to spoil everything.'

Dinner and the evenings generally became intolerable. One night, bereft of ideas and fearing a row at home, Léopold took along with him his friend Frédéric Morel, the man with whom he had almost fought a duel. Soon Morel was a friend of the family and the respected counsellor of both husband and wife alike.

Only six months remained before the deadline at which the million was to be donated to charity. Little by little, Léopold's attitude towards his wife changed. Now it was he who had become the aggressor, making veiled insinuations designed to hurt and referring mysteriously to other fellows' wives who really knew how to help a husband's career. From time to time he would report the unexpected rise in fortune of some secretary or other: 'Young Ravinot . . . only a copy clerk five years ago . . . Look at him now, deputy head of section . . .'

Madame Bonnin would retort: 'Unlike you of course, completely useless as usual . . .'

Léopold would shrug his shoulders. 'Ah, well of course
he's got an intelligent wife, that's the thing. She knows how to
get round the head of department. She can get anything she
wants. If you want to get on in life you can't let things get on
top of you.'

What exactly did he mean? What did she take him to mean?
What was this all about? They each had a calendar on which
they marked off the days leading up to the fateful date. Every
week they felt an increasingly mad, desperate rage and such total
exasperation that they would have been capable, if necessary, of
committing any crime in the world.

But what did happen was that one morning Madame Bonnin,
her eyes shining and her face radiant, placed her two hands on
her husband's shoulders and looking steadily and joyfully deep
into his soul said quietly: 'I think I'm pregnant.'

His heart leapt so that he nearly fell over backwards. He
seized his wife in his arms, showered her with kisses, sat her on
his knee and hugged her again and again like an adored child
till finally he gave way to his emotion, wept and sobbed.

Two months later there was no longer any doubt. He took
her to a doctor to have her condition attested to and took the
certificate to the notary who held the will. This representative
of the law declared that since the child existed, born or unborn,
he acceded and would defer the execution of the will until the
end of the pregnancy.

A boy was born. Following an ancient royal tradition they
called him Dieudonné.[2]

They became rich.

Then one night when Monsieur Bonnin came home for a
dinner at which Frédéric Morel was to be their guest his wife
said simply:

'I have just asked our friend Frédéric not to set foot in this house
again. He has behaved . . . inappropriately . . . towards me.'

He looked at her for a second with a grateful smile, then
opened his arms. She flew into them and the couple embraced
over and over again like the dear husband and wife that they

were, so tender, so close and so honourable towards each other.

And you should hear Madame Bonnin when she gets going about wives who stoop to conquer and get carried away by a surge of passion into adultery!

FEMME FATALE

The restaurant, Le Grillon,[1] Mecca of the entire local boating community, was now slowly emptying. At the main entrance a large crowd of people were calling and shouting out to each other. With oars on their shoulders, strapping great fellows in white jerseys waved and gesticulated. Women in light spring frocks were stepping cautiously into the skiffs moored alongside and, having settled themselves in the stern of each, were smoothing out their dresses. The owner of the establishment, a tough-looking, red-bearded man of legendary strength,[2] was helping the pretty young things aboard and with a practised hand was holding steady the gently bobbing craft.

The oarsmen then took their places, playing to the gallery and showing off broad chests and muscular arms in their sleeveless vests. The gallery in this case consisted of a crowd of suburbanites in their Sunday best, as well as a few workmen and some soldiers, all leaning on the parapet of the bridge and watching the scene below with keen interest. One by one the boats cast off from the landing stage. The oarsmen leaned forward and with a regular swing pulled back. At each stroke of the long, slightly curved blades the fast skiffs sped through the water making for La Grenouillère[3] and growing progressively smaller till they disappeared beyond the railway bridge and into the distance.

Only one couple now remained. The slim, pale-faced young man, still a relatively beardless youth, had his arm around the waist of his girl, a skinny little grasshopper of a creature with brown hair. They stopped from time to time to gaze into each other's eyes.

The owner cried: 'Come on, Monsieur Paul, get a move on!'

The couple moved down closer. Of all the customers, Monsieur Paul, who paid regularly and in full, was the best liked and most respected. Many of the others ran up bills and frequently absconded without settling them. The son of a senator, he was also an excellent advertisement for the establishment. When some stranger asked, 'And who's that young chap over there with his eyes glued to the girl?' one of the regulars would murmur, in a mysterious, important sort of way, 'Oh, that's Paul Baron, you know, the son of the senator.' Then the stranger would inevitably have to comment, 'Poor young devil, he's got it bad.' The proprietress of Le Grillon, a good businesswoman and wise in the ways of the world, called the young man and his companion 'my two turtle doves' and looked with tender indulgence on the love affair which brought such glamour to her establishment.

The couple ambled slowly down to where a skiff called the *Madeleine* was ready. Before embarking, however, they stopped to kiss once more, much to the amusement of the audience gathered on the bridge. Finally, Monsieur Paul took up the oars and set off after the others also making for La Grenouillère.

When they arrived it was getting on for three and here too the vast floating café was swarming with people. It is in effect one huge raft with a tarpaulin roof supported by wooden columns. It is connected to the charming island of Croissy by two narrow footbridges, one of which runs right through to the centre of the café itself. The other connects at the far end with a tiny islet where a single tree grows and which is nicknamed the Pot-de-Fleurs. From there it connects with the land again via a bathing pool.

Monsieur Paul moored his boat alongside the café, climbed up to its balustrade then, holding his girl's two hands, guided her up also. They entered, found a place for two at the end of a table and sat down opposite each other.

Lining the towpath on the opposite side of the river was a long string of vehicles. Fiacres[4] alternated with the flashy carriages of gay young men-about-town. The first were lumbering great hulks whose bodywork crushed the springs beneath and to which were harnessed broken-down old hacks with drooping necks. The other carriages were streamlined, with light suspension and fine, delicate wheels. These were drawn by horses with slender, straight, strong legs, heads held high and bits snowy with foam. Their solemn, liveried drivers, heads held stiffly inside huge collars, sat ramrod straight with their whips resting on their knees.

The river banks were crowded with people coming and going in different kinds of configurations: family parties, groups of friends, couples and individuals. They idly plucked at blades of grass, wandered down to the water's edge then climbed back up to the path. Having reached a certain spot they all congregated to wait for the ferryman whose heavy boat plied constantly back and forth, depositing passengers on the island.

The branch of the river, incidentally called the dead branch, which this floating bar dominates, seemed asleep, so slowly did the current move there. Flotillas of gigs, skiffs, canoes, pedaloes and river craft of all kinds streamed over the still water, mingling and intersecting, meeting and parting, running foul of each other, stopping, and with a sudden jerk of their oarsmen's arms and a tensing of their muscles, taking off again, darting this way and that like shoals of red and yellow fish.

More were arriving all the time; some from Chatou upstream, some from Bougival, downstream. Gales of contagious laughter carried from one boat to another and the air was full of insults, complaints, protestations and howls. The men in the boats exposed their muscular, tanned bodies to the glare of the sun and, like exotic water-plants, the women's parasols of red, green and yellow silk blossomed in the sterns of their craft.

The July sun blazed in the middle of the sky and the atmosphere was gay and carefree, while in the windless air not a leaf stirred in the poplars and willows lining the banks of the river. In the distance ahead, the conspicuous bulk of Mont-Valérien loomed, rearing the ramparts of its fortifications in the glare of the sun. On the right, the gentle slopes of Louveciennes, following the curve of the river, formed a semi-circle within which could be glimpsed, through the dense and shady greenery of their spacious lawns, the white-painted walls of weekend retreats.

On the land adjoining La Grenouillère strollers were sauntering under the gigantic trees which help to make this part of the
island one of the most delightful parks imaginable. Busty women
with peroxided hair and nipped-in waists could be seen, made
up to the nines with blood red lips and black-kohled eyes.
Tightly laced into their garish dresses they trailed in all their
vulgar glory over the fresh green grass. They were accompanied
by men whose fashion-plate accessories, light gloves, patent-
leather boots, canes as slender as threads and absurd monocles
made them look like complete idiots.

The part of the island facing La Grenouillère is narrow and
between it and the opposite bank where another ferry plies,
bringing people over from Croissy, the current is very strong
and very fast. Here it swirls and roars, raging like a torrent in a
myriad of eddies and foam. A detachment of pontoon-builders
wearing the uniform of artillerymen was camped on the bank
and some of the soldiers, side by side on a long beam of wood,
sat watching the river below.

A noisy, rambunctious crowd filled the floating restaurant.
The wooden tables, sticky and awash with streams of spilt
drink, were covered with half-empty glasses and surrounded by
half-tipsy customers. The crowd sang and shouted and brawled.
Red-faced, belligerent men, their hats tipped at the backs of their
heads and their eyes glassy with booze, prowled like animals
spoiling for a fight. The women, cadging free drinks in the
meantime, were seeking their prey for the night. The space
between the tables was filled with the usual clientèle – noisy
young boating blades and their female companions in short
flannel skirts.

One of the men was banging away at the piano using his
feet as well as his hands. Four couples were dancing a quadrille
and watching them was a group of elegantly dressed young
men whose respectable appearance was ruined by the hideous
incongruity of the setting.

The place reeked of vice and corruption and the dregs of
Parisian society in all its rottenness gathered there: cheats, con-
men and cheap hacks rubbed shoulders with under-age dandies,
old roués and rogues, sleazy underworld types once notorious

for things best forgotten mingled with other small-time crooks and speculators, dabblers in dubious ventures, frauds, pimps, and racketeers. Cheap sex, both male and female, was on offer in this tawdry meat-market of a place where petty rivalries were exploited, and quarrels picked over nothing in an atmosphere of fake gallantry where swords or pistols at dawn settled matters of highly questionable honour in the first place.

Every Sunday, out of sheer curiosity some of the people from the surrounding countryside would drop in. Every year would bring a fresh batch of young men, extremely young men at that, keen to make useful contacts. Casual cruisers would amble by and every so often a complete innocent would become embroiled.

La Grenouillère lived up to its name. There was a place for bathing between the tarpaulin-covered raft where drinks were served and the Pot-de-Fleurs. Women with the requisite curves came there to display their wares and their clients. Those less fortunate who required padding and corsetry to pass muster looked disdainfully on as their rivals cavorted and splashed about.

Awaiting their turn to plunge in and thronging around a small diving board were swimmers of every shape and size: some slim and straight as vine-poles, some round as pumpkins, some gnarled as olive-branches, some with bodies curved forward over pot-bellies, some whose vast stomachs threw the body backwards. Each was as ugly as the other as they leapt into the water and splashed the customers drinking at the café next door.

Despite the proximity of the river and the huge trees shading it, the place was suffocatingly hot. Mingling with the fumes of spilt drinks came the smell of flesh and the cheap perfume with which the skin of those trading in sex was drenched. Underlying all these smells was the slight but persistent aroma of talc, which wafted with varying intensity as if an unseen hand were waving some gigantic powder-puff over the entire scene.

All eyes were on the river where the comings and goings of the boats attracted everyone's attention. Girls sprawled in the stern opposite their strong-wristed menfolk looked with contempt at those still prowling about the island in search of a male to buy them dinner that night. Sometimes when a crew in full swing flashed past their friends ashore would shout and were joined by the crazy, yelling crowd inside the restaurant. At the bend of the river near Chatou boats were constantly coming into view. As they approached and grew more distinct, faces became recognizable and more shouts went up.

A boat with an awning and containing four women came slowly downstream towards them. The woman at the oars was small, lean and past her prime. She wore her hair pinned up inside an oilskin hat. Opposite her a big blonde dressed in a man's jacket was lying on her back at the bottom of the boat with a foot resting on the thwart on either side of the oarswoman. The blonde was smoking a cigarette and with each jerk of the oars her bosom and her belly quivered. At the very stern of the boat under the awning two beautiful, tall, slender girls, one blonde the other brunette, sat with their arms round each other's waists watching their two companions.

A shout went up from La Grenouillère: 'Aye-aye! Lesbos!' and suddenly a wild clamour broke out. In the terrifying scramble to see, glasses were knocked over and people started climbing on the tables. Everyone began to chant 'Lesbos! Lesbos! Lesbos!' The words merged into a vague howl before suddenly starting up again, rising into the air, filling the plain beyond, resounding in the dense foliage of the tall surrounding trees and echoing in the distance as if aimed at the sun itself.

During this ovation the oarswoman had calmly come to a halt. The big blonde lying at the bottom of the boat turned her head languorously and raised herself on her elbows. The two in the stern started laughing and waving to the crowd. At this there was even more of a hullabaloo and the place shook with the noise. The men raised their hats and the women waved their handkerchiefs. Every voice, deep and shrill alike, chanted in unison 'Lesbos!' This motley collection of undesirables seemed to be saluting a leader, as warships give a gun salute to their passing admiral. From the flotilla of boats also there was wild acclamation for the women's boat which now continued at its leisurely pace, to land a little further off.

Monsieur Paul's reaction was unlike that of the others. Pulling a key from his pocket he started using it as a whistle and blew hard. His girl, looking nervous now and even paler than before, pulled his arm to make him stop. This time when she looked into his eyes, it was with fury. But he was beside himself with male jealousy and a deep, instinctive ungovernable rage. His lips trembling with indignation he stammered: 'Shouldn't be allowed! They should be drowned like puppies with stones round their necks!'

Madeleine suddenly lost her temper. Her shrill voice became piercing as she lashed out at him: 'Mind your own business, will you! They've got a perfect right to do whatever they want. They're not doing any harm to anyone. Why don't you just shut up and leave them alone . . .'

He cut her short. 'This a matter for the police! If it was up to me I'd have them locked up in Saint-Lazare!'[5]

She gave a start. 'Oh you would, would you?'

'Certainly I would. And in the meantime I forbid you to have anything to do with them. I absolutely forbid it, do you understand?'

She shrugged her shoulders at this and said in a suddenly calm voice: 'Listen, dear, I shall do exactly as I please. If you don't like it you know what you can do. Get the hell out. Now. I'm not your wife, so shut up.'

He remained silent and they stood staring each other out, breathing rapidly, their mouths set.

At the other end of the café the women were now making their entrance. The two dressed as men led, one gaunt and weatherbeaten, ageing and very mannish. The other, more than amply filling the white flannel outfit with her large bottom and her huge thighs encased in the wide trousers, waddled forward like a fat, bow-legged goose. The two friends followed and the whole boating community surged forward to shake hands.

The four had rented a riverside cottage and lived together there as two couples. Their vice was public, official and perfectly obvious to all. It was referred to quite naturally as something entirely normal. There were rumours about jealous scenes that took place there and about the various actresses and other famous women who frequented the little cottage near the water's edge. One neighbour, scandalized by the goings-on, alerted the police at one stage and an inspector accompanied by one of his men came to make enquiries. It was a delicate mission: there was nothing the women could be prosecuted for, least of all prostitution. The inspector was deeply puzzled and could not understand what these alleged misdemeanours could possibly be. He asked a whole lot of pointless questions, compiled a lengthy report and dismissed the charges out of hand. The joke spread as far as Saint-Germain.

Like queens they now walked slowly the entire length of La Grenouillère. They seemed happy to be in the limelight and delighted with the attention paid to them by all this riff-raff. Madeleine and her lover watched them, and as they approached the girl's face lit up.

When the leading couple reached their table Madeleine cried 'Pauline!' and the big girl, turning round, stopped, still arm in arm with her midshipwoman.

'Well good heavens! Madeleine! Darling! Come and join us for a bit. We must catch up!'

Paul tightened his grip on his girl's wrist but she said, 'You know what you can do, sweetheart, shove off.'

He kept quiet and let her be. Standing huddled together the women continued their animated conversation *sotto voce*. Pauline from time to time cast furtive glances at Paul and flashed him an evil, sardonic smile. Finally, unable to bear it a minute longer he suddenly stood up and trembling in every limb leapt towards her. He seized Madeleine by the shoulders and said: 'Come with me, do you hear? I said you were not to speak to these beastly women!'

Raising her voice, Pauline began to swear at him like a fish-wife. People around started laughing. Others stood on tip-toe to get a better look. Under the hail of filthy abuse he was speechless. Feeling contaminated by it and fearing there might be worse to come he retreated, retraced his steps and went to lean on the balustrade overlooking the river, turning his back on the three triumphant women. He stayed there looking at the water and every so often brusquely wiping away the tears that sprang to his eyes.

The fact was that despite himself, without knowing why or how it had happened and very much against his better judgement, he had fallen hopelessly in love. He had fallen as if into some deep and muddy hole. By nature he was a delicate and sensitive soul. He had had ideals and dreamed of an exquisite and passionate affair. And now he had fallen for this little cricket of a creature. She was as stupid as every other woman and not even pretty to make up for it. Skinny and foul-tempered, she had taken possession of him entirely from tip to toe, body and soul. He had fallen under the omnipotent and mysterious spell of the female. He was overwhelmed by this colossal force of unknown origin, the demon in the flesh capable of hurling the most rational man in the world at the feet of a worthless harlot. There was no way he could explain its fatal and total power.

Behind his back now he could feel something evil brewing. Their laughter pierced his heart. What should he do? He knew very well but had not the courage. He stared fixedly at the opposite bank where an angler was fishing, his line perfectly still. All of a sudden the man jerked out of the water a little silver fish which wriggled at the end of his line. Twisting and turning it this way and that he tried to extract his hook, but in vain. Losing patience he started pulling and, as he did so, tore out the entire bloody gullet of the fish with parts of its intestines attached. Paul shuddered, feeling himself equally torn apart. It seemed to him that the hook was like his own love and that if he were to tear it out he too would be gutted by a piece of curved wire hooked deep into his essential self at the end of a line held by Madeleine.

Feeling a hand on his shoulder he started and turned round. Madeleine was standing beside him. Neither spoke. She simply put her elbows on the balustrade beside him and leaned with him, staring out at the river. He tried to think of something to say but failed. He was incapable of analysing what was going on inside him. All he felt now was joy in the very nearness of her and a shameful cowardice on his own part. He wanted to forgive her, to let her do anything in the world she liked provided she never left him again.

After a while in a very gentle voice he asked, 'Would you like to leave now? We'll be better off in the boat.'

'All right my pet,' she said.

Awash with forgiveness and with tears still in his eyes he held her two hands tightly and helped her on board. Basking in the warmth of the afternoon they rowed upstream again past the willows and the grass-covered banks. When they reached Le Grillon once more it was not yet six, so, leaving their skiff, they set off on foot towards Bezons across the meadows and past the high poplars bordering the banks.

The wide hayfields waiting to be harvested were full of flowers. The sinking sun cast a mantle of russet light over all and in the gentle warmth of the day's end the fragrance of the grass wafted in on them mingling with the damp smells of the river and filling the air with easy languor and an atmosphere of blessed well-being.

He felt soft and unresistant, in communion with the calm splendour of the evening and with the vague, mysterious thrill of life itself. He felt in tune with the all-embracing poetry of the moment in which plants and all that surrounded him revealed themselves to his senses at this lovely restful and reflective time of day. He was sensitive to it all but she appeared totally unaffected. They were walking side by side when suddenly, bored by the silence, she began to sing. In a squeaky, unmodulated voice she sang one of the catchy tunes of the day which jarred violently with the deeply serene mood of the evening. He looked at her and felt between them an unbridgeable abyss. She was swinging her parasol through the grass with her head down, looking at her feet as she sang, drawing out the notes and adding the odd little trill.

So behind the smooth little brow which he so much adored there was nothing! Absolutely nothing! Its sole concern at the moment was this caterwauling. The thoughts which from time to time passed through it were as vapid as the music. She had no understanding of him. They were as separate and distinct as if they had never met. His kisses had touched her lips only and nothing deeper within.

When, however, she raised her eyes to meet his and smiled,

he felt himself melt. Opening his arms out wide to her in a surge of renewed love he clasped her passionately to him. Since he was crushing her dress as he did so, she eventually broke free saying consolingly, 'Yes, yes, I love you, my pet, now that's enough.' In a mad rush of relief he grabbed her round the waist and started to run, dragging her with him. He kissed her on the cheeks, the temples and the neck, all the time dancing with joy. They threw themselves down at the edge of a thicket incandescent in the light of the setting sun. Even before catching their breath they came together. She could not understand the rapture he felt.

Walking back hand in hand they suddenly saw through the trees the river and on it the boat containing the four women. Big Pauline must have caught sight of them at the same time since she straightened up, blew kisses at Madeleine and shouted, 'See you tonight!'

'See you tonight!' shouted Madeleine in reply.

Paul felt his heart turn suddenly to ice. They returned for dinner and settling down in one of the arbours at the side of the water they began to eat in silence. When darkness fell, a candle enclosed in a globe was brought which shed a feeble, glimmering light on the two. All the time they could hear bursts of laughter coming from the large room on the first floor where the boat-trippers were. The couple were just about to order dessert when Paul, taking Madeleine's hand tenderly in his own, said: 'Darling, I feel so tired. Shall we make an early night of it?'

But she saw through his little ploy and shot him an enigmatic glance, one of those treacherous looks that so often appear in women's eyes. She thought for a second, then said, 'You're perfectly welcome to go to bed if you like but I've promised to go to the dance at La Grenouillère.'

Attempting to mask his misery he gave her a pitiful smile and answered in a coaxing, wheedling tone: 'Be a darling. Let's both stay here. Please.'

She shook her head without saying a word. He tried again. 'Please, sweetheart . . .'

She cut him off. 'You know what I said. If you're not happy, you know where the door is. Nobody's stopping you. But I've promised, and I'm going.'

He put his two elbows on the table, sank his head into his hands and sat brooding. The trippers were coming down the stairs, yelling as usual before setting off for the dance at La Grenouillère. Madeleine said to Paul: 'Make up your mind. If you're not coming I'll ask one of these gentlemen to take me there.'

Paul rose. 'Come on then,' he muttered before they too set off. The night was dark and the sky full of stars. Around them the air was still hot and the atmosphere heavy with seething, unseen activity. The warm breeze caressed their faces, its hot breath stifling their own and making them gasp slightly. The skiffs set off, each with a Venetian lantern in the prow. It was too dark to see anything of the boats themselves except for the little patches of colour in the night bobbing and dancing like frenzied glow-worms. Voices sounded from the shadows on all sides as the young couple's skiff glided gently along. Sometimes when another overtook they would catch the flash of the oars-man's white-jerseyed back illuminated by his lantern. As they came round the bend of the river, La Grenouillère came into sight in the distance.

In gala mood, the place was decorated with bunting and with strings, clusters and garlands of fairy lights. On the surface of the Seine large barges moved slowly about, representing domes, pyramids and all kinds of monuments picked out in variously coloured lights. Illuminated festoons hung down as far as the water itself, and here and there an enormous red or blue lantern suspended from an invisible rod hung like a huge star in the sky.

All these illuminations shone on the café and floodlit the great trees on the bank whose trunks stood out pale grey and whose leaves were milky green against the deep, pitch black of the fields and of the sky. A band consisting of five local players blared shrill, syncopated music across the water and, hearing it, Madeleine began to sing along. She wanted to go in right away. Paul would have preferred to make a tour of the island first but had to give in. The clientèle had thinned out a little by this time, still consisting mostly of boatmen with the odd sprinkling of middle-class couples and a few young men flanked by girls. The director and organizer of the can-can[6] strutted in his faded black suit and cast round the audience the world-weary, professional eye of a cheap music-hall master of ceremonies. Paul was relieved to see that Big Pauline and her chums were nowhere to be seen.

People were dancing. Couples faced each other and capered about madly, kicking their legs as high as their partners' noses. The women, who appeared to have double-jointed legs and hips, leapt about in a frou-frou of lifted skirts, flashing their knickers and kicking their legs up over their heads with amazing agility. They wriggled their bellies and shook their bosoms, spreading about them the powerful smell of female flesh in sweat. The males squatted like toads in front of them making faces and obscene gestures. They cavorted and turned cartwheels, posturing meanwhile in hideous parody, as one strapping maid and two waiters served the audience drinks.

Since the café-boat was covered by a roof only and had no side walls to separate it from the outdoors, the whole rumbustious dance was performed against the backdrop of the peaceful night and a firmament dusted with stars. Suddenly Mont-Valérien in the distance lit up as if a fire had started behind it. The glow deepened and spread, describing a wide, luminous circle of pale light. Then a ruby-coloured shape appeared, grew large, and glowed like red-hot metal. The circle widened further still and seemed to be emerging from the earth itself, as the moon, breaking free of the horizon, sailed gently upwards into space. As it rose, its crimson glow dimmed and turned to an increasingly light then bright yellow. As the planet climbed higher it grew smaller and smaller still in the distance.

Paul, lost in long contemplation of this sight, had become oblivious of his girl. When he turned round she had disappeared from view. He looked for her in vain. Having searched anxiously and systematically up and down the rows of tables he started asking people. No one had seen her. He then began to wander about wretchedly until one of the waiters said: 'If you're looking for Madame Madeleine, she went off a little while ago with Madame Pauline.'

Simultaneously, he caught sight of the midshipwoman and the two beautiful girls sitting at the opposite end of the café, arms round each other's waists, watching him and whispering.

Realizing what had happened, he ran off like a madman towards the island. Chasing first in the direction of Chatou, he stopped at the edge of the plain, turned and retraced his steps. He began to search the dense coppices, wandering about aimlessly and stopping every so often to listen. All he could hear around him was the short, metallic croak of frogs. Towards Bougival an unfamiliar bird sang a song which reached him faintly from a distance. Over the broad fields the moon shed a soft, filmy light. It filtered through the foliage, silvering the barks of the poplars and casting a shower of brilliant moonbeams on the shimmering tops of the tallest trees. Despite himself Paul was enchanted by the intoxicating loveliness of the night. It penetrated the terrible anguish he was feeling and stirred in his heart a fierce sense of irony. He longed with all his gentle and idealistic soul for a faithful woman to worship – someone in whose arms he could express all his love and tenderness as well as his passion.

Choked by racking sobs, he had to stop in his tracks. Having recovered a little he went on, only to feel a sudden stab in his heart. There, behind that bush . . . a pair of lovers! He ran forward and saw their silhouettes united in a seemingly endless kiss before they quickly ran off at his approach. He dared not call out, knowing full well that his own girl would not respond. He was desperately afraid now of coming upon them all of a sudden. The music of the quadrilles with its piercing solo cornets, the mock gaiety of the flute and the scraping of the fiddles pulled at his own heartstrings and deepened the pain he continued to feel.

Suddenly it occurred to him that she might have gone back in! Yes, that was it! She must have returned. He had lost all sense of proportion, he was stupid, he had been carried away by all the silly suspicions and fears that always haunted him. In one of those periods of strange calm which occur during periods of the blackest despair he turned and began to make for the café again.

He took in the whole room at a single glance. She was not there. He checked all the tables, and once again came face to face with the three women. He must have looked the picture of dejection for the three burst out laughing. Rushing out again,

he ran back to the island. He threw himself into the coppices
and stopped to listen once more. It was some time before he
could hear anything save the roaring in his own ears. Finally,
however, he thought he could hear some way ahead a shrill little
laugh he knew only too well. Creeping forward he fell to his
knees and crawled on, parting the branches cautiously as he
went. His heart was beating so wildly in his chest that he could
hardly breathe. Two voices were murmuring. He could not
make out what they were saying. Then they fell silent again.

He had a sudden furious desire to run away, not to see, not
to know and to keep on running to escape from the raging
passion with which he was consumed. He would return to
Chatou, catch a train and never come back. He would never see
her again. Just as suddenly her face appeared in his mind's eye.
He saw her as she was waking up next to him in their warm bed.
He saw her snuggle up to him and throw her arms round his
neck. Her hair was loose and a little tangled over her brow. Her
eyes were still closed and her lips parted, waiting for the first
kiss of the day. The thought of this morning's embrace filled
him with unbearable regret and frantic desire.

They were talking again. He approached bent double. Then
a cry rose from under the branches close to him. That cry!
It was one of those he had come to know from their most
tender, their most passionate love-making. He crept even closer,
drawn irresistibly, blindly, despite himself ... and then he
saw them.

Oh! If only the other person had been a man! But this! He
was transfixed by the loathsome sight before him. He remained
there overwhelmed by shock. It was as though he had just
stumbled upon the mutilated body of a loved one. It was a crime
against nature, a monstrous and wicked desecration. Suddenly
flashing into his mind's eye this time came the image of the little
fish whose entrails he had earlier seen ripped out. Madeleine
was moaning 'Pauline', exactly as she used to moan 'Paul' to
him. Hearing it, he felt such pain that he turned and fled. He
hurtled into one tree and ricocheted into another, fell over a
root, picked himself up and ran again until suddenly he found
himself at the edge of the river. The raging torrent made whirls

and eddies on which the moonbeams now played. On the opposite side the bank loomed over the water like a cliff, leaving a wide band of black at its foot from which the sound of the swirling water rose in the darkness. Clearly visible on the other side were the weekend homes at Croissy.

Paul saw all this as if in a dream or as something remembered. He was no longer thinking. He understood nothing now. Everything including his own existence seemed vague, distant, forgotten and finished. There was the river. Did he know what he was doing? Did he want to die? He had lost his mind. Nevertheless he turned round to face the island where she was. Into the night in which the faint but persistent beat of the dance-band still throbbed back and forth, he shouted, 'Madeleine!'

His heart-rending call pierced the great silence of the sky and echoed, lost in the distance. Then with a furious animal-like leap he plunged into the river. The water splashed then closed over the spot setting up a series of ever-widening circles which rippled in the moonlight as far as the opposite bank. The two women had heard. Madeleine got up and said, 'That's Paul.' A suspicion arose suddenly in her mind. 'He's drowned himself,' she said and rushed towards the bank where Pauline caught up with her.

A heavy punt with two men in it was circling over and over around the same spot. One of the men rowed while the other was plunging a long pole into the water evidently looking for something. Pauline shouted: 'What's happened? What are you doing?'

A stranger's voice cried: 'A man's just drowned himself.'

With haggard faces the two women huddled together and watched the boat's manoeuvres. The music from La Grenouillère pounding in the distance provided a grim counterpoint to the movements of the solemn fishermen. The river, now containing a corpse in its depths, continued to swirl in the moonlight. The search was prolonged and Madeleine, waiting in horrible suspense, shivered. Finally, after a good half-hour, one of the men announced: 'I've got him!'

Very gradually he pulled in the boathook. A large mass appeared at the surface of the water. The other boatman left his oars and between the two, each heaving with all his strength, they managed to haul the inert body and bring it tumbling into the boat. They soon reached the bank and found an open, flat space in the moonlight. As they landed, the women approached.

As soon as she saw him Madeleine recoiled in horror. In the light of the moon's rays he looked green already and his mouth, his eyes, his nose and his clothes were full of the river's slime. The stiff fingers of his clenched fist looked hideous. Black, liquid silt covered his entire body. The face looked swollen and from his hair now plastered down with ooze a stream of filthy water ran. The two men examined him.

'You know him?' asked one.

The other, the Croissy ferryman, hesitated.

'Seems to me I know the face . . .,' he said, 'but it's difficult to tell seeing him like this . . .'

Then suddenly: 'Oh! I know! It's Monsieur Paul!'

'Who's Monsieur Paul?' his friend asked.

The first went on: 'You know! Monsieur Paul Baron. Son of that senator. The kid who was so hooked on that girl, you remember?'

The other added philosophically: 'No more girls for him now, eh? Poor sod. And with all that money too!'

Madeleine, having collapsed on the ground, was sobbing. Pauline approached the body and said, 'I suppose he really is dead . . . there's no chance he might . . . ?'

The men shrugged their shoulders.

'After that length of time no question.'

Then one of them asked: 'Was he staying at Le Grillon?'

'Yes,' said the other. 'We'd better take him back there. Handsome tip, mate.' Re-embarking they set off, moving slowly against the rapid current. Long after they had disappeared from the two women's sight the regular sound of their oars could still be heard.

Pauline took poor, weeping Madeleine in her arms, kissed and rocked her for a long time and then said: 'Now look. As long as you know it's not your fault. You can't stop men doing stupid things. It was his decision so it's just too bad, that's all.'

Then lifting her to her feet, she added, 'Come on darling!

Come and sleep at the house. You can't go back to Le Grillon tonight.' She kissed her again. 'Come on, you'll feel better with us,' she said.

Madeleine got up, still sobbing, but less violently. She leaned her head on Pauline's shoulder. Seeming to find there a safer, warmer refuge and a closer, more intimate affection, she walked slowly away from the scene.

MONSIEUR JOCASTE

Do you remember, Madame, that great argument we had one night in the little Japanese drawing room, about the father who committed incest? Remember how angry you were at the time? How you insulted me? What a wave of righteous indignation you were riding? Can you remember all I said in his defence? This is my appeal against the guilty verdict you then pronounced. In your view no one in the world can absolve anyone else of the infamous crime I was defending then. So now I'd like to bring the whole drama out into the public arena. Perhaps we will find someone who, without ever denying the brutal, distasteful facts of the matter, will nevertheless understand that one cannot always overcome certain inevitabilities, certain freak circumstances with which Nature, in all her rich variety, sometimes presents us.

This particular girl had been married off at the age of sixteen to a hard-nosed old businessman keen to get his hands on her dowry. She was a pretty little blonde creature, a cheerful, idealistic sort of girl who longed for perfect happiness. Her heart, aching from early disillusionment, finally broke. Suddenly she realized that all her hopes for the future had been destroyed. The only desire left in her soul was to have a child to whom she could devote all the abundant love she had within her.

None came.

Two years passed. She fell in love. He was a young man of twenty-three who loved her and would have done anything for her. For a long time she resisted his advances strenuously. Then one winter evening when he had dropped in for a cup of tea and they were alone in the house, the two of them had sat down together on a low seat by the fireside. They were so transfixed by desire that they could scarcely speak. Each pair of lips thirsted desperately for the other and their arms trembled with the need to open wide and embrace. A lace-shaded lamp cast an intimate glow on this scene in the silent room. Equally embarrassed, they exchanged the occasional word but each time their eyes met their hearts leapt violently. What is the use of fine feelings when pitted against the power of instinct? And what chance does modest restraint have against that of natural desire?

Their fingers touched by chance. And that was it. The brutal force of their senses hurled the couple together. They clung to each other and she gave herself to him.

She became pregnant. How could she tell whether by her husband or her lover? More than likely the latter. From then on she was haunted by a dreadful fear. She became convinced that she would die in childbirth. Time and again she made the man who had possessed her promise to look after the child as long as he lived, to refuse the child nothing, to be everything to it, and to do anything, legal or illegal, which would ensure its happiness.

This became a kind of obsession with her and she approached her term in a state of wild exaltation.

She died giving birth to a girl.

The young man's despair was so deep and so appalling it could not be concealed. The husband, whether because he suspected or knew the child was not his own, shut the door on the man who considered himself the child's father. He had her hidden from him and brought up in secret.

Many years passed.

As in time all is forgotten, Pierre Martel forgot. But though he became rich he never again fell in love and never married. His life was unexceptional, peaceful and happy. He heard no more about the husband he had cuckolded nor about the young girl he supposed to be his own.

One day, however, he received from a third party a letter in which was casually mentioned the death of his former rival. A feeling of guilt swept over him. What would become of his child? Perhaps there was something he could do. He made enquiries. Apparently she had been taken in by an aunt. She was living in dire poverty verging on destitution. He wanted to see and help her.

He got in touch with the only relative of the orphan. His name meant nothing to this person. He was a young-looking forty. Fearful of arousing suspicion he said nothing of his relationship with the girl's mother and was duly received.

When she walked into the little parlour where he was anxiously waiting, he had a violent, terrifying shock. It was she! The other girl! The dead girl! She was the same age, had the same eyes, the same hair, the same figure, the same smile, and even the same voice. The resemblance was so great that he nearly went out of his mind. He felt himself going completely mad. All his previous love came surging up from the depths of his heart. She, too, was cheerful and open. They shook hands and became friends immediately.

When he returned home he realized that the old wound had re-opened and, with his head buried in his hands, he wept inconsolably. He wept for the other girl. He was haunted now by the memory of her and by the old familiar things she used to say. Suddenly he was plunged again into the blackest despair.

He returned to the house where the young girl lived. He could no longer live without her and her laughing conversation, the rustle of her dress as she moved, the tone of her voice as she spoke. He could no longer distinguish in either his heart or his mind between the dead girl and the living. Regardless of the distance, the passage of time, and even death, he loved his old love in this one and loved in her the memory of the first. No longer did he even try to understand. No longer did he wonder whether or not she could be his own.

He was tortured by the thought of the poverty and destitution surrounding the woman he loved. Equally agonizing for him was the love itself, coming as it did so mysteriously and incomprehensibly from twin sources. What could he do? Offer money? But how? By what right? Take on the role of tutor? He looked hardly older than she was; they would be taken for lovers. Marry her off to someone else? This thought suddenly rearing up in his mind terrified him. Then he calmed down. Who would want to marry her when she had nothing, literally not a *sou* to bring as dowry?

The aunt watched as he returned again and again. She knew that he loved the girl. Still he waited, knowing not at all what for.

One night they found themselves alone. They were chatting quietly side by side on the settee in the little sitting room. Suddenly in a fatherly way he took her hand. He kept hold of it, struggling against a bitter, unwelcome anguish in both his heart and his mind. He dared not relinquish the hand she had given. Yet he knew if he kept it he was lost. All of a sudden she let herself fall into his arms. She had inherited her mother's fatal passion and already loved him to distraction. Overcome with emotion he placed his lips on the tresses of her blonde hair and, as she raised her head in order to flee, their mouths met. There are certain moments when people go mad as these two did just then.

When he found himself out in the street again he walked blindly straight ahead, not knowing what he was going to do.

I remember, Madame, your indignant voice crying, 'He should have killed himself there and then.' But what good would that have done her? Should he have killed her too? This young girl loved him deeply, loved him to distraction. An inevitable, inherited passion had thrown this innocent virgin in a bound of joy into this man's arms. She had acted under the influence of selfless, unpremeditated passion, the power of heedless instinct which flings the male and the female of the species together. And if he had killed himself what would have become of her? She would have died dishonoured, hopeless and in hideous torture. What should he do? Provide her with a dowry? Find her a husband? She would have died of a broken heart, surely. She would not have accepted his money or his offer of a husband other than himself. It was to him that she had given herself, not to anyone else. He would have ruined her life, destroyed all her hopes of happiness. He would have condemned her to eternal abandonment, despair, tears, isolation and possibly death.

And of course he loved her, too! He loved her with an agonizing passion. Supposing she were his daughter, what of it? For
had it not been the random laws of fertility, the blind power of
reproduction, a momentary contact that had made a daughter
of this being to which no legal tie bound him, whom he cherished
as he had cherished her mother and in whom was now incarn-
ated the two passions of his life? Besides it was not even certain
she was his daughter. What if she were? Who would know? And
returning to him came the memory of the promises he had made
to the dying girl. He had promised to give his life, to do anything,
legal or illegal, to secure the happiness of the child. He loved
her again, reliving the memory of the sweet and terrible pledge
he had made, and was torn apart by pain and desire. Who would
know . . . since the other . . . the father . . . was dead?

Right! he said to himself, this wretched secret could consume
me for the rest of my life. Since she could never dream what
happened I shall carry the burden of it entirely on my own.

He asked for her hand and married her.

I don't know if he was happy, Madame. All I do know is that
I would have done exactly the same.

TWO FRIENDS

Paris, under siege, was starving and breathing her last.[1] The sight of a sparrow on a rooftop was rare and even the sewers were increasingly depopulated. People were eating anything they could lay their hands on.

One bright January morning Monsieur Morissot, a watch-maker by trade but under the present circumstances a man of enforced leisure, was walking disconsolately along the outer boulevard with an empty stomach and his hands in his uniform[2] trouser pockets when he stopped in his tracks, recognizing a comrade-in-arms, an old angler friend of his, Monsieur Sauvage.

Every Sunday before the war Morissot used to leave home at daybreak carrying a bamboo fishing rod in his hand and a tin lunch-box on his back. He would take the Argenteuil train, get off at Colombes and walk to the island of Marante.[3] The minute he arrived at this, for him, idyllic spot he started to fish and went on fishing till night fell. There too, every Sunday, he used to meet a jolly, portly little man by the name of Monsieur Sauvage, a haberdasher on the rue de Lorette[4] who was also a keen fisherman. Many a half-day they spent sitting side by side with their fishing-rods in their hands and their feet dangling over the water. Over the years they had become great friends.

Some days they would spend the whole time in silence. Sometimes they would have a chat. Having very similar tastes and feeling very much the same way about things in general, they got on well without the need for a great deal of talk.

On spring mornings at about ten o'clock when a fine mist was rising and drifting over the smooth surface of the river and the sun of the new season felt deliciously warm on the backs of the

two happy fishermen, Morissot would say to his companion:
'This is the life, eh?'

And Monsieur Sauvage would reply: 'This is the life all right.'

That was all they needed to say for a perfect and respectful understanding to exist between them. In the autumn, towards the end of the day when the setting sun reddened the
sky, stained the river crimson and reflected scarlet clouds upon
water, when the fiery flames of the horizon lit up the profiles of
the two friends and gilded the trees, already russet and shivering
as though it was winter, Monsieur Sauvage would smile at
Monsieur Morissot and declare: 'What a sight, eh?'

And Morissot, marvelling too but with one eye always on his
float, would reply: 'Beats the old boulevard every time, don't
you think?'

As soon as they recognized each other they shook hands
warmly, each struck by such a huge change in their circumstances. Monsieur Sauvage heaved a deep sigh and murmured,
'Some mess we're in!'

Morissot groaned in reply: 'Some weather, too! First fine day
we've had all year.'

The sky was indeed a bright, unclouded blue.

They walked on side by side, both sad and thoughtful.

'Remember the fishing?' Morissot continued. 'Those were the
days, eh?'

Monsieur Sauvage asked, 'I wonder if we'll ever get back,
don't you?'

They went into a little bar and drank an absinthe together.
Then they resumed their stroll along the pavement.

Morissot suddenly stopped again.

'What about another one?'

'I'm with you on that,' concurred Monsieur Sauvage.

So they went into another small bar.

Coming out, they both felt extremely giddy, not surprisingly
for people drinking on an empty stomach. The weather was
mild and a slight breeze fanned their faces.

It went straight to the head of an already tipsy Monsieur
Sauvage who, stopping in his tracks, said: 'Come on, let's go.'

'Where to?'

'Fishing, of course.'

'But where?'

'Our island, of course, where else? The French outposts are just by Colombes. I know Colonel Dumoulin. They'll let us through, no problem.'

Morissot was quivering with excitement: 'Right! You're on!'

In an instant they split up and went off to collect their tackle.

An hour later they were walking side by side along the highway. They reached the villa used by the colonel as his headquarters. He smilingly indulged their whim and they set off once again, this time armed with a pass.

They soon crossed the line of outposts, passed through the deserted village of Colombes and found themselves at the edge of the small vineyards sloping down towards the Seine. It was about eleven o'clock.

At Argenteuil on the opposite side of the river there was no sign of life. The heights of Orgemont and Sannois dominated the whole countryside, and the vast plain which stretches as far as Nanterre was entirely empty apart from bare cherry trees and grey fields.

Pointing to the high ground Monsieur Sauvage murmured: 'That's where the Prussians are, up there.'

Looking at this wholly deserted expanse, the two friends were seized by paralysing anxiety.

'The Prussians!' Not one of them had they ever seen but their invisible, all-powerful presence had been felt for several months around Paris, bringing ruin on France, looting, murdering and starving the population. A superstitious terror was now added to the hatred they felt for this unknown race of conquerors.

Morissot stammered: 'What if ... what if we came across some of them? What would we do?'

With typical, irrepressible Parisian cockiness, Monsieur Sauvage replied: 'We'd give them plenty of fish to fry, don't you worry!'

But, intimidated by the deep silence of everything around them, they hesitated to venture into the open country. Finally Monsieur Sauvage came to a decision.

'Oh, come on, let's get going! Keep your head down!' he said.

They went down, sometimes bent double, sometimes crawling on hands and knees into a vineyard where, straining for any sound and with their eyes nervously darting from right to left, they took advantage of the cover of the bushes. There was just one strip of open ground to cross before reaching the riverside. Running for it, they reached the bank and crouched, hidden, among the dry rushes. Morissot pressed his ear to the ground for any sound of marching in the vicinity. He heard nothing. They were alone, completely alone. As their confidence returned they began to fish.

Opposite them the deserted island of Marante hid them from the other bank. The little restaurant there was closed and looked as if it had been abandoned for years. It was Monsieur Sauvage who took the first gudgeon. Monsieur Morissot followed with a second and every few minutes one or the other lifted his line to find a small silvery creature wriggling on the end: it was a little miracle of a catch. Carefully they slid each one into a fine-meshed net bag at their feet and as they did so a delicious feeling of joy swept over them, the sort of joy you feel when, after having been deprived of a certain pleasure for a very long time, you discover it anew. The kindly sun spread its warmth between their shoulders. They heard nothing and thought of nothing; the world ceased to exist as they simply fished.

Suddenly, however, a dull, apparently subterranean roar made the ground shake. The big guns were firing again. Morissot, turning his head, saw on the left, above the river bank, the great shape of Mont-Valérien now sporting a white plume of the smoke it had just spat out. Almost immediately another puff of smoke was emitted from the top of the fortress, to be followed in a few moments by the growl of a second detonation. More followed, and now every second the mountain belched out its deadly breath, sending milky puffs up into the peaceful sky and forming a cloud over it.

Monsieur Sauvage shrugged his shoulders: 'There they go again,' he said.

Morissot, looking with concern at the feather on his float bobbing up and down, felt a sudden wave of anger, like any peace-loving man, against these idiots who would insist on fighting each other.

'Killing each other like that. Talk about stupid,' he muttered.

'Worse than animals,' said Monsieur Sauvage.

Morissot, who had just hooked a chub, declared: 'That's the government for you.'

Monsieur Sauvage cut in: 'The Republic would never have declared war . . .'

Monsieur Morissot interrupted.

'With a monarchy you've got war abroad. With a republic, you've got war at home.'

They settled down to a friendly debate, setting the world to rights with all the sweet reasonableness of two modest, peaceful men and agreeing on one point – that humankind would never be free. Mont-Valérien continued to thunder on, relentlessly destroying French homes with its shells, ruining lives, crushing bodies and shattering dreams, expectations and hopes of happiness. It inflicted wounds that would never heal in the hearts of girls, wives and mothers in other lands as well.

'That's life,' said Monsieur Sauvage.

'That's death, more like,' Monsieur Morissot retorted with a laugh.

Suddenly, however, both gave a start of terror as they became aware of footsteps immediately behind them. Looking round they stared into the barrels of four guns aimed squarely at them by four large, bearded men dressed like liveried servants and wearing flat caps on their heads. The two lines slipped from their hands and floated downstream.

In a few seconds they were seized, bound, marched off and bundled into a boat in which they were ferried across to the island. Behind the house they had thought deserted, twenty or so German soldiers could now be seen. A hairy giant of a man, sitting astride a chair and smoking a large porcelain pipe, asked them in excellent French: 'Well, gentlemen. And have you had a good day's fishing?'

At this, one of the soldiers deposited at the officer's feet the mesh bag full of fish which he had taken care to bring along with them. The Prussian smiled.

'Ah! I see you weren't doing too badly. But that's neither here nor there. Listen to me and you'll have nothing to worry about. I have to consider you as two spies sent to see what I'm up to. I capture you and shoot you. Fishing was your cover which I have just blown. That's your bad luck. War is war. But since you've come through your own lines you must have a password to get back. You give me that and I'll spare your lives.'

The two friends, ashen-faced and with slightly trembling hands, stood side by side and said nothing.

'No one will ever know about it,' the officer went on. 'You will return home quietly and the secret remains with you. If you refuse, you die here and now. Your choice.'

They remained motionless, not saying a word. Still calmly, the Prussian pointed at the water.

'Just think what it will be like in five minutes to be lying at the bottom of that river. In five minutes! I presume you've got relatives at home?'

Mont-Valérien thundered on.

The two fishermen stood there in silence. The German gave orders in his own language. Then he shifted his chair so as not to be too close to the prisoners. Twelve men came and took up their positions at twenty paces, rifles at the ready. The officer spoke again.

'I give you one minute. Not a second more.'

He got up suddenly, approached the two Frenchmen and, taking Morissot by the arm, drew him aside, whispering: 'Quick! Give me that password. Your friend won't know . . . I'll pretend I've relented.' Morissot made no reply. The officer then drew Monsieur Sauvage to one side and put the same proposition to him. Monsieur Sauvage said nothing. They found themselves together again side by side. The officer began issuing orders. The soldiers raised their rifles. Just then Morissot's glance happened to fall on the bag full of gudgeon which was lying on the grass a few feet away. A ray of sunlight glistened on the catch of fish which were still wriggling. He suddenly weakened and despite his best efforts his eyes filled with tears.

'Goodbye Monsieur Sauvage,' he stammered.

'Goodbye Monsieur Morissot,' Monsieur Sauvage replied.

Trembling uncontrollably from head to foot they shook hands.

'Fire!' the officer shouted.

The twelve shots rang out as one.

Monsieur Sauvage fell forward like a log. Morissot, being taller, swayed, swivelled round and fell across his friend. He remained with his face to the sky while blood gushed out from the holes in the chest of his tunic. The German issued fresh orders. His men dispersed and returned with rope and stones which they tied to the feet of the two dead men. Then they carried them to the river bank. Mont-Valérien growled on, covered now with a mountain of its own smoke.

Two soldiers took Morissot by the head and feet. Two others picked up Monsieur Sauvage the same way. The bodies were swung energetically backwards and forwards, then flung as far away as possible. They described a curve and then, weighted by the stones, plummeted feet first into the river.

The water splashed, bubbled and eddied, then became calm once more as a few tiny wavelets reached the banks on either side. A little blood floated to the surface. Unperturbed, the officer commented to himself that it was now the fishes' turn. And he set off back to the house. Suddenly he noticed the net full of gudgeon lying in the grass. He picked it up, looked at it, smiled and cried: 'Wilhelm!'

A soldier in a white apron came out and ran up to him. The Prussian tossed him the catch of the two executed men and ordered: 'Fry these little creatures up for me while they're still alive, will you? They'll be delicious.'

And with that he relit his pipe.

AWAKENING

She had been married for three years and never once left the valley of Ciré, where her husband owned two cotton mills. They had no children and she led a quiet, happy life in a house which was hidden by trees and which his employees referred to as 'the château'. Monsieur Vasseur, her much older husband, was a good man whom she loved with absolute faithfulness. Her mother came to spend the summers at Ciré, and returned to Paris as soon as the leaves began to fall.

Every autumn, Jeanne would develop a cough when for five months the narrow valley through which a river wound was shrouded in mist and fog. Initially, a light mist would cover all the meadows so that they looked like a great pond from which rooftops protruded. Then, like a rising tide, this thick cloud would envelop everything in sight. The valley became a ghostly place where mildewed trees stood dripping with moisture and men who knew each other well could pass unrecognized within ten feet of each other.

People crossing the slopes on either side and looking down into the white hole which was the little valley could always see emerging from a great mountain of fog the two giant chimneys of Monsieur Vasseur's establishments belching out into the sky, night and day, two columns of black smoke. This was the only sign of life in what appeared to be a hollow filled with a cloud of cottonwool.

One year, as October came round, her doctor advised the young woman to spend the winter in Paris at her mother's, since the air in the valley was becoming too dangerous for her health. Accordingly, she left. During her first few months away she thought constantly about the house and the routine she had abandoned. She missed the familiar pieces of furniture and the quiet tenor of her life there. Eventually, however, she began to very much enjoy all the parties and the dinners, all the dances and the entertainments and became accustomed to her new way of living.

Until then there had always been something underdeveloped about her, a certain hesitancy, a little adolescent dreaminess. She had been slow to engage with people and to smile. But now she became gay, vivacious and full of fun. Men flirted with her. She enjoyed the light banter and the compliments and took none of it seriously. Through marriage she had learned enough about love to find it slightly repulsive. The thought of submitting her body to the clumsy caresses of these bearded creatures made her laugh in pity and shudder a little with repugnance. She was at a complete loss to understand how women could consent to this kind of degrading contact with strangers. Surely one's own husband was quite enough. She would have loved hers more if they had been able to live together as friends, limiting their intimacy to chaste kisses soulfully exchanged.

But she did enjoy men's gallantry and loved seeing desire, unreciprocated though it might be, flash into their eyes. She enjoyed the bold advances, the declarations hurriedly murmured in her ear as she withdrew to the salon after an exquisite dinner. She loved hearing words stammered so softly they had sometimes to be guessed at, but her heart was unmoved. Unconsciously, however, though she herself was unaroused, these encounters tickled her vanity and sparked off in her a little warm contentment. Her face would light up and a smile would play on her lips. She found it thrilling to be, as every woman should be, the object of adoration.

She loved a little firelight *tête-à-tête* in the drawing room before the lamps were lit, when the man, stammering and trembling, would become more insistent and fall on his knees. For her it was a new and exquisite pleasure to feel a passion which she did not share, and through the movements of her head and her lips, to convey refusal, to draw away her hands, to rise and ring for the lamps and see the man, furious and embarrassed, rise off his knees before the servant arrived.

She had a cold little laugh at which words of burning passion would freeze on her admirer's lips; harsh words which acted like a bucket of icy water dashed on ardent protestations of love. Her glacial tones would drive a man who loved her madly to think instead of suicide.

She had two particularly keen admirers who were as different as chalk and cheese. One, Monsieur Paul Péronel, was tall, bold and gallant. He was a wealthy, urbane young man who knew how to bide his time. The other, Monsieur d'Avancelle, trembled when she was near but otherwise hardly dared allow her to guess his feelings. He followed her like a shadow and expressed his desperate desire for her through beseeching glances and by his constant presence. The first she nicknamed 'Captain Thunder' and the other 'Little Lamb'. Never out of sight, and treated by her like a servant, the latter became gradually a kind of slave to her.

She would have laughed her head off at the suggestion that she might fall in love with him. But love him she did, in a strange sort of way. He was constantly by her side and just as one becomes used to the people with whom one lives, she became accustomed to his voice, his gestures and everything about him. Quite often his face would haunt her dreams. She would see him as he was in real life – gentle, sensitive and humbly passionate. She would awaken still under the influence of the dream and imagine she could still hear his voice and feel him close to her. One night (she might possibly have had a temperature at the time) she dreamed she was with him in a little wood where they were both sitting down on the grass. He was saying lovely things to her, squeezing her hands and kissing them. She felt the warmth of his skin and his breath on her. As if it were the most natural thing in the world, she was stroking his hair. In dreams we are quite different from our daily selves. She felt herself now full of a deep, calm affection for him and glad to be touching his forehead and holding him close to her. Gradually, he went on to take her in his arms, and to kiss her cheeks and eyes while she made no attempt to free herself. Their lips met and she gave herself to him.

It was a moment of intense, rapturous happiness, a super-human and unforgettable uniting of body and soul. She woke suddenly, distraught, and tingling in every limb. She could not get back to sleep. She felt completely taken over and possessed by him. When she next saw him, unaware though he was of the turmoil he had caused within her, she felt herself blush. As he spoke timidly of his love she could think of nothing but that ecstatic moment in the dream. She loved him with a very particular affection which combined the sensual and the ideal and which was based principally on the memory of her unconscious. However, she still feared any realization of the desire now kindled in her heart.

Eventually, he became aware of her feelings. She told him all, including her fear of his kisses. She made him promise to respect her. And respect her he did. Together they would spend long hours of platonic love during which their souls alone embraced. They parted feeling on edge, weak and exhausted. At times their lips would meet and, closing their eyes, they would enjoy a long, lingering but nevertheless chaste kiss.

Realizing that she would be unable to resist for long, and since she had no wish to succumb, she wrote to her husband saying that she wished to return home to him and take up again her former quiet and isolated life. He wrote an excellent letter in response, urging her against returning in the middle of winter and exposing herself through too sudden a change of climate to the freezing fogs of the valley. She was dismayed and felt indignant at the confidence of this man who obviously failed to understand her and could not imagine how hard she was having to struggle.

February was bright and mild, and although she now avoided being alone with Little Lamb for long, she did occasionally consent to a carriage ride with him around the lake at twilight. On this particular night, the breeze was warm and the sap was rising, both literally and metaphorically. The little coupé[1] had slowed to a walking pace and the shadows were beginning to gather. They were pressed close to each other, holding hands. She said to herself: 'That's it! I'm done for! I'm lost!' She felt desire rising within her and a desperate yearning for that rapturous feeling which in her dream had been so complete. All the time, their mouths feverishly sought and found each other, no sooner separated than frantically together again. He dared not escort her indoors but left her exhausted and trembling with emotion on the threshold of the house.

In the little unlit salon Monsieur Paul Péronel was waiting. As soon as he touched her hand he could tell that she was on fire. He began to speak to her in a low murmur, flattering and soothing her exhausted spirit with tender words of love. She listened to him silently. All the time he spoke, she was thinking of the other, hearing his voice, feeling his body close to her, all in a kind of hallucination. She saw no one but him. For her now no other man existed. When the three syllables 'I love you' fell upon her eager ear it was as though the other spoke. It was he who now kissed her hands and he who pressed her breast close to his, just as earlier on in the carriage. It was his triumphant kisses which now rained down on her lips, it was he around whom she flung her arms and whom she now held tightly. It was to him that she now appealed with all the love in her heart and all the fierce desire of her body.

When she came to, she uttered a terrible cry.

Captain Thunder, on his knees beside her, was thanking her profusely and covering her hair, now unpinned, with passionate kisses.

'Go away! Go away! Go away!' she cried.

As, uncomprehending, he tried once more to put his arms around her waist she twisted away and panted: 'You're despicable! You've robbed me! Go away!'

He rose to his feet in a daze, took his hat and left.

The following day, she returned to the valley of Ciré. Surprised, her husband reproached her for having acted so impetuously.

'I couldn't bear being without you any more,' she said.

He found her personality had changed. She was sadder than before. When he asked, 'What's the matter, then? You seem unhappy. What can I get you?' she would reply, 'Nothing. Only my dreams.'

Little Lamb came to see her the following summer. She received him calmly and with no regrets, realizing all of a sudden that she had only ever loved him in a dream from which Paul Péronel had awakened her.

But the young man, who still adored her, reflected as he returned: 'Really strange, complex . . . unfathomable creatures, women.'

THE JEWELS

The minute Monsieur Lantin met a certain young girl at a party given by the deputy head of his department, he fell hopelessly and head over heels in love. She was the daughter of a provincial tax inspector long since deceased. After his death she and her mother had moved to Paris where they became part of a circle of neighbouring middle-class families within whose ranks the mother hoped one day to marry her young daughter. They were poor but worthy, quiet and sweet-tempered ladies. The young girl was exactly the kind of virtuous young woman any decent young man would aspire to make his wife. Her unassuming beauty and modesty were charming and the faint but angelic smile which hovered constantly on her lips reflected the very purest of hearts.

Everyone sang her praises. All those who knew her always said: 'Whoever marries her will be a lucky man. They really don't come any better.'

Monsieur Lantin, then a chief clerk at the Ministry of the Interior, with an annual salary of 3,500 francs, asked for her hand in marriage and was accepted.

He was extremely happy with her. She ran his household so cleverly and with such thrift that they always seemed to live in the lap of luxury. She was so sweet, so kind and so loving towards her husband that six months after their first meeting he was more in love with her than ever.

The only two faults he could find with her were that she was mad on both the theatre and on imitation jewellery. Her friends, the wives of various minor bureaucrats, would pass on tickets to her for all the fashionable plays, and, like it or not, he would have to accompany her to these wretched productions even after a hard day at the office. After a while he begged her to find some lady friend to go with who could drop her off afterwards. At first she demurred, saying it was hardly the correct thing to do, but after a while she gave in and he was infinitely grateful.

Soon, however, going to the theatre led to dressing up whenever she went. Her outfits remained simple and always in very good taste. The modesty of her manner and her irresistible gracefulness were in fact enhanced by the simplicity of the dresses she wore. But after a while she began to wear two great big rhinestones dangling from her ears, strings of imitation pearls around her neck, pinchbeck bracelets on her arms and in her hair various combs decorated with all sorts of cheap, fake stones.

Her husband, shocked a little by the vulgarity of his wife's taste, would often say: 'My dear, if we cannot afford real jewels then you must wear the rarest gems of Nature, that's to say your very own grace and beauty.'

But she merely smiled her sweet smile at him, saying, 'I can't help it. I just adore them. I know you're right, but that's the way I am. Of course I'd love the genuine article but chance is a fine thing!'

She would run the strings of pearls through her fingers, hold up the facets of cut glass to catch the light and say, 'Don't they look good! You'd swear they were genuine, wouldn't you?'

And he would smile back, saying, 'You're a real little gypsy, that's what you are!'

Sometimes, as they were chatting by the fire of an evening, she would put on the tea-table between them the leather jewel box in which she kept what Monsieur Lantin referred to as her baubles. She would sit and examine these trinkets with passionate attention and a deep, secret delight all of her own. She would insist on draping some of them round her husband's neck, then burst out laughing.

'You look such a scream,' she would say, then fling herself into his arms and shower him with kisses.

She went to the Opéra one winter night and came back shivering with cold. The following day she developed a cough. A week later she died of pneumonia.

Lantin nearly followed her to the grave. He fell into such a deep depression that within a month his hair had turned completely white. He wept from morning till night and his heart almost broke under the unbearable pain he was suffering. He was haunted by his dead wife's smile, her voice, and of course her charm.

Time did not heal. Often at work, as his colleagues were chatting away about nothing in particular, they would see his face fall, his nose wrinkle and tears well up in his eyes. His face would become contorted with grief and he would break into sobs.

He had kept his wife's room just as she had left it and every day he would lock himself in there and think about her. All her furniture and even her dresses were left exactly as they had been on the last day of her life.

His finances were becoming increasingly difficult too. The income he earned, so cleverly managed by his wife, had in her day been sufficient for all the needs of the household. Now he could hardly make it do for one. Now that he could no longer afford it, he wondered how on earth she had always managed to provide him with the finest wines and keep such an excellent table.

Like many in reduced circumstances he ran up debts and tried to scrape together as much money as he could from any source. One morning, with not a *sou* to his name and a full week to go before the end of the month, he wondered if he should not perhaps try to sell something. He went immediately to fish out the baubles belonging to his wife. In his secret heart of hearts the tawdry things still managed to irritate him. The mere sight of them every day used to come between him and the memory of his beloved.

He spent a long time looking through the pile of trinkets she had left, for she had continued collecting right up to the end of her life and nearly every evening had come back with some new piece or other. He decided on a long necklace which had been one of her favourites. It must be worth at least six or eight francs he thought, because for an imitation piece the workmanship was very good. He put it in his pocket and went to the office at the Ministry via the boulevards, where he looked out for a reliable-looking jeweller.

At length he saw one and went in, a little ashamed of having to make such an open display of need by selling something so worthless.

'Monsieur,' he said to the dealer, 'I'd like you to value this piece for me if you'd be so kind.'

The man took the article, examined it, turned it over, weighed it, took up a magnifying glass to look at it more closely, called his assistant, murmured a few words to him, put the necklace back on the counter and stepped back to see what it looked like from a distance. Monsieur Lantin was a little embarrassed by all this ceremony and was about to say, 'Look, don't worry, I'm pretty sure it's got no value at all to it,' when the jeweller announced: 'Monsieur, I would put it at between 12,000 and 15,000 francs. However, I could not purchase it from you without knowing its exact provenance.'

The widower opened his eyes wide and gaped uncomprehendingly. Finally he stammered: 'You're saying . . . I mean, are you sure . . . ?'

The jeweller misinterpreted his astonishment and said crisply: 'Of course Monsieur is perfectly free to try for a higher price elsewhere. But my best offer would be 15,000. Do come back later if you wish.'

Stupefied, Monsieur Lantin took back the necklace and left the shop. He felt vaguely that he needed to be by himself to think for a while. As soon as he was in the street again he broke into nervous laughter thinking, 'The fool! The stupid fool! Supposing I'd taken him seriously! Just goes to show . . . even jewellers aren't always so expert in their field!'

He went into another jeweller, this time in the rue de la Paix.[1] As soon as he saw the piece the goldsmith there cried out: 'Well I'm dashed! I know this necklace well . . . it came from us!'

Monsieur Lantin, extremely puzzled, said, 'Well how much is it worth?'

'Monsieur, I sold it for 25,000. I can buy it back for 18,000. That's if you can provide me with your legal title to it, of course.'

This time Monsieur Lantin was so stunned that he had to sit

down. 'Please . . . please look at it very carefully . . .,' he said,
'. . . I've always thought it was . . . imitation . . .'

The jeweller answered: 'Would you be good enough to give
me your name, Monsieur?'

'Certainly. It's Lantin. I'm at the Ministry of the Interior and
my home address is 16, rue des Martyrs.'[2]

The dealer opened up his account ledgers, searched for a
while, then said: 'Yes, here we are. The necklace was sent to the
home of Madame Lantin, 16 rue des Martyrs on 20 July 1876.'

The two men looked each other in the eye, the clerk lost in
amazement, the dealer beginning to smell something fishy.

He went on: 'Would you mind leaving it with me for twenty-
four hours, Monsieur? I should be more than happy to make
out a receipt for it, of course.'

Monsieur Lantin stammered: 'Yes . . . yes, of course.'

He left the shop, folding up the piece of paper given to him
and putting it in his pocket. He crossed the road, walked
some way down it, noticed he was in the wrong street, went
down as far as the Tuileries, crossed the Seine, then, realizing
where he was, retraced his steps again and walked all the way
up the Champs Elysées without once having a single clear
idea in his head. He made an effort to construct some sort of
reason, to try and understand. His wife would never have been
able to buy such a valuable piece on her own. Absolutely not.
So. It had to be a gift then. A gift! But a gift from whom? And
whatever for?

He stopped stock still in the middle of the avenue. A horrible
suspicion flashed through his mind. Not her, surely! Because if
so, what about all the other jewels? They had to be gifts too!
The ground heaved beneath his feet. A tree leaned as if to fall
over. He stretched out his arms and collapsed in a dead faint.

He regained consciousness in a pharmacy to which he had
been carried by some passers-by. He had himself driven back
home and locked himself indoors. All day long he wept in
despair, biting his handkerchief to stop himself wailing.
Exhausted with emotion he put himself to bed and eventually
fell into a deep sleep.

A ray of sunlight awoke him the following day and he got up

slowly to go to the Ministry. It was hard to go to work after such an emotional upheaval. It occurred to him that he might send word to his superior, excusing himself from his duties that day. Accordingly he wrote a note. Then he remembered that he had to go back to the jeweller. Turning crimson with shame, he stayed where he was for a long time just thinking things over. He could hardly leave the necklace with the fellow after all. Finally he got dressed and went out.

It was a lovely day with a blue sky over the entire city, which seemed to be in a carefree mood. Strollers were ambling by with their hands in their pockets. As he watched them pass, he said to himself: Great to have money, isn't it? With money in the bank, you can just shake off all your worries, all your troubles, go where you like ... travel ... have fun ... God I wish I was rich.

He noticed that he was hungry, not having eaten for nearly two days now. But his pockets were empty. Again he remembered the necklace. Eighteen thousand francs! Eighteen thousand francs! Serious money, that was!

He reached the rue de la Paix and began to walk up and down the pavement opposite the shop. Eighteen thousand francs! He must have made at least twenty attempts to go in but each time shame stopped him. He was really hungry by now, however – ravenous in fact and without a *sou*. Coming to a sudden decision, he raced across the road and, before he could change his mind again, rushed into the jeweller's shop.

As soon as he saw him, the dealer began to dance attendance and with a polite smile offered him a chair. Even the assistants gathered, looking sideways at Lantin with a gleam of amusement in their eyes and a half-smile playing on their lips.

The jeweller declared: 'I have made the necessary inquiries, Monsieur. If you still wish to offer it for sale I am in a position to offer you in turn the sum we mentioned earlier.'

The clerk stammered: 'Yes ... yes ... certainly ... I do.'

From a drawer the jeweller drew out eighteen large bills, counted them out and presented them to Lantin, who signed a receipt chit, and, trembling, pocketed the money.

Then as he was leaving he turned again towards the jeweller

who was still smiling. Lowering his eyes, Lantin said: 'I've also come into some other jewellery . . . in the same . . . the same way. Would you be interested in purchasing them as well?'

The dealer bowed.

'But of course, monsieur.'

One of the assistants, unable to contain his laughter, ran off. Another blew his nose loudly.

Ignoring this, Lantin, serious and blushing, said: 'Then I shall bring them to you.'

He took a fiacre and went to fetch the jewels.

An hour later when he returned with them he had still not eaten. They examined the pieces meticulously one by one, evaluating each in turn. Nearly all were from the dealer's own firm. As time went on, Lantin began to query the valuations, affected annoyance and made them open the account books for him. As the sum grew larger his voice became louder.

The large diamond earrings were worth 20,000 francs; the bracelets, 35,000; the brooches, rings, medallions and lockets, 16,000; the set of emeralds with sapphires, 14,000; the pendant comprising a solitaire diamond on gold chain, 40,000 – making a grand total of some 196,000 francs.

'Well, this is somebody who *really* invested in jewellery,' said the jeweller in a slightly teasing tone.

'Perfectly sound policy, I'd say,' Lantin replied gravely.

He left, having agreed for the buyer to get a second opinion the following day.

Out in the street again, he looked at the colonne de Vendôme[3] and felt an overwhelming desire to shin up it as if it were a greasy pole. He felt so light he could have leapfrogged over the statue of the Emperor perched up there at the top.

He lunched at Voisin's[4] and ordered a bottle of wine costing twenty francs.

After that, he called a fiacre and went for a turn in the Bois. He looked with contempt at certain carriages there and barely suppressed the desire to shout out 'Me too! Me too, I'm rich! I've got 200,000 francs!'

He remembered the Ministry and ordered himself to be driven there. Striding resolutely into his boss's office he announced: 'I have come, Monsieur, to offer my resignation. I've just inherited 300,000 francs.'

He went to shake hands with his former colleagues and shared with them the plans he was making for his new life. He then went and dined at the Café Anglais.[5]

Finding himself sitting next to a distinguished-looking gentleman he could not resist the temptation of telling him, not without a certain degree of pride, that he had just inherited 400,000 francs. For the first time in his life he went to the theatre and enjoyed it. Following that he spent the night with some prostitutes.

Six months later he married again. His second wife was extremely virtuous but difficult to get on with. She gave him a very hard time indeed.

TRAIN STORY

I

At Cannes the compartment had filled up, and since everyone knew each other there was naturally a good deal of talk. As we passed through Tarascon[1] somebody said: 'Isn't this where those murders were?' The conversation then turned to the mysterious and elusive murderer who, for the past couple of years or so, had taken to bumping off the occasional passenger on this line.[2] Everyone had, if not their own pet theory, at least something to say about it. The women looked out into the darkness beyond the windows, shuddering at the thought that a man might suddenly appear at their carriage door. People started telling scary stories of various unpleasant encounters they had had at one time or another – a conversation in an express train with someone clearly off his head; hours spent sitting opposite some suspicious character or other elsewhere, and so on and so forth.

Each of the men had some tale of valour that starred himself. Each had either sent off or sent sprawling, or in some cases strangled, some villain or other under extraordinary circumstances in which they themselves had shown remarkable bravery or presence of mind. After this, a doctor who spent every winter in the south of France added a story of his own.

'Personally,' he said, 'I have never had the opportunity to test my own courage under those sorts of circumstances. However, I did know a woman, a patient of mine, now dead, to whom the most extraordinary thing in the world happened. It's one of the most mysterious as well as one of the most touching tales I ever heard.

She was a Russian countess, Marie Baranow, a very grand lady and a great beauty too. You know how beautiful Russian women are, at least to us:[3] those fine noses, the delicate mouths, the close-set eyes of . . . how *can* one describe that lovely grey-blue colour and that distant, almost cold look they have. There's something wildly attractive about them, some combination of the severe and the gentle which we Frenchmen find absolutely irresistible. Maybe it's just the charm of the exotic that makes us see so much in them, I don't know . . .

At any rate, her doctor, considering that she had a danger-ously weak chest, had for many years been trying to persuade her to come to the south of France. She, however, was never willing to leave Petersburg. Finally last autumn, fearing the worst, the doctor informed her husband who immediately ordered his wife to Menton. She went by train, she by herself in one compartment with another one reserved for her entourage. She was leaning against the window, looking out a little sadly as the train passed through different parts of the country. She felt very much alone and rejected. She had no children, no relatives to speak of, and a husband whose love for her having died was now packing her off on her own to the ends of the earth, just like an ailing servant rushed off to hospital in the back of beyond.

At every stop her own manservant, Ivan, would come and see if his mistress needed anything. He was an ancient retainer, blindly devoted and happy to do anything in the world for her.

Night fell and the train was now travelling at top speed. She was far too wide-awake to think of trying to sleep. However, it suddenly occurred to her that she ought to count the gold coins in French currency her husband had put into her hands at the last minute. She opened her little bag and poured on to her knees a pool of the gleaming metal.

Suddenly a gust of cold air hit her in the face. Surprised, she raised her head. Someone was opening the door of the compartment. The Countess Marie, distraught, flung her shawl over the money she had spread out on her dress and waited. A few seconds went by and then a man appeared, bare-headed, breathless and wounded in the hand. He was wearing evening dress. He shut the door after him and sat down. His eyes were feverishly bright as he looked at his neighbour then proceeded to wrap a handkerchief around his bleeding wrist.

The young woman felt herself grow faint. Obviously the man had seen her counting her gold and intended to steal it and kill her. Still out of breath he stared at her. His face was convulsed. Clearly he was about to pounce on her, she thought. Suddenly he said: "Madame . . . please . . . don't be afraid!"

She said nothing. Unable to open her mouth, she could hear her heart pounding and a buzzing in her ears.

He went on: "I'm not a thief or anything like that, Madame."

Still she said nothing but as she made a sudden movement, bringing her knees together, her gold cascaded to the carpet like water into the gutter. Surprised, the man looked at this river of coins and quickly bent down to pick them up. She rose, terrified, letting the remains of her entire fortune fall to the ground. She made a dash for the door of the compartment as if to throw herself out. Guessing her intention, he hurled himself after her. He clasped her in his arms, forced her to sit down and, gripping both her wrists, said: "Listen to me, please, Madame. I am not a thief or anything like that at all, I assure you. To prove it I am about to pick up all this money and return it to you. However, I myself am practically done for. I am a dead man unless you help me cross the frontier. I can say no more. In one hour's time we shall be at the last station on Russian territory and in one hour and twenty minutes we shall be crossing the frontier of its Empire. Unless you come to my aid I am doomed. And yet, Madame, I have killed no one and I have stolen nothing. I swear to you I have done nothing at all dishonourable. But I can tell you no more than that."

Kneeling, he picked up all the coins, including some he found rolled far under the carriage seats. Then when the little leather bag was full once more, without a word he handed it over to his neighbour and returned to sit in the opposite corner of the compartment.

Neither of them stirred. She remained silent and rigid, still terrified out of her mind but gradually becoming more reassured as time went by. As for the man, he made no movement, not even a gesture but sat upright, looking straight ahead, as pale as death. From time to time she cast a quick glance in his direction then turned away again. He was an extremely good-looking man of about thirty with every appearance of a gentleman.

The train hurtled through the darkness, its heart-rending wails piercing the night as it went. Sometimes it slackened pace before picking up speed again. Suddenly it slowed down, and this time came to a complete halt. Ivan appeared at the door awaiting orders. The Countess Marie, trembling, looked over one last time at her strange companion then, suddenly brisk, said to her manservant: "Ivan, you must return to the Count. I no longer need you with me."

Dumbfounded, the man opened his eyes wide. He stammered: "But *barinya* . . ."

She went on: "Yes that's right . . . I have changed my mind. You needn't come any further. I'd rather you remained here in Russia. Here . . . take some money for the return journey . . . and . . . give me your hat and coat before you leave."

Terrified, the old servant was nevertheless used to accepting unquestioningly any whim or change of mind on the part of his masters. Removing his hat and coat and handing them over to her, he left with tears in his eyes. The train moved off once more and sped towards the frontier.

The Countess Marie then said to her neighbour: "These articles are for you, Monsieur. You are now my servant Ivan. All I ask in return is this: that in future you will never once speak to me. Not a word, either of thanks or anything else."

The stranger bowed his head in silence. Soon they stopped again and uniformed officials boarded to inspect the passengers. The Countess handed them her papers and, pointing to the man sitting in the corner of the compartment, said: "That is my manservant Ivan. Here is his passport."

The train set off again. Throughout the night they remained together, never once exchanging a word. When morning came and they stopped at a German station the stranger began to disembark. Pausing as he stood at the door, he spoke: "Forgive me, Madame, for breaking my promise but I have deprived you of your servant and it is only fair that I should replace him. Is there anything you need?"

Coldly she replied: "Go and fetch my maid."

Having done so, he disappeared. From then on, whenever she ate at one of the station buffets en route she was aware that from a distance he was watching her. Finally they arrived at Menton.'

II

The doctor remained silent for a moment then continued.

'One day as I was seeing my patients at my surgery a tall fellow walked in and said to me: "Doctor, I've come to ask after the health of the Countess Marie Baranow. She doesn't know me but I'm a friend of her husband."

I replied: "She's not got long to live. She will certainly not be able to make the journey back to Russia."

The man suddenly burst into sobs. Then he rose and staggered out as if drunk.

That very evening I informed the Countess that a stranger had been to see me inquiring after her health. She seemed touched and related to me the story I've just told all of you. She added: "This man, who is a complete stranger to me, follows me like my own shadow. I see him every time I go out. He looks at me full of curiosity but he has never addressed a single word to me."

She thought for a while, then added: "In fact I would bet he's outside the hotel as we speak."

She rose from her chaise longue, drew back the curtains and showed me the same man who had come to see me. He was sitting on a promenade bench opposite. Seeing us, he rose and left without a backward glance.

I was witnessing the saddest and most extraordinary relationship: unspoken love between two perfect strangers. He loved her with all the devotion of a rescued animal, constant and grateful unto death. Every day he would come and ask "How is she?" And as he watched her grow paler and weaker with every passing day, he would weep inconsolably.

She would say to me: "I've only spoken to this extraordinary man once, yet I feel I've known him for twenty years."

When they met, she would return his salutation with a charming, serious smile. I felt that this dying and rejected woman was happy to be loved in such a respectful and constant way, in this exaggeratedly romantic manner and with such unconditional devotion. And yet it was with something akin to rapture that she was determined to keep to her word. She was desperate, adamant in her refusal to receive him, to know his name or speak a word to him.

"Oh no!" she would say, "that would spoil the very special nature of the friendship for me. We have to remain strangers to one another."

He himself was sufficiently quixotic not to make any attempt to approach her. He wished to keep to the very end the absurd promise he had made, never to address a single word to her. Often, during the long hours of her illness, she would rise from her chaise longue and open the curtains a chink to see if he was there beneath her window. And when she saw that he was sitting as usual, motionless on his bench, she would go back and rest with a smile on her lips.

She died one morning at about ten o'clock. As I was leaving the hotel he came up to me, his face distraught. He already knew.

"I'd like to see her, just for a moment, with you there," he said.

I took his arm and went back into the building. Standing at the dead woman's bedside, he seized her hand and kissed it for the longest possible time. Then he ran off like a thing possessed.'

Again the doctor paused, then said: 'That's certainly the most extraordinary train story I've ever heard. You have to admit, men do the maddest things sometimes.'

One of the women quietly murmured: 'Those two weren't as mad as you might think. They were . . . they were . . .'

But she was weeping too much to go on. We changed the subject so as to take her mind off it. As a result we never did find out what she had meant to say.

REGRET

Monsieur Saval, popularly known in Mantes[1] as Old Saval, has just got up. It is raining on a sad autumn day. Leaves are falling. They fall slowly like a different, denser and more leisurely kind of rain. Monsieur Saval is not in the best of spirits. He paces from his fireplace to his window and back to his fireplace again. It is one of life's darker days. And for him now, dark days are all there will be for he is sixty-two! He is a lonely old bachelor with no one in his life close to him. How sad it will be to die like this, all alone, with no one to love and with no one in turn devoted to him.

He thinks how bare, how empty his life is. He remembers the dim, distant past, his childhood, the house with his parents in it, school, outings, his days as a law student in Paris. Then he remembers his father's illness and subsequent death. Saval had returned to live with his mother. The two of them had shared a perfectly happy, peaceful life together. Then she too had died. Oh, how sad life is!

He was left all alone. And now soon he too would die. He would just disappear and that would be that. No more Monsieur Paul Saval on the face of the earth. What a terrible thing! Other people carrying on living, loving and laughing. Yes, other people having fun and he would be no more! Isn't it strange how people can laugh and have fun while the certainty of death remains constant? If it were merely probable, you could still live in hope, but no, it is inevitable, as inevitable as night follows day.

If only his life had at least been a full one. If he had done something, tasted pleasure or success or experienced some satisfaction or other. But no, he had had nothing like that either. He had never done anything at all except get up in the morning, eat at the same time every day and then go to bed. And that is how he had reached the age of sixty-two. He had not even married, as other men had done. Why was that? Yes, why had he never married? He could have done, he had enough capital. Was it lack of opportunity? Maybe that was it! But people *make* opportunities, don't they? He was obviously just too casual about things, that's all. Being casual about things had been his greatest fault, the biggest flaw in his character, his weakness, you might say. How many people fail in life through being too casual about things? But, on the other hand, it's just so difficult for certain personalities to get up and do things, take some initiative, say things, think things through, and so forth.

He had not even been loved. No woman had gone to sleep with her head on his chest in the complete abandonment of love. He had never known the exquisite pain of waiting for someone to come, the heavenly thrill in the squeeze of a hand or the ecstasy of triumphant passion. What heavenly happiness must flood into your heart when lips meet for the first time, when four arms combine into a single being, the supremely happy unity of two creatures madly in love.

Monsieur Saval sat down in his dressing-gown and put his feet up close to the fire. No doubt about it, his life was a failure. A total failure. And yet he himself had loved. He had loved in secret, painfully and of course casually, as usual. Yes, he had been in love with Madame Sandres, the wife of his old chum Sandres, and now herself his old friend too. Oh, if only he had known her as a young woman! But he had been too late. When he met her she was already married. He would certainly have proposed to *her*, no question of that. And despite that, how he had loved her, constantly, from the very first day they had met! He remembered how he had felt every time he saw her and how sad he was to leave her side. He remembered now all the sleepless nights of his life that he had spent thinking about her. In the mornings he always used to wake up feeling a little bit less in love. Why was that?

How pretty she was in those days – a sweet, blonde, curly-headed little thing always bubbling with laughter. Sandres was

not the man she ought to have married. Now she was fifty-eight.
She seemed happy. Oh if only *she* had loved him back then.
If only she had loved him! And why should she not have?
Considering how much Saval loved Madame Sandres.

Saval began to wonder about a thousand more things. He
went back over his entire life trying to recall a whole host of
details. He remembered all the long evenings playing *écarté*[2]
at Sandres' house when she was full of youthful charm. He
remembered things she had said to him, the tone of her voice
and the gentle, meaningful smiles she would give him. He
remembered how the three of them used to go for walks along
the banks of the Seine, the picnics they used to have, always on
a Sunday, since Sandres worked in the administration.

Suddenly a vivid memory came back to him of one afternoon
he had spent with her in a little wood that ran alongside the
river. They had all set off in the morning, taking a packed lunch.
It was one of those brilliant spring days which go completely to
your head. Everything smells wonderful and the world is a
happy place. The birds sing more merrily than ever and even
their wings seem to flutter faster. The three had sat down on the
grass to eat, under some willows, near the water which flowed
slowly in the heat of the sun. The air was warm around them
and full of the smell of sap. They drank it all in. What a day
that was! What a day!

After lunch, Sandres had lain flat on his back and fallen asleep.
'Best nap of my life,' he had said when he awoke from it. Madame
Sandres had taken Saval's arm and the two of them had set off
along the river bank. She was leaning on him, laughing and
saying: 'I'm tipsy you know my dear, quite, quite tipsy!'

Quivering all over with emotion, feeling himself grow pale
and fearful lest he appear too bold or lest his trembling hand
betray his secret, he looked at her.

She had made a coronet of greenery and water-lilies and asked
him: 'There! What d'you think of me in this then?'

And as he said nothing – since he could think of no response
except possibly to fall on his knees – she began to laugh an
unhappy little laugh in his face: 'You great lummox! Can't you
think of *anything* to say?'

And still, though he was close to tears, not a word would come out.

All this returned to him now in every minute detail. Why had she said, 'You great lummox, can't you think of *anything* to say?' like that?

And he remembered with what tenderness she had leaned on him. Passing beneath an overhanging branch he had actually felt her ear against his, *his* cheek, imagine it! He had drawn back quickly in case she thought he had engineered the contact. When he had wondered aloud whether it was time they were getting back she had given him a very peculiar sort of look. Yes, really a very strange look indeed. He had thought nothing of it at the time but now it was all coming back to him.

'Just as you like, my dear. If you're tired, let's go back.'

And he had replied: 'It's not that, but don't you think Sandres will have woken up by now?'

Shrugging her shoulders, she said, 'Oh of course if you're afraid my husband might have woken up, that's different. That means we *must* go back, of course!'

She had said nothing as they returned. She had no longer leaned on his arm, however.

Why was that?

He had never before wondered why that was. It was beginning to seem as if he was on the verge of discovering something hitherto unknown to him.

Could it be that . . . ?

Monsieur Saval could feel himself colouring and he leapt to his feet. It was as if he had heard Madame Sandres say, thirty years earlier, 'I love you.'

Could that be the case? What was dawning on him was sheer torture. Was it possible that he had not seen, not even guessed? Oh . . . if only it were true! Imagine if he had been so close to happiness . . . and just not able to grasp it! I must know, he said to himself. I can't bear not knowing. I must find out!

He got dressed hurriedly, flinging on his clothes and thinking, I'm sixty-two, she's fifty-eight. Surely at this stage I can ask her. And he went out. Sandres' house was on the other side of the

street, almost directly opposite his own. He banged on the
knocker and the little parlourmaid opened the door. She was
astonished to see him there so early.

'Monsieur Saval! At this time of day! Is anything the matter?'

Saval replied: 'No, love, nothing. Just go and tell the mistress
I'd like a word with her straight away.'

'I'm afraid Madame's busy at the stove making her stock of
pear jam for the winter. She's not, like, dressed properly, you
know.'

'Never mind about that – doesn't matter. Tell her it's very
important.'

With long, nervous strides, but no feeling of embarrassment,
Saval began to pace the salon. He would ask her for this information just as he would ask for a recipe. He was sixty-two, for
heaven's sake!

The door opened and she appeared. She was now a plump
roly-poly of a woman with round cheeks and a ringing laugh.
She walked in, holding her hands well away from her sides. Her
bare arms in their rolled-up sleeves were sticky with sugary juice.
Concerned, she asked: 'My dear, what's the matter? You're not
ill, I hope?'

'No, my dear friend, not at all,' he replied, 'but there's something which is very important to me that I'd like to ask you.
Promise you'll give me an absolutely honest answer?'

She smiled.

'I'm always honest. Ask away.'

'Well, this is the thing. I've loved you from the day I first saw
you. Did you ever have any idea?'

There was something of the old tone in her voice when she
laughingly replied: 'You great lummock! Of course I did, from
the word go!'

Saval began to tremble. He stammered: 'You knew . . .
So . . . ?' He stopped.

'So . . . what?' she asked.

'Well I mean . . .,' he went on, 'what did you think . . . what
would you have said if . . . ?'

She laughed even more. Drops of the syrup were dripping off
her fingertips on to the parquet floor.

'Me? You never asked me. It was hardly up to me to make a declaration.'

At this he took a step towards her.

'Tell me ... tell me ... you remember that day Sandres fell asleep after lunch ... when we went as far as that bend together ... ?'

He waited for her to speak. She had stopped laughing and was looking him straight in the eye.

'Of course I remember.'

He went on, trembling slightly: 'Well ... that day ... if I'd shown a bit of initiative ... what ... what would you have done?'

She began to smile the smile of a happy woman who has no regrets in life and replied frankly, with a touch of irony in her voice: 'I would have been yours of course.'

With this she turned on her heel and fled back to her jam.

Saval went out into the street again, pole-axed as if by the news of some disaster. Looking straight ahead, he strode like a robot through the rain down to the river. When he reached the bank he turned right and followed it as if driven by some instinct. His clothes were wringing wet and his hat, limp and shapeless as a rag, dripped like a roof. On and on he walked until he came to the place where they had lunched on that distant day he remembered with such anguish. There, surrounded by the leafless trees, he sat down and allowed his own tears to fall.

MINOR TRAGEDY

Half the pleasure of travel, surely, is the possibility of the chance meeting. Which of us has not to our great delight discovered 500 miles away from home a fellow-Parisian, say, or someone we went to the school with or who lives in the same county? Who has not spent the night wide awake as the stagecoach jingles its way through places as yet untouched by the railway, while sitting next to an unknown young woman glimpsed only by lamplight as she entered the carriage outside a white-painted house in some little town or other? When morning comes and one's ears are still full of the sound of harness bells and the shattering rattle of window panes, what a delightful feeling it is to see one's charmingly dishevelled companion open her eyes and look about her. We watch as she runs her dainty little fingers through her tousled hair, feels to make sure that her bodice has not twisted around too much in the night, sets the waist to rights and smoothes out the creases in her skirt. And she of course steals a glance, albeit of cold curiosity, at you, before settling herself back into her corner and appearing totally absorbed by the passing scenery.

Despite yourself you watch her constantly. And despite yourself you speculate about her all the time. Who can she be? Where does she come from? Where is she going? Despite yourself again, you start to draft a little novel about her. She's pretty. She looks lovely. Happy the man who ... Maybe she is the woman of your dreams, the woman made for you alone. Maybe your life would be one long and exquisite pleasure with this woman at your side.

Equally keen is the resentment you feel as you watch her

alight at the gate of some house in the country. A man is there
waiting for her with two children and two maids. He lifts her
into his arms, kisses her and sets her on her feet. She leans
down to hold the little ones who are stretching out their
arms to her. She strokes them tenderly and they set off together
down a drive while the maids pick up all the parcels thrown
down by the driver. Gone for ever! Goodbye! You'll never see
her again, never in your life. Goodbye to the young woman who
has spent the entire night at your side. Still you do not know
her. Never did you speak. And yet you are sad to see her go.
Goodbye!

   Oh the countless travellers' tales I could tell you! Some sad,
some happy, so many . . . !

I was in the Auvergne once, wandering on foot around those
friendly, familiar French peaks of ours which are neither too
high nor too difficult to negotiate. I had climbed Sancy[1] and was
in a little inn near a pilgrim chapel called Notre-Dame-de-
Vassivière[2] when I noticed, sitting by herself at the far end
of the dining room, a slightly eccentric, certainly odd-looking
elderly woman. She must have been at least seventy and was tall,
austere and angular, with white hair drawn into old-fashioned
wings at the temples. She was dressed in the casual manner of
the English lady traveller, that's to say with no regard at all for
style, and was eating an omelette with which she was drinking
water. There was something quite extraordinary about her. Her
eyes were full of pain and she looked like someone whom life
had treated rather badly. I kept looking at her in spite of myself,
wondering who she might be, what sort of life she led and why
she was wandering about these mountains entirely alone.

   She paid and rose to leave, fixing about her shoulders an
unusual little shawl, the ends of which now dangled over her
arms. From a corner she picked up a walking stick covered with
place-names in poker-work, and with a stiff yet purposeful
stride walked out. A guide was waiting for her at the door.
They moved off and I watched them descend the valley along a
path marked by tall wooden crosses. She was taller than her
companion and seemed to move more quickly than he did.

Two hours later I was climbing the slopes of the high volcanic crater in whose wonderfully vast green bowl grow trees, bushes, greenery, rocks and flowers and in the middle of which lies Lake Pavin[3] so perfectly round as to seem drawn by a compass, and as clear and blue as a sea of azure descended from the sky. The view is so enchanting that you want to move immediately into the little hut on the wooded hill that dominates the sleeping crater full of cold, still water. She was standing there motionless, contemplating the transparent surface of the lake lying within the now extinct volcano. She looked deep into its unknown depths populated, according to legend, by giant trout which have devoured all the other fish within. As I passed her I thought I saw two tears roll down her cheeks. But she strode off to join her guide who had remained in the little lodge at the foot of the rise leading to the lake.

I saw nothing more of her that day.

The following evening as night fell I arrived at the Château de Murol.[4] The earth-coloured tones of the old fortress appeared in the shape of a gigantic tower forming a peak in the middle of a wide valley at the junction of three smaller vales. Though bruised and battered it still showed softly rounded contours from the large circular base up to the crumbling rooftop of its turret. It is an unusual ruin because of its great size and simplicity and because of the majesty of its ancient, powerful, sombre appearance. It stands alone as high as a mountain, like a dead queen rising still above the sleeping valleys below. It is reached by a slope planted with firs and is entered through a narrow gap beyond which the visitor stops at the foot of the walls forming the outward fortification.

Within lie the remains of rooms, disintegrated staircases, spaces where who knows what once stood, foundation stones, dungeons, shattered walls, seemingly unsupported vaults and a maze of fissured stones where grass grows and animals roam.

Wandering alone through this ruin I was suddenly aware of a ghostly presence, the spirit, as it were, of this ancient, ruined dwelling. I gave a start of surprise mixed with fear before recognizing the old woman I had already seen twice before. She was weeping huge tears and clutching a handkerchief. I turned to leave her in peace but she spoke, ashamed at having been caught off guard.

'Yes, Monsieur, I'm weeping, as you can see. It doesn't often happen, but . . .'

Embarrassed, and not knowing what to say in the circumstances, I stammered: 'I'm so sorry to have disturbed you. Obviously something terrible has happened to . . .'

'Well, yes . . . and no . . . it's just that . . . I'm at a complete loss . . .'

Dabbing her eyes, she sobbed. I took hold of her hands to try and calm her down and was moved in turn by her tears. Suddenly, as if she could no longer bear to carry the burden of it alone, she began to tell me her story.

'Oh! . . . Monsieur . . . if only you knew what misery . . . what great misery I am in . . . I used to be happy . . . I used to have a house . . . back at home . . . but I can't . . . I *can't* go back to it. I will not go back. It's just too hard for me.

I have a son. And all this is about him! My son! Oh, children have no idea, do they! There's so little time to really live! And do you know, I'm not even sure I'd recognize him now! I loved him so much even before he was born when I could feel him stirring inside my own body. And so much afterwards! How I loved him, adored him, cherished him. If you knew how many nights I spent watching as he slept, thinking about him. I loved him to distraction. When he was eight, his father sent him away to prep school. That was the end. He was no longer mine. Oh, my God! He was allowed home on Sundays, that's all. After that he went to boarding school in Paris. He was allowed home no more than four times a year. So every time I was amazed at how much he had changed. I could always see how much he'd grown but I never saw him growing! I was robbed of his childhood, of his trust and of the tenderness which he could always have felt towards me. All the joy of seeing him develop, of growing into a young man, all that was taken away from me. Imagine, seeing your own son four times a year! Every time he visited he was a different person. His body, his appearance, his movements, his voice, his laugh, none of them was ever the same. He was no longer mine. Children grow so quickly and when you're not there to see them it's just so terribly sad ... you can never have that back. One year he arrived with down on his cheeks! My son! I was so stunned, so sad that ... it's unbelievable ... but I hardly dared give him a kiss! Was this really my dear, my darling little baby that I'd dandled in napkins on my knee, who had drunk my milk with his greedy little lips? Was my baby this great dark-haired chap who couldn't snuggle up to me any more, who seemed to love me mainly out of duty, who called me 'Mother' and kissed me formally on the forehead, when all I wanted to do was enfold him in my arms?

First my husband, then my parents died. After that I lost my two sisters. When death comes to someone's home it's as if it wants to get as much done as quickly as possible to save coming again for a long time. It often leaves only one or two to mourn the others. I never remarried. My son was now doing law and I hoped I could live and die not far from him. I moved near him so we could live closer to each other. But of course by then he was a young man, he'd got his own life and he let me know I was in the way. So I left. Maybe that was a mistake, but I hated to feel surplus to requirements. I went back home.

I hardly ever saw him again. Hardly ever. Then he was to get married. Wonderful! Now we would all be together forever. I would have grandchildren! But he had married an English girl who took an instant dislike to me. Maybe she sensed that I loved him too much. So again I found myself alone. Yes ... that's how it was, Monsieur. Then he left for England. He was going to live with *them*, his wife's parents. Can you understand what that meant? It meant that they've robbed me of him! He's theirs now! He writes to me once a month. There was a time when, instead of that, he used to come and see me. Not any more. Never.

It's now four years since I saw him. He had white hair. Wrinkles. How did that happen? How could this man verging on old age be my son, my little pink and white babe? It's quite likely that's the last I shall ever see of him. So I just keep on travelling all year round. I travel here, there and everywhere as you see, with no one for company. I am, as I say, completely bereft. Goodbye, Monsieur. Don't stay, I beg of you. I feel badly enough already for having unburdened myself of all this to you.'

And as I walked back down the hill again, turning round once I caught sight of the old woman standing tall on top of one of the ravaged battlements and contemplating the mountains, the long valley and Lake Chambon[5] in the distance. The lower part of her skirt together with the strange little shawl she wore around her shoulders were fluttering in the wind like flags.

THE CHRISTENING

At the door of the farm, men were waiting, dressed in their Sunday best. The May sun was shining brightly on the apple trees in blossom. Round and fragrant like enormous pink and white bouquets, they formed a roof of flowers over the entire yard. A constant snowstorm of fine petals swirled and eddied as they fell into the tall grass now flecked with blood-red poppies and blazing yellow dandelions. Near the dungheap a sow dozed, her vast belly and full teats surrounded by a litter of piglets with tightly curled tails.

Suddenly from far beyond the farmland trees, the church bell pealed. In the distance, the sound of its iron tongue rang faintly in the clear air. Swallows darted like arrows across the blue space enclosed by huge, motionless beeches. Stable smells wafted, mingling with the sweet, soft breath of the blossom.

One of the men standing round the door turned towards the house and yelled: 'Come *on*, Mélina! Can't you hear the bell?'

He was about thirty, a tall farmer of upright bearing, unbent as yet by long years of toil in the fields. His bandy-legged father, with hands and arms as gnarled as an old oak, declared: 'That's women for you. Never ready.'

The old man's other two sons began to laugh and one, turning to his elder brother, the man who had shouted, said: 'Go on in and get them moving, Poly. Else we'll be here till noon.'

The young man went into his house.

A gaggle of geese, pausing near the farmers, hissed and flapped their wings before proceeding with slow, measured gait towards the pond.

Just then, at the newly opened door, a buxom woman

appeared carrying a baby of some two months. The snowy strings of her tall bonnet dangled on her shoulders about which she wore a flame-red shawl. The baby, swaddled and swathed in white, lay comfortably across the nurse's ample belly.

Then on her husband's arm out came the mother, a tall strong-looking girl of barely eighteen, fresh-faced and smiling. The two grandmothers, wizened like old apples, followed, their backs bent and twisted by patient, daily labour. One, a widow, took the arm of the other grandfather, who had stayed outside the door. These two, heading the rest of the procession, followed the baby and the midwife. The others followed behind, the youngest carrying paper bags full of sugared almonds.[1]

The little bell continued to peal in the distance, calling as loudly as it could for its tiny baby. Children climbed on the hedgerows, people came out to their gates and dairy maids set down their yoked pails of milk to watch the procession pass by. The nurse, carrying her living burden in triumph, stepped carefully to avoid the puddles in the rutted path between banks planted with trees. The old folk walked ceremoniously and a little crookedly on account of the aches and pains of their old age. The young men, in dancing mood, eyed the girls who had come out to see them pass. The father and mother walked with grave and solemn steps following the child who would eventually take their place and himself bring back into the community again the well-known name of Dentu.

They came out into the open plain and, leaving the long way round by road, took a short cut across the fields. Now the church with its pointed steeple came into view. An opening just above its slate roof showed something moving quickly to and fro inside, appearing and reappearing behind the narrow window. It was the bell still ringing and calling the newborn child to come for the first time into the house of God. A dog had begun to follow. Sugared almonds were thrown at it as it gambolled around. The church door was open. The priest, a tall red-headed fellow, lean and powerful, was himself a Dentu, one of the father's brothers and therefore uncle to the baby. He was waiting at the altar. According to the rites of the Church he christened his nephew Prosper-César. On tasting the holy salt, the baby began to cry.

Once the ceremony was over the family waited in the porch while the priest divested himself of his surplice. They then set off again. This time, with the prospect of the feast to come, they walked quickly. All the children from the neighbourhood followed behind. Each time they were flung a handful of sugared almonds there was a wild scramble to pick them up. They fought and pulled each other's hair while the dog, piling in and even more determined than they were, was tugged by the tail, the ears and the paws. The nurse, tiring a little by now, said to the priest, who was walking beside her: 'Here, Father, if you don't mind, carry your nephew a bit for me, will you, so's I can have a bit of a stretch. Nearly got cramp holding him, I have.'

The priest took the child, whose white gown looked dazzling against the black of his cassock. He kissed him, then, all elbows, carried the little bundle awkwardly ahead. Everyone started to laugh. One of the grandmothers said: 'Crying shame isn't it, Father, you never going to have none of your own.'

The priest made no reply. He was striding ahead looking into the eyes of his charge and longing to give his little round cheeks another kiss. Finally he gave in, lifted his nephew to his face, and gave him a big kiss.

The father cried: 'Here Father, you want one? You just say the word, mate.'

As farmers will, they started in on the crude old jokes. As soon as they sat down to eat, ponderous humour produced gales of laughter in the countryfolk. The two other sons were also soon to be married. After the ceremony, their fiancées had come to join them for the meal. The guests made constant allusion to the generations to come that were heralded by these happy unions. Unremitting earthy banter couched in even coarser language made the blushing girls giggle and the men, yelling and pounding the table, fall off their chairs, laughing. The father and grandfather kept the jokes coming, every one a filthy gem. The mother smiled, the old folk joined in the ribaldry and put in the odd crack themselves.

The priest, used to these Brueghelesque scenes, was sitting next to the nurse and tickling his nephew's lips to make him laugh. He seemed astonished by the sight of this child as if he had never properly seen one before. He looked at him with close attention and a deep, thoughtful seriousness. Mingled with it was a tenderness itself new born within him, and not felt by him before – an intense and poignant tenderness towards this fragile little creature who was his brother's son.

Oblivious of his surroundings, he contemplated the child. He would have liked to pick him up again and put him on his lap. He could still feel against his chest and within his heart the sweet sensation of carrying him earlier, back from the church. In his contemplation of this miniature of a man, he was moved as if by some ineffable mystery unprecedented in his life, a holy, sacred mystery which was the incarnation of a new soul. Here in essence was the great mystery of burgeoning life; of love awakening and with it the survival of mankind; the onward march of humanity.

The nurse in mid-feast, her face red and her eyes gleaming, was having difficulty reaching the table with the baby in her lap. The priest said to her: 'Give him to me. I'm not hungry.'

And again, he picked up the child. Once more, for him, all else faded and then disappeared from view. He gazed at the chubby, pink face and gradually the warmth of the little body through its swaddling and through the cloth of his own cassock reached his lap and came through to him as a very light, very chaste and delicious caress, so full of goodness that his eyes filled with tears.

The noise of the revellers at table became deafening. The child, disturbed by all the roistering around him, began to cry. A voice called out: 'Go on, Father! Give him the breast.'

The room reverberated with their laughter. But the mother rose, picked up her son, and carried him off to an adjoining room. She came back in a few minutes saying that he was now fast asleep in his cradle.

The meal continued. Men and women went out into the yard from time to time, then returned to the table. Meat and vegetables, cider and wine disappeared down the guests' gullets, swelling stomachs and putting a gleam in the eye. The festivities reached their peak.

Night was falling as coffee was served. The priest, to no one's

great surprise, had long since disappeared. Finally, the young
mother got up to see whether the baby was still asleep. It was
now dark and she fumbled her way through the room with arms
stretched out in front of her so as not to bump into the furniture.
Suddenly a strange sound made her stop in her tracks. She
ran out terrified, certain that she had heard someone move.
Extremely pale and trembling she returned to where everyone
was eating and said so. The men rose as one with an angry,
drunken roar. The father, seizing a lamp, rushed in. At the
cradle's side, his head on the pillow where the baby's lay, the
priest knelt, sobbing.

COWARD

Generally referred to as Beau Signoles, his full title was the Vicomte Gantron-Joseph de Signoles. As an orphan with a sizeable fortune to his name he was highly eligible as well as dashing and physically attractive. Possessed not only of natural dignity and a distinctly aristocratic bearing but also of great wit, he was much sought after by the ladies, who admired his handsome moustache and were drawn to the gentle expression always to be seen in his eyes.

Much in demand by salon society, he was particularly popular with the waltzers. Men regarded him with the amused tolerance often shown to the more attractive among them and there was also talk of one or two love affairs, which added even further lustre to his name. He led a happy not to say charmed and morally blameless life and enjoyed a reputation as both an excellent swordsman and an even better shot.

'In a duel,'[1] he would say, 'I should always choose pistols. Then I'd be sure of my man.'

One night, as it happened, he had taken two young lady friends together with their husbands to the theatre. After the show he suggested ices at Tortoni's.[2] They had been sitting there for ten minutes before he noticed a man at a nearby table staring hard at one of his own companions. She looked uncomfortable and embarrassed. After a while she said to her husband: 'There's a man there staring at me. I've no idea who he is, have you?'

The husband, who had noticed nothing, looked over at the man. 'No, no idea.'

The young woman went on, half amused but half annoyed too, 'It's too bad. It's spoiling my ice for me.'

The husband shrugged his shoulders: 'Forget it. Just don't take any notice. It happens all the time.'

The Vicomte, however, got up immediately. He could not allow this complete stranger to spoil an ice bought by himself. The insult was directed at him, he felt. Since it was he who had brought them to this café, it was his responsibility entirely.

He went up to the man and said: 'I cannot allow you to keep staring at these ladies. Be so good as to stop it this minute.'

The other man replied: 'Why don't you just mind your own business.'

The Vicomte replied through clenched teeth: 'Take great care, Monsieur, that you don't force me to take this any further.'

The man answered with just one word. The obscenity rang from one end of the café to the other and produced an instantaneous reaction in every single customer. All those who had their backs to the man turned round. Everyone looked up. Three waiters spun on their heels like tops. The two women behind the counter started and wheeled round like a pair of twin robots.

A heavy silence fell. Then suddenly a crack was heard. The Vicomte had slapped the man's face. Everyone rose to intervene. Cards were exchanged.

On his return home the Vicomte strode nervously up and down his room for a few minutes. He was too upset to think. The word 'duel' filled his head so completely that he was as yet unable to attach any emotion to it. He had done what he had to do. He had behaved as a man should. Talking to himself, as one does in times of great stress, he said aloud: 'What a brute of a fellow!'

He then sat down to think. First thing tomorrow morning he would have to find seconds. Who should he ask? In his mind he went through the most respectable and most responsible of his friends. Finally he chose the Marquis de La Tour-Noire and Colonel Boudin. That was good: one from the aristocracy and one from the military. Their names would look good in the papers. He realized that he was thirsty and drank three glasses of water one after the other before beginning to pace the floor again. He felt full of energy. If he showed himself hard and determined to see the thing through right to the end, if he demanded the most dangerous and rigorous conditions, then more than likely his opponent would back down.

He looked again at the piece of card he had taken out of his pocket and tossed on to his table. As his glance had revealed in the café, and as every gaslight passed in the cab on the way home had confirmed, the name he read was Georges Lamil, 51, rue Moncey. He looked at this collection of letters which appeared to contain some hidden mystery: Georges Lamil? Who was this man? What did he do? Why had he stared at that woman like that? Wasn't it appalling to think some complete stranger could suddenly come storming into your life just because he had the nerve to stare at a woman? The Vicomte said aloud again, 'What a brute!'

He stopped and eyed the card once more, speculating. He was suddenly angry with the scrap of paper, and, mingled with his anger and loathing, was a strange feeling of unease. So stupid, the whole thing! He took up his open penknife and, as if he were stabbing the man, stuck it in the middle of the printed name.

So! It had come to a duel, had it? As the injured party, should he choose swords or pistols? There was less danger with swords but on the other hand the threat of pistols might make his opponent retract. Very rarely is a swordfight fatal since the two duellists make sure they never fence close enough to each other for the swordpoint to go in very deep. With pistols he would be taking a very serious risk with his life but he might also get out of the affair with his honour intact and possibly without even having to meet the man.

'Must be firm. Frighten him off,' he said.

The sound of his own voice gave him such a shock that he looked round to see who was there. He felt extremely nervous, drank another glass of water then got undressed ready for bed.

As soon as he was in bed he blew out the candle and closed his eyes. He was thinking, 'I've got all day tomorrow to arrange things. Sleep's the best thing now. Got to keep up my strength.'

He felt very hot between the sheets and simply could not drop off. He tossed and turned, five minutes on his back, five more on his left side, then his right, and so on.

He felt thirsty again and got up for a drink. A sudden thought set him worrying: 'Could it be that I'm frightened?'

Why did his heart start to beat wildly every time he heard the most ordinary noises in the room? When the clock was about to strike, the sound of the spring just beforehand made him jump. He had to breathe through his mouth for a few seconds to recover. He began to weigh the possibilities: 'Could I be scared?'

Of course not! He couldn't be scared if he was so determined to see it through! He couldn't be frightened if he had willed himself to fight and not to waver. But he was so worried that he now began to entertain a further possibility: 'Could a man be frightened in spite of himself?'

He was overwhelmed now, first by doubt, then anxiety and finally terror. What if a force stronger than his own will-power overcame him? What would happen then? No doubt he would make it to the appointed spot because he wanted to. But what if he was shaking? What if he passed out? He thought of his position in society, his reputation, and his good name.

A sudden, bizarre impulse made him get up again to go and look at himself in the mirror. He relit his candle. When he saw his face in the polished glass he hardly recognized himself. It was as if he had never seen himself before. His eyes were enormous and he was as pale as a ghost.

He remained standing in front of the mirror and was about to stick out his tongue to check his state of health, when suddenly a thought struck him like a bullet:

'This time the day after tomorrow I could be dead.'

His heart began to pound furiously again.

'This time the day after tomorrow, this person in front of me, this me I see in the mirror will be no more. What? Here I am looking at myself, feeling myself living, and in twenty-four hours I could be lying over there in that bed, dead, with my eyes closed – cold, lifeless, gone!'

He turned towards the bed, and could distinctly visualize himself lying there on his back under the same sheets as a moment ago. He had the hollow-faced look of the dead and his hands the lifelessness of those which will never move again. He became frightened of his bed, and to avoid looking at it he went through into his smoking room. Mechanically he picked up a cigar, lit it and started pacing up and down again. He felt cold and was just about to ring for his manservant when he stopped, his hand on the bell-pull. 'The man will see I'm frightened.'

So instead of ringing he lit a fire, his hands trembling every time they touched anything. His head spun and his thoughts became fleeting, sudden and painful. A kind of intoxication overwhelmed him and he felt as if he had been drinking.

'What shall I do? What is to become of me?' he kept wondering. His entire body was convulsed with shakes. He rose, went to the window and opened the curtains.

Dawn was breaking on a summer's day. The pink sky cast a rosy tinge over the roofs and walls of the city. A great sweep of warm light, like a caress from the rising sun, enveloped the waking world. With it a sudden, bright, cheerful ray of hope lit up the Vicomte's heart. Was he mad to let himself be paralysed with terror before a single thing had been decided, before his seconds had even paid a call on this Georges Lamil, and before he knew that a duel was even going to take place?

He washed, dressed and strode purposefully out. As he walked he said to himself: 'I must keep active, very active. Have to show I'm not frightened.'

His seconds, the Marquis and the colonel, put themselves at his disposal and, after shaking hands vigorously with him, discussed conditions. The colonel asked: 'Do you want this to be a proper, serious duel?'

'Very serious,' the Vicomte replied.

'You insist on pistols?' the Marquis went on.

'Yes.'

'Do we have your permission to see to everything else?'

The Vicomte in a terse, clipped tone replied: 'Twenty paces. At the command. The weapon to be raised not lowered. Exchange of fire to the point of serious injury.'

'Excellent conditions,' replied the colonel, sounding satisfied. 'You're a good shot. Everything looks good, I'd say.'

They duly left. The Vicomte returned to his place to wait for them there. His agitation, momentarily calmed, now returned with a vengeance as the minutes ticked by. In all his limbs, in his arms and his legs, in his chest and all over his body, he felt a constant shaking and trembling. He could not remain in one position for long, either sitting or standing. There was not a trace of saliva in his mouth and he kept making a dry sound with his tongue, which stuck constantly to his palate.

He would have liked some lunch but could not manage to eat. It occurred to him that a drink might give him some courage. He ordered a small carafe of rum to be brought in to him and drank six small glasses of it in swift succession. A warm, burning glow spread through him and soon afterwards his thoughts became slightly muddled.

'That's the answer. Now I shall be all right,' he said to himself.

But within an hour he had emptied the carafe and was feeling even more nervous. He felt desperately like rolling on the floor, yelling and biting into something. The evening shadows began to gather. A ring of his bell gave him such a fright that he was unable to rise and greet his seconds. He no longer dared speak to them, say good evening or utter a single word for fear that his voice would give everything away.

The colonel announced: 'Everything has been arranged according to your wishes. At first your opponent claimed the privileges of injured party but almost immediately he agreed to all your conditions. His seconds are two officers.'

'Thank you,' said the Vicomte.

The Marquis continued: 'Don't mind if we just come and go. We have hundreds of things to attend to. We need a good doctor since the duel will continue to the point of serious injury and as you know bullets don't mess about. We have to decide on a place near a house where the injured man may be carried if necessary, and so on and so forth. Anyway we shall be busy for the next two to three hours.'

A second time the Vicomte said: 'Thanks.'

'Are you all right?' the colonel inquired. 'Feeling quite calm, are you?'

'Yes, perfectly, thank you.'

The two men took their leave.

Left alone once more, the Vicomte nearly went mad. After

his manservant had lit the lamps he sat down at his table to write some letters. Having written at the top of one page: 'This is my last will and . . .', he rose brusquely and walked away, incapable of putting two thoughts together. He could think about nothing, decide on nothing. So! He was going to fight a duel! There was no avoiding that now. What was happening to him then? He wanted to fight, he had that resolve, that determination. And yet he knew all too well that, despite his best efforts and all the will-power he could muster, he no longer had the strength even to go to the rendezvous. He tried to visualize the combat, to envisage how he and his opponent would behave. From time to time his teeth chattered, making a dry little clacking sound in his mouth. He tried to read, and picked up Châteauvaillard's duelling code.[3] He wondered: 'Does my opponent practise? Is he a recognized shot? How is he rated?'

How could he find out? He remembered the Baron de Vaux's book of marksmen[4] and read it from cover to cover. Georges Lamil was not listed. But if the man was not a good shot he would never have agreed immediately to such dangerous weapons and these deadly conditions. Passing a table on which lay a case marked Gastine-Renette,[5] he took out one of the pistols, assumed a firing stance and raised his arm. He was shaking so much the gun pointed all over the place.

He said to himself: 'It's impossible. I can't fight a duel like this.'

He looked down the barrel of the gun into the little black hole which spits out death. He thought of the disgrace. He thought of what people would whisper about him. He thought of the sniggers in the salons and of the women's contempt. He thought about what the papers would say and all the insults cowards would be able to cast at him. He was still looking into the weapon and raising the safety catch when he noticed a little primer inside glowing like a small red flame. By chance, someone had forgotten to unload the pistol. This gave him a vague, inexplicable pleasure. If he failed to behave with calm dignity in confronting his opponent he was finished forever. He would be tainted, shamed and rejected. And he knew now that he would be unable to muster what was necessary. He felt it in his bones. Yet he was brave since he did want to fight! He was brave, since . . . The thought which began at that moment to enter his mind remained incomplete. Instead, opening his mouth wide and ramming the barrel of the gun into the back of his throat, he pulled the trigger.

When his manservant, hearing the shot, reached him, he was lying on his back, dead. Blood had spurted on to the white paper on the table, making a large red stain under the words: 'This is my last will and . . .'

ROSE

The two young women are practically buried beneath a layer of blossom. They have all to themselves a huge landau[1] filled to the brim with bouquets and looking like a gigantic flower basket. On the front seat are two wickerwork panniers lined with white satin and full of Nice violets. On the bearskin rug covering their knees, a huge pile of roses, mimosa, stocks, marguerites, tuberoses and orange-blossom all tied with silken favours appears to crush the two delicate figures, so that from this dazzling, perfumed bed, only the shoulders and a glimpse of two bodices, one blue and one lilac, are seen to emerge.

The handle of the coachman's whip is trimmed with anemones, the horses' harnesses festooned with gillyflowers and the wheel-spokes with mignonette. Instead of lanterns, two enormous round bouquets stare out like a strange pair of eyes on this lumbering beast created entirely of blooms.

At a brisk trot, the landau skims along the procession route, the rue d'Antibes, preceded and followed by an accompanying flotilla of similarly garlanded floats carrying women submerged beneath seas of violets. It is the festival of flowers at Cannes.[2]

They reach the field of battle, the boulevard de la Fonçière, where, on either side of the immense avenue, a double row of flower-bedecked coaches weaves back and forth in an endless ribbon. Flowers are thrown from one side to the other, flying in a shower through the air, landing on fresh young faces, then swirling and falling to the ground where a crowd of urchins swarms to pick them up.

A different, dense crowd standing on the pavements is held back by mounted police who roughly boot back the over-curious, making sure none of this riff-raff mixes with the quality. Noisy but good-humoured, the onlookers watch from the sidelines. From the carriages friends call out greetings and pelt each other with a hail of roses. All eyes are drawn to an attractive carriage full of young women all dressed in Mephistophelian red. A gentleman resembling Henri IV is having the time of his life tossing back and forth an enormous bouquet he has attached to a length of elastic. The young women shield their eyes against the barrage and the men bow their heads; the elegant missile describes a graceful curve and returns to its owner, who immediately aims it at yet another target.

The two young women empty their arsenal by the handful and receive another onslaught in return. After an hour or so of exchanges they are by now a little tired. They order their coachman to take them along the coast road, the Route du Golfe Juan.

The sun disappears behind the mountain of Esterel and its long, lace-edged silhouette is etched in black against a blazing sunset. A calm, bright blue sea stretches as far as the horizon where it merges with the sky. Ships of the fleet, anchored in the middle of the bay, ride motionless on the water like a flock of hunchbacked and armour-plated beasts of the Apocalypse, crested with slender, plume-like masts, and with eyes that glow in the dark.

The two young women, stretching out under the heavy rug, languidly survey the scene. Finally one speaks. 'Everything's so lovely, isn't it, Margot? Specially on a beautiful evening like this!'

'I suppose so, yes,' the other replies, 'but there's always something missing, don't you think?'

'Like what? I'm perfectly happy as I am. Can't think of anything else I'd like.'

'Can't you really? Then you're just not thinking. However relaxed I feel, my heart always yearns for . . .'

'A little love?' says the other, smiling.

'Yes, a little love.'

They fell silent looking directly ahead. Then the one called Margot murmurs: 'Life's just not worth living without it. For me, anyway. I need to be loved, if only by a dog. I'm sure we're all like that, whatever you might say, Simone.'

'No, darling. I'd rather not be loved at all than by just anybody. Can you *imagine* what it would be like to be loved for example by . . . by . . .'

She looks round for a likely person, letting her gaze wander over the vista ahead. After scanning the horizon her eyes fall on the two gleaming metal buttons on the coachman's back: 'Well . . . by my coachman,' she laughingly concludes.

Madame Margot gives a weak smile and declares, *sotto voce*: 'Do you know, it's really rather fun to have one of your servants in love with you. It's happened to me more than once. They make such eyes at you, my dear, it's too killing! The keener they are, of course, the more distant you have to be. In the end, naturally, you have to find some reason to send them away. I mean it would be too frightful if anyone were to suspect.'

Madame Simone listens, looking straight ahead, then announces: 'Well I wouldn't like it, I can assure you. Having my footman in love with me wouldn't seem like much of a conquest. Anyway, how can you tell?'

'Same as with other men. They just go a bit daft.'

'*I* don't think they're daft when they're in love with me – other men, I mean . . .'

'Completely potty, my dear. They can't think of a thing to say. Can't take a thing in.'

'But what about you? How did you feel when you had a servant in love with you? Touched? Flattered . . . or what?'

'Touched, no. Flattered, yes, a little. One is always flattered by a man's love, whoever it is, don't you think?'

'Oh, Margot! Really!'

'Oh yes you are, you know! Listen, I must tell you. The strangest thing happened to me once. You'll see how weird and confused you can feel when something like that happens.'

'Four years ago this autumn I found myself without a personal maid. I'd tried five or six in succession and they were all hopeless. I was beginning to think I'd never find one, when I read this advertisement in a magazine. A young woman who could sew, embroider and do hairdressing was looking for a job. She could provide the highest references. On top of all that, she could speak English.

I wrote to the address she gave and the following day this person came to the house. She was quite tall, slim and a little pale. She seemed terribly shy. Beautiful big dark eyes, lovely complexion. I took to her straight away. Asked for her references. She gave me one written in English, since apparently her last appointment had been in the household of Lady Rymwell where she had been employed for ten years. The reference confirmed that this young lady was leaving of her own accord since she now wanted to come back and live in France. Throughout the lengthy period of her employment, apart from what was referred to as a certain French *coquetterie* she had given absolute satisfaction. I was slightly amused by the prim phrasing of the English letter and hired her on the spot.

She began her employment with me the very same day. She was called Rose, and within a month I was practically in love with her. She was phenomenal. A treasure. Fabulous. She was an incredibly good hairdresser, a near-professional milliner, particularly when it came to lace, and she wasn't a bad dressmaker either. I was amazed at what she could do. I'd never had a servant like her. She used to dress me in no time at all and with such astonishing lightness of touch! I *hate* being touched by my maid but never once was I aware of this young woman's fingers on my skin. After a while, I became extremely lazy, so much did I love this tall shy girl to dress me from top to toe, from undergarments to gloves, blushing as she always did, and never saying a word. When I used to get out of the bath, there she would be, waiting to rub me down and give me a massage while I sometimes dozed off on a divan. I tell you, it got to the stage where I used to think of her more as a friend from a slightly inferior class than just a servant.

Well, one morning my concierge asked if he could have a word. He was very mysterious about why he wanted to see me. I was surprised and asked him in. He was absolutely reliable, an ex-soldier, my husband's former batman, in fact. He seemed embarrassed to speak. Then finally he blurted out that he'd

got the local commissioner of police downstairs. I asked him
outright what this chap wanted.

"He's got a warrant to search the house."

Now I know how necessary the police are, but personally I
can't stand them. Seems like an undignified profession to me.
So I was both offended and annoyed by this.

"What's the warrant for? I refuse to let him in until I know
exactly what this is all about!"

The concierge went on: "Apparently they have reason to
believe that someone wanted by the police is living in hiding
here."

Alarmed by this news, I asked for the commissioner to be
brought in to me so that he could explain. He turned out to be
quite a well-educated sort of chap, Légion d'honneur and all
that. He was very sorry, most apologetic in fact, then told me
that I would find I was harbouring a convict in my household!

I was absolutely revolted. I said I could answer for my entire
domestic staff and I got them all to come up.

"This is the concierge, Pierre Courtin, an ex-military
man . . ."

"No, that's not him."

"This is my coachman, François Pingau, from the Champagne, son of one of my father's tenant farmers . . ."

"Not him."

"This is the headman at my stables, also from the Champagne,
son of other tenants also known to me. And of course the
footman you've just seen . . ."

"Not them."

"Well you can see for yourself now, can't you, there's
obviously been some mistake."

"I beg your pardon, Madame, there's no mistake whatsoever.
We're talking about a notorious criminal here, and under the
circumstances I would be most grateful if you could call in your
entire staff for us to interview."

I was unwilling to begin with but then I gave in and called
every single member of the household, male and female alike.
The commissioner cast a quick glance over them all and
declared: "Not everyone is present."

"Forgive me, Monsieur, but the only person not present is my own personal maid, a young lady you're hardly likely to take for a convict, I imagine?"

"May I see her too, please?"

"Of course."

I rang for Rose, who came immediately. She had hardly stepped into the room when the commissioner gave a signal and two men I hadn't noticed hidden behind the door pounced on her, grabbed both her hands and tied them with rope. Furious, I cried out and would have leapt to her defence if the commissioner hadn't stopped me.

"This girl, Madame, is in fact a man. He is called Jean-Nicolas Lecapet. He was sentenced in 1879 for murder preceded by rape. His sentence was commuted to life imprisonment. Four months ago he escaped and we have been searching for him ever since."

I was stunned. Flabbergasted. I couldn't believe it. Laughing, the commissioner went on: "There's only one proof I can offer you. He has a tattoo on his right arm."

The sleeve was rolled up and, lo and behold, there was a tattoo. Then the police officer added, in rather poor taste, I thought actually: "I should leave any other proof to us if I were you."

And away they led my personal maid!'

'The thing is, believe it or not, what I felt at the time was not anger at having been tricked like that, deceived, you know, made to look a bit of a fool. Nor did I feel ashamed at having allowed myself to be dressed and undressed, handled and touched by this man. I felt a much deeper humiliation . . . a female humiliation . . . Can you understand that?'

'I don't know what you mean, exactly.'

'Listen. Just think a minute. He'd been found guilty of rape, this fellow! I was thinking about the woman he'd raped . . . and it was *that* I felt humiliated by . . . that's what I mean. Do you see now?'

Madame Simone gave no response. She was looking fixedly and with the enigmatic smile women sometimes wear at the two gleaming livery buttons directly before her eyes.

IDYLL

The train had just left Genoa en route for Marseille and was following the long curves of the rocky coast. It slithered like an iron snake between the mountains and the sea, past beaches of yellow sand lapped by little silver waves, before being swallowed up into the mouth of a tunnel like an animal bolting into its lair.

In the last carriage a plump woman and a young man were sitting opposite each other in silence, stealing the odd surreptitious glance at each other. She was about twenty-five and sitting on the door side of the carriage, looking out at the passing scenery. She was a stocky, chubby-cheeked Piedmontese peasant woman with black hair and a full bosom. Having pushed several parcels under the wooden seat she was now holding a basket on her knees.

The young man was about twenty, very thin and with the deep tan of someone who works in the fields under a blazing sun. Beside him tied up in a bundle was his entire fortune: a pair of shoes, a shirt, a pair of breeches and a jacket. Under his seat he had stowed a pick and shovel tied together with rope. He was hoping to find work in France.

The sun as it rose poured a rain of fire over the coast. It was late May and delightful fragrances filled the air and wafted through the lowered carriage windows. Orange and lemon trees in blossom breathed upwards into the peaceful sky sweet, pervasive, honeyed scents which mingled with the perfume of the roses growing wild along the track, rambling over the rich gardens they passed, around the doors of tumbledown country cottages and in the open country too. This coast is their natural habitat. They fill the place with their light yet powerful fragrance and turn the air itself into something both sweeter than wine and equally intoxicating.

The train was moving slowly as if it wanted to linger and savour the gentle charm of this Eden. It kept stopping at small stations where a few white houses stood. Then, after giving a long whistle, it continued on its leisurely way. No one ever got on. It was as if the entire population was dozing and reluctant to move at all on that hot morning in spring.

From time to time the plump woman's eyes would droop then quickly fly open again as she just managed to save the basket from falling off her knees. She would examine the contents for a while then nod off again. Beads of sweat stood like pearls on her forehead and she was breathing with difficulty as if she were suffering from some painful constriction. The young man's head had fallen forward on to his chest and he was sleeping the deep, sound sleep of a country lad.

Suddenly, as they were leaving a small station, the peasant woman seemed to revive. Opening her basket she took from it a hunk of bread, some hard-boiled eggs, a flask of wine and some beautiful, crimson plums. She began to eat. The young man, having also awoken, watched her, following the progress of each mouthful from her knees to her lips. He sat with his arms folded, his eyes fixed and his own lips pressed together. His cheeks were hollow.

The woman ate with huge gusto, swigging at the wine flask greedily to help the hard-boiled eggs down, then stopping to get her breath back. She devoured the lot – the bread, the eggs, the plums and all the wine. As soon as she had finished her meal the boy closed his eyes again. The woman loosened her bodice to be more comfortable and he suddenly looked up at her again. With not a trace of self-consciousness she went on unbuttoning her dress. The pressure of her bosom stretched the fabric so that, as the opening widened, a flash of white undergarment and a little of her skin were revealed. Feeling much more at ease now the woman said in Italian: 'So hot you can't breathe, hardly.'

The young man replied in the same language and with the same accent as her own: 'Good weather for travelling.'

'You from Piedmont?' she asked.

'Asti.'.

'I'm from Casale.'[1]

Immediately, they started chatting together as neighbours. For some time, as is often the case among ordinary people not much used to making conversation with strangers, their exchanges were stiff and formal. They then discussed local affairs and discovered mutual acquaintances. As the list of people they had each recently bumped into grew, the two became friends. Brief, hurried words with sonorous endings fell from their lips in lilting Italian. They moved on to personal matters.

She was married with three children who were now in the care of her sister. She herself had found a good job as wet-nurse to a French lady living in Marseille. The man was looking for employment. He too had been told he was sure to find some there since apparently there was a good deal of construction work on offer.

They then fell silent.

The heat beating down furiously on the carriage roofs was becoming unbearable. A cloud of dust raised by the train drifted in. The smell of the orange and lemon trees as well as of the roses became stronger, yet more pervasive and heavier. The two passengers fell asleep once more.

When they opened their eyes again it was simultaneously. The sun was sinking towards the sea and casting a brilliant sheen on its blue waters. The air freshened and became a touch lighter. Even with her bodice loosened, the wet-nurse was panting. Her cheeks looked flabby and her eyes lacklustre. She said in a weak voice: 'I haven't given the breast since yesterday. I feel so giddy with it. Almost faint.'

Not knowing what to say, he made no reply.

'When a woman produces as much milk as I do she has to give the breast three times a day. If not it gets very painful. It's like a weight pressing down on me. Stops me breathing. Does me in. That much milk's a real problem.'

'I'm sure,' he said, 'it must be a nuisance for you.'

She did look in a very bad way indeed, as if she might pass out any minute.

'I've only got to press for the milk to come gushing out like a fountain. It's amazing. Unbelievable. At Casale all the neighbours used to come and watch.'

'Oh really?' he said.

'Yes really. I'd show you now only it wouldn't be any help to me. Not enough comes out that way.'

She fell silent.

The train stopped at a little halt. Standing behind the barrier was a thin woman dressed in rags and carrying a crying baby in her arms. The wet-nurse looked at her sympathetically.

'Now there's a woman I could help. And that baby'd give me some relief, I can tell you! I'm not a rich woman else I wouldn't be leaving my home like this, and my people and my darling little youngest to find work away, but I'd give five whole francs quick as a flash to have that kid for ten minutes and give it the breast. I'd be a new woman.'

Again she fell silent. Several times she raised her hot hand to wipe her forehead which was dripping with sweat. She groaned: 'I can't stand it any more. I'll die in a minute.'

With an unselfconscious movement she opened her dress completely, revealing her enormous, taut right breast with its brown nipple. The poor woman was moaning: 'Oh my God! I don't know what to do! What can I do?'

The train had set off again and was continuing its journey amid the flowers whose fragrance now deepened in the warmth of the evening. From time to time a fishing boat would appear, sleeping on the surface of the blue sea, its motionless white sail reflected in the water like its own double, upside-down.

Embarrassed the young man stammered: 'Madame ... perhaps I could ... perhaps I could help you ...'

In a broken voice she replied: 'Oh yes if you will. That'd be a great help. I can't ... I really can't stand it any more!'

He knelt down in front of her. She leaned towards him and with a practised gesture pushed the dark tip of her breast towards his mouth. With the movement she made with both hands to proffer her breast to the man a drop of milk appeared at the crown. He licked it greedily then, as if on a fruit, closed his lips on the heavy breast. Regularly and deeply he began to suck. He put both arms around the woman's waist so as to bring her closer to him and drank in long, slow draughts, making movements with his neck like a baby.

Suddenly she said: 'There, that's enough on that side. Take the other one now.'

Obediently he moved to the other breast. She put her two hands on the young man's back and was now breathing deeply and contentedly, enjoying the fragrance of the flowers mingled with the gusts of air that blew into the carriage as they moved.

'Smells lovely round here,' she said.

He made no reply and continued to drink at the human fountain, his eyes closed as if to savour the pleasure of it. Gently, however, she pushed him away.

'That's enough. I feel much better now. It's put new life in me.'

He got up, wiping his mouth with the back of his hand. As she replaced inside her dress the two living gourds of her bosom, she said, 'That was a great help, Monsieur. Thanks very much.'

Gratefully, he replied, 'My pleasure, Madame, I'll tell you. I've had no food for two days.'

MOTHER SAUVAGE

It was fifteen years since I had been in Virelogne, then one autumn I went back for some shooting at the invitation of my friend Serval. During the war the Prussians had destroyed his château there and restoration work on it was now complete.

I loved this part of the world with a passion. It is one of those places the very sight of which brings an almost sensual pleasure. For those of us who love landscape, to conjure up in one's mind's eye certain springs, certain woods, certain pools maybe, or certain hills is like recalling some of the happiest events in one's life. Sometimes the thought of a particular forest glade, a patch of river bank or an orchard carpeted with flowers seen maybe just once on a lovely day, is as poignant and unforgettable as the sight of a woman dressed in sprig-muslin for spring, and glimpsed in the street for an instant. Body and soul are left with a feeling of longing, as if happiness were for once just within arm's reach.

At Virelogne, I loved every aspect of the land, the forests scattered here and there and the rivers criss-crossing its surface like so many veins carrying life-blood to the earth. With crayfish, trout and eel for sport, it was a fisherman's paradise. There were places to bathe, and snipe were often to be found in the tall grass growing on the banks of the narrow rivers and streams.

I was bounding along like a mountain goat one day, some way behind my two dogs which were snuffling about in the undergrowth. A hundred metres to my right old Serval was beating in a field of lucerne. I had just reached the hedge at the boundary of the Saudres woodland when I came across the ruins

of a cottage. All of a sudden I remembered the last time I had
seen it. This was in 1869[1] when it was completely intact, covered
with vines and with a few hens pecking round the door.

Is there any sight sadder, I wonder, than a dead house with
its sinister, broken skeleton exposed to the wind and the rain? I
also remembered that the woman who lived there had given me
a glass of wine one day when I was extremely tired and it was
then that Serval had told me about her family. Her husband, an
inveterate old poacher, had been killed by the police. And the
son, whom I had sometimes caught sight of on my wanderings,
was a big, tall fellow and an equal force to be reckoned with
when it came to bagging game. The family was called Sauvage,
and we wondered whether this was their real name or their
nickname.

I called Serval and he came towards me with his long, wading-
bird stride.

'What happened to the people who used to live here, then?'
I asked.

He proceeded to tell me the following story.

When war was declared, the Sauvage son, then aged thirty-three,
enlisted, leaving his mother alone at home. No one was particularly sorry for her since it was a well-known fact that she was
quite comfortably off. She lived all by herself in this very isolated
spot on the edge of the wood and far away from the village
itself. Of the same stock as her husband, she was a fearless,
tough old bird, tall, skinny and very dour. Not the sort of person
you could have a laugh with – like a lot of peasant women in
that respect. Let the menfolk laugh if they find things so funny,
is their philosophy. But as for themselves, living as they do an
unrelievedly bleak life, their attitude to the world is tight and
constrained. The peasant man does sometimes get a bit merry
at the café-bar and have the occasional guffaw, but his better
half stays sober in every sense of the word. Her facial muscles
seem never to have learned what it is to smile.

So Mother Sauvage carried on as usual in her cottage which
was soon covered with snow. She used to come into the village
once a week to fetch bread and a little meat and then return

home. There were rumours of wolves about and so she slung over her shoulders her son's rusty old rifle with its well-worn butt. She was a curious sight trudging slowly through the snow with the rifle-barrel sticking up behind the close-fitting black bonnet she wore clamped over her invisible but presumably white hair.

One day the Prussians arrived. They were billeted on local householders according to the latter's means and resources. The old woman, who was known to be relatively prosperous, was given four soldiers.

They were stout, blond fellows with blue eyes and light skin. They had stayed on the heavy side despite all hardships endured so far and, although representative of the occupying forces, they were good lads on the whole. Left alone with this elderly woman, they were kindness itself and spared her as much effort and expense as they possibly could. The four of them could be seen in the mornings washing at the well, in the cold, snowy light splashing water on their pink-and-white northern flesh as Mother Sauvage moved about inside preparing the day's soup. You would see them cleaning the kitchen, polishing the floor tiles, chopping firewood, peeling potatoes, doing the washing and all the other necessary household chores. All in all they behaved as good sons would towards their mother.

She, however, thought constantly of her own son; her tall, hook-nosed, brown-eyed boy, with the thick moustache lying there on his upper lip like a big black roll. Every day she would ask: 'Do you know where the 23rd Infantry have got to? That's what my son's with.'

'Ve don't know,' they would answer. 'Ve really don't know.'

Having mothers back home themselves they could sympathize with her and understand why she was so anxious and worried. They did all sorts of things for her and in time she became fond of her four official enemies. Peasants very rarely feel patriotic loathing for others. Those sorts of feelings, they believe, are reserved for their social superiors. The least warmongering are the poor, humble people whom war affects most because they can least afford any extra charges. The least jingoistic are those who are killed in their thousands and form the real cannon-fodder of battle. The people who suffer the greatest misery and deprivation in times of conflict are always the weakest and most vulnerable. They are the ones for whom national honour and glory mean nothing and they form the bulk of the populations on both sides of war. In six months it exhausts both victors and vanquished alike.

When Mother Sauvage's four Germans came up in conversation local people would say, 'Now those four got a cushy billet all right!'

One morning when the old woman was at home by herself, she saw a man in the distance coming towards the house. In a little while, she recognized the local postman. He gave her a piece of folded paper and, having put on the spectacles she used for sewing, she read:

Madame Sauvage,
This letter brings sad news. Your son Victor was killed yesterday by a cannonball which effectively cut him in half. I was close to him when it happened since we are next to each other in the company. He asked me to let you know the same day if anything should ever happen to him. I took his watch from his pocket and will return it to you when the war is over.
Greetings from your friend,
Césaire Rivot. Recruit. 23rd Infantry.

The letter was dated three weeks earlier.

Madame Sauvage did not weep. She stood stock still, so shocked and paralysed by the news that she felt as yet no pain. She simply thought, 'Victor's dead now.' Then little by little tears came to her eyes as she was overwhelmed with grief. Ideas came into her mind one after another. Dreadful, appalling thoughts began to creep in. She would never hold her lovely boy in her arms again! The police had killed his father – now the Prussians had killed her son. He had been sliced in two by a cannonball! She could visualize the whole horrifying scene. She imagined his head falling forward, his eyes still wide open as he stood chewing the end of his moustache as he always did when he was angry. What had they done with his body afterwards? If only they had given her her child back, as they had her husband, even with the bullet-hole in his forehead!

She heard the sound of voices. It was the Prussians returning from the village. She quickly hid the letter and dried her eyes carefully before greeting them as she always did. They were in excellent spirits, having managed somehow to get hold of a rabbit, more than likely stolen. They made signs to indicate that they had something good to eat and she began to prepare the midday meal. When it came to killing the creature, however, despite the countless times she had done so in the past, her courage failed her now. One of the soldiers stunned it with a blow behind the ears. Once the animal was dead she pulled its red body out of its skin. But the sight of the blood as she did so and as it covered her hands, the feel of the warm blood as it cooled and coagulated, made her tremble from head to foot. In her mind's eye she saw her own darling boy's red flesh being torn in two while, like that of the rabbit, his body still continued to throb with life.

She sat down at the table with the Prussians but could not touch a thing. They devoured the rabbit without paying too much attention. She looked at them out of the corner of her eye, silently mulling over an idea which had come into her head. Her face was expressionless. They suspected nothing. Suddenly she said:

'Do you realize, we've been together here now for a whole month and I don't even know your names.'

With some difficulty they managed to understand what she was getting at and told her what they were called. She wanted more. They must write it down, as well as the addresses of their families back home. Fixing her spectacles on her large nose, she looked at the unfamiliar handwriting, then folded the paper they had written on and put it in her pocket alongside the note informing her of her son's death.

When the meal was over she said to the men, 'I've just thought of something that might be of some help to you,' and started carrying up hay into the loft where they slept each night. They were surprised to see her doing this but when she explained that it was to keep them warmer they willingly gave her a hand.

Between them, they piled up bales as high as the thatched roof, making a kind of large bedroom with walls of warm, fragrant straw within which they would sleep like babies.

At supper that night one of them was a little concerned to see Mother Sauvage still not eating. She explained that she was suffering from stomach cramps and made up the fire to keep herself warm also. Eventually, climbing up the ladder they used every night, the four Germans retired to their quarters. As soon as the trap-door was shut, the old woman took away the ladder. Then opening the outside door again she fetched in more bales of straw and filled the kitchen with them. She tip-toed back and forth in the snow barefoot so as to make no noise. From time to time she could hear the loud, irregular snores of the four sleeping soldiers.

When preparations were completed to her satisfaction she tossed one of the bales into the hearth and, once the straw had caught fire, started spreading it over the others. She then went outside again and stood watching. In a few seconds the whole of the interior was lit by a blinding incandescence and in a few more this turned into a terrifying brazier, a gigantic furnace the light of whose flames cast a dazzling glare through the narrow window and on to the snow outside. Then a cry went up from the top of the house followed by the hideous clamour of human screams and heartrending cries of terror and agony. Then, the trap-door having collapsed into the kitchen below, a whirling tornado of flames flew up towards the loft, shot through the thatched roof and like some giant, flaming torch, leapt into the sky as the cottage crumbled and collapsed.

Nothing more was heard except for the crackling of the fire, the shattering of walls and the crump of rafters hitting the ground. Suddenly, as the roof finally fell in, the blazing carcass of the house threw a great burst of sparks into the air amid a cloud of smoke. The white landscape, illuminated by the fire, gleamed like a silver cloth shot through with red.

In the distance a bell began to peal.

Mother Sauvage remained in front of her ruined house, standing with her son's rifle ready in case any of the men escaped. When she saw that it was all over she threw the weapon into the blaze and a shot rang out. People, both locals and Prussians, began to arrive at the scene. They found the woman sitting on a tree-trunk with a look of calm satisfaction on her face. A German officer who spoke fluent French asked her: 'Where are your soldiers?'

She lifted a skinny arm in the direction of the fire's red heart, now beating its last, and answered confidently, 'In there!'

People crowded round her. The Prussian continued: 'And how did the fire start?'

'I started it myself,' she said.

No one believed her. They thought the disaster had affected her mind. And so, while everyone gathered round to listen, she told the whole story from beginning to end, from the arrival of the letter to the last cry of the men burned to death inside. She omitted no detail either of what she had felt or what she had done.

When she came to the end she pulled out two pieces of paper from her pocket. Then, again adjusting her spectacles to see which was which, she said, showing the first: 'That's the one about Victor's death.'

Next, showing them the other and nodding her head towards the red ruins of her home, 'And that's their names so you can write to their families.'

To the officer now holding her by the shoulders she calmly passed the sheet of white paper, saying: 'Tell them exactly what happened and don't forget to tell their relatives that it was me Victoire Simon, the Sauvage, who did it.'

The officer shouted out some orders in German. She was seized and thrown against the still warm walls of her house. With great despatch, twelve men took up position at a range of twenty metres away from her. She stayed quite still, understanding perfectly, and awaiting her fate. An order rang out, followed immediately by a long burst of fire and one late shot.

The old woman did not fall. She crumpled to the ground as if her legs had been scythed from beneath her. The Prussian officer approached. She had been virtually cut in half and in her clenched fist still held a blood-soaked letter.

My friend Serval added: 'It was by way of reprisal for this incident that my château was destroyed by the Germans.'

My own thoughts were for the mothers of the four gentle boys burned inside and of the terrible heroism of the other mother executed against the wall before me.

I stooped and picked up a little pebble still blackened from the fire.

MADAME HUSSON'S
ROSE KING[1]

We had just come through Gisors where I had woken at the sound of porters' voices shouting out the name of the station. I was just about to slide gently back to sleep again when a violent jerk of the train sent me flying into the lap of a stout lady sitting opposite. One of the engine wheels had broken and the engine itself was now lying across the track. The tender and the luggage van, also derailed, lay next to the dying creature as it expired, wheezing and croaking, whistling and spitting the while. Like a horse collapsed in the street with its chest and flanks heaving and nostrils steaming, the whole shuddering body was totally incapable of struggling upright again.

The train had barely got up steam when the accident happened and there were neither fatalities nor casualties apart from a few cases of concussion. We all looked sadly at the poor crippled iron beast[2] incapable now of carrying us an inch further. It was going to obstruct the rail for some considerable time since more than likely an emergency locomotive from Paris would have to be sent for.

It was ten o'clock in the morning and I decided immediately to walk back in the direction of Gisors where I might possibly find some lunch. As I walked along the track I thought to myself, 'Gisors . . . Gisors . . . don't I know somebody in . . . haven't I got a friend living in Gisors?' Suddenly the name Albert Marambot flashed into my mind. He was an old schoolfriend of mine whom I had not seen for at least twelve years and who was now practising medicine at Gisors. He had often written asking me to stay. I had always said I would one day, but never had. Now was the time to take him up on it.

I asked the first person I met where Dr Marambot lived and got an immediate response in a Normandy drawl. He lived on the rue Dauphine. And there indeed, on the door pointed out to me, I could see a brass plate engraved with the name of my old chum. I rang. The young, blonde servant girl who answered looked a little dim and kept repeating, ''E's not in.' However, in the background I could hear the clink of glasses and cutlery. 'Hey Marambot!' I shouted. A door opened and a fat man with whiskers appeared, holding a table napkin in his hand and looking not best pleased.

I would never have recognized him. He looked at least forty-five, and in one second I could see reflected in his face all the dullness and tedium of provincial life. In a single flash as instantaneous as my own handshake I knew everything about his way of life, his approach to existence, the sort of mentality he would have developed and his views on the state of the world. I could visualize the lengthy meals contributing to his paunch, the after-dinner snoozes in a cognac-induced haze, the cursory examinations he would give patients while his thoughts strayed to the chicken roasting on the spit at home. I could hear all the conversations about food, about cider, about brandy and about wine; about the best way to cook a certain dish, to blend a certain sauce. All was revealed to me as I took in his florid complexion, his thick lips and his dull, lacklustre eyes.

'You don't recognize me, do you?' I said. 'I'm Raoul Aubertin.'

He opened his arms wide and nearly crushed me to death. His first words were: 'You haven't had lunch yet, I hope?'

'No.'

'Wonderful! I'm just sitting down to an excellent trout. Come and join me.'

Five minutes later I was seated opposite him and tucking in to lunch.

'So you never married?' I asked.

'Good heavens no!'

'And you like it here?'

'Oh yes! Always busy, always something to do. Patients, friends. I eat well. I'm in good health. Lots of good laughs.

Good hunting. What more could a man desire? Not much, in my view!'

'And you don't get bored living in such a small place?'

'Not for a minute. Plenty going on always. Small town's just like a large one, I'd say. There's less variety in the way of entertainments but then each one becomes more exciting as a result. You know fewer people but you see them oftener. When you know every window in a small place, each individual one is more interesting than a whole streetful in Paris. You can have a very nice time, a very, very nice time indeed in a small town, you know. I mean, take this one for example, Gisors, I know its history backwards, from the earliest times to the present day. And I tell you it's absolutely fascinating.'

'Are you from Gisors yourself?'

'Not Gisors, no. I'm from Gournay. That's its sister town, and its rival. Gournay is to Gisors what Lucullus was to Cicero.[3] In Gournay, the big thing is food. People refer to the inhabitants as the "Gournay Guzzlers". Gisors looks down its nose at Gournay. But of course the people of Gournay laugh at Gisors. It's absolutely hilarious!'

I realized that what I was eating was truly exquisite: soft-boiled eggs enveloped in a slightly chilled, herb-flavoured meat jelly. Smacking my lips appreciatively I said, 'This really is very good indeed.'

My host smiled.

'Two things you've got to have: proper meat jelly – not so easy to find as you might think – and decent eggs. Decent eggs are few and far between, you know. You want one with a slightly reddish yolk, nice and tasty. I've got two separate hen houses as a matter of fact. One for laying hens. One for chickens for the table. I give my layers a special feed. I'm very particular. With eggs, just as with chicken meat and of course with beef and lamb, with milk, with everything in fact, you've got to be able to taste the sap, the quintessence of what the animal itself has been feeding on. We'd have much better food if we just bore that in mind a bit more.'

I laughed. 'Keen on food then, are you?'

'Good God, only idiots aren't keen on food! Being keen on

food is like being keen on the arts, keen on education, keen on
poetry, what have you! The sense of taste, my dear chap, is as
delicate a sense, as sensitive and as reliable a sense as sight and
hearing. To be deprived of taste is to lose an exquisite faculty,
the capacity to discern quality in food just as in literature or in
works of art. If you don't have that, you're deprived of an
essential sense, one of the ones that constitute human superiority
over animals. Without it, you'd be one of the many insensitive,
lumpen, brutish kinds of creatures our race is generally made
up of. To have an insensitive palate is like having a dull mind.
A man who can't tell the difference between a crayfish and a
lobster, say, or a herring – that wonderful multi-flavoured fish
which contains every known taste of sea-life – a man who can't
tell a herring from a mackerel, a Crassane pear from a Duchesse,[4]
is like a man who can't distinguish between Balzac and Eugène
Sue,[5] between a Beethoven symphony and a military march, or
who can't make a distinction between the Apollo of Belvedere
and the statue of General Blanmont.'[6]

'Who's General Blanmont?'

'Oh, of course you wouldn't know. You're not from Gisors,
obviously. Did I tell you the inhabitants of Gisors are known as
the "Glorious of Gisors"? Never was the term more appropriate.
But let's finish lunch first. Then I'll tell you all about the town
as we go round it. From time to time he stopped talking to take
a long slow sip of his half-glass of wine which he looked at with
tenderness as he replaced it on the table.

He was quite a comical sight with his napkin knotted around
his neck, his red cheeks, his gleaming eyes and his whiskers now
framing beautifully his ever-busy mouth. He made me eat till I
was fit to burst. Then, since I needed to get back to the station,
he grabbed my arm and guided me through the streets of the
town. A fine example of the provincial style, it was dominated
by a fortress, one of the most curious military structures in
the whole of France. It overlooked a long, green valley on
whose pastureland lumbering Norman cattle grazed and chewed
the cud.

'Gisors,' said the doctor 'population approximately 4,000,
situated on the borders of the Eure, is mentioned as early as

in Caesar's *Commentaries*: Caesaris ostium, then Caesartium, Caesortium, Gisortium, Gisors. I shan't take you up to the Roman camp, the ruins of which are visible to this day.'

Laughing, I replied: 'My dear fellow, it looks to me as though you're suffering from a disease which as a medical man you might be interested in. It's called parochialism.'

He stopped in his tracks.

'Parochialism, my friend, is nothing other than natural patriotism. I love my house, my town, and by extension my province because it still upholds the traditions of my village. In the same way I love the frontier and am happy to defend it should a neighbour encroach upon it, because my own house is threatened and because the frontier, though it may be unfamiliar ground to me, represents the path to my province. In other words I'm a Norman through and through. I might happen to have a grudge now against the Germans. I might want to get revenge on them. But I don't actually hate them. I don't loathe them as instinctively as I do the English, who are my real, my traditional enemy. It's the English who set foot on the soil of my ancestors and raped and pillaged here from time immemorial. The aversion I have for those deceitful people is something given to me at birth by my father . . . Oh, by the way, here's the statue of the general.'

'Which general was that?'

'General Blanmont, of course! We had to have a statue. We're not called the Glorious of Gisors for nothing! So we found General Blanmont. Look over here.'

He dragged me towards the window of a bookshop in which fifteen or so volumes bound in yellow, black and red immediately drew the eye. The titles made me giggle. They read:

Gisors, its Past and its Future, by Monsieur X, member of several learned societies
The History of Gisors, by the Abbé A.
Gisors from Caesar's Day to Our Own, by Monsieur B, proprietor
Gisors and District, by Dr C. D.
The Glories of Gisors, by some researcher or other.

'My dear fellow,' Marambot went on, 'do you know not a year goes by, not one year without the publication of some new history of Gisors. We have some twenty-three altogether.'

'And what exactly are these glories of Gisors?' I asked.

'Oh, there are so many! I couldn't list them all. I'll just tell you the main ones. First of all, we have General Blanmont, then the Baron Davillier, the famous ceramicist who went on expeditions to Spain and the Balearic Islands and brought back wonderful examples, collectors' pieces of Hispano-Arabic pottery.[7] In literature, we've got the late, great journalist Charles Brainne, and among those very much alive and kicking we have the eminent editor-in-chief of the *Nouvelliste de Rouen*, Charles Lapierre[8] . . . and many, many more . . .'

We were going up a long, slightly sloping street, the entire length of which was now being warmed by the June sun from which most of the inhabitants had escaped indoors. All of a sudden, at the other end of this street a man appeared, staggering and obviously drunk. His head was stuck forward as he lurched, with unsteady legs and his arms dangling on either side of his body, in a series of three, six or ten little steps at a time, followed by a rest. When his brief burst of energy took him into the middle of the road he stopped dead and teetered, hesitating between collapse and a fresh surge. Then off he went at a tangent again. He ran straight into the wall of a house and seemed for a moment glued there as if he expected to be drawn in by suction. Then, with a shake he turned round and stared fixedly ahead, slack-jawed, his eyes blinking against the glare of the sun. Jerking his back off the wall he set off once more. A scrawny little yellow mongrel followed him, barking, stopping and starting in accompaniment.

'Well, well,' said Marambot, 'there's Madame Husson's Rose King.'[9]

I was extremely surprised and asked: 'Madame Husson's Rose King? What do you mean by that?'

The doctor began to laugh.

'Oh, it's what we call drunkards round here. It's an old story that's become a bit of a legend locally. Even though every word of it is true.'

'Good story?'
'Very funny indeed.'
'Tell me then.'
'With pleasure.'

'In this town, there used to live a very proper, correct old lady who was a great believer in virtue. Her name was Madame Husson.[10] These are real names that I'm telling you – I'm not making them up. Madame Husson was particularly involved with good works, helping the poor, encouraging the worthy, that sort of thing. She was small and took tiny little steps. She wore a black silk wig and was on very good terms with the Almighty in the person of the abbé Malou. She abhorred vice of any kind but particularly the one the Church refers to as lust. The idea of any kind of intimacy before marriage incensed her. She used to be beside herself at the thought of it.

Just about this time there were a lot of Rose Queens being crowned on the outskirts of Paris, and it occurred to Madame Husson that it might be a good idea for Gisors to have one of its own. She told the abbé Malou about her idea and he immediately drew up a list of candidates. Now Madame Husson had in service with her an elderly maid called Françoise, who was equally strict in her views. As soon as the priest had gone, her mistress called her and said: "Now look, Françoise, here's a list of the girls Monsieur le curé recommends for their virtue. Try and find out what other people think of them, will you?"

Françoise applied herself to the task with vigour. She gathered together every scrap of gossip and tittle-tattle she could find and every hint of suspicion, however small. In case she should forget any details, she wrote them all down in her household expense book where, having adjusted her spectacles on her thin nose, Madame Husson would read:

Bread	four sous
Milk	two sous
Butter	eight sous

Malvina Lavesque seen out last ear with Mathurin Poilu.

Leg of lamb	twenty five sous
Salt	one sou

Rosalie Vatinel seen with Césaire Piénoir in Riboulet wood by
  Madame Onésine, laundress and presser on twentieth july at
  dusc.

Radish	one sou
Vinegar	two sous
Sorrel salt	two sous

Joséphine Durdent tho not believed to have fallen nonobstant in
  corraspondance with the Oportun boy now in servise in Rouen
  and he send her by diligence a present of a bonnet.

No girl emerged from this rigorous inquiry intact. Françoise
asked everybody – neighbours, tradesmen, the infant-school
teacher and the sisters at the convent school. She sniffed out the
smallest scrap of information. And since there isn't a girl in the
world totally untouched by gossip, not a single young girl could
be found in the entire district with no hint of scandal attached
to her name.

Madame Husson, however, was determined that the Rose
Queen of Gisors, like Caesar's wife, should be entirely above
suspicion. She was staggered and appalled by what she read in
her maid's expense book and began to despair of ever finding a
suitable girl. The catchment area was enlarged to include a
greater number of neighbouring villages. Still no one could be
found. The Mayor was consulted. His own protégées also failed
the test as did those of Dr Barbesol, despite the rigorously
scientific nature of his assurances.

Then one day on her return from the shops Françoise said
to her mistress: "You know, Madame, if you want to crown
somebody local, it's going to have to be Isidore."

This set Madame Husson thinking.

She knew Isidore very well. He was the son of Virginie who
kept the greengrocer's shop. His amazing celibacy was now
Gisors' pride and joy. It was also an interesting topic of conversation throughout the town and a source of great amusement to
the girls, who teased him mercilessly about it. He was past
twenty now, tall and gangling, shy and a bit slow in his manner.

He helped his mother in the business and spent most of his time sitting on a chair near the shop door preparing the fruit and vegetables for display.

He was scared witless by girls and immediately lowered his gaze if one of them gave him a smile when she came into the shop. This well-known timidity of his made him the easy butt of every joke in town. Anything vaguely rude or risqué made him blush so quickly that Dr Barbesol called him his modesty thermometer. His neighbours took malicious delight in speculating whether he knew anything or not. What was it exactly which affected the greengrocer's son so deeply? Was it plain indignation at the necessarily messy contact required by love for its full flowering? Or was it shame for his ignorance about something mysterious and unknown?

Little urchins would run up and down in front of the shop yelling obscenities, simply to see him lower his gaze. Girls passed back and forth, whispering wicked things which would force him to retreat indoors. The bolder ones teased him openly for the hell of it, asking him for dates and making terrible suggestions.

Anyway, as I say, Madame Husson was giving it much thought. It was certainly true that Isidore was a remarkable, not to say a famous, example of virtue. Totally unimpeachable. No one, not even the most sceptical, even the most suspicious mind could cast any doubt whatsoever on Isidore's complete moral integrity. He had never once been seen in a café and never out in the street at night. He went to bed at eight and got up at four. He was a pearl among men. Perfection itself.

Still Madame Husson hesitated. The idea of substituting a Rose King for a Rose Queen still worried and dismayed her a little. She decided to consult the abbé Malou.

The abbé replied: "What is it you wish to reward, Madame? Virtue, is it not? Virtue pure and simple. In which case, what does it matter if it be male or female? Virtue is eternal. It transcends birth and gender. It is *Virtue*."

Thus encouraged, Madame Husson went to see the mayor. He was in total agreement.

"We shall have a beautiful ceremony," he said. "Then another year if we find a woman as worthy as Isidore we shall crown a woman. I would go so far as to say that this could act as a lesson to Nanterre. *We* do not exclude. Let *us* be the ones who welcome merit of every kind."

Isidore when he was told blushed deeply and appeared very happy. The coronation date was fixed for 15 August, the Feast of the Virgin Mary, dedicated also to the Emperor Napoleon. The municipality decided to make a big splash on this occasion and accordingly a platform was built on what became known as the Coronation Gardens, a lovely extension of the old fortress's ramparts which I'll show you in a minute.

In a natural reversal of public opinion Isidore's virtue, hitherto ridiculed and mocked in some circles, became overnight universally acknowledged as enviable and respectable, especially now that it was carrying off a prize of 500 francs as well as a savings book. Not to mention all the honour and glory. The girls were sorry they had been so coarse and vulgar. A little smile of satisfaction now played on Isidore's lips, reflecting his inner happiness.

On the eve of 15 August the entire rue Dauphine was decked with flags and bunting . . . Oh! I forgot to tell you why this street is called the rue Dauphine. Apparently the Dauphine, I'm not sure which one, was visiting Gisors one day. She had been kept in the public eye for so long accepting all the formal presentations and formalities that suddenly, in the middle of the procession through the town, she stopped in front of one of the houses on this street and cried: "Oh what a lovely house! How I should love to visit it! Pray who is the owner?" The owner was named and found and, covered in glory and confusion, brought before the princess. She got out of her carriage, entered the house, declared her intention to inspect its every nook and cranny and even asked to be left closeted in one of the upstairs rooms by herself for a few minutes. When she re-emerged, the people, flattered by the honour shown to a citizen of Gisors, yelled, "Vive la Dauphine!" However, a local wag composed a little ditty and the street was renamed after her royal highness's title. It went:

With no holy water
The king's lovely daughter
Baptized it alone
With some of her own.

But I digress. To get back to Isidore. Flowers were strewn all along the route of the procession, just as on the day of the Fête Dieu.[11] The National Guard was in attendance under its commander-in-chief, Major Desbarres, a stalwart old veteran of the *grande armée*.[12] Next to the framed Cross of Honour given to him by the emperor himself, he used to proudly display the beard of a cossack sliced from its owner's chin in one fell swoop of Desbarres' sword during the retreat from Russia. The corps under his command were some of the crack troops of the entire province. The famous Gisors Grenadiers were called in on every important occasion within a radius of at least fifteen to twenty miles. It's said that King Louis-Philippe, as he was reviewing the troops of the Eure, stopped in amazement when he came to the Gisors company and cried, "Oh, who are these fine grenadiers?" "They are from Gisors", the general replied, at which the king is alleged to have commented, "I might have known it!"

So there was Desbarres leading his men behind a military band to escort Isidore from his mother's shop. After a little fanfare had been played under his windows, the Rose King himself appeared on the threshold. He was dressed from head to toe in white drill and wore a straw hat, on the brim of which lay a little circlet of orange-blossom. The question of costume had been a source of great worry to Madame Husson. She was torn between the sober black jacket of First Communion and a whole suit of pure white. It was Françoise, her adviser, who made her plump for the white suit, saying it would make the Rose King look as graceful as a swan.

From behind him his guardian angel and godmother, Madame Husson, appeared in triumph. She took his arm to proceed forward and the Mayor positioned himself on the Rose King's other side. The band played a drum-roll, Major Desbarres shouted, "Present arms!" and the procession moved off towards the church amidst a vast crowd of people who had come from outlying communes for miles around. After a brief Mass was said and a touching address given by the abbé Malou, they proceeded again, this time towards the Coronation Gardens where a banquet was to be served in a marquee. Before taking his seat the Mayor made a speech. I have learned it by heart, it's so beautiful.

> Young man [he said], a worthy lady of charity, beloved of the poor and respected by the rich, Madame Husson, to whom I offer thanks on behalf of the entire community, has conceived the idea – the happy and munificent idea – of founding in this town a prize for virtue intended to act as a precious encouragement to the inhabitants of our beautiful region.
>
> You, young man, are the first to be elected, the first to be crowned in this dynasty of wisdom and charity. Your name will head the list of the most meritorious. Your life, mark this well, your entire life must follow in the spirit of this most auspicious of beginnings. Today, in the presence of this noble woman who rewards your conduct; in the presence of our soldier-citizens who took up arms to defend the honour of those such as you; in the presence of this congregation gathered here in love to acclaim you, or rather, virtue made manifest in you, you make a solemn pledge with this town and with all of us here to follow unto death the excellent example you have hitherto shown in youth. Never forget, young man, you are the first seed to be sown in the soil of hope. Bring to us the harvest we have come to expect of you.

The Mayor took three steps forward towards Isidore who was now sobbing, opened his arms wide and embraced him warmly. The Rose King wept, he knew not why, with mixed emotions of pride and a sort of simple joy. The Mayor placed in one of his hands a silken purse in which solid gold clinked – 500 francs in gold! Having placed in Isidore's other hand a savings book, he declared in a solemn voice: "All honour, glory and wealth to virtue!"

Major Desbarres cried "Bravo!", the grenadiers echoed him in chorus and the people burst into applause. It was now Madame

Husson's turn to wipe tears from her eyes. They then took their places at the table where the banquet was being served. It was both magnificent and interminable. Course after course was brought. Yellow cider and red wine flowed in and out of convivial glasses and reached appreciative throats. The clatter of crockery, the sound of voices and that of music in the background provided a constant, resonant buzz which faded as it rose into the sky where swallows now flew.

From time to time Madame Husson adjusted her black silk wig, which had a tendency to keel over and remain beached on her ear. She chatted amicably with the abbé Malou while the Mayor in a state of high excitement talked politics with the major. Isidore ate and drank as he never had before! He took helpings and second helpings of everything on offer and realized for the first time how wonderful it is to feel one's stomach fill with things that have already tasted heavenly in the mouth. He had slyly undone the buckle of his trouser-belt which was straining under the pressure of his rapidly distending belly. Silent now, and a little worried about a wine stain on his white drill jacket, he stopped eating and brought to his lips a glass which stayed there for some time as he slowly savoured its contents.

It was time now for the toasts. There were many, each applauded with great enthusiasm. Night was beginning to fall and they had been at table since noon. Already, over the valley fine, milky mists were forming as the rivers and the meadows put on their gauzy nightgowns. The sun sank slowly towards the horizon, cattle were lowing in the distant hazy pastures and people were beginning to amble down home to Gisors. The procession broke into little groups for the return leg and Madame Husson, having taken Isidore's arm, was giving him much urgent and no doubt invaluable advice. Finally they arrived at the greengrocery door and the Rose King was deposited at his mother's house.

She, however, was not yet back. Having been invited by relatives to a family celebration of her son's triumph she had followed the procession as far as the banqueting marquee then gone on to lunch at her sister's. Isidore was therefore on his own in the shop as night fell. His head spinning with pride and the effects of the wine, he sat on a chair and looked about him. Carrots, cabbages and onions filled the enclosed space with their strong earthy, vegetable smell. Mingling with it was the sweet, pervasive fragrance of strawberries and the fleeting scent that wafted from a basket of peaches. The Rose King took one and bit into it eagerly even though his belly was as round as a barrel. Then in a sudden surge of joy he leapt to his feet and began to dance. As he did so, something clinked in his jacket. Surprised, he plunged his hands into the pockets and from one drew out the purse containing the 500 francs. He had completely forgotten them. Five hundred francs! A fortune! He poured the louis on to the counter and, with a loving gesture, spread them out so that he could see them in all their glory. There were twenty-five coins in all. Twenty-five solid gold coins! All gold! In the gathering darkness they gleamed on the wood as he counted and recounted them over and over again. He put a finger on each murmuring, 'One, two, three, four, five, hundred; six, seven, eight, nine, ten, two hundred.' Then, putting them back in the purse, he stowed it safely away in his pocket again.

We will never know and who could ever tell what a terrible struggle between good and evil then took place in the Rose King's soul. What violent attack did Satan make upon him? What wicked temptation did he plant in this timid, virgin soul? What ideas, what suggestions, what desires did the Devil invent for the chosen one? Who knows? But Madame Husson's golden boy grabbed his hat with the little coronet of orange-blossom still resting on its brim. Slipping out through the back door he disappeared into the night.

Having been informed that her son had returned, Virginie the greengrocer came back at once and found the house empty. Initially unconcerned, after an hour had passed she started making inquiries. Her neighbours in the rue Dauphine had seen Isidore come home and not seen him go out again. They began to look for him. In vain. Worried now, the greengrocer ran to the Mayor's house. All the Mayor knew was that the Rose King had been escorted safely home.

Madame Husson had just gone to bed when the news was brought to her that her protégé had disappeared. She immediately put on her black silk wig again, got up and went to Virginie's herself. Virginie, a simple and emotional soul, was crying her eyes out surrounded by her cabbages, carrots and onions.

It was feared he might have had an accident. What sort, they wondered? Major Desbarres alerted the police who made a search of the entire town. On the road to Pontoise they found the little coronet of orange-blossom. It was placed on the table around which the authorities were now deliberating. The Rose King must have been the victim of some practical joke or, worse, of someone acting out of jealousy. What means had been employed to kidnap the innocent boy and what was the motive behind the kidnapping? Exhausted by the search they all went to bed, leaving Virginie to wait in tears alone.

The following night when the diligence returned from Paris, Gisors learned to its horror that its Rose King had flagged the coach down not 200 metres outside the parish boundary. He had got in, paid for his seat with a golden louis for which he was given change, and had got down in the very centre of the big city.

Feelings ran high at home. Letters were exchanged between the Mayor and the Paris chief of police but no further news came. Day followed day until finally a week passed. Then, out early one morning Dr Barbesol noticed a man sitting on someone's doorstep. He was dressed in a grey suit and, with his head propped up against the wall of the house, was fast asleep. The doctor approached and recognized the man as Isidore. He tried to wake him but failed. The former Rose King was in a worryingly deep, impenetrable slumber. The doctor was puzzled and called for help to carry the young man to Boncheval, the pharmacist. As they lifted him up an empty bottle rolled out from underneath him. Sniffing it, the doctor declared that it had held brandy, which was useful to know as they tried to bring him round. Eventually they succeeded.

Isidore was drunk. Sodden with drink in fact. After a week-long binge he was a complete wreck. His beautiful white drill

suit was now a greyish yellow, filthy, torn, and covered in grease
and stains; his breath and his entire body stank to high heaven
of all the squalor and mess he had wallowed in for all that time.

He was washed, lectured and locked indoors for four days.
He seemed ashamed and contrite. His purse containing the 500
francs had disappeared as had the savings book and even his
silver watch, a precious heirloom bequeathed to him by his
father the fruiterer.

On the fifth day he ventured out into the rue Dauphine.
Curious looks followed him as he walked past the houses, head
down, glancing furtively about him. He disappeared as he left
town, making for the valley beyond. Two hours later he
reappeared, giggling and bouncing from one wall to the other.

He never went back on the straight and narrow.

His mother kicked him out and he became a carter, driving
coal trucks for Poigrisel and Co. – still in business today, as a
matter of fact. His notoriety spread far and wide. As far away
as Évreux people talked about Madame Husson's Rose King
and it's become the local term for a drunkard.

All of which just goes to show – no charitable act ever goes
entirely to waste.'

Dr Marambot rubbed his hands together as he came to the end
of his story. I asked him if he had ever known the Rose King
personally.

'Indeed I did. I had the honour of closing his eyes for the last
time.'

'What did he die of?'

'Delirium tremens, of course.'

We had reached the old fortress, a mass of ruins now dominated by two towers, one called Saint Thomas of Canterbury's
Tower and the other Prisoner's Tower. Marambot told me how
this prisoner had managed, using a nail and the position of the
sun as it filtered through an arrow-slit, to cover the entire surface
of the walls of his cell with carvings.

I then learned that Clotaire II had given the town of Gisors to
his cousin, the holy Bishop Romain of Rouen; that Gisors had
ceased to be the capital of the Vexin region after the treaty of

Saint-Clair-sur-Epte; that the town occupies the most strategically important position for this particular part of France and that accordingly it had been taken and re-taken times without number. Under orders from Guillaume the Red, the famous military engineer Robert de Bellesme had built a strong fortress there which was later attacked by Louis the Fat, then by various Norman barons; it had been defended by Robert de Candos and finally ceded to Louis the Fat by Geoffroy Plantagenet; then it was taken by the English as a result of a Templar betrayal; it was disputed by Philippe-Auguste and Richard Coeur de Lion, burned by Edward III of England who failed to take the castle; it was taken again by the English in 1419 and later bequeathed to Charles VII by Richard Marbury; taken once more by the Duke of Cabria, occupied by the Ligue, lived in by Henri IV, etc., etc., etc.

Marambot was now well into his stride.

'The bloody English, I tell you! What a bunch of drunks they are, my friend. They're all Rose Kings over there, the hypocrites!'

Then after a moment's silence he stretched out an arm in the direction of the narrow river gleaming in the pastureland below.

'Did you know, by the way, that Henry Monnier[13] was one of the keenest anglers ever to fish from the banks of the Epte?'

'I didn't, actually.'

'And Bouffé, my dear chap, Bouffé, the stained-glass artist.[14] He did some work here, too.'

'You don't say!'

'He certainly did. I'm really amazed at how little you know about the world!'

ENCOUNTER

It happened by chance, quite by chance. Since all the Princess's apartments had been thrown open for this gala evening, the Baron d'Etrailles, tired of standing, walked away from the brightly lit salons and into the relative darkness of a deserted bedroom.

Certain that his wife would not wish to leave before dawn, he was looking for somewhere he could lounge and doze till then. From the doorway, he made out a wide bed of azure gilded with flowers, which, standing as it did in the middle of the room, suggested to him a catafalque where love might lie entombed. The Princess was no longer young. Behind this, a large patch of light gave the impression of a lake viewed from some high window. It was a vast yet discreet mirror with dark hangings which could either be closed or, as was more likely, left open. The mirror cast a conspiratorial eye over the bed. Like a castle haunted by the ghosts of the dead, it too might contain memories and regrets. Across its blank and empty face one could easily imagine the lovely shapes of women's naked thighs and the gentle movements of their entwining arms.

The Baron stood at the threshold, smiling a little wistfully at the sight of this chamber of love. All at once, as though the ghosts just imagined had suddenly risen up before him, something appeared in the mirror. A man and woman, seated on a low divan hidden in the shadows, were rising to their feet. The polished crystal reflected their image as they stood kissing each other on the lips, then separating.

The Baron recognized his wife and the Marquis de Cervigné. With strong, manly self-control, he turned on his heel and left.

He waited for daybreak to come and, with it, the Baroness. Sleep was no longer on his mind.

As soon as he was alone with her, he said: 'Madame, I saw you earlier in the Princesse de Raynes' chamber. I need say no more. I have no wish to be reproachful, or violent, or ridiculous. To avoid all that, we shall quietly separate. The solicitors will follow my orders regarding your future situation. Since you will no longer be under my roof you are free to live as you choose. However, since you will continue to bear my name, if ever any hint of scandal is attached to it, I shall be forced to take sterner measures.'

She tried to speak but he stopped her, bowed, and returned home.

He felt more surprised and saddened than unhappy. He had been very much in love with her during the early years of their marriage but his passion had gradually cooled. Now, though in a way he still found the Baroness attractive, he was frequently involved with other women, sometimes from the theatre, sometimes from wider afield. She was extremely young, not quite twenty-four, small, strikingly blonde and slim, not to say skinny. A little Parisian doll with fine, delicate features, she was smart and flirtatious, but endowed with more charm than real beauty. Joking familiarly with his brother about her, he would say: 'My wife, you know . . . she's attractive, alluring and all that, but . . . there's nothing *to* her, you know? She's like an over-frothy glass of champagne. Too much bubble, not enough substance.'

He paced worriedly up and down his room thinking of a million things at once. Every so often a wave of anger surged over him and he felt a savage desire to go and beat the daylights out of the marquis or go and slap his face publicly at his club. Such bad taste though, he reflected – people would laugh at him, not at the other fellow. Wounded pride, not a broken heart, he thought, going to bed, but not to sleep.

A few days later, the word around Paris was that the Baron and Baroness d'Etrailles had come to an amicable agreement to separate on grounds of mutual incompatibility. Nothing untoward was suspected. There were no ugly rumours and no real surprise was felt. Nevertheless, in order to avoid possibly painful encounters, the Baron travelled abroad for a year. The following summer he was at various coastal resorts, then in the autumn went hunting. He returned to Paris for the winter but never once did he see his wife. He knew that no gossip surrounded her name. At least she was being careful to keep up appearances and that was all he asked.

He grew bored, travelled yet again, then had restoration work done to the Château de Villebosc, which he owned. This took two years and after that he held a series of house parties there which kept him busy for at least another fifteen months. Finally, when the constant round of pleasure had become a little tedious, he returned to his town house in the rue de Lille, just six years after the separation. He was now forty-five years old, with more than a dusting of white hair, more than a slight paunch, and the slightly melancholy look that people who were once attractive, sought-after and loved have about them as each day wreaks some further havoc on their person. A month after his return to Paris he caught cold as he was going home from his club one night. The cold developed into a cough and his doctor ordered him to spend the remainder of the winter in Nice. Accordingly, one Monday night soon afterwards, he set off, taking the express train.

He arrived late, just as it was beginning to move. There was space in a coupé,[1] into which he climbed. One passenger was already settled in the farthest seat but was so bundled up with coats and fur coverings that there was no way of guessing if the passenger was male or female. Resigned to ignorance, the Baron too put on his travelling hat, unrolled his own coverings, snuggled into them and, stretching out, fell fast asleep. It was dawn before he awoke and looked immediately over at his companion. The latter had not moved all night and appeared to be still deep in sleep. Monsieur d'Etrailles took this opportunity of performing his morning toilet, brushing his beard and recomposing the face which, as one grows older, night ravages so deeply.

'How triumphant are the mornings of the young!', as the poet has it.[2]

What magnificent awakenings there are indeed in youth, when

we rise fresh-faced and bright-eyed, hair glossy with the sap of life. With age come the lacklustre eyes, the red, puffy complexion, the coated tongue, the unkempt beard, the tangled hair, all spelling staleness, fatigue and exhaustion – 'the day's disasters in his morning face'. The Baron, having opened his travelling-case, gave a few final touches to his appearance and waited.

The whistle blew and the train stopped. His neighbour shifted. Awake, no doubt. Then the train moved off again. A shaft of sunlight slanted into the compartment and fell directly across the sleeper who moved again, butting the air a few times like a chick coming out of an egg, then calmly emerged.

It was a fresh young blonde woman, plump and very pretty. She sat up.

The Baron looked at her and was stupefied. He was not at all sure he could believe his eyes. Honestly, he could have sworn it was . . . it was his wife! But extraordinarily changed! Changed so much . . . but so much for the better! She was so much fuller . . . like himself no doubt but to her far, far greater advantage. She looked at him calmly without any apparent recognition and began methodically to extricate herself from her outer coverings. She showed the quiet confidence of a self-assured woman somewhat rudely awakened but conscious of being in the full, fresh prime of her life.

The Baron was going mad.

Was it his wife? Or was it some other woman who happened to look exactly like her? It was six years since he had seen her, after all. He could be wrong. She yawned. Her gestures were familiar to him. But again, as she turned her gaze towards him, it was unperturbed and indifferent, a blank look which she now fixed upon the countryside. He was totally bewildered and in an agony of doubt. He waited again, keeping a steady watch on her out of the corner of his eye. *Of course* it was his wife, damn it all! How could he possibly imagine otherwise? How many other women had that nose? A thousand memories came crowding in, memories of her caresses, the finer detail of her body, a beauty spot on her thigh, a matching one on her back. How often he had kissed them! He felt himself fall into the old intoxication, remembering once again the smell of her skin, her smile as she threw her arms around his neck, the gentle tone of her voice, and all her graceful, winning ways. But how altered she was, how very much more beautiful. It was she and yet no longer she. He found her more mature, more womanly, more attractive, more desirable, more adorably desirable. To think that this stranger, this unknown woman whom he had met by chance in a railway carriage, was legally his. He had only to say the word.

He used once to sleep in her arms and live surrounded by her love. Now he found her so changed that he hardly recognized her. She was simultaneously herself and someone else. She had been reborn, reshaped, and had grown into a different woman during the time since he had left her. Yet she was also the woman he had possessed and whose behaviour he now saw altered. Her features were more developed, her smile was less simpering and her gestures more confident. She was two women in one, a mixture of the largely unknown and the fondly remembered. There was something very special about the combination, something disturbing and exciting. It was the mystery of love clouded in delightful vagueness. It was his wife in a new body, made of new flesh which his lips had yet to trace.

In six years, he reflected, everything about us changes. Only the outline remains the same and sometimes even that goes. All is reconstituted and renewed differently – blood, hair, skin, everything. When a long time goes by before you see someone again, you find them quite different, though they are obviously the same person and have the same identity. So it is with the heart, which can also change, and with ideas, which are constantly altered or replaced. In forty years of living, through ceaseless, slow transformations, we can become four or five completely new and different human beings. He searched his soul. Thinking back suddenly to the night when he had surprised her in the Princess's bedchamber, he felt no trace of anger. The woman before him was no longer the skinny little flibbertigibbet of yesteryear.

What should he do? How should he speak to her? What should he say? Had she recognized him? The train was stopping

again. He rose, bowed and spoke: 'Berthe, is there anything you
need? Could I bring you . . . ?'

She looked him up and down and replied with neither embarrassment nor anger but calm indifference: 'No. Nothing,
thank you.'

He jumped down and took a few steps on the platform as if
to get his balance back after a fall. What was he to do now? Get
into another carriage? That would look too much like running
away. Pay court and dance attendance? She might think he was
begging for forgiveness. Be masterful? Crude thought. Besides,
if he was honest, he had already forfeited that right. He climbed
in and took his seat again. She in turn had taken advantage of
his absence to quickly perform her own toilet. She was now
comfortably relaxed in her seat looking both radiant and
unapproachable.

He turned to her and said: 'My dear Berthe, just because
fate has so strangely thrown us together again after six years'
separation, peaceful separation at that, must we carry on behaving like sworn enemies? Here we are, thrown together, as I say.
It's up to us, but I'll tell you one thing – I'm certainly not getting
out. Couldn't we just have a little conversation together . . . like
. . . like . . . I don't know . . . like friends? Till we get to wherever
we're going?'

'If you wish,' she replied calmly.

He fell silent, at a loss for words. Then, daringly, he moved
closer, sat himself down on the middle seat next to her and
began with practised charm: 'I see I'm going to have to woo you
all over again. Can't say I mind. In fact I shall relish it. You
really are devastatingly attractive, you know. You can't imagine
what an improvement there is in you! I tell you I know no other
woman who could have given me the sort of thrill I felt just
now, seeing you emerge from those furs. Really, I would never
have believed such a change . . .'

Without moving her head or looking at him, she said: 'I'm
afraid I can't return the compliment. You've gone decidedly
downhill.' He blushed with embarrassment and unease, then,
with a resigned smile said: 'You're a hard woman.'

'Why?' she asked, turning towards him. 'I speak my mind,

that's all. You're not about to offer me your love, are you? So it should be a matter of complete indifference to you what I think you look like. But I see this is a painful subject for you. Let's talk about something else. What have you been doing since I last saw you?'

He had lost his composure and was stammering.

'Me? I've been travelling. Hunting. Getting old. As you see. What about you?'

Serenely she replied: 'I have been keeping up appearances as you instructed.'

He bit back the unkind words that sprang to mind. Taking his wife's hand in his, he kissed it. 'And I'm grateful for that.'

She was surprised. He really was strong and still just as self-controlled.

He went on: 'Well you've agreed we can talk, at least. But can't it be without all this bitterness?'

She made a little gesture of contempt.

'I feel no bitterness, I assure you. You're a complete stranger to me. I'm simply trying to keep up a somewhat difficult conversation.'

He continued to gaze at her, attracted despite her rudeness, feeling a savage desire to break down her defences and an irresistible urge to master her.

Sensing rightly that she had drawn blood she pressed her advantage.

'How old are you now, by the way? You must be younger than you look.'

He grew pale.

'I'm forty-five,' he said, then added, 'I forgot to ask if you have news of the Princesse de Raynes. Do you still see her? How is she?'

She threw him a glance full of loathing.

'Yes. Still. She's very well, thank you.'

And so they remained, sitting side by side, their hearts and minds in angry turmoil.

Suddenly he announced: 'My dear Berthe, I've just had a change of mind. You're my wife and I wish you to return today under my roof. I find that you've improved in both character

and beauty and I'm taking you back. I am your husband and I
have the right to do so.'

Stunned, she looked at him searchingly, trying to fathom his
meaning. His face was impassive, expressionless and set.

She replied: 'I'm so terribly sorry but I have a previous
engagement.'

He smiled. 'How very unfortunate for you . . . I warn you,
I have the force of the law behind me and, should I need to,
I shall not hesitate to use it.'

They were approaching Marseille. The whistle blew and the
train began to slow down. The Baroness rose, briskly rolled up
her furs and turned to her husband.

'My dear Raymond, do not attempt to prolong this little
tête-à-tête which I arranged ahead of time. In order to comply
with your wishes I needed to take certain precautions so that
whatever may happen in the future I should have nothing to
fear from either you or from society. You're going to Nice,
I believe.'

'I'm going wherever you are.'

'On the contrary. Once you've heard what I have to say you
will leave me in peace, I can assure you. In a few moments you
will see waiting for me on the platform the Princesse de Raynes
and the Comtesse Henriot, together with their respective husbands. I wished us to be seen together, you and I, and for people
to know that we spent the night together in this carriage. Don't
worry, the ladies will make sure such interesting news spreads
like wildfire. I told you earlier I have followed your instructions
in every particular. I have been careful to keep up appearances.
We may draw a veil over the rest, I'm sure. And it is precisely so
as to continue keeping up those appearances that I had to make
sure we would meet like this. You ordered me to avoid scandal
at all costs, and that, my dear, is precisely what I am doing
because I'm . . . I'm . . .'

Before finishing she waited for the train to come to a complete
halt and for the little group of friends to rush to open the
carriage door.

'I'm afraid I'm pregnant.'

The Princess was opening her arms ready to embrace. Pointing to the Baron, who was now dumbfounded and reeling with incomprehension, the Baroness said to her: 'Don't tell me you didn't recognize Raymond? He has changed, to be sure. Wasn't it sweet of him to come along with me? Rather than let me travel all alone. We often take off on little excursions like this. We are the greatest of friends but can't possibly live together! Anyway, this is where we come to the parting of the ways. He's had enough of me already!'

She offered him her hand which he took automatically. Then she jumped on to the platform and into the midst of her waiting friends. The Baron slammed the carriage door, too upset to speak or think. He heard his wife's voice and her joyful laughter grow ever fainter in the distance.

He never saw her again.

Had she lied or was she telling the truth? He was never to know.

HAPPINESS

Dusk was falling at the time before the lamps were brought in at the villa which looked out on to the sea. Above it the sun, now out of sight, had left in its wake a sky of pink with a dusting of gold. The Mediterranean, without a ripple on its surface and gleaming still in the light of the dying day, lay ahead like a boundless sheet of polished metal.

To the right in the distance the black lace-edged silhouette of the mountains stood out against the pale mauve of the sunset. The talk was on the age-old subject of love and the same was being said as had been said countless times before. In the gentle, melancholy twilight the conversation was leisurely and wistful. The word 'love', constantly repeated now by a strong, masculine voice, now in the lighter tones of a woman, seemed to fill the little drawing room, its spirit floating and hovering birdlike over the scene.

Was it possible to stay in love over a long period of years? Some people said yes, others no. Examples were given, definitions attempted, cases cited. Everyone, men and women alike, seemed moved by the memories, some disturbing, some long since buried, which came flooding back. Each spoke with great feeling and conviction about the most commonplace yet the most important aspect of life: the mysterious bond of affection between two human beings.

Suddenly one of the group who had been looking out into the distance, shouted: 'Oh look! Over there! What on earth is that?'

Rising from the ocean on the far horizon a huge grey mass could be seen. The women left their chairs and gazed uncompre-

hendingly at this amazing phenomenon which none of them had
ever seen before.

Someone said: 'It's Corsica! Just once or twice a year you can
see it. The atmospheric conditions have to be absolutely right,
and that doesn't often happen. The air has to be completely
transparent. Otherwise mists form and normally at that distance
they obscure it.'

Mountain crests could just about be distinguished and some
people thought they could see snowy summits. Everyone was
amazed and a little disturbed, even frightened by the sudden
appearance of this land, rising like a phantom from the deep. It
was the sort of strange sight explorers such as Columbus must
have seen in days of old.

Just then an elderly gentleman, who had not spoken before,
said: 'As a matter of fact that island appearing suddenly like
that before us as if to take part in our discussion has reminded
me of something quite extraordinary. It was there that I once
came across a wonderful example of constant and unbelievably
happy love.'

'Five years ago I was travelling in Corsica. That wild island is
more distant and unknown to us than America, even though
she can sometimes be seen as she is today from our very own
French shores. Imagine a world still in primeval chaos. Imagine
a great eruption of mountains separated by narrow ravines full
of raging torrents. Not a single plain, just huge waves of granite,
great reefs of land covered with bush and tall forests of chestnut
and pine.

It is virgin soil, uncultivated and deserted apart from the
occasional village which looks like a pile of rocks perched on
top of a hill. No culture, no industry, no art. You never come
across so much as a carved piece of wood or stone; no trace,
however sketchy, of any desire on the part of early man here to
create style or beauty. This is the most striking aspect of the
place. It's a magnificent, rough land, utterly indifferent to the
attraction of form which we call art.

You've got, on the one hand, Italy where every palazzo is
full of masterpieces and which is itself a masterpiece. There,

marble, wood, bronze, iron and every other kind of metal and stone are transformed to reflect the genius of man. Even the most insignificant of objects discovered in the ruins demonstrates a spiritual yearning. We all love Italy, we cherish the place precisely because it attests to, is visible living proof of, the effort, the greatness, the power and the triumph of creativity in man.

And directly opposite you have Corsica, which has remained as it was from the very beginning. Its inhabitants live in their crude habitations, oblivious of everything but the very basic necessities of life and family vendettas. It has retained both the qualities and the defects of primitive man: violence, hatred and mindless savagery. Yet the people there are hospitable, generous, loyal and innocent. They will open their doors to passing strangers and offer unconditional friendship at the first sign of camaraderie.

For a month I had been wandering about this splendid country, feeling myself at the ends of the earth. Not a single inn, no cafés, no roads. It is only by mule track that you can reach the hamlets clinging to the sides of the mountains which look down into tortuous gulleys. From these in the evening a constant clamour rises which is the deep, distant roar of rapids. You knock on someone's door. You ask for a night's lodging and food till the next day. You sit down at a modest board and sleep under a humble roof. The following day you shake the hand offered to you by your host who will have accompanied you as far as the village boundary.

It happened that one night after ten hours' walking, I came across a lonely little dwelling at the bottom of a narrow valley two or three miles inland. The two steep sides of the mountain, covered as they were with bush, fallen rocks and tall trees, enclosed this sombre, lugubrious ravine like two dark walls. Around the cottage were a few vines, a little garden and, further off, a few chestnut trees – more than enough to live on in this impoverished land. The elderly woman who received me looked somewhat severe, but unusually clean. The man who had been sitting in a rush-bottomed chair got up to greet me, then sat down again in silence. His companion said to me: "Do excuse him. He's deaf now, I'm afraid. He's eighty-two." She spoke proper French, which surprised me.

"You're not from Corsica, then, I gather?"

"No, we're from the Continent originally. But we've lived here for fifty years."

A feeling of fear and anguish gripped me at the thought of fifty years spent in this dark hole so far from towns and people. An old shepherd came to join us and we sat down to a single course – a thick soup of cabbage, potato and bacon.

When this brief meal was over I went to sit outside the front door. I was in low spirits as I contemplated the bleak landscape and was saddened as travellers sometimes are on certain evenings in a desolate place. You get the feeling that everything – human existence and the universe itself – is about to come to an end. You're suddenly struck by the misery of life, the isolation in which we all live, the nothingness of it all and the desperate loneliness in hearts deluded by dreams until death.

The old woman joined me. Even in the pessimistic mood I was in I could feel keen curiosity stirring within me.

"So you're from France, are you?" she said.

"Yes, I'm here for pleasure."

"Are you from Paris, by any chance?"

"No, from Nancy."

This news seemed to have an extraordinary effect on her. It wasn't anything you could put your finger on, just an impression I got.

She continued, speaking very slowly: "From Nancy, did you say?"

The man appeared at the door, impassive as the deaf inevitably are.

She went on: "Never mind. He can't hear." Then, after a few moments: "So, do you know many people in Nancy?"

"Oh yes. Practically everybody."

"The Saint-Allaizes?"

"Very well. They were friends of my father."

"What's your name, did you say?"

I gave it. She stared at me, then, in the low voice with which we speak our memories, she said: "I know that name very well.

Very well indeed. What about the Brisemares, what's become of them, then?"

"All dead now, I'm afraid."

"Ah! And the Sirmonts, do you know them?"

"Yes. The latest Sirmont's now a general."

This time she spoke in a voice trembling with emotion, anguish and some other indescribable but powerful feeling. It seemed like an almost religious desire to confess, to say everything, to talk about things which she had been bottling up for years and about people the mere mention of whose name had such an overwhelming effect upon her.

"Yes, Henri de Sirmont. We're talking about my brother."

I raised my eyes and looked at her in astonishment. Then all of a sudden it hit me.

The whole affair had in its day scandalized the entire aristocracy of Lorraine. A beautiful, rich young girl had eloped with a non-commissioned officer from her father's regiment. He was a handsome fellow of peasant stock who looked well in the blue uniform of the Hussars. She had no doubt noticed him on parade, picked him out from all the others and fallen in love with him. But how she had managed to speak to him, how they had been able to see and get to know each other, how she had dared let him know that she loved him no one was ever to know.

No one suspected a thing and it happened quite without warning. One night when the soldier's tour of duty had come to an end he disappeared with her. They were hunted but never found. No news was ever received from them and eventually it was as if they were dead.

And here she was living in this sinister valley.

Now it was my turn to speak: "I remember very well. You must be Mademoiselle Suzanne."

She nodded. Tears had welled up in her eyes and were now coursing down her cheeks. Then, indicating the old man standing motionless on the threshold she said: "That's him."

I realized that she was still in love with him. She still saw him with the same eyes as always.

"Well at least you've been happy?" I asked.

"Oh yes! Very happy! He has made me very happy! I've never had a single regret."

I gazed at her, feeling moved, astonished and marvelling at the power of love. This wealthy girl had followed a peasant and become a peasant herself. She had adapted herself to this basic, charmless existence with no luxuries and no comfort of any sort. She had conformed to his simple ways. And still she loved him. In her bonnet and her thick cotton skirt she had become a country wife. She ate a broth of cabbage, bacon and potato from an earthenware bowl off a scrubbed wooden table, sitting on a simple rush-bottomed chair. At night she slept beside him on a straw mattress.

Nothing else mattered except him. She had missed none of the finery, the costly materials, the elegance, the comfortable chairs, the fragrant warmth of the tapestry-hung bedrooms, the restful, welcoming softness of the bedding. She had never needed anything apart from him. He was all she wanted. As long as he was there she was happy. Early on she had given up the life she was used to and the people who had brought her up and loved her. She had come on her own with him to this wild ravine. He had been everything to her; all that she desired, all she dreamed of, all she always wished and ever hoped for. He had filled her life to the brim with happiness. She could not have been more content.

All night long I heard the harsh breathing of the old soldier on his pallet with, beside him, the woman who had followed him so far. I thought what a strange yet simple adventure it must have been to create such complete happiness with so little.

I left at dawn having shaken hands with the old married couple.'

The man telling the story had come to the end of his tale. One woman said, 'It's quite obvious she had no standards, this woman. She had very simple, basic needs, easily met. She must have been an idiot.'

Another said slowly, 'What does it matter? She was happy, that's what counts!'

And now on the far distant horizon the vast shadow faded

into the night, sliding gently into the sea, and with it Corsica, which had appeared as if to tell in person the story of the two simple lovers welcomed to her shores.

A BIT OF THE OTHER

Before their marriage they were a pair of chaste, starry-eyed lovers who had met by happy chance at a seaside resort. Against the background of the ocean's vast horizon he had noticed passing him this delightful girl with the pink and white complexion, in her cool-looking dresses and shaded by her gay parasol. He had fallen in love with her, framed as she was then by blue waves and huge skies. The tender expansiveness which this girl on the threshold of womanhood awakened within him was closely associated in his mind with the vague but powerful feeling aroused in his soul, his heart and in his veins by the clear, salt air and the huge sunlit seascape upon which he gazed.

She in turn had fallen in love with him because he courted her and because he was young, fairly well-off, charming and attentive. And as young girls regularly fall for young men who whisper sweet nothings in their ear, she had fallen in love with him. For those three months they had been inseparable, walking about hand in hand and gazing into each other's eyes. Though their lips had never met, the savour of future kisses was strong in the greetings they exchanged before each morning bathe and again in their evening farewells on the sand, under the stars, and in the warmth of the deep calm night. They awoke in the mornings and fell asleep at night thinking only of each other. Without admitting it their souls yearned and their bodies were full of mutual desire.

After the wedding they had worshipped each other in the garden of earthly delights. With tireless, frenzied energy they made love at first with passion and tenderness in a kind of exaltation, and then, with experience, knowing caresses and a rapturous feeling of wickedness. Every glance they exchanged by day was charged with erotic significance and every gesture a hint of the torrid night before.

Now, however, though they hesitated to admit it, they were becoming, unconsciously perhaps, just a touch bored. Of course they were still fond of each other, but neither had anything more to reveal. There was nothing they had not done many times before, nothing in which either could initiate the other. Not so much as an endearment was new, no fresh gesture, no unexpected intonation came to add piquancy or meaning to their oft-repeated exchanges.

They tried hard to fan the dying embers of their passion into flame. Every day they devised some new kind of play, a new game, sometimes childish, sometimes sophisticated, in a series of desperate attempts to rekindle the once inextinguishable fire that had consumed them during the days and nights of their honeymoon. Every so often they whipped up their desire enough to enjoy an hour or so of feigned frenzy. Immediately afterwards, however, they were filled with a kind of weary revulsion.

They had tried everything – moonlit walks through the forest in the soft air of the night; romantic wanderings along the river bank in the mist; they had even on occasion joined in with the dancing in the streets. Then one day Henriette said to Paul: 'Will you take me one night to a cabaret?'[1]

'Certainly darling.'

'A real one . . . you know.'

'Of course.'

He looked at her with curiosity, realizing she had something in mind which she could not bring herself to say.

She went on: 'You know what I mean, the sort of place . . . a private room . . . where you can have a . . . an assignation . . .'

He smiled. 'I know exactly what you mean . . . a private cubicle in a . . . private restaurant.'

'Yes, but I mean where they know you. Where you've already been. Where you've been for supper . . . no . . . dinner . . . I mean a place where we could . . . I can't say it . . .'

'Come on darling! Tell me what you mean! You can share it with *me*, surely!'

'Well, I'd like to pretend ... I'd like to pretend to be your lover. I'd like the waiters not to know we're married ... and to think I'm your lover. And for you to think so too, while we're there ... where you remember being before with someone else ... That's what I'd like! And I want to pretend to *myself* that I'm your lover and that I'm having an affair with somebody ... that I'm being unfaithful to you ... with you! There, isn't that wicked of me! But I'd really like to ... don't make me blush ... I know I'm blushing ... you can't imagine how exciting it would be for me to have supper with you in a terribly disreputable kind of place like that ... a private cubicle where people come to make love every night ... every night! How wicked! I'm as red as a beetroot. Don't look at me!'

Highly amused he replied with a laugh, 'We'll go tonight. I'll take you to a very special place. Where I'm ... shall we say known.'

At seven o'clock they were climbing the stairs to the first floor of a well-known boulevard café, he grinning triumphantly, and she wearing a shy but delighted smile. As soon as they entered a private room furnished with four large easy chairs and a large red velvet divan, a dark-suited maître d'hôtel came in with the menu. Paul passed it to his wife.

'What do you feel like eating?'

'Well I don't know. What's usually good here?'

He read the whole menu as he was taking his coat off and handing it to another attendant. Then he said, 'We'll have something spicy tonight, I think. *Potage bisque, poulet à la diable, rable de lièvre, homard à l'américaine*, and we'll have a spicy vegetable salad with that before dessert.'

The maître d'hôtel smiled as he looked at the young lady then took back the menu murmuring, 'And would Monsieur Paul like tisane or champagne tonight?'

'Champagne please. Very dry.'

Henriette was thrilled by the fact that the man had addressed her husband by name. Having sat down side by side on the divan they began their meal by the light of ten candles reflected in a massive mirror whose surface was dulled by thousands of names scratched by diamonds and which looked as though a huge cobweb had been spun across its clear glass.[2]

Already a little tipsy after the first couple of glasses, Henriette drank more and more to get herself in the mood. Paul, whose eyes were shining with the excitement of so many memories the place brought back to him, kept kissing his wife's hand. She in turn was beginning to feel the atmosphere of impropriety delightfully, wickedly exciting. They were swiftly and quietly served by two solemn, silent waiters accustomed to seeing all and immediately blanking it out. These men knew when to make an entrance and when, if interrupting moments of passion, discreetly to retire.

Halfway through dinner Henriette was more than a little drunk. In fact she was decidedly tipsy and Paul, also very merry, was by this time squeezing her knee hard. Her cheeks were flushed, her eyes bright and sparkling and she was talking animatedly now, with no inhibitions.

'Come on then Paul. Tell me everything. I want to know.'

'About what, darling?'

'You know . . . don't make me spell it out.'

'Spell what out?'

'Did you have lots of women . . . before you met me?'

He hesitated, undecided whether to brag about his conquests or cover them up.

She continued: 'Oh, please! Tell me. Lots?'

'A few, yes.'

'How many?'

'I really don't know. Never thought about it.'

'You mean you never counted how many?'

'Of course not.'

'So . . . a lot, then.'

'Of course.'

'Roughly how many? Just roughly.'

'I really don't know, darling. Some years lots, some years a lot less.'

'So. How many a year, about?'

'Oh, I don't know. Twenty or thirty one year, four or five another.'

'Oh! So over a hundred all told.'

'I suppose about that.'

'That's disgusting!'

'What do you mean, disgusting?'

'Precisely that, disgusting. When you think of all those women . . . naked . . . for the same reason. That really is disgusting, that is, more than a hundred women!'

He was shocked that she should find it so and replied with the arrogance men use to persuade women they are talking nonsense.

'What a ridiculous thing to say! There's nothing more disgusting about having a hundred than there is to having one.'

'Oh yes there is!'

'How?'

'Because with one woman, you're in a relationship, you have a bond, through love. Whereas a hundred women, that's just plain immoral. Plain filthy lust. I don't understand how a man can be intimate with a lot of dirty tarts.'

'I can assure you, they're extremely clean!'

'They can't be, considering what they do.'

'On the contrary. It's precisely what they do that requires them to be clean.'

'Oh come off it. Just think . . . yesterday, they were doing the same thing with some other man. It's indecent.'

'Look. It's no more indecent than drinking from this glass – who knows who was drinking from it this morning? And which was washed a darn sight less carefully, I'm sure!'

'Oh do be quiet. You're revolting.'

'Well, why did you start all this business anyway?'

'I was coming to that. Who were they? Were they all prostitutes, all hundred?'

'Of course not.'

'What then?'

'Oh, I don't know. Actresses, some of them . . . working girls . . . some society women . . .'

'How many society women?'

'Six.'

'Only six?'

'Yes.'

'Were they pretty?'

'Yes, of course.'

'Prettier than the prostitutes?'

'No.'

'Who did you prefer, the society women or the prostitutes?'

'The prostitutes.'

'You pig! Why?'

'Don't like amateurs.'

'Oh stop it! You're wicked, you know that? And did you enjoy flitting from one woman to another like that?'

'Of course.'

'A lot?'

'Very much.'

'What was so enjoyable about it? Weren't they all the same?'

'Of course not.'

'Oh I see. Women aren't all the same, then.'

'Absolutely not.'

'Not in any way?'

'No way, no.'

'How amazing! In what way are they different?'

'Every way.'

'Physically?'

'Yes, of course physically.'

'Every woman's body is different?'

'Yes.'

'How else?'

'Well . . . how they kiss. How they speak. What sort of small talk. You know . . .'

'Ah! And it's fun to ring the changes?'

'Great fun.'

'And are men different too?'

'I haven't the faintest idea.'

'No idea?'

'None.'

'They must be.'

'I expect so, yes.'

She remained pensive for a while holding her glass of champagne in her hand. It was full and she drank it off in one draught. Then placing it back on the table she threw her two arms around her husband's neck and murmured into his mouth, 'Oh darling! I love you so much!'

He clasped her in a passionate embrace. A waiter on the point of coming in quickly retreated, closing the door behind him and allowing a discreet interval of five minutes or so to elapse. When the maître d'hôtel reappeared bearing fruit for their dessert she had a fresh glassful in her hand. She looked deep into the clear, yellow liquid as if she might find within it things she had hitherto seen only in her dreams.

'Yes,' she was murmuring, 'I bet that's a lot of fun too!'

LOVE

Three Pages from *The Diary of a Hunting Man*

I have just been reading in the paper the account of a *crime passionel* involving a man who killed the woman he loved and then turned the gun on himself. The personalities do not matter; what counts is the passion. I was interested in the story not because it touched me or because it gave me pause for thought but because it reminded me of something that happened to me once on a hunting trip during my youth. Just as the cross allegedly appeared in the sky to some of the early Christians, so love sailed into my own view out of the blue on this particular occasion.

I was born with all the instincts and senses of primitive man but these have been tempered with time by both the reasoning and the sensibilities of his civilized successor. I am passionately fond of hunting yet a bleeding animal, a bird with blood on its feathers, or even the sight of blood on my own hands often makes me feel faint.

One particular year towards the end of autumn, when the cold had set in really early, I got an invitation from one of my cousins, Karl de Rauville, to go duck-shooting with him down on the marshes by dawn. My cousin was a strapping great fellow with red hair and a huge beard, a very hale and hearty outdoor type, a bit of a rough diamond really, but for all his faults extremely good company. He lived in a kind of country-house-cum-farm in a wide river valley. On the slopes to the right and left of it was ancient woodland with magnificent trees where some of the rarest game-birds in that part of France were often to be found. Sometimes eagles had been shot there, and certain birds of passage which almost never visited our overpopulated regions invariably stopped over among its age-old boughs as if they knew or somehow recognized in it a little vestige of primeval forest remaining there to shelter them on their brief, nocturnal landfall.

The valley was made up of wide pastures irrigated by channels and separated by hedges. The river, itself a channel up to this point, spread out here into a vast area of marshland. This marsh, the best hunting-ground in which I have ever shot, was the pride and joy of my cousin who maintained it with as much care as if it were parkland. Through the great masses of rushes with which it was covered and which endowed it with a rustling, turbulent life of its own, narrow passages had been formed where flat-bottomed boats propelled by poles slid silently on the dead water, brushing against bullrushes, causing fish to dart quickly under the tall grass and moorhens, with their pointed black heads, to dive quickly out of sight.

I am wildly and passionately fond of the water. I love the sea despite its being too vast and uncontrollable ever to be really mastered; I love rivers and their evanescent beauty as they flow out of sight; in particular I love the marsh, where a whole world of invisible aquatic life seethes. The marsh is, as I say, a universe apart, with its own permanent inhabitants, its own migratory creatures, its own voice, its own sounds and above all its own sense of mystery. There is nothing that makes one more wary, more uneasy, nothing more frightening sometimes, than a swamp. What is the fear that hovers over these low, watery plains? Is it the vague murmur of the reeds, the strange fireflies, the deep silence enveloping all on calm nights, the weird mists shrouding the rushes, or is it perhaps the barely audible lapping of the water, so soft, so gentle and yet sometimes more terrifying than human gunfire or thunder from above. Is it all this which makes the marsh a nightmarish spot, a place of fear, concealing perhaps a dangerous and unfathomable secret?

No, there's something else to it. A different secret, even deeper and older, still floats on the dense fogs. Perhaps it contains the secret of creation itself! For was it not in stagnant, muddy water and the heavy humidity of wet land warming in the heat of the sun that the first stirrings, the first movements and the beginnings of life itself were felt?

It was evening when I reached my cousin's house and cold enough to split stone. During dinner, my cousin, wearing a sealskin jacket and looking like some exotic Siberian animal, told me about the arrangements he had made for starting out that very night. We ate in the great hall where every sideboard, every wall and even the ceiling were festooned with stuffed birds – sparrow-hawks, herons, owls, nightjars, buzzards, harriers, vultures and falcons, some with wings outstretched, some perched on branches which were themselves hooked on to nails.

In order to reach the place chosen for our shoot by half past four we were to leave at about three-thirty in the morning. A shelter made of blocks of ice had been built there to keep out the terrible wind of the hours before daylight. It is the sort of wind which is so cold that it cuts into your flesh like a saw, pinches like a pair of pliers, stings like a poisoned dart and burns like fire.

My cousin was rubbing his hands.

'I've never known such a frost,' he said, 'we were down to twelve below zero at six this evening.'

Directly after supper I plunged straight into bed and went to sleep by the light of an enormous fire blazing in my hearth. As three struck, I was awoken. I put on a sheepskin and Karl when I met him was wrapped in a bearskin. After we had each drunk two cups of boiling hot coffee followed by two glasses of liqueur brandy we set off, accompanied by a keeper and by our two dogs, Plongeon and Pierrot.

As soon as I stepped outside I was frozen to the marrow. It was one of those nights when the world seems dead with cold. The frozen air becomes an almost tangible presence so badly does it hurt. Not a breath of wind stirs; all is rigid, motionless. The atmosphere bites, cuts, dries up and kills all trees, plants and insects; sometimes small birds fall dead to the frozen ground where they too stiffen at once in its icy embrace.

The pale moon in its last quarter and tilted to one side seemed to hang half-dead in space, too weak to go on and itself paralysed by the severity of the weather in the heavens. Casting a weak, mournful light on the world it shed the usual pale glimmer it gives each month at the end of its resurrection.

Karl and I walked side by side, backs hunched against the cold, our hands in our pockets and guns under the arm. Our shoes had been wrapped in wool so that we could walk without slipping on the frozen river. Now they made no sound and as we walked on I watched the breath of our dogs rise as white steam beneath us.

We were soon at the edge of the marsh and turned into one of the pathways of dry rushes leading through this miniature forest. Our elbows brushing against the long, ribbonlike leaves made a soft sound. I was gripped as never before by the very powerful and particular emotion which the marsh produces within me. This one felt stone dead of cold as we trod on its surface through the dried-up reeds.

Suddenly, as we came round a bend in one of the pathways, I saw the ice hut constructed to shelter us. I went in, and since we had an hour to wait before any stray bird might awaken I rolled myself up in my wrap and tried to get warm. Lying on my back I began to look at the crooked moon which, distorted through the semi-transparent walls of this igloo, looked like four horns in the sky. Soon the cold from the frozen marsh together with the condensation coming off the walls and dropping on us from above had got so deep into me that I began to cough. My cousin Karl became suddenly worried.

'Never mind if we don't have much of a bag today,' he said. 'I certainly don't want you to catch cold. Come on let's build a fire.'

He ordered the keeper to cut us some rushes. We piled them up in the middle of the shelter in whose roof a gap was left to let out smoke. When the red flames licked the clear crystal walls within, they began to melt little by little as if in a gentle sweat. Karl, who had remained outside, cried out, 'Come and see!'

I came out and was lost in wonder. Our cone-shaped cabin looked now like a diamond with a fire at its heart crystallizing suddenly out of the frozen water of the marsh. Inside could be seen the fantastical shapes of our two dogs as they too tried desperately to get warm.

A strange cry, the cry of a lost wanderer, passed over our heads. The glow from our hearth was beginning to wake the

birds of the wild. Nothing stirs me more than that first anony-
mous clamour of life carrying so fast and so far before the first
light appears on the winter horizon. In the icy dawn, to me that
fleeting cry borne on the wings of a bird becomes the sigh of the
soul of the world.

'Put out the fire,' Karl was saying, 'here comes the dawn.'

The sky was indeed beginning to grow pale, and across it
skeins of ducks sketched long, sudden lines, which in an instant
disappeared. A flash burst out in the darkness. Karl had just
fired a shot and the two dogs were off. From then on, every
minute or so changing position, one or other of us would aim
as soon as the shadow of a flying formation appeared above the
rushes. Pierrot and Plongeon, breathless and ecstatic, retrieved
for us the bleeding creatures whose eye sometimes looked at
us still.

Dawn had broken on a clear and cloudless day. The sun was
appearing at the bottom of the valley and we were thinking of
leaving when two birds with necks and wings outstretched
passed suddenly over our heads. I fired a shot. One, a teal with
a silvery breast, fell practically at my feet. Then from the space
above my head came the terrible cry of a bird. It was a heart-
breaking lament, repeated over and over. The little creature
which had been spared began to wheel and circle against the
blue of the sky above us looking down at his dead mate which
I held in my hands.

Karl, on his knees, the gun at his shoulder and a glint in his
eye, was watching, waiting for it to come close enough.

'You shot the female,' he said, 'the male will never leave now.'

Nor did he. He circled and cried around us and never did a
cry of pain pierce my heart like that grief-stricken sound, the
sorrowful reproach of a poor creature lost now in the heavens
above. At times he would flee under threat from the gun trained
upon him. Sometimes he looked as though he were about to go
on alone. But never could he bring himself to leave. Always he
came back for the female.

'Put her out on the ground,' Karl instructed. 'He'll come back
in a while.'

Heedless of danger and distraught with love for the mate I

had killed, the bird approached again. Karl fired. It was as though a cord holding the bird aloft had been cut. I saw a black object fall and heard it land in the rushes. Pierrot brought it back to me.

I put them both, cold already, in the same gamebag. And that same day I left for Paris.

HAUTOT & SON

The house, half farm and half manor, was one of those combinations often found in the country of a property once vaguely seigneurial and now owned by farmers themselves rich in land. In front of it the dogs tied to the farmyard apple trees were barking and yelping as the keeper and some small boys arrived carrying gamebags.

It was the opening day of the season and in the vast kitchen which served as dining room Hautot senior, Hautot junior, Monsieur Bermont the tax-collector and Monsieur Mondaru the lawyer were having a drink and a bite to eat before setting off on the day's shoot. Hautot senior, very proud of his property, was telling his guests ahead of time what excellent game they would find on his land. He was a big-boned, ruddy-faced Norman, the powerfully built sort of man who can carry a whole barrel of apples on his shoulders. Somewhat authoritarian in manner, he was wealthy, respected and highly influential. He had sent his son César to school up to the fourth form so that he should have some education, then removed him lest he become so much of a gentleman that he no longer cared about his land.

César Hautot was nearly as tall as his father, but leaner. He was an easy-going, happy-go-lucky young man, a good son to his father whom he greatly admired and to whose every wish and opinion he was happy to defer.

Monsieur Bermont, the tax-collector, was a stout little man on whose red cheeks a maze of violet-coloured veins looked like a network of tortuous rivers and tributaries as might be seen on maps in an atlas. He asked, 'And hare? Will there be . . . hare?'

Hautot senior replied, 'As much as you like! Specially round Puysatier.'

'Where shall we start?' enquired the lawyer, a portly, well-fed man trussed up now in a new shooting jacket bought the previous week in Rouen.

'Down at the bottom, I think. We'll get the partridge out on the plain and then put them up from there.'

With this, Hautot senior rose. Following suit they all stood up and stamped their feet to bring warmth and suppleness to the leather of their newly-donned and tight-fitting boots. They collected the guns propped up in various corners of the room, examined the locks, then left the house. Outside, the dogs, still leashed, were now jumping up on their hind legs, yelping shrilly and pawing the air.

They set off towards the lower grounds and a small valley which was no more than a dip of poor-quality land left purposely uncultivated. It was criss-crossed with gullies and covered with fern – an excellent place for game. The guns spread out, with Hautot senior on the far right, Hautot junior on the far left and the two guests in the middle. The keeper and two gamebag carriers followed. Nervously fingering their triggers and with their hearts beating fast they stopped and stood waiting in solemn silence for the first shot of the season to ring out.

There it was! Hautot senior had fired. They saw one partridge fall away from the headlong flight of birds and come down in a gully covered with thick brush. Highly excited, Hautot leapt up and ran off, tearing up everything in his way and finally disappearing into the undergrowth to pick up his quarry. Almost immediately a second shot rang out.

'The lucky devil!' cried old Bermont. 'He's picked off a hare while he's at it!'

They all waited, eyes fixed on the dense, impenetrable undergrowth. Cupping his hands round his mouth, the lawyer yelled: 'Have you got them?'

Since no answer came from Hautot senior, César, turning to the keeper, said: 'Go and give him a hand, Joseph, will you? We must spread out in line. We'll wait for you.'

Joseph, a great gnarled tree-trunk of a man, set off calmly

down towards the gully. Like a fox he carefully reconnoitred the easiest way through the brush. Having found it and disappeared, he cried out suddenly: 'Come quick! Quick! There's been an accident!'

Each man tore through the bushes towards the scene. When they got there they saw Hautot lying on his side, unconscious, clasping his stomach from which long streams of blood were flowing inside his bullet-torn jacket and into the grass. His fallen partridge within reach, Hautot must have dropped the gun to pick it up and in so doing triggered a second shot which shattered his own entrails. They dragged him from the ditch and on removing some of his clothing found a terrible wound now spilling out his intestines. They ligatured him as best they could and carried him home where the doctor they had sent for was waiting, along with a priest.

When the doctor saw him he shook his head gravely, and turning to Hautot's son who was sobbing in a chair, said, 'My poor boy, I'm afraid it doesn't look at all good.'

But when a dressing had been applied, the injured man moved his fingers, opened his mouth, then a pair of haggard eyes, and cast a few anxious glances around him. He seemed to be searching his mind for something and then, when the whole sequence of events came flooding back, murmured: 'Christ almighty! I've had it now.'

The doctor took his hand.

'No! Certainly not! All you need is a few days' rest and you'll be absolutely fine.'

Hautot went on: 'No, I know the score. Shattered stomach. I've had it.'

Then suddenly: 'I want to talk to my son if I've got time.'

Young Hautot whimpered like a little boy: 'Papa! Papa! Oh, poor Papa!'

In a firmer tone his father said: 'Listen, stop crying. Doesn't help. I've got to talk to you. Come close, it'll only take a minute. Then I'll feel much better. You lot, can we have a minute or two if you don't mind?'

The others went out of the room, leaving father and son together. As soon as they were alone the father spoke: 'Listen,

my boy, you're twenty-four, I can tell you everything now. Not
that there's much to tell. Anyway you know when your mother
died seven years ago I was . . . well I'm forty-five now. I was
married at nineteen by the way, right?'

'Yes I know.'

'So when she died she left me a widower at thirty-seven. Can
you imagine? Chap like me. Can't be a permanent widower at
thirty-seven, can you my boy?'

'No father, of course not.'

The father's face was pale and contorted with pain.

'God, I'm in agony here. Anyway, to continue. A chap can't
live entirely on his own yet I couldn't remarry. I'd promised
your mum. So . . . are you following?'

'Yes father.'

'So. I took up with this girl in Rouen. Rue de l'Éperlan,
number 18, third floor, second door. You are taking all this in I
hope? This girl, she's been so good to me, you know. I couldn't
have wished for a sweeter little wife. Loving, devoted, you get
the picture my boy?'

'Yes father.'

'Well, anyway, if I should pop off I reckon I owe her. A lot.
Enough to set her up. You understand?'

'Yes, father.'

'When I say she's a good kid, I mean really good. If it hadn't
been for you, and out of respect for your mother's memory, if
it hadn't been for this house, and us having lived here, the three
of us, I'd have brought her home here and married her, no
question. Listen, listen, my boy. I could have made a will but I
didn't. Didn't want to. Never put things down in writing. Not
that sort of thing anyway. Upsets the family. Makes everything
too complicated. Everybody at each other's throats. Who needs
legal documents? Don't ever use them. That's how I've made
my money, such as it is. Understand, my boy?'

'Yes, father.'

'Listen again, carefully. So I haven't made a will. Didn't need
to. Because I know you. You've got a good heart, you're not . . .
careful . . . tight-fisted, you know what I mean? So I thought
when the end came I'd just tell you how things stood and I'd

ask you not to forget the girl: Caroline Donet, rue de l'Éperlan, number 18, third floor, second door, don't forget. Listen again. Go straight there when I've gone . . . and make sure she's seen all right by me. You'll have plenty. You can do it. I'm leaving you enough. Listen. She won't be there most of the week, she works for Madame Moreau, rue Beauvoisine. But go on Thursday. That's when she expects me. That's my day, has been for six years now. Oh the poor girl! She's going to be so upset! I'm telling you all this because I know you, my boy. Not the sort of thing you tell everybody. Not the lawyer and not the curé. It happens, everybody knows that, but you don't discuss it. Not unless you have to. So, no strangers in on it. Just the family that's all. You understand?'

'Yes father.'

'Promise?'

'Yes father.'

'Swear?'

'Yes, father.'

'I beg of you, my boy, please. Please don't forget. You mustn't.'

'I won't father.'

'Go in person. You're in charge of everything.'

'Yes, father.'

'Then you'll see what she says. I can't talk any more. Swear to me.'

'Yes father.'

'That's good, my boy. Come and give me a kiss goodbye. I'm nearly finished. This is it. Tell them they can come in.'

Moaning, the younger Hautot kissed his father and, obedient as always, opened the door. The priest appeared wearing a white surplice and carrying the holy oils. But the dying man had closed his eyes and refused to open them again. He refused to reply and refused to give any sign that he knew what was going on.

He had talked enough and could not say another word. Besides, he felt relieved now. He could die in peace. What need was there for him to confess to this delegate of God since he had already confessed to his own son who really was family?

The last rites were administered, and he was given communion in the midst of his kneeling friends and servants with never a movement of his face to indicate that he was still alive. He died at around midnight after four hours of spasms indicative of appalling pain.

The season had opened on the Sunday and Hautot was buried the following Tuesday. Having returned from taking his father to the cemetery, César Hautot spent the rest of the day in tears. He hardly slept that night and was so miserable the next day that he wondered how he could carry on living. Nevertheless he spent the whole day thinking that, if his father's last wish was to be carried out, he should go to Rouen the following day and see this Caroline Donet at the rue de l'Éperlan, number 18, third floor, second door. He had repeated this like a mantra so many times so as not to forget it, that now he could think of little else. Both his mind and his ear were hypnotized by the phrase. Accordingly, the next morning around eight o'clock, having ordered Graindorge harnessed to the tilbury,[1] he set off at a brisk pace behind the heavy Norman horse on the main road from Ainville to Rouen. He was wearing his black frock-coat, a tall silk topper and his trousers with the straps under the soles. In the circumstances he decided not to wear over his handsome suit the loose blue smock which, flapping in the wind, protected his better clothes against any dust or spots and which he normally shed as soon as he jumped down on arriving at his destination.

He got to Rouen just as ten o'clock was striking and went as usual to the Hôtel des Bons-Enfants, rue des Trois Mares. There he was embraced by the proprietor, the proprietor's wife and their five sons, all of whom had heard the sad news. After that he had to tell them exactly how the accident had happened and this set him off crying again. He turned down their offers of comfort, all the more insistent now that he was a man of substance, and even refused their invitation to dinner, which really offended them.

Having dusted off his hat, brushed down his frock-coat and given his boots a quick wipe, he set out to find the rue de l'Éperlan. He dared not ask for directions lest he be recognized and suspicions raised. Finally drawing a complete blank, he spotted a priest and counting on the professional discretion of a clergyman found out from him the way to the address. It was very close. In the next street on the right in fact.

He began to feel a little hesitant. Until this moment he had been blindly following his dead father's instructions. Now he felt a confusing mixture of sorrow and shame as he thought of himself, a son, soon to be face to face with the woman who had been his father's mistress. All the old moral strictures lying buried in his unconscious under layer after layer of conventional, received wisdom handed down from generation to generation, everything he had learned from his catechism years and since about loose women and the instinctive mistrust men have of them even if they marry one – all these ignorant, peasant values clamoured inside him, held him back and brought a blush of shame to his cheeks.

Nevertheless, he thought, I promised my father. Mustn't let him down. The door marked 18 was ajar so he pushed it open and saw beyond it a dark stairway which he climbed as far as the third floor. There he saw first one door, then a second with a bell-pull which he now tugged. The tinkle which he heard echo into the room beyond made his heart sink. The door was opened and he found himself standing opposite a very well-dressed, fresh-faced brunette who was staring at him in astonishment.

He had no idea what to say and she, unaware of anything untoward and expecting his father any minute, did not invite him in. They looked at each other for a full thirty seconds, at the end of which she said: 'Can I help you, monsieur?'

He murmured, 'I'm Hautot, the son.'

She started, turned pale and stammered as if she had known him all her life: 'Oh! Monsieur César?'

'Yes.'

'What . . . what's . . . ?'

'I have a message for you from my father.'

She said, 'Oh my God!' and took a step backwards to let him in. He then saw a little boy playing with a cat on the floor in front of a stove where several dishes were cooking.

'Sit down,' she said.

He sat down.

'Well?' she asked.

He was struck dumb, his eyes on the table in the middle of the room laid for three including a child. He looked at the chair with its back to the fire, the plate, the napkin, the glasses, one bottle of red wine, already drunk from, and one unopened bottle of white. That must be his father's usual place with his back to the fire! He was still expected by her! That would have been his father's bread with all the crust removed because of his poor teeth. Raising his eyes, he saw hanging on the wall a large photograph of his father taken at the Paris Exhibition,[2] the duplicate of one which hung over the bed in the master bedroom at Ainville.

The young woman went on: 'So? Monsieur César?'

He looked at her. She was pale with dread and her hands were trembling fearfully as she waited for him to speak. Eventually he gathered up enough courage to do so. 'Well Mam'zelle, I'm afraid Papa died on Sunday on the opening day of the shooting season.'

She was shocked literally rigid. After a few moments' silence she said in a barely audible voice, 'Oh no! He can't have!'

Then suddenly her eyes filled with tears. She raised her hands to cover her face and began to sob. The little boy, seeing his mother burst into tears and deducing that this stranger was the cause, hurled himself on César, grabbed him by the trouser-leg with one hand and started smacking him on the thigh as hard as he could with the other. César, frantic with grief himself, his own eyes still swollen with crying, was moved at the sight of this woman weeping for his father and the little boy defending the mother. He felt almost overwhelmed with emotion and, in order to keep from breaking down himself, started to speak: 'Yes,' he said, 'the tragedy occurred on Sunday morning at eight o'clock . . .'

He went on, assuming she was hearing it all and forgetting no detail, omitting not the smallest incident in a painstaking, plodding peasant way. The little boy continued to smack him and had now begun to kick him on the ankles. When Hautot junior came to the part where Hautot senior had talked about her, the young woman, hearing her own name, uncovered her face and asked: 'I'm sorry. Could you start again please? I wasn't taking it in . . . I really want to know what happened . . .'

He began again, using exactly the same words: 'The tragedy occurred on Sunday morning at eight o'clock . . .'

Again he told her everything, stopping every now and then to punctuate the story with little asides of his own. She listened attentively. With the sensitive perception of a woman, she seized every implication of each twist and turn of events, shuddering with horror and saying 'Oh my God' from time to time. The little boy, seeing his mother had calmed down, stopped hitting César and was now holding her hand, listening too as if he understood every word. When he came to the end Hautot junior said: 'And now what we must do is make sure his wishes are carried out. I'm in a comfortable position. He's left me property so . . . I wouldn't want you to feel in any need . . .'

She broke in abruptly: 'Oh, please, please, Monsieur César! Not today! My heart's breaking! Another time, another day, perhaps. But not today. And if I were to accept, I do want you to know it would not be for me, oh no, no, no, I swear I wouldn't want anything for myself but for the little one. We'll put any money in his name.'

César was aghast. Then the penny dropped. He stammered, 'You mean . . . he's his?'

'Oh yes,' she said.

Hautot junior looked at his half-brother with a mixture of emotions, all deeply painful. After a long silence, for she had begun to weep again, César was at a complete loss as to what to do. He said: 'Well then, Mam'zelle Donet, I'd better be going. When would you like us to meet and talk about arrangements?'

She cried out: 'Oh don't go! Please! Please don't leave me and Émile on our own. I'd die of grief. I've got nobody now except my little boy. Oh it's awful, Monsieur César, it's terrible! Please, please sit down! Talk to me some more. Tell me about what he used to do when he was away from here, when he was back home with you.'

And so César, obedient as always, sat down again. She drew her chair up close to his in front of the stove where the food was still cooking. She put Émile on her lap and asked César hundreds of little intimate questions about his father from which he could see or rather feel instinctively that this poor young woman had loved Hautot with all her heart.

The conversation naturally kept returning to the accident and he told her all over again what had happened, in the same detail. When he said, 'The hole in his stomach was so big you could have put both hands in it', she gave a sort of cry and began sobbing yet again. This time César too broke down with her and started to weep. Softened by his own tears he leaned down towards Émile whose forehead was within reach and kissed it. His mother struggled to get her breath back.

'Poor little mite,' she said, 'he's fatherless now.'

'Me too,' said César.

At this, each stopped talking. Suddenly the young woman became the practical housewife who thinks of everything and everyone.

'I don't suppose you've eaten a thing all morning, have you, Monsieur César?'

'No, Mam'zelle.'

'Oh, you must be hungry! Will you have something to eat?'

'No thank you,' he said, 'I'm not hungry. Too upset.'

'Oh, but you've got to eat in spite of everything, you'll grant me that. Do stay a bit longer. I don't know what I'll do when you leave.'

After a few attempts at resistance, he sat down opposite her, and in the chair with its back to the fire he settled down to a dish of the tripe that had been sizzling in the oven, and to a glass of red wine. Several times he wiped the mouth of the little boy who had dribbled sauce all over his chin. As he rose to leave, he said: 'When would you like me to come back and talk business, Mam'zelle Donet?'

'If it's all the same to you, Monsieur César, next Thursday. It'll save me taking time off. I've always got Thursday off anyway.'

'That's fine with me. Next Thursday.'

'You'll have lunch, won't you?'

'Oh, I don't know . . . really.'

'It's much easier to talk over a meal. Saves time too.'

'All right then. Let's say twelve o'clock.'

After giving little Émile another kiss and shaking Mademoiselle Donet's hand he left.

The week passed very slowly for César Hautot. He had never been on his own before and solitude seemed unbearable to him. Until then, he had shadowed his father all his life, following him into the fields, seeing that his orders were carried out, then, after a little while apart, he would see him again at dinner. In the evenings they would sit opposite each other smoking their pipes and talking about horses, cows and sheep. Their morning handshake was an expression of deep family attachment.

And now César was alone. He wandered about in the ploughed fields of autumn, all the time expecting to see the tall silhouette of his father waving to him from some field or other. To kill time he would drop in on neighbours, describe the accident to anyone who had not heard what had happened, and retell the story to those who had. Sometimes when he had run out of things that needed thinking about or doing he would sit down at the side of a cart track and wonder how much longer he could carry on.

He thought often of Mademoiselle Donet. He had liked her very much. He thought she was a very nice person indeed, a good, kind girl as his father had said. Yes, she was a lovely girl. A really lovely girl. He was determined to do her proud and to give her 2,000 francs in interest on capital to be settled on the child. He was rather pleased that he had to go and see her the following Thursday to sort things out with her. The thought of this brother, this new little fellow was a bit of a worry. It bothered him a little, yet at the same time it gave him a warm sort of feeling. There was a bit of kin for him there. The kid born on the other side of the blanket would never be called Hautot, but he was a bit of family with no pressure attached, a bit of his father after all.

When he found himself once more on the way to Rouen on Thursday morning, with these and similar thoughts in his head and the sound of Graindorge's rhythmical clip-clop, his heart was lighter and his mind calmer than at any time since the accident. As he entered Mademoiselle Donet's apartment he saw that everything was laid exactly as it had been the previous Thursday with one single exception – the crust of the bread at his place had not been removed.

He shook hands with the young woman, kissed Émile on both cheeks and sat down feeling both very much at home and extremely emotional. Mademoiselle Donet seemed slightly thinner and slightly paler. She must have cried her little heart out. This time she was a bit awkward in her manner towards him as if she had realized something she had been unable to absorb on that first occasion when she was still taking in the enormity of what had happened. She was extremely attentive to his needs and humble in her approach, as if trying to pay back in devotion and service towards him some of the generosity he was showing her. They took a long time over lunch and discussed the business which had brought him there. She did not want so much money. It was too much, far too much. She earned enough to keep herself; all she wanted was that Émile might have something to look forward to when he reached his majority. César, however, stuck to his guns and even added a present for herself as a token of mourning. As he finished his coffee, she asked, 'Do you smoke?'

'Yes, I've got my pipe here , , .,' he began.

He patted his pockets. Damnation. He had left it at home! He was just about to bemoan the fact when she produced one belonging to his father which she had kept tucked away in a cupboard. He took it from her and recognized it. Sniffing it and with emotion in his voice, declaring it to be one of the best, he filled and lit it. Then he put Émile on his knee and played ride-a-cock-horse with him while she cleared the table, stacking the dirty dishes in the sideboard to wash later after he had gone.

At about three, when he rose regretfully, he hated the idea of leaving.

'Well, Mamz'elle Donet,' he said, 'I'll wish you a very good afternoon. I'm delighted to have made your acquaintance like this.'

She remained standing in front of him, blushing and near to tears. As she looked at him she thought of his father.

'Are we not to see each other again then?' she asked.

He replied simply: 'We can, Mam'zelle, if that's what you'd like.'

'It most certainly is, Monsieur César. Shall we say next Thursday, if that's convenient for you?'

'Indeed it is, Mam'zelle Donet.'

'You'll come for lunch, of course?'

'Well, if you're offering I wouldn't say no.'

'Very well, Monsieur César. Thursday next it is, at twelve o'clock, like today.'

'Twelve o'clock on Thursday then, Mam'zelle Donet!'

NEW YEAR'S GIFT[1]

Jacques de Randal, having dined alone at home, gave his man-servant the evening off and sat down at his desk to write some letters. It was a custom of his to spend the last night of the year alone doing precisely this and taking mental stock. He thought over the things which had occurred since the previous New Year's Eve, things that were now finished and done with, and said a kind of goodbye to them. As the faces of his friends rose up in his mind's eye he wrote each a few lines wishing them a very happy new year.

Having sat down, he opened a drawer and drew from it the photograph of a woman. He looked at this for a few moments, kissed it, then placing it next to a fresh sheet of paper, he began:

My dear Irene,
You must have received by now the little token I sent earlier which I addressed to the woman in you. I have shut myself in tonight in order to write and tell you . . .

Here the pen stopped moving. Jacques got up and started pacing the room. For ten months now he had had a mistress. Quite unlike other women of the kind, she was no adventuress and not at all the sort who could be picked up at the theatre, say, or on the street. This was a woman with whom he had fallen in love and whom he had eventually won. Though no longer in the first flush of youth he was still young in years, took life very seriously and approached it in a practical and positive way.

Accordingly, just as every year he assessed the state of his friendships, some of which fell by the wayside while others were newly formed, he now tried to assess this passion of his. Now that the first ardour of his love had turned into a calmer sort of emotion, like a careful tradesman he tried to gauge the extent of his feelings for her and predict what they would be in the future.

What he found in his heart was great and deep love, much tenderness and gratitude, together with a thousand tiny attachments such as were likely to form a strong and enduring bond between them.

The doorbell rang, making him jump. He wondered what to do. Should he go and open it? Yes, he thought, on New Year's Eve you should always open the door to whatever stranger might be first-footing. Picking up a candle, therefore, he crossed the hall, drew back the bolts and turned the key. As he pulled the door open towards him he saw his mistress leaning with her hands against the wall and looking as pale as death.

'What on earth's the matter?'

'Are you alone?' she asked.

'Yes.'

'Without the servants?'

'Yes.'

'You weren't going out?'

'No.'

She walked into the familiar surroundings and as soon as they reached the drawing room collapsed on the divan. Burying her face in her hands, she began to weep bitterly. He fell on his knees in front of her, trying to prise her hands away and look into her eyes. 'Irene, Irene,' he kept saying, 'I beg of you tell me what on earth is the matter.'

Between sobs she began to mumble, 'I can't go on living like this, I can't . . .'

Uncomprehending, he said: 'What do you mean, like this? Like what?'

'I can't . . . can't go on as things are . . . at home . . . You don't know . . . I've never told you . . . it's terrible . . . I can't go on any longer . . . just now . . . he hit me . . .'

'Who? Your husband?'

'My husband, yes.'

'Oh, the . . . !'

Never having suspected him to be violent, Jacques could not believe his ears. The man moved in the most select of circles, was a member of the best clubs, rode, fenced and had the ear of influential politicians. With impeccable manners, a mediocre mind unburdened by either education or real intelligence, and a firm grasp of all the right prejudices – all the hallmarks of a gentleman in fact – he was well liked, much quoted and respected by all.

Like every other rich man of good family he appeared to take as much interest in his wife as was required. He knew the state of her health, her taste in clothes, and various other things. Apart from that, he left her pretty much to her own devices. Once Randal became a friend of Irene, he was given the warm handshake any sensible husband reserves for his wife's close friends. Once he became her lover his relations with the husband were even more cordial, as is perfectly right and proper. He had never suspected any difficulties within the marriage and was therefore staggered by this unexpected revelation.

'How did it happen? Tell me.'

She began to recount the whole long story of her married life since its beginning. Triggered by a trivial disagreement at first, a rift had begun to grow, widening every day between their two diametrically opposite characters. Further quarrels followed, and then a virtual separation which was never made public. After that, her husband had become aggressive, quick to anger and finally violent. Now he was jealous, jealous of Jacques, and that very day, after a scene, had struck her.

Once again she said with conviction: 'I'm never going back to him. You can do what you like with me.'

Jacques went to sit down opposite her. Their knees touched as he took both her hands in his.

'My dearest, that would be a *very* foolish, a *hopelessly* foolish move. If you really do want to leave your husband then you must make sure it is *he* who is entirely in the wrong. Then your reputation as a woman of the highest honour will remain intact.

Casting an anxious glance at him, she said: 'What exactly do you advise me to do, then?'

'Go back home and just try to bear it until you can get either a separation or a divorce, but keep your reputation beyond reproach.'

'Don't you think that's a little cowardly?'

'No, I don't. I think it's the wisest, most sensible thing to do. You have a position to maintain, your honour to protect, friends you want to keep and relatives to think of. You must not forget all these considerations by acting on impulse . . .'

She rose and violently burst out, 'No, no, no! I can't do it. I tell you it's over, finished, once and for all!'

Then, placing her hands on her lover's shoulders and looking deep into his eyes, she said: 'Do you love me?'

'Yes.'

'Truly?'

'Yes.'

'Then take me in.'

'Take you in? Here? In my house? Are you mad? I'd lose you forever! Finally and definitively! Have you taken leave of your senses?'

Slowly, and seriously she continued, weighing every word carefully: 'Listen, Jacques. He has forbidden me to see you again. I do not intend to play games. I will not come and see you on the sly. You must take me or lose me.'

'In that case, my dear Irene, get your divorce and I will marry you.'

'That's in, what, two years? At the earliest. Your impatience is flattering.'

'Listen, please. If you stay here, he'll come and pick you up tomorrow. He's your husband. He has the law on his side. He'd be acting within his rights.'

'I wasn't asking you to keep me here, Jacques. I meant take me away with you, anywhere. I thought you loved me enough to do that. I see I was wrong. Goodbye.'

She turned on her heel and made for the door. She moved so fast that he only caught up with her on the threshold of the drawing room where he seized hold of her. 'Irene, listen!'

She struggled, refusing to hear another word. Her eyes were full of tears as she stammered: 'Leave me . . . leave me . . . leave me alone! Let me go!'

He forced her to sit down and once again knelt down in front of her. He tried every means in his power to convince her of the folly and the danger of doing what she was contemplating. His arguments were comprehensive and he searched deep in his heart for reasons to dissuade her from this course.

Still she remained icily silent. He begged and implored her to listen to him, to believe what he said and to take his advice. When he had finished speaking, she said:

'*Now* will you let me go? Take your hands off me and let me get up.'

'Irene, listen . . .'

'I *said*, let me go, will you?'

'Irene, are you really going to leave him?'

'Let me go, I tell you!'

'Just tell me if you actually mean to go through with this plan of yours, this stupid plan which you will bitterly regret.'

'Yes, I do. Let me go.'

'Very well then, stay. You know this is your home. We'll leave first thing in the morning.'

She wrested herself from his grasp and rose, saying: 'No! Too late! I don't want any noble sacrifices from you.'

'Stay, please. Now that I've said what I ought to, now that I've done what I ought to do, I've discharged my duty towards you and my conscience is clear. Tell me what you want and I'll do it.'

She sat down again, gazed at him for a very long time, then, in a newly calm voice, asked: 'Well? What was all that about?'

'What do you mean? What is there to explain?'

'Everything. Tell me what it was that made you change your mind. Then I'll know what to do.'

'I don't know. I just know that I had to tell you it was a stupid idea. But if you really mean it, then I want to be part of it. In fact, I demand to be part of it.'

'A man doesn't do a volte-face just like that.'

'Listen, my dearest. It's not a question of noble sacrifice or anything like that. The day I realized I loved you, this is what I

said to myself and I think anyone in love in the same circumstances must do the same:

'A man who loves a woman, who does his very best to win
her, who does so and who has her, engages in a very solemn
contract both with himself and with her. That's in the case of a
woman like you, I mean, not a woman of easy virtue. The
institution of marriage is of great social value, great legal value,
too, but it doesn't seem to me, given the way things usually are,
it doesn't seem to me to have any great moral value. So when a
woman is tied by a legal bond to a husband she does not and
cannot love, when a woman like that whose heart is still free
meets a man whom she does love and gives herself to him and
is taken by him, I say the two of them are entering into a
commitment to each other more binding, because of the mutual
free consent between them, than that of an "I do" in front of an
officiating mayor. I believe that if they are both people of honour
the commitment they make is closer, stronger and healthier than
if they had received all the sacraments on offer elsewhere. That
woman risks everything. Precisely *because* she is well aware of
the possibly dire consequences, *because* she gives all she has,
her heart, her body and her soul, *because* she knows only too
well what deprivations are in store for her, what dangers and
catastrophes may be round the corner, *because* she commits this
act boldly and fearlessly and is ready to face up to everything,
including a husband who has the right to kill her and society
that has the power to reject her – because of all these considerations the conjugal infidelity she commits is in my view highly
respectable. And it's for that reason too that her lover in taking
her must also take all of these things into consideration and
himself forsake all others, come what may. That's all I have to
say. I spoke to you first as a circumspect man ought, someone
whose duty it was to warn you. But now you hear me speak
simply as a man who loves you and who is yours to command.'

She was radiant, and closed his mouth with her lips, murmuring quietly: 'Darling, none of it was true. Nothing's wrong. My
husband isn't in the least bit suspicious. But I wanted to see . . .
I wanted to know what you would do . . . I suppose I wanted

some kind of token ... from your heart ... a different kind of token from the necklace you sent earlier. And you have given it! Thank you! Thank you! Oh God, I'm so happy!'

THE HORLA[1]

Doctor Marrande, one of the most eminent psychiatrists in the country, had invited three of his colleagues and four others in the field of the natural sciences to spend an hour at his clinic considering the case of one of his patients. When they were all gathered, he said to them: 'I should like to present to you the strangest and most disturbing case I have ever come across. I shall say nothing ahead of time about this patient, but let him speak for himself.'

The doctor rang and a man entered, accompanied by a member of staff. He was extremely thin, cadaverous even, as some madmen look when they are consumed by an obsession. Their bodies seem ravaged by one sick thought which devours them faster than any disease or consumption. Having greeted the company and sat down, the man spoke.

'Gentlemen, I am well aware of what brings you here. I am happy to comply with Dr Marrande's request for me to give you my history. For a long time he himself believed I was mad. Today he is not so sure. Some time in the near future you will realize that, unfortunately, not only for myself but for you and all the rest of humanity, my mind is as healthy, clear and as lucid as your own. Let me first of all give you the facts.

I am forty-two years old and unmarried. My income is sufficient for me to live a fairly luxurious kind of life. I live in a property which I own on the banks of the Seine at Biessard, near Rouen. I like hunting and I like fishing. Beyond the rocky hillsides behind my house lies one of the most beautiful forests in the whole of France, the forest of Roumare. And in front of the house, which is very large and very old, lies one of the most beautiful rivers in the world. Moreover, the house itself is attractive: it is painted white and stands in the middle of parkland which extends as far as the rocky hillsides I mentioned earlier.

My staff consists, or rather consisted, of a coachman, a gardener, a manservant, a cook and a laundry-cum-scullery maid. All these people had lived there with me for between ten and sixteen years. They were long familiar with my ways, with the running of the house, with the neighbourhood, everything. They made an excellent, harmonious team, a point which it is important to bear in mind in what follows.

I should add that since the Seine, as you probably know, is navigable as far as Rouen, on the stretch of it in front of my house I used to see daily all kinds of sea-going vessels from all over the world pass up and down stream, some under sail, some under steam.

Well, about a year last autumn, I suddenly began to suffer inexplicable spells of a strange malaise. To begin with, I was prey to a kind of nervous anxiety which kept me awake for entire nights at a stretch, a kind of hypersensitivity which made me jump at the least little sound. I began to have periods of moodiness and sudden fits of anger for no apparent reason. I consulted a doctor who prescribed cold showers and potassium bromide.

I followed his advice and took a shower morning and evening, as well as the bromide. Quite soon I did in fact manage to start sleeping again, but this time sleep turned out to be even more intolerable than the insomnia. As soon as my head hit the pillow, my eyes closed and I was out. I mean out completely. I fell into absolute nothingness, a void, a total blank. My self became completely dead until I was suddenly, horribly awoken by the most appalling sensation. An unbearable weight was lying on my chest and another mouth was sucking the life out of me through my own. I shall never forget the terrible shock of it! Just imagine a man asleep and in the process of being murdered. He wakes with the knife in his throat. He can hear his own death-rattle, feel his own blood ooze out of him. He cannot breathe. He knows he is going to die but not why – that's exactly what it felt like!

I was losing a dangerous amount of weight all the time and suddenly realized that my coachman, a big, solid sort of fellow, was doing the same thing. I said to him in the end, "Look, Jean, there's definitely something wrong with you. What d'you think is the matter?" "To tell you the truth, monsieur," he said, "I think I've caught whatever you've got. My nights seem to be eating into my days." I began to think that there was something noxious permeating the house, something poisonous, maybe, emanating from the river.

I had decided to spend two or three months away, despite the fact that the hunting season was in full swing, when something strange happened. I might easily have missed it, so trivial did it at first seem but it led to a series of such unbelievable, fantastical events that I decided after all, to stay.

One night, being thirsty, I drank half a glass of water and noticed when I did so that the carafe on my bedside table had been full up as far as its glass stopper. During the night I had one of those terrible awakenings I just mentioned. Still shaking, I lit my candle and was about to take another drink of water when I noticed to my stupefaction that the carafe was now empty. I could not believe my eyes. Either someone had come into the room or I was acting unconsciously in my sleep.

The following night I wanted to see if the same thing would happen. This time I locked my door to make sure no one could come into the room. I went to sleep and woke up as I did every night. *Someone* had drunk all the water I had seen there with my own eyes only two hours before. But *who*? Myself, obviously, and yet I could have almost sworn that I had made no movement in my deep and painful sleep.

I resorted to various stratagems in order to convince myself that I was not doing these things unconsciously. One night I put next to the carafe a bottle of vintage claret as well as a glass of milk, which I hate, and a piece of chocolate cake, which I love. Both the wine and the cake remained intact. But the water and the milk disappeared. None of the solid foodstuffs had had inroads made in them, only the liquids – the water and milk especially.

I was still in agonizing doubt. Maybe it was still I myself who was getting up without any consciousness of it. Maybe it was I who even drank the liquids I detested. My senses could have been so drugged that in sleep they were completely altered. In that state it was possible for me to have shed my former dislikes and acquired new tastes altogether.

I tried another way to catch myself out. I wrapped everything which was likely to be touched in thin muslin, which in turn I covered with the finest linen napkins. Then, just before getting into bed, I rubbed my face, hands and moustache all over with black lead. When I awoke, the materials were still spotless. They had, however, been moved. The napkins lay differently from the way I had placed them, and, more importantly, both the water and the milk had been drained off. This time my door had been locked with an extra security key, the shutters had been padlocked also just in case, and no one therefore could possibly have come into the room. So I had to ask myself the terrifying question of who it was that was in there with me every night.

I see you smile, gentlemen. You have already decided that I am mad, I can see. I have rushed you somewhat. I should have described in greater detail the feelings of a man with a completely clear mind, safe inside his own house, seeing water disappear from his carafe while he's asleep. I should have conveyed to you better the kind of torture I experienced every morning and every evening. I should have described how annihilating the sleep was and how hideous the awakening. But let me continue.

Quite suddenly, these inexplicable occurrences ceased. Nothing was touched in my room. It was over. I began to feel much better in myself. I felt a sense of relief return, particularly when I learned that Monsieur Legite, one of my neighbours, was showing many of my own earlier symptoms. Once more I was sure it must have something to do with our location and that it was something in the atmosphere. My coachman, incidentally, had become extremely ill and had stopped working for me a month earlier.

Winter had passed and it was now early spring. One day I was walking near one of my rose-borders when I saw, I tell you I saw with my very own eyes and right next to me at that, the

stalk of one of the most beautiful roses break off exactly as
though an invisible hand had plucked it. The flower described
the curve which an invisible arm would have made to bring it
to someone's face, then hung terrifyingly suspended in mid-air
all by itself, no more than three feet away from my eyes. Scared
witless, I lunged forward to grab it. Nothing! Gone! I suddenly
became furious with myself. No man in his right mind could
have hallucinations like that! But was that what it was? I looked
for the stem of the rose again and found straight away where it
had been broken off between two other blooms on the same
branch. I knew there had been three earlier on. I had seen them.

I went indoors, shaken to the core. I assure you, gentlemen, I
am quite clear about this. I do not now and never have believed
in the supernatural. But from that moment onwards, I knew as
surely as I know night follows day that somewhere near me was
an invisible being. It had haunted me before, left me for a while
and was now back.

A short while later I had proof.

My staff began to quarrel among themselves every day. It was
always over seemingly trivial matters, but for me they were full
of significance. One day one of my best glasses, a beautiful
Venetian piece, fell for no apparent reason from the dining room
dresser and smashed into smithereens. My manservant blamed
the maid who in turn blamed somebody else, and so it continued.
Doors firmly locked in the evening were found next day wide
open. Every night milk was stolen from the pantry . . . and so
on and so forth ad nauseam. What was all this about? What
on earth was happening? I vacillated, terrified, torn between
wanting to know and dreading what I might learn. Once again
the house returned to normal and once more I began to think I
must have dreamed the whole thing, until the following events
occurred.

It was nine o'clock on the evening of 20 July and very warm.
I had left my window open wide and light from a lamp on my
table fell on a volume of Musset[2] open at *Nuit de Mai*.[3] I myself
was stretched out on a sofa and had nodded off. After about
forty minutes or so, awakened by a strange sort of feeling, I
opened my eyes again but kept perfectly still. At first nothing

happened. Then, as I watched, one of the pages of the book turned over, seemingly by itself. Not a breath of air had wafted through the window. Puzzled, I waited and in another four minutes or so I saw, I saw with my own eyes, gentlemen, another page rise and place itself over the first, exactly as if turned by invisible fingers. The armchair next to it seemed unoccupied but I knew perfectly well *it* was there. I leapt across the room to grab it, touch it, to seize hold of it somehow or other. But before I reached it, the chair, seemingly of its own accord, turned over backwards as if fleeing from me. The lamp also fell and went out, its glass smashed. The window was suddenly flung back against its hinges as if by some intruder making his escape . . . oh, my God! I rang the bell furiously and when my manservant came, said, "I've knocked all this stuff over and smashed it. Go and fetch another lamp will you?"

I slept no more that night. Yet I could still have made some sort of mistake. When you wake from a snooze you're always a little bit befuddled. Could it have been I who turned the armchair over and upset the lamp, rushing about like a mad thing? No! Of course it was not! I had not the slightest doubt about that. Yet that was what I wanted to believe.

Now. What should I call this . . . Being? The Invisible One? No, that would not do. I decided to call it the Horla. Don't ask me why. So I was going to be stuck with this Horla indefinitely. Night and day I could feel it there. I knew it was close to me the whole time, yet totally elusive. I also knew for certain that with each passing hour, each passing minute, even, it was drawing the life out of me. I was driven to distraction by the fact that I could never see it. I lit every lamp in the house. Maybe given proper illumination it could be exposed.

Then, finally, I saw it. Believe it or not, I saw it.

I was sitting with some book or other in front of me, not really reading. With every nerve on edge, I was waiting and watching for this being I could feel near me. I knew it was there somewhere. But where? What was it doing? How could I get hold of it? Opposite was my bed, an old oak four-poster. To my right was the fireplace. On the left the door, which I had made sure was locked. Behind me was a very large, mirrored wardrobe before which I shaved and dressed every day. Whenever I passed it I could see myself full length. So there I was, pretending to this presence which I knew was spying on me that I was reading. All of a sudden I felt it reading over my shoulder, brushing against my ear. Leaping to my feet, I turned round so quickly that I nearly fell over. Believe it or not, though the room was bright as day, there was no sign of me in the mirror. It was empty, clear and full of light. But my reflection was not in it, despite the fact that I was standing directly in front of it. I looked at the large glass, clear now from top to bottom. I looked at it in terror. I dared not take a step forward, knowing that this being was in between. I knew that although it would slip away from me again, its own invisible body had absorbed my own reflection. I was so frightened! Then suddenly I saw myself begin to appear from the misty depths of the mirror, rising as if from a body of water. The water itself seemed to shift slowly from left to right revealing, second by second, an increasingly sharper reflection of myself. It was like the end of an eclipse. What was concealing me looked like an opaqueness gradually turning transparent. Finally I could see myself clearly again, as I do when I look in the mirror every day. But now I had seen it. The terror of that moment remains with me and makes me tremble still. The following day I came here and asked to be admitted.

And now, gentlemen, I come to the end of my story. Having been fairly sceptical for some time, Dr Marrande decided to make a little unaccompanied trip to my part of the world. It transpires that three of my neighbours are now in a similar condition to the one I have described, isn't that so?'

'Absolutely true!' the doctor replied.

'You instructed them to leave out some milk or water in the bedroom every night to see if these liquids disappeared or not. They did. They disappeared just as they did in my house, didn't they?'

With great seriousness the doctor replied, 'They did indeed.'

'So, gentlemen, a Being, some new Being which, like ourselves, will undoubtedly multiply and increase, is now on earth. What? Why are you smiling? Because the Being is still invisible? But, gentlemen, what a primitive organ is the eye! It can barely spot our basic needs for survival. It misses the infinitesimal as well as the infinite. It does not perceive the millions of tiny organisms present in a drop of water. It does not perceive the inhabitants, the plants and the earth of the planets closest to us; it does not apprehend what is transparent. Put it in front of a piece of non-reflecting glass and it fails to notice. We go careering straight into it as a bird trapped inside a house will continue to beat its skull against the window panes. It fails to perceive solid but transparent objects. Yet these things exist. It cannot see air which is essential to human life; wind, which is the most powerful force in nature, capable of lifting men off their feet, flattening buildings, uprooting trees, and raising the sea into mountains of water which pulverize cliffs of solid granite. Why should we be surprised if it cannot make out a new kind of body to the human, and different from it only in that it does not emit light. Do you see electricity? Yet of course it exists. What is this being, gentlemen? I believe it is what the earth is waiting for, to supersede humanity, to usurp our throne, to overwhelm and perhaps feed on us as we feed now on cattle and wild boar. We have sensed and dreaded it for centuries. We have heard its approach with terror. Our forefathers have been haunted forever by the Invisible.

It has come.

All the legends of spirits, hobgoblins and evil, elusive riders in the sky were about it. It is his arrival which man has been dreading with such trepidation. And you yourselves, gentlemen, all the activities you have been engaged in in the last few years – hypnotism, the power of suggestion, magnetism – all point towards the Invisible. And I tell you he is here. He roams about anxiously, just as primitive man did, ignorant as yet of his full power and potential which will be realized soon enough! Finally, gentlemen, here is an excerpt from a newspaper article which I have come across, published in Rio de Janeiro:

An epidemic of apparent insanity appears to have been raging for some time in the province of São Paulo. The inhabitants of several villages have fled their homes and abandoned their crops in the belief that they are being hunted and eaten by invisible vampires living off their sleeping breath and drinking nothing but water or occasionally milk.[4]

I should add that a few days before my own first attack of the disease which nearly killed me, I distinctly remember having seen a three-master pass, flying the flag of Brazil . . . I told you that my house is situated near the river bank . . . No doubt he was hidden somewhere aboard that ship. That's all I have to say, gentlemen.'

Dr Marrande rose to his feet and murmured, 'I am in as much of a quandary as you all. I cannot tell if this man is mad or whether we both are . . . or whether . . . man's successor is already in our midst . . .'

DUCHOUX

The atmosphere inside his club as the Baron de Mordiane
descended the stairs was like a hothouse and he left his fur coat
open. Now, as the great front door closed behind him, the cold
pierced through him painfully like a sudden stab of sorrow. Not
only had he lost a little money that evening but also he had been
having a little stomach trouble lately and had to be careful what
he ate. He was just about to go home when the thought of his
huge, empty apartment, where his valet would be asleep in
the ante-room, and of his bathroom where water would be
simmering on the gas burner in readiness for his evening ablu-
tions, and finally of the ancient, sombre bed waiting for him like
a mortuary slab, cut deep into him even more painfully than the
icy air.

For some years now the burden of solitude had begun to
weigh heavily on him as on many another bachelor grown old.
There was a time when he had been strong, agile and full of life,
when he spent all day on sports and all night at parties. Now he
felt weighed down by everything and nothing gave him very
much pleasure any more. Exercise tired him too much, suppers
and even dining out he found a pain, and women now bored
him as much as they had entertained him before.

The monotony of the same kind of evening – with the same
friends in the same places at the club where they played the
same games in which losses and gains cancelled each other out
after a while; the same conversations on the same topics, the
same badinage, the same jokes and the same gibes about the
same women – sickened him almost to the point of suicide. He
could no longer go on with his empty life which was as regular

as clockwork and equally meaningless and which, while it appeared on the surface an easy, carefree existence, was actually becoming a real burden. He was looking for something that would soothe and calm him, something comfortable. He had no idea what it might be.

Certainly not marriage. He could not bear the idea of sentencing himself to a life of miserable conjugal servitude. He had no stomach for the odious coexistence of two human beings yoked together for life and knowing each other so well that not a word spoken by one was unpredictable by the other, not a gesture unanticipated and not a thought or a wish or an opinion not easily guessed in advance. It was his belief that people were interesting to the extent that they were unknown, hidden and still mysterious. He would have needed a kind of non-family, in which he lived only part of his life. Once again the thought of his son came to haunt him.

He had been thinking about him constantly for a year now and the irresistible desire to see and get to know him had only increased with the passage of time. He had been born as the result of a dramatic love-affair when the Baron himself was young. The child had been sent to the south of France and brought up near Marseille without ever knowing who his father was.

The latter had paid first for a nurse, second for his education, then for the period during which he sowed his wild oats, and finally had sent sufficient money for the boy to make a reasonable sort of marriage. A discreet notary had acted as intermediary and revealed nothing throughout this period.

The Baron de Mordiane knew only that someone with his blood in his veins was living on the outskirts of Marseille; that he was apparently bright and well brought-up; that he had married the daughter of an architect entrepreneur in whose footsteps he had followed. He had also apparently made quite a lot of money.

Why not go, incognito, and see this stranger son of his, just to see what he was like and make sure that, if need be, the Baron had an acceptable sort of family he could relax with.

He had distributed largesse in the past. The generous wedding

cheque had been gratefully accepted so the Baron did not antici-
pate any proud desire for independence on the part of his son.
This idea, this desire of his to go to the south of France came to
him every day now. It was beginning to get under his skin and
become a real obsession. A curious wave of self-pity washed
over him as he thought now of the warm, happy home close to
the sea. He could picture his young and lovely daughter-in-law
ready to welcome him; grandchildren, their arms outstretched,
running to meet him; and a son to remind him of the brief, sweet
affair of his long-distant youth. His only regret was that he had
already given so much money. Since his son had used it wisely
to make more, the Baron would seem now less of a benefactor
than he would like to appear.

These were the thoughts that went through his mind as he
walked on, his shoulders hunched up inside his fur collar. He
hailed a passing fiacre and had himself driven home. Rousing
the valet who came to answer the door he said: 'Louis, we're
leaving tomorrow night for Marseille. We shall probably
stay for about two weeks. Make the necessary preparations,
would you?'

The train was running alongside the sandy banks of the Rhône,
then across golden plains, past whitewashed villages, and finally
into a wide tract of land bound in the far distance by bare
mountains. The Baron de Mordiane, awake now after a night
in his sleeper, was looking sadly at himself in the little mirror of
his travelling case. The bright glare of the southern sun showed
him hitherto unsuspected lines and a decrepitude in his face
which had remained hidden in the relative darkness of his Paris
apartments.

He looked at the wrinkles at the corners of his eyes, at the
folds in his eyelids and at his bald temples and forehead.

'Dammit!' he said, 'I'm not just getting on, I'm a wreck!'

He suddenly longed once again for rest, and for the first time
ever to dandle grandchildren on his knee. At about half-past
one in the afternoon, having hired a landau[1] in Marseille, he
arrived at one of those southern houses whose whiteness standing out in this case against an avenue of plane trees is almost

painfully dazzling to the eyes. He smiled as he walked up the drive, saying to himself, 'Well! This *is* good!'

Suddenly a little urchin of five or six appeared from behind a bush and stood at the side of the drive looking at the gentleman.

Mordiane went up to him: 'Hello, my boy!'

The child made no reply. So the Baron leaned down and picked him up to give him a kiss. All at once a great wave of the garlic which seemed to permeate the child's entire body made the Baron quickly set him down on the ground again and murmur: 'Must be the gardener's child.'

He walked on towards the house. Washing hung on a line outside the front door; shirts, napkins, dishcloths, aprons and sheets. Festooned across one whole window like strings of sausages in a charcuterie were line upon line of socks.

The Baron called.

A typically southern-looking maid appeared. She looked dirty and her unkempt hair was constantly falling into her eyes. Her skirt, despite the spots and stains upon it, was garish in colour and reminiscent of the fairground or the circus.

'Is M. Duchoux[2] at home?' he asked.

This was the name which, as an already cynical young man, he had jokingly given to the foundling baby so that no one should query its provenance.

'You want M. Duchouxe?'[3]

'Yes.'

'Inside. Doing his plans.'

'Could you tell Monsieur Duchoux that Monsieur Merlin would like a word, please?'

She looked astonished.

'Come on in if you want to see him,' she said, then yelled: 'M. Duchouxe! Visitor!'

The Baron walked into a large room in semi-darkness with its shutters half-closed. He got a vague impression of squalor in both the people and the things inside. Standing in front of a table cluttered with all sorts of objects a short, bald man was drawing on a large sheet of paper. He stopped working and came forward a couple of steps. Judging by his open waistcoat, unbuttoned waistband and rolled-up sleeves, he was feeling very hot. The muddy shoes on his feet suggested rain in the previous few days. In a strong Midi accent, he asked: 'To whom do I have the honour . . . ?'

'Monsieur Merlin. I've come about a plot of land to build on.'

'Ah! ah, very good!'

Duchoux turned to his wife who was knitting in the shadows. 'Joséphine, clear a chair will you?'

Mordiane then saw an already old-looking young woman. Twenty-five is old in the country where there is no time to primp and preen, to clean or generally titivate. In the country there is little tradition of preserving youthful charm and beauty well into middle age. Wearing a fichu[4] about her shoulders, her thick, dark hair all over the place, she removed with work-worn hands a child's frock, a knife, a length of string, an empty flower-pot and a greasy plate from the seat of a chair which she then offered the visitor.

He sat down and noticed that on Duchoux's work-table as well as books and papers there were two freshly picked lettuces, a bowl, a hairbrush, a table napkin, a revolver and several dirty cups. The architect intercepted his glance and said laughingly: 'Sorry about the mess in here. Children, you know.'

He drew his chair closer to the customer.

'So. You're looking for a plot on the outskirts of Marseille?'

His breath, even at a distance, wafted over to the Baron a strong smell of garlic which is as natural to a southerner as fragrance to a flower.

Mordiane enquired: 'Was that your son I met under the plane trees?'

'Yes indeed. My second.'

'You have two?'

'Three, monsieur. One a year.'

Duchoux seemed proud of the fact. But the Baron thought to himself: if they all reek like this I shudder to think what the bedroom smells like. He continued: 'Yes, I'd like an attractive little plot by the sea near a relatively secluded beach.'

Duchoux began to expound. He had twenty, no, fifty, possibly even a hundred plots like that, at all kinds of prices and to suit a vast variety of tastes. He spoke nineteen to the dozen, smiling confidently and swaying his round, bald head this way and that as he spoke.

Mordiane remembered a slim, somewhat melancholy little blonde girl saying to him tenderly, 'My darling love . . .' He could feel his pulse quicken at the mere thought of her. She had loved him, madly, passionately for three weeks. Then when she became pregnant during the absence of her husband, the governor of a colony abroad, she had run away in terror, then gone into hiding until the birth of the baby whom Mordiane had taken away one summer night and whom neither of them had ever seen again.

She had died of tuberculosis three years later in her husband's colony where she had rejoined him. And now here in front of Mordiane was their son, with this grating accent of his, saying: 'This particular plot, Monsieur, is very special . . .'

Mordiane could hear the other voice, as soft as the breeze, murmuring, 'My darling love, we must never part . . .' He remembered the deep, gentle devotion in her blue eyes as he now looked into the round, blue, but essentially expressionless eyes of this ridiculous little man who took after his mother, yet . . . with every second he could see more and more of a resemblance in the tone of the man's voice, in his gestures, in everything about him. He did resemble her, but as a monkey resembles a man. And there were other characteristics he had inherited from her, too: a thousand irritating, even revolting traits which were indisputably hers. The Baron was in anguish. This terrible similarity, increasing horribly and unbearably, began to assume the proportions of a nightmare torturing him with dreadful remorse.

He stammered: 'When can we go and see this plot?'

'Well, tomorrow, if you like.'

'Fine, tomorrow. What time?'

'One o'clock?'

'Very well.'

The child he had met in the drive appeared at the open door and shouted 'Papou!' No one took any notice. But Mordiane was already on his feet, his legs unsteady, desperate to get out of the place! That 'Papou!' had struck him like a bullet. The garlicky, southern 'Papou!' touched a nerve in him! Oh how delicate had been her fragrance all those years ago!

Duchoux was seeing him to the door. 'Is the house yours?' asked the Baron.

'Yes, Monsieur, I bought it not so long ago. And very proud of it I am too. I was born a love-child, I'll make no bones about it. Proud of that too. I'm a self-made man, I am. Don't owe a thing to anybody. Everything I've done, I've done on my own.'

The child, still standing where they had left him, called out again, this time in the distance 'Papou!'

Mordiane, panic-stricken and trembling in every limb, could not wait to be gone. He's going to guess, any minute, who I am, he thought, he's going to clasp me in his arms! He'll plonk a garlic-flavoured kiss on each cheek and call me 'Papou'!

'Till tomorrow, then, Monsieur.'

'One o'clock it is.'

The landau sped along the white road.

'The station, driver!'

In his head two voices alternated. One, distant and soft, said in the faint, sad voice of the dead, 'My darling love . . .' The other bellowed insistently 'Papou!' as accusingly as one yells 'Stop thief!' after a robber.

The following night as he went into the club the Comte d'Etreilles stopped him and said: 'Haven't seen you for few days. Have you been ill?'

'Yes, not been too good. I get these migraines, you know, every so often . . .'

THE *LULL-A-BYE*

Calm as a millpond and with its surface now burnished by the morning sun, the stretch of the Seine lying directly in front of my house flowed broadly ahead in a long sheet of silver. In the fluttering of the leaves, in the river's rippling reflections, and palpable in the very air itself, a fresh and happy sense of life renewed was throbbing.

After the postman's call, the papers were brought to me and with them I sauntered down to the river for a quiet read. In the very first I opened, my eye was drawn to a column entitled 'Suicide Statistics' which contained the information that during the previous year alone some 8,500 human beings had taken their own lives.[1] Accompanying images sprang immediately to my mind's eye and I visualized a hideous, self-inflicted massacre of desperate people at the end of their tether. I saw people bleeding, a broken jaw, a smashed skull, a chest shattered by a bullet. I pictured individuals, alone perhaps in some poky hotel room, dying slowly not so much from their wounds as from the relentless pressure of unhappiness in their lives.

I saw some with a slit throat, some disembowelled, the razor or the kitchen knife still clutched in their hand. Others I saw sitting with a box of matches in front of them, and others still with a red-labelled bottle to hand. Motionless, they sat and stared before draining the glass and waiting. Then the contorted face, the twisted lips, the eyes gazing wildly about in terror. So much unimagined pain before the end! One of them stood up to walk, stopped dead in his tracks, clutched his belly, felt his organs consumed by the fire within, till finally he fell unconscious. I saw others hanging from a nail in the wall, from a window catch, an attic rafter, the branch of a tree in the evening rain. I could imagine everything they had been through before reaching their present state – lifeless, and with lolling tongues. I felt the anguish in their hearts as last-minute doubts crept in, as they tied the rope, tested it, slipped the noose over the head and as they finally let go.

I saw others lying on miserable beds; mothers with children; elderly people near starvation; young girls tortured by the results of sex – all stiff corpses now, strangled or suffocated while the night burner smoked on in the middle of the room. Most sinister of all, I pictured those loitering by night on deserted bridges. The water flowed with a gentle murmur under the arches . . . unseen . . . but how close was its cold, dank smell! Feared and desired at the same time. They dare not! Yet they must. A distant clock chimes and suddenly in the vast, shadowy silence, the sound of a body hitting the water, a few cries, more splashes as arms flail the surface. Sometimes not even that, but if the hands are bound, or a stone tied to the feet, the simple slice of a clean dive.

Oh those poor people! Those poor, poor people! How I felt for them! How many deaths I died with them. Reading on, I suffered all their pain, endured all their torments. I knew everything that had brought them to such a pitch. I knew only too well how vile and hideous life can be. None better. How easily could I understand these weak creatures, poor victims of unfortunate circumstance alone, with their loved ones lost perhaps and all hope of restitution gone. Gone too was any belief in a once harsh but now merciful God, and gone for them all dreams of happiness or joy. They had had enough. They wanted simply to end either the unremitting tragedy of their lives or the shameful absurdity of it all.

Suicide. The one power left to the powerless, the one hope of the hopeless, the single sublime act of courage left to the defeated. Of course there is a way out of this life. We need only open the door and pass through to the other side. Nature has taken pity and left us a loophole after all. We are no longer her captives. The desperate give thanks! Those now bereft of all illusion may still walk on with minds and hearts at ease. They have nothing to fear while there is still a way out. If they wish to leave there is always that door in reserve which not even the gods can close to them forever.

As I visualized the great host of those dead by their own hand, those 8,500 in the last year alone, it was as if I could hear them unite in a prayer to the world, a simple plea for something which will come in the future when we have more understanding. I could hear all those tormented souls, those who had cut their own throats, poisoned, hanged, suffocated or drowned themselves, all unite in one terrifying horde, clamouring to society: 'Let us at least have an easy death! Help to die those you have not helped to live! See how many of us there are. In these enlightened days of freedom when every man has a choice, give those abandoning life a death which is neither hideous nor horrifying!'

My thoughts began to wander around this idea in a miasma of weird, bizarre daydreams. For a while I was in some beautiful city, Paris I think, but the period was unclear. I was strolling along the streets looking at various houses, theatres and public buildings when suddenly I came across a large, very attractive and extremely elegant building standing on one side of a square. I was surprised to read on its façade, emblazoned in gold letters the words, 'Institute of Voluntary Death'. How extraordinary are our waking dreams in which the mind enters an unreal yet perfectly believable world of its own. In it we are amazed or shocked by nothing and our unbridled imagination makes no distinction between the comic and the grotesque.

I moved closer towards the building in the vestibule of which I could now see footmen in knee-breeches seated in front of a cloakroom, just as in the entrance-hall of any gentleman's club.[2] As I went in to have a look, one of them rose and said: 'May I help you, Monsieur?'

'Yes, I was just wondering . . . what sort of a place this is, actually.'

'That's all you want to know?'

'That's all, yes.'

'In that case, allow me to take Monsieur to the Secretary of the Institute.'

I hesitated, then went on to say, 'Are you sure it's not an intrusion?'

'Oh, no, Monsieur. Part of his job is to make himself available to anyone wishing to make enquiries.'

'In that case, do lead on.'

He led me through a series of corridors in which several elderly gentlemen were chatting. I was then ushered into an elegant though somewhat sombre office with ebony furniture. Inside, a portly young man with a paunch was in the process of writing a letter while smoking what smelt like a very expensive cigar. We bowed to each other and after the footman had left he asked: 'And how may I be of service to you, Monsieur?'

'You'll forgive any indiscretion on my part. None intended, I assure you, but this is the first time I've noticed this establishment and the words on the front of the building rather took me aback. I'd very much like to know what goes on here.'

He gave a smile of satisfaction before replying:

'My dear Monsieur, for those who wish to die, we provide a clean ... I hesitate to say agreeable, but at any rate an easy death.'

I was in no way shocked by this. It seemed to me the fairest and most natural thing in the world. What did surprise me was that such an enterprise, reflecting as it seemed to me a highly developed level of civilization, should have come to exist on this planet of ours which I knew to be base, materialistic and self-interested and whose principles I knew to be far from embracing any notion of real freedom. I went on: 'How did you manage to bring such a thing into existence?'

'The rate of suicides, Monsieur,' he replied, 'had increased so much in the five years following the Great Exhibition of 1889[3] that the situation became urgent. People were killing themselves all over the place – in the street, at parties, in restaurants, at the theatre, on trains, and even at presidential receptions, everywhere, in fact. It was not only a rather unedifying spectacle to those who, like myself, are actually rather keen on living, but also it gave a bad example to children. So it became necessary to, as it were, centralize the procedure.'

'Why had the rate gone up so dramatically?'

'I've no idea really. I suppose people are a bit more mature these days. They've only just begun to see what it's all about when they realize they can't come to terms with life. Fate, the government, it's all the same nowadays I suppose. People realize it's a big con and once they've realized that they decide to chuck it in. When they see that providence is just as likely to lie, to trick, to steal and betray human beings as their elected representatives, they get mad. They can't give a new kind of providence a trial period of three months, and then change it as they could their embers of parliament, if you'll forgive my little joke, so they get the hell out of what they see as a pretty wretched situation.'

'Really!'

'Well, it's not my own view, as I say, but . . .'

'Would you mind telling me how this institute of yours actually functions?'

'It would be a great pleasure, Monsieur. You could yourself join, of course, any time you liked. It's just like any other club.'

'Club?'

'Absolutely, Monsieur. Founded by some of the most eminent men in the country. The most generous of souls. The finest minds.'

With a hearty laugh, he added: 'And I can assure you, Monsieur, that a very good time is had by all!'

'What, here?'

'Oh yes, Monsieur, here most especially.'

'You do surprise me.'

'But when you think, Monsieur! The whole thing is . . . none of our members has to experience fear of death. That's what spoils every imaginable pleasure on earth!'

'But if they belong to this club, how is it they don't actually commit suicide?'

'Oh, that's not a prerequisite to membership. You don't have to kill yourself to belong.'

'Well how does it work then?'

'Let me explain. Given the unacceptably high and rising rate of suicide and given the appalling spectacle it offers to the public at large, a charitable society was formed whose sole mission was to provide a haven for the desperate and a means whereby they

could avail themselves of peaceful death which would also be
. . . how shall I put it . . . *undreaded.*'

'Who on earth could you get to authorize something like
that?'

'Oh, General Boulanger,[4] during his brief period in power.
He was hugely generous over this. In fact, it was probably the
only good thing he managed to achieve, as it happens. So, as I
say, a charity was set up by a body of well-informed, clear-
sighted, and . . . unsentimental men. They decided to build, right
in the middle of Paris, a kind of temple of contempt for death.
To start with people were extremely frightened of this place.
Nobody would come near it. Then the founders put on a big gala
evening on the premises to launch it. Madame Sarah Bernhardt
attended it, as well as Judic, Théo, Granier and a number of
other stars including Monsieur de Reszké, Coquelin, Mounet-
Sully, and Paulus.[5] Following that, they produced a series of
concerts. And finally a season of plays. They put on Dumas,
Meilhac, Halévy and Sardou.[6] We only had one flop and that
was a piece by Monsieur Becque[7] which was seen as a bit of a
downer here but it went on to become a huge success at the
Comédie Française[8]. In the end, *le tout Paris* came and the place
took off from then on, really.'

'Party time! How macabre!'

'Not at all. Death needn't be sad. Simply neutral or indifferent,
that's all. We've even made it fun! We've made it fragrant! We've
made it flowery! We're learning by doing. People see there's
nothing to it, after all!'

'I can see how people might come for a bit of a celebration
but . . . did anybody come for . . . that?'

'Not immediately, no. People were afraid.'

'But what about later on?'

'Yes, people came.'

'Lots?'

'Masses. We've had more than forty a day. Almost as many
as drownings in the Seine.'

'Who started the whole thing off?'

'Oh, one of our members, actually.'

'A real enthusiast, then?'

'Not really, no. He was in deep trouble. Huge debts. He'd been losing heavily at baccarat for three months.'

'I see.'

'The second was an eccentric sort of Englishman. We took out advertisements in the press, you see. We explained our procedures. Offered all kinds of different deaths. Choice. The greatest response came, I have to say, from the poor.'

'But, I mean, how do you actually set about it? What do you actually do?'

'Perhaps you'd like a tour of the place? I can explain as we go along.'

'Yes, thank you.'

He picked up his hat, opened the door for me and went on to usher me into a gaming room full of gentlemen at the tables much as in any other club. We then passed through various reception rooms where there was a great deal of animated conversation going on. I had rarely been in such a lively atmosphere. Very gay and convivial it all was. As I said as much, the secretary replied:

'Oh it's a top spot. Anybody who's anybody belongs. To show how much contempt they have for death. And once they're in, lest anyone think they really are afraid of it, they feel an obligation to show how relaxed and happy they feel. It makes for an extremely good atmosphere. Lots of laughter and fun, you know. Wit is very highly prized. Here you've either got it or you learn it. It's arguably *the* place to see and be seen in the whole of Paris. So much so that there'll soon be an annexe for women. They insist on being part of the whole thing.'

'Despite the fact that you've got a lot of suicides going on all the time here?'

'Yes, as I mentioned, between forty and fifty per day. Very few from the upper échelons of society, admittedly, quite a few middle-class types and then plenty of the other poor devils.'

'And tell me, how does it actually work?'

'Asphyxiation. Gradual, of course.'

'How do you do it?'

'By gas. It's one we invented ourselves. We've taken a patent out on it. On the other side of the building you'll find the public entrances. Three inconspicuous little doors leading in from the back streets. When a man or a woman comes to us, we start off by asking a few questions. Then we offer help, support and a measure of protection. With the client's agreement, we open up an enquiry and quite often we are able to rescue them.'

'Where does the money come from?'

'We have generous funds in our possession. The cost of membership is extremely high. And of course a lot of prestige comes from making donations to the cause. The names of all sponsors are published regularly in the *Figaro*[9]. On top of that, every wealthy would-be suicide has to pay 1,000 francs. It's means-tested, with no charge at all for the poor.'

'How do you test for poverty?'

'That, Monsieur, is usually pretty obvious! Besides which, they are required to provide a certificate of need from their local chief of police. I can't tell you how gruesome it is when those sorts of people arrive. I've only actually been to that side of the building once, and I shan't go back in a hurry, I can tell you. As a venue, so to speak, it's as good as here, only perhaps not quite as elegant and comfortable. But the people! You should see what sort appear! Old men and women in rags who've come simply to finish off what they've been doing slowly for months on end, that's to say, dying of poverty, existing on handouts, living a dog's life on the margins of society; women come in, all skin and bone in tattered clothing, sick, paralysed some of them, with no chance in the world. They tell us their story, then they say more or less I can't go on like this. I'm not good for anything any more, can't even scrape a living. We had one woman who came to us aged eighty-seven. Lost all her children and grand-children. She'd been sleeping rough for six weeks. I tell you it turned my stomach, that one. But all sorts come, as I say. Some, as soon as they come in, they don't mince words. "Where is it?" they ask, and we take them there straight away and get it over with as soon as possible.'

I was feeling pretty nervous myself by this stage and heard myself say: 'And . . . where *is* it, exactly?'

'Here.'

He opened a door, saying: 'Go in, do. This part is for the

exclusive use of club members. It's the one we use least frequently. So far, we've had only eleven extinctions here.'

'Is that what you call them? Extinctions?'

'That's right, Monsieur, do go in.'

I hung back for a moment, then finally entered. The room was the most delightful kind of conservatory, with stained glass windows of the palest blue, the softest pink and a beautiful apple green. Between them hung tapestries showing pastoral scenes. All around the room were divans, superb potted palms, and flowers, mostly fragrant roses. There were books on occasional tables, copies of the *Revue des Deux Mondes*,[10] boxes of excellent cigars and, most oddly of all to my mind, Vichy pastilles[11] in a little *bonbonnière*.

As I expressed my surprise, my guide explained: 'Oh yes, people come in here simply to talk,' he said, adding, 'And the public rooms are very similar, just a little more simply furnished.'

'How does it work?' I asked.

He pointed to a chaise-longue covered in cream crêpe-de-chine picked out with white embroidery. It was positioned under a large shrub, of a variety unknown to me, but which was underplanted with a circle of mignonette.

The secretary added in a quieter tone: 'The flower and the fragrance are customized. The gas, which is odourless, gives death the perfume of the person's favourite flower. We volatize it with various essences to produce this effect. Would you like a taster?'

'No thanks!' I said hurriedly. 'Not yet.'

He started laughing: 'Oh dear me, Monsieur, there's absolutely no danger involved. I've tried it out myself, many times!'

Not wishing to look like a coward, I said: 'Oh all right, then . . .'

'Just stretch out on the *Lull-a-Bye*.'

None too confidently, I first sat, then stretched out on the crêpe-de-chine-covered chair. Almost immediately, a delicious haze of mignonette wafted all around me. I opened my mouth, the deeper to breathe it in. I was now so relaxed that I could feel myself drifting into the most exquisite oblivion, the first stage of asphyxiation by a powerful and irresistible opiate.

Then I felt my arm being shaken.

'Monsieur! Monsieur!' the secretary was calling gleefully. 'I think you were really getting into it there!'

Another voice, real this time, with nothing remotely hazy about it, was calling in less refined tones: 'Monsieur? You all right, Monsieur?'

My dream vanished into thin air. I saw the Seine shimmering before me in the sun, as up the path came stomping the local *garde-champêtre*,[12] his right hand now touching the silver-braided peak of his black uniform cap.

'Good morning to you, Marinel. And where are you off to then?' I replied.

'Got to register a drowning fetched up near Morillons. Another one just chucked himself in the drink, Monsieur. Even taken off his trousers, this one had, to tie round his legs, I don't know, indeed . . .'

MOTHER OF INVENTION

I

An elegant victoria[1] to which were harnessed two superb black horses was waiting in front of the steps leading up to the town house. It was about half-past five on a late June evening and between the roofs which enclosed the main courtyard the sky looked bright, clear and inviting.

The Comtesse de Mascaret appeared at the top of the steps just as her husband, returning home, passed under the carriage entrance. He stopped and grew pale at the sight of his wife. She looked extremely beautiful, svelte and distinguished with her long, oval face, her honey-and-ivory complexion, grey eyes and dark hair. Without acknowledging or even seeming to notice him, she got into the carriage with such grace and style that he felt a deep pang of the old jealousy which had consumed him for so long. Approaching, he greeted her: 'Going for a ride?' he asked.

Contemptuously she spat out a mere five words: 'What does it look like?'

'To the Bois?'

'More than likely.'

'And might I be allowed to accompany you?'

'It's your carriage.'

Unsurprised by her tone he got in, sat down next to his wife and called out: 'To the Bois!'

The footman leapt up on to the seat by the coachman, and the horses, after pawing the ground and nodding as trained, trotted out into the street. The couple remained side by side in silence. He was about to start a conversation but her face was so stubbornly set that he did not dare. Finally he slid his hand stealthily towards the gloved hand of his wife and touched it as if by chance. The gesture she made to remove her arm was so brusque and conveyed such aversion that he beat a hasty and anxious retreat. This was most untypical of his usually highly authoritarian, not to say tyrannical character.

'Gabrielle!' he murmured.

'What do you want?' she asked, without turning her head.

'I think you're adorable.'

She said nothing in response but leaned back in her carriage like an irritated queen. They were driving now up the Champs Élysées towards the Arc de Triomphe de l'Étoile. The huge monument at the end of the long avenue spread its colossal arch across a sky of red. The sun appeared to be setting directly on top of it, casting a haze of fire on the horizon as it sank. The stream of glittering carriages with glints of copper and silver in the harnesses reflected in the dazzling crystal of the coach lanterns, flowed in two separate currents, one towards the Bois, the other towards the city.

The Comte de Mascaret continued: 'Gabrielle, my dear . . .'

Unable to bear it a moment longer, she turned round to him in exasperation.

'Oh leave me *alone*, will you? Can't I even go off on my own in the carriage any more?'

He ignored her and continued: 'You've never been prettier than you are today.'

Losing patience entirely, she could no longer contain her rage.

'It's a pity you should think so because I swear to you here and now – I shall never again be yours.'

What she said amazed him and for a moment he was dumbstruck. Very quickly, however, he changed from supplicant lover to brutal master of the situation. His violent nature began to reassert itself as he snapped: 'What's that supposed to mean?'

She repeated her words quietly even though neither of the servants could have heard above the deafening rumble of the wheels.

'That's more like you: "What's that supposed to mean?" Do you really want me to tell you?'

'Yes.'

'You want me to tell you everything?'

'Yes.'

'Everything I've always felt in my heart ever since I became the victim of your appalling selfishness?'

He flushed with a mixture of astonishment and annoyance. Through clenched teeth he snarled, 'Go ahead.'

He was a tall, broad-shouldered man with a large red beard. People thought him good-looking, a gentleman and a man of the world. He also had the reputation of being a perfect husband and a model father. For the first time since leaving the house she turned and looked him straight in the eye.

'You're not going to like what you hear, but let me tell you this. I'm prepared for the worst. I'm ready to face whatever I have to. I'm not afraid of a single thing any more. Least of all, at this moment, you!'

He too was looking her straight in the eye. Already he was beginning to tremble with rage. He murmured, 'You're mad!'

'No I'm not! But I refuse from now on to be put through the dreadful torture of motherhood which you have inflicted on me for the last eleven years! I want to live, at last, as my own woman, as I have every right to, as every woman has a right to!'

He grew pale again and stammered: 'I don't understand.'

'Oh yes you do. It's now three months since I last gave birth. Despite all your efforts at disfigurement I'm still beautiful, as you just pointed out. Now that you find me attractive again I suppose it's time to make me pregnant once more.'

'You're out of your mind.'

'No I'm not. I'm thirty and we have seven children. We've been married for eleven years and I expect you'd like us to carry on like this for another ten. After that, maybe, you might just stop feeling jealous of me.'

He gripped her by the arm and pulled her roughly to him.

'I will not allow you to speak to me like that a minute longer!'

'And I don't intend to stop till I've said everything I have to say to you. If you try and stop me I shall raise my voice so that

the servants can hear. The only reason I let you in was because
these two could witness what I have to say and restrain you if
necessary. Listen. You've always been repellent to me and I've
been perfectly honest with you about it. I never lie, Monsieur.
You married me against my wishes. You forced my needy
parents to hand me over to you because you were rich. They
made me do it and I have to say I wept. So in effect you bought
me. And as soon as you had me in your power, as soon as I
became your companion, someone who was attached to you,
who had to put up with your intimidation and your manipu-
lation, as soon as I became your devoted wife and tried to love
you as much as it was possible for me to do, you turned jealous.
You became the most jealous man that's ever lived. You spied
on me. You were low. Your methods were base. You behaved
in a way degrading to yourself and insulting to me. I hadn't been
married more than eight months before you started thinking me
capable of all kinds of affairs. You said so to my face. The
shame of it! And since you could hardly prevent me from being
beautiful and attractive, to be considered in every drawing room
and by every newspaper one of the prettiest women in Paris,
you looked for ways to remove me from this atmosphere of
adulation. You hit on the disgusting plan of making me perman-
ently pregnant so that in the end men would be put off. Don't
try and deny it! I didn't realize for a long time. I never guessed.
But you even bragged about it to your sister. She told me. She's
fond of me and she thought it was barbaric and obscene! Don't
pretend you've forgotten all those fights! The locks you forced,
the doors you broke down. What a life you made me endure for
eleven years! A brood mare in your stud. And as soon as I did
get pregnant, you yourself found me unattractive and I never
saw you for months. I was packed off to the country, to the
family château. Put out to grass, to pasture, till I dropped
the foal. And then when I reappeared, fresh and pretty again,
indestructible and still an object of attraction, when at last I
could hope to live as a wealthy young woman of the world,
once again you would become jealous. Again you would start
pursuing me with that wretched desire with which you're consumed this very minute as you're sitting there. It's not a desire

to possess me – I would never have refused you that – it's the desire to disfigure me! And something else happened which was equally despicable. It was a mystery to me and it took me a long time to discover what was going on. But in the end I became expert at knowing how your mind worked. I realized that the bond between you and your children was based on the security they gave you while I was expecting them. Your love for them was in direct proportion to your hatred for me. They represented the temporary removal of your cowardly fears. It was with glee that you watched me grow big with them. How often did I feel that glee in you! I saw it in your eyes! I knew it. You love your children as victories over me, not as your own flesh and blood. They are your triumphs over my youth and charm. They counteracted all the compliments I received, as well as those made outside my hearing. You were proud of the children. You paraded them with you, took them for rides in the Bois, for donkey rides at Montmorency.[2] You took them to matinées where you could be seen surrounded by them and where everybody would say over and over again what a marvellous father you were . . .'

Suddenly he grabbed hold of her wrist with brutal savagery and gripped it so hard that she stopped speaking, stifling a scream. Quietly he said to her: 'Listen to me. I love my children! What you've just said is shameful coming from a mother. You're *mine*, I tell you! I am master here. Your master! I can make you do exactly what I want . . . whenever I want. I have the law on my side!'

He tried to crush her fingers in his huge, muscular fist. White with pain, she made an effort to extract her hand from his vice-like grip. It hurt so much that she was breathless. Tears came to her eyes.

'You see?' he went on, 'you see now who is the master? Who is the stronger?'

When he loosened his grip slightly, she spoke again: 'Would you call me a practising Christian?'

Surprised, he stammered: 'Of course I would.'

'Do you think I believe in God?'

'Of course.'

'Do you think I could lie to you while I was swearing to something with my hand on the altar containing the body of Christ?'

'No.'

'Will you come with me then to a church?'

'Whatever for?'

'You'll see. Will you?'

'If you insist.'

Raising her voice she cried: 'Philippe!'

The coachman, without taking his eyes off the horses, turned his head slightly and seemed to incline his ear towards his mistress alone.

'Take us to the church of Saint-Philippe du Roule!'

The victoria, having just reached one of the entrances to the Bois, turned round and headed back towards Paris. Husband and wife exchanged not a word throughout the return trip. When the carriage stopped in front of the entrance to the church, Madame de Mascaret jumped down and went in, closely followed by the Comte.

She went directly to the choir railings, fell on her knees in front of a chair and began to pray. She prayed for a long time. Standing behind her, he noticed she was weeping. She wept silently as women do in moments of particularly painful sorrow. Her whole body moved in a kind of ripple, ending in a small sob which she tried to stifle with her fingers. Considering that this had gone on long enough, the Comte de Mascaret tapped her on the shoulder. She recoiled from the contact as if touched by fire. Getting to her feet she looked him once more straight in the eye.

'You can do what you like, I'm not afraid. You can kill me if you feel so inclined but this is what I have to tell you: one, just one of the children, is not yours. I swear this to you before God who is my witness here. It was the only revenge I could take on you and the only defence against your abominable male tyranny, the forced labour of giving birth to which you sentenced me. And who was my lover? You will never know! You will suspect every man and you will never find out. I gave myself to him with neither love nor pleasure but simply so as to deceive you. Which child is his? You will never know that either. There are seven, take your pick! I had intended to tell you this much later. Revenge is never complete till the person knows. But you forced me to confess today and that's what I've done.'

She fled through the church to the open door and out into the street. She kept expecting to hear behind her the footsteps of the husband she had so openly defied and to be hurled on to the pavement by a stunning blow from his fist. Hearing nothing, however, and leaping into the carriage, tense and panting with fear, she called to the coachman 'Home!' and the horses set off at a brisk trot.

II

Closeted in her room, the Comtesse awaited dinnertime as a condemned man waits for the hour of execution. How would he react? Had he returned? She was well used to his rages, his violence and his domineering manner but still she wondered what he had planned, what was in store for her and what decision he had come to. The house was silent. She looked every few minutes at the hands of the clock. Her maid, having dressed her for dinner, had now left.

Eight o'clock struck. Almost immediately there were two knocks at her door.

'Come in.'

The butler appeared, saying: 'Madame la Comtesse, dinner is served.'

'Has the Comte returned?'

'Yes, Madame la Comtesse. Monsieur le Comte is in the dining room.'

For a few seconds she wondered whether or not to take with her the little revolver she had bought some time previously in anticipation of the scene she imagined might soon take place. Then remembering that all the children would be present she took only a bottle of smelling salts.

When she entered the dining room her husband was standing by his chair, waiting. They bowed to each other curtly and sat down. The children then took their places: the three sons with their tutor, the abbé Marin, to the right of their mother, the three daughters with their English governess, Mademoiselle Smith, on her left. The youngest child, a baby of three months, remained upstairs in its room with a nurse.

The three girls, ranging in age from ten years old downwards, were all blonde and wore blue frocks trimmed with white lace. They looked like three exquisite little dolls. Already pretty, each one showed every sign of becoming as beautiful as her mother as she grew. The three sons, two with chestnut-coloured hair and the nine-year-old eldest already dark, looked likely to grow into tall, sturdy, broad-shouldered men. There was a strong family resemblance between them and the same strong, vigorous blood flowed in their veins.

The abbé said grace as usual when no guests were present. When strangers were entertained the children did not eat with their parents. The Comtesse was in the grip of a feeling she had not anticipated. She kept her eyes lowered as the Comte, with anguish and doubt in his own, looked from one to the other, first of the three boys, then of the girls. Suddenly, as he put down his wineglass, it shattered and pink liquid spread over the tablecloth. The sound of this slight accident made the Comtesse leap from her chair. For the first time husband and wife looked at one another. From then on, despite the wave of loathing which rose every time their eyes met, they kept raising and levelling them at each other like a pair of pistols.

The abbé, aware of an atmosphere between the couple but unaware of its cause, tried several times to get a conversation going. He tried one topic after another, eliciting not the slightest response. No one spoke a single word.

The Comtesse, with instinctive feminine diplomacy and aware of her social obligations, tried several times to reply. In vain. She could not string two sentences together such was the turmoil within her. Her own voice frightened her in the silence of the vast room where only the clink of silver on porcelain could now be heard.

Leaning forward towards her the Comte suddenly said: 'Here and now, surrounded by your children, will you swear to me that what you told me earlier on is true?'

The hatred now seething in her veins gave her the courage to stand up suddenly and respond to the question. Raising both her hands, one towards her sons and one towards her daughters, she said unfalteringly in a firm and resolute voice: 'On the heads of my children I swear that what I told you is true.'

He got up and threw his napkin on the table in fury. Turning, he hurled his chair against the wall and without another word left the room. Heaving a great sigh of relief as if after some great victory, she went on calmly: 'Pay no attention, my darlings. Your father has just received some very bad news. He is in great distress as a result. It will pass in a few days.'

She then began to talk to the abbé and Mademoiselle Smith. She brought the children into the conversation and spoke tenderly to them, filling their little hearts with the sweetness that comes from a mother's devoted attention. When dinner was over she moved with everyone else to the drawing room. She got the older ones talking and told the little ones stories. When bedtime came for them all she gave them each a long kiss. Then, having sent them off to bed, she retired alone to her room.

She felt certain he would come. With her children out of the way, she decided to defend her body the same way she had preserved her dignity earlier on. In the pocket of her dressing-gown she slid the revolver, this time loaded. The clocks chimed the hours as they passed. Eventually every sound in the house ceased. All that could be heard was the noise of the fiacres in the street beyond, filtering through the heavily tapestried walls of her room as a distant, muffled rumble.

She waited, alert and expectant, with all fear gone. She was ready for anything now and felt something akin to triumph. She had found something that would torment him every hour of the day for as long as he lived. The first light of dawn crept through the fringes at the bottom of her curtains and still he had not come to her room. Stupefied, she realized now he had no intention of doing so. Having locked herself in and shot the bolt she had had fixed for security, she climbed into bed and lay with her eyes open, thinking, wondering and trying to guess what his plan might be.

Later, as she brought in her mistress's tea, the maid gave her a letter from the Comte. In it he wrote that he was going on a long journey, adding in a postscript that his lawyer would see that she had everything she needed...

III

Six Years Later

In the coupé[3] carrying them home from a performance at the Opéra, the Comte and Comtesse de Mascaret, sitting side by side, were again silent. Suddenly the husband said to his wife: 'Gabrielle!'

'What is it?'

'Don't you think this has gone on long enough now?'

'What has?'

'The torture you've been putting me through for the past six years.'

'I can't help that, I'm afraid.'

'Tell me which one. Please.'

'Never.'

'Just try and imagine what it's like for me. I can't set eyes on my children, I can't feel them around me, ever, without this terrible doubt crushing the life out of me. Tell me which one and I promise to forgive, to treat him or her exactly like the others.'

'I can't. I have no right.'

'Don't you see I can't bear it any longer? It's destroying me. This question always, always torturing me every time I see them. It's driving me insane.'

'You've suffered a lot, have you?' she asked.

He replied in a small, sad voice: 'I've just told you. Every day is an unbearable torment to me. Why do you think I came back? Why, if I didn't love each and every one of them, do you think I returned to this house and lived here with both you and them? Oh, you've been so cruel to me! You know very well I love my children with all my heart. I'm an old-fashioned father to them just as I'm an old-fashioned husband to you. I'm a man of instinct, a man of nature, an old-fashioned type of man. I do admit you made me hideously jealous because you're a woman. You're practically a different race. You have a different kind of soul, different needs. Oh I'll never forget what you said to me! From then onwards I didn't care what happened to you. I didn't kill you because you were the only means on earth I had of discovering which of our . . . sorry, which of *your* children was not mine. I held back but I've suffered more than you can possibly imagine. I dare not love them now apart from the two elder ones, possibly. I daren't look at them or call them or kiss them. I can't take any of them on my knee any more without wondering: Is this the one? For six years, you have to admit, I've behaved well, even generously towards you. Tell me the truth and I swear I won't do you any harm.'

In the darkness of the carriage interior he sensed that she was beginning to yield, that she might after all speak.

'Please, please,' he said, 'I implore you.'

She murmured: 'You may find that I have been more guilty than you think. But I could not, I could no longer carry on with that terrible life of pregnancy after pregnancy. I had only one way of driving you away from my bed. I lied before God, and I lied on the heads of my children. I have never been unfaithful to you in my life.'

In the shadows he grabbed her arm and held it as he had on that terrible drive to the Bois. He stammered: 'Oh will it never end? Am I to be racked by doubt forever? How can I believe you now? How can any woman be trusted? I'll never know what to think in future! I'd rather you'd said it was Jacques or it was Jeanne!'

The carriage was pulling into the courtyard. As it stopped in front of the steps the Comte got down and as usual offered his wife his arm to mount the steps. When they reached the first floor, he said: 'May I have a few more minutes with you?'

'Certainly,' she replied.

They went into the little drawing room where a footman, surprised, lit candles for them. When they were alone again the Comte continued: 'How can I know which is the real truth? I begged you a thousand times to tell me but you kept silent. You were inflexible and inexorable. There was no way I could get through to you. And now you say you were lying all along. That for six years you let me believe such a dreadful thing. No! It must be today that you're lying, perhaps because you feel sorry for me, I don't know.'

With both conviction and sincerity ringing in her voice she replied: 'Had I not done so, I should have had another four children by this time.'

'What a way for a mother to speak!' he cried.

'Look,' she said, 'I have no maternal feelings whatsoever for babies I never had. It's quite enough to be mother to the ones I already do have and to love them with all my heart. We are women of the civilized world, Monsieur. We refuse, absolutely, to remain the repopulation machines of the world. As she rose to leave he took both of her hands in his.

'One word, just one, Gabrielle. Tell me the real truth will you?'

'I have just told it to you. I was never once unfaithful to you in my life.'

He looked at her directly. She was so beautiful with her grey eyes like the winter sky. In the deep, dark night of her hair a tiara with a dusting of diamonds shone like the Milky Way. Suddenly he had a strong, instinctive feeling that this human being standing before him was no longer a woman whose destiny in life was to ensure the survival of the species. He suddenly saw her as the strange and mysterious incarnation of all our complex desires accumulated over the centuries. It was this being which diverted man from his primitive notion of predestination and towards a more mystical kind of beauty, evanescent and impalpable. Some of this beauty blooms in our dreams alone, made lovelier still by everything with which civilization has surrounded woman: she embodies the spirit of poetry and idealism which we crave even more than the satisfaction of our other appetites.

Her husband remained standing before her, stunned by this belated and complex discovery. Though he could not quite understand it all yet, he knew that it had something to do with the cause of his former jealousy.

Finally he spoke: 'I believe you. I sense that you are not lying. Before, I thought you were lying all the time.'

She held out her hand to him.

'Well? Friends?'

He took her hand. Kissing it, he replied: 'Friends. Thank you, Gabrielle.'

He left, looking at her still and wondering that she could remain so beautiful. Stirring within him he could feel a strange emotion, perhaps more awesome, he thought, than good old-fashioned love itself.

WHO KNOWS?

I

My God! I can't believe it! At last, at long last, I am actually going to put down in black and white what happened to me! That's if I am able! If I dare! The whole story is so weird, so impossible to explain, so . . . crazy!

If I were not absolutely certain of what I saw and sure that there is no gap in the chain of events I am about to relate, if I were not totally convinced that there is no possibility of a mistake about what happened, I would simply think it was a hallucination or that I had been fooled by some sort of strange illusion. And when all is said and done, who knows anyway?

I am at present in a psychiatric clinic but I came here voluntarily as a precautionary measure because I was afraid. Only one other human being knows my history and that is the doctor here. I am going to write it down, though quite why, I am not sure. Perhaps to get it off my chest. The weight of it on my mind all the time is practically unbearable. It's a waking nightmare. These are the facts.

I have always been something of a loner, a bit dreamy, you might say, but well-meaning, unambitious, with no particular animosity towards my fellow human beings and fairly content with my lot. I have always lived alone because of a certain creeping unease I feel in the presence of other people. I don't know how to explain it. I am not averse to seeing people – I mean, I go out and eat with friends and so forth but if I feel they have been near me for any prolonged period of time, even the closest begin to get so much on my nerves that I have this overwhelming, increasingly urgent desire to see them gone or to go off and be by myself.

It is actually more than a desire. It is a real need, something absolutely essential to me. If I were forced to stay in company, and if I had to stay not so much listening as simply hearing the conversation of other people, I know that some kind of accident would happen to me. I'm not sure what exactly. Who knows, after all? I'd probably faint, I suppose, yes, that's it, I'd pass out!

I love my solitude so much that I cannot even bear to have others sleeping under the same roof as me. I could never live in Paris, for example. I die a slow death when I'm there. It's a kind of annihilation of the spirit for me; both my mind and my body are tortured by the consciousness of a vast, seething mass of humanity living around me there, awake or asleep. I tell you, other people's sleep is even more painful to me than their speech! I can never rest while I know, while I can feel behind that wall, say, the existence of others whose powers of reasoning are temporarily and regularly shut down.

Why am I like this? Who knows? Perhaps the reason is very simple. Maybe I just tire very quickly of anything that is not happening to myself. And there must be thousands like me. There are two kinds of people in the world. First there are those who need others and who are entertained, distracted, even soothed by company. Solitude for this kind of person is a huge, unremitting burden to bear, something as difficult and daunting as crossing a desert or climbing a dangerous glacier. Then there's the second type of person who gets tired, irritated and finally bored stiff in the company of others. For this kind of person, solitude is a balm, something they can lie back and bask in while their thoughts are allowed to roam free.

In other words we're talking about a perfectly normal psychological given. Some people are good at living extrovertly, others introvertly. I happen to be one of those whose capacity for attention to the outside world is very small and quickly exhausted. As soon as it reaches its limit I feel this intolerable unease throughout both my mind and my body.

As a result of this I have become, or rather had become, very attached to inanimate objects which were as important to me as human beings. My house has, or had, become a world in which I lived a solitary yet active life, surrounded by familiar objects, furniture and *bibelots* as lovable to me as human faces. Little by little I filled my house with these things and lived in their midst as happily as in the arms of a beloved woman whose warm, familiar embrace has become a prerequisite to a calm, untroubled existence.

I had had the house built within an attractive garden by which it was set back a little way from the road. It was situated on the outskirts of a town to which I could go whenever I felt like a little social life. All my servants lived in a building some way off at the end of a vegetable garden surrounded by a high wall. So beautifully soothing to me was the dark enfolding of the night in the silence of my secluded home, nestling as it did under the leaves of the huge surrounding trees, that every evening I used to put off going to bed the longer to savour it.

This particular night, they were putting on a production of *Sigurd*[1] at the local theatre. It was the first time I had heard this beautiful, fairytale opera and I enjoyed it enormously. I was walking happily home, my ears full of the lovely arias, in my mind's eye seeing again the magical scenery. It was very, very dark indeed, so dark, in fact, that I could hardly see the road, and several times nearly fell into the ditch. From the tollgate to my house it's about a kilometre, maybe more – in other words, about a twenty-minute gentle walk. It was between one and half past one in the morning. The sky cleared a little above me and the sad old crescent moon of the last quarter appeared. The new crescent moon, the one which rises at about four or five in the afternoon, is bright and cheerful like polished silver but the one rising after midnight is a dismal, reddish, rather gloomy one, a real Sabbath moon. Anybody with nocturnal habits will tell you that, I'm sure. The first, however slender, however threadlike, throws a shining brilliance that fills the heart with delight and casts sharp shadows on the earth. The last hardly sheds more than a dying glow and that so dull as to make hardly any shadow at all.

I could see in the distance the dense mass which was my garden when, out of nowhere, it seemed, a sort of unease began to creep over me at the thought of entering it. I slackened my pace. The air was balmy. The great clump of trees ahead looked like a tomb beneath which my house lay buried.

I opened my gate and began to walk up the long avenue of sycamores leading to the house, arched to make a vault-like tunnel, with banks of flowers on either side, then lawns where flowerbeds formed vague ovals among the pale shadows. As I approached the house, I was gripped by a strange feeling of foreboding. I stopped in my tracks. There was not a sound to be heard. Not a leaf rustled. What on earth was the matter with me, I wondered. I had been coming home like this for ten years with never a hint of any anxiety in my mind. I was not frightened. I have never been afraid of the night. Had I spotted some prowler or burglar, anger would have translated itself into physical action and I would have hurled myself at him without the slightest hesitation. Besides, I was armed. I had my revolver on me. But I never touched it. I knew that I needed to control by myself the fear I could feel stirring into life within me.

What was it? Some premonition? The mysterious kind of premonition which grips a man's senses when they are about to witness something inexplicable? Perhaps so. Who knows? As I moved forward, my flesh began to creep. When I reached the outside walls of my vast house with its closed shutters I felt I needed to wait a few minutes before opening the front door and going in. I sat on a garden seat under my drawing room windows. Trembling a little, I leaned my head against the wall and focused on the shadowy bushes beyond. For the first few moments I noticed nothing unusual. I had a little roaring in the ears but I get that often. It's as if I can hear trains passing, bells ringing, or the stamp of a crowd on the march.

Soon, however, this roaring became more distinct, sharper in tone and more specific. I had been wrong in thinking this was the usual sound of blood coursing through my arteries. This was a very particular sound which, however difficult to define, was coming, there was no doubt about this now, from within my house itself.

Through the wall I could hear it continuously, more of a tremor than a noise, the vague shifting of a host of things, as if all the furniture were being picked up, shaken, then dragged quietly off. Well! As you can imagine, for a very long time I wondered whether I was hearing things. But having glued my ear to the shutter to try and find out what this disturbance inside my home was, I came to the firm conclusion that something incomprehensible and abnormal was going on. I was not so much frightened as ... how can I put it? ... terrified with astonishment. I did not load my revolver, guessing quite correctly, as it turned out, that there was no earthly reason to do so. I waited.

For a long time I continued to wait, not knowing what to do, with a mind perfectly clear though full of trepidation. By now I was standing listening to the noise increase at times to an ear-shattering pitch. At other times, too, this mysterious upheaval sounded like a growl of impatience or even of anger. Suddenly ashamed of being such a coward, I got hold of my bunch of keys, chose the one I needed, rammed it into the lock, turned it twice, then flung the door open with such force I sent it crashing against the interior wall.

It sounded like gunshot as the noise echoed from top to bottom of my entire house, from which came now a thunderous reverberation. It was so sudden and so deafening that I recoiled a few paces in horror. Although I knew it was still useless, this time I did take my revolver out of its holster.

Again, I waited for ... I don't know how long ... a little while I suppose. What I could now hear was the extraordinary sound of steps coming down the stairway and on to the parquet and the carpets – the sound not of shoes or of human footwear but the clatter of wooden and iron crutches clashing like cymbals, or so it seemed. Suddenly, what should I see waddling over the threshold of my own room but the big armchair in which I used to sit to read. It came out into the garden. Others from the drawing room followed it and were followed in turn by low settees crawling crocodile-like along on their squat little legs. All my other chairs leapt out like goats, with footstools lolloping alongside.

You can imagine what I felt like! I slid behind some shrubbery and remained crouching there watching the procession continue to pass by, for they were all leaving, one after the other, quickly or slowly, according to size and weight. My piano, my full-size grand piano galloped wildly past me with a musical murmur in its flank; the smallest objects such as hairbrushes and crystal chandelier droplets crawled like ants on the ground accompanied by glass goblets on which the moonlight cast little glow-worms of phosphorescence; curtains, hangings, tapestries spread like pools and stretched out octopus-like tentacles of fabric as they swam past. My desk hove into view, a rare eighteenth-century piece now containing some photographs and all the letters tracing the sad history of my painful love-life.

I suddenly lost my fear. I threw myself on it and held it down as if it had been a burglar or a woman attempting to flee. However, there was no stopping it and despite all my angry efforts I could not even slow down its inexorable progress. In my desperate struggle against this appalling power I was thrown to the ground, then rolled over and dragged along the gravel. In no time, the rest of the furniture in its train began to trample all over me, bruising my legs in the process. When I let go of the desk the rest of the pieces careered over my body as a cavalry charge mows down a fallen rider.

Frightened witless, I managed to drag myself away from the avenue and hide myself again behind the trees, from which position I watched everything down to the smallest, the most modest of my former possessions, including some of whose existence I was not even aware, all disappear.

Then in the distance, from within my home now echoing as empty houses do, I heard a tremendous noise of doors shutting. My house from attic to cellar rang with the sound of slamming until the door which I myself had just recently opened in terror finally also closed.

I too now fled and ran towards the town. I did not regain any degree of composure until I was again in the streets where late-night revellers were making their way home. I went to a hotel where I was known and rang the bell. I dusted myself down before going in to explain that I had lost my keys, among them the one for the garden gate where my servants slept in the separate house within the fence protecting my fruit and vegetables from thieves.

I dived into the bed they gave me and covered myself up to the eyes. I could not sleep, however, and as I lay waiting for daylight I could hear my heart pounding. I had ordered my servants to be alerted at dawn, and at seven o'clock my manservant came knocking at the door.

He looked devastated.

'Something dreadful happened in the night, Monsieur,' he said.

'Oh? What was that?'

'Monsieur has been robbed of every single article in the house, every single one, down to the very smallest piece.'

This news pleased me. I have no idea why. Who knows? I felt perfectly in control, certain that I could pretend and that I need tell no one what I had seen. I was sure I could keep this terrible secret hidden in my subconscious. I replied: 'It must be the same people who stole my keys. We must let the police know at once. I shall join you in a few minutes after I've got dressed.'

The inquiry lasted five months. Nothing was discovered. Not a single piece of mine was recovered and not the slightest trace of robbers ever found. My God! Imagine if I'd said what I knew! If I'd said a word about that, it would have been myself rather than any robbers who would have been locked up for believing such a thing! Oh yes, I kept my mouth shut all right! But I never refurnished the house. That would have been pointless. The whole business would have started up again. I wished never to return there. I stayed away therefore and never saw the place again.

I came and lived in a hotel in Paris where I consulted doctors about the state of my nerves which had been giving me a lot of trouble ever since that appalling night. They recommended that I do some travelling and I followed their advice.

II

I started with a trip to Italy, where the sun did me good. For six months I wandered about between Venice, Florence, Rome and Naples. Then I toured through Sicily admiring its wildlife and the monuments left by the Greeks and others. I went on to Africa and made a leisurely crossing of the great, calm, yellow desert. Here I saw camels roam, as well as gazelles and Arab vagabonds, and on its light, transparent air no trace of animosity ever seems to be felt, either by day or by night.

I returned to France via Marseille where, despite traditional Provençal gaiety, the relative diminution in light cast a tinge of sadness over me. Returning to this continent I felt strangely like an invalid who, though allegedly cured of his illness, knows from the dull ache that he feels that it is merely dormant within him.

Then I came back to Paris. After a month I was bored with it. It was autumn, and before winter set in I wanted to make a tour of Normandy, then still unfamiliar territory to me. I started in Rouen, of course, and for a week wandered around enthusiastically, finding fresh delights in the medieval city of Gothic monuments which is such an astonishing and wonderful museum in itself.

One afternoon at around four o'clock I turned in to an incredible street where a river called Eau de Robec flowed with water as black as ink. While I was looking with great interest at the bizarre architecture of the houses there, my attention was drawn to a series of antique shops set all in a row, one next door to the other. Those crooked old dealers in antiquity had certainly picked the right place. The street was eerie, with its pointed tile and slate roofs where ancient weather vanes still creaked on high. Stored in the dark interiors of these shops could be seen carved sideboards piled high, one on top of the other, Nevers pottery,[2] Moustiers ware,[3] painted statuettes, carved oak figures, crucifixes, Madonnas, saints, church ornaments, chasubles, copes and even one or two holy vases, as well as a tabernacle conveniently vacated by the Godhead. What amazing places they were, these huge, tall houses like Aladdin's caves crammed to bursting with all kinds of objects of seemingly finite use, but which had long survived their first owners and endured through their century, their times and fashions, to be bought as curiosities by the generations that followed!

My fondness for such things was revived in this enclave of the ancient. I went from shop to shop, crossing in two strides the little bridges made of four worm-eaten planks thrown across the evil-smelling Eau de Robec. God help me! What a frightful shock I was soon to get! On one side of a vault packed tightly with stuff and looking like the entrance to the catacombs of some furniture cemetery, what should appear before my eyes but one of my own most beautiful cupboards! I approached, trembling in every limb, so much so in fact that at first I dared not touch it. Tentatively I stretched out my hand. Yes, it was mine all right; a unique, Louis XIII piece, once seen never forgotten. Suddenly, peering into the darkest depths of this gallery I saw three of my armchairs covered in petit point, and farther on still, my two Henri II tables, such rare examples that people used to come from Paris to look at them.

Imagine! Just imagine what I felt like!

On I went nevertheless. Half-dead with fright, still I advanced. I'm brave, I'll say that for me! Nearly paralysed with dread by now, I inched forward like a knight from the dark ages making his way through the enchanted forest. As I moved on, with every step I gradually found everything that had once belonged to me – my chandeliers, my books, my pictures, my curtains, rugs, armour, everything except the desk full of love-letters, of which there was no sign anywhere.

Farther in still I went, descending into the deepest of the dark galleries below, then climbing up to the upper storeys. I was alone. I called but never an answer came. I was alone. There was no one else in the vast, winding labyrinth of a house. Night fell and, reluctant to leave, I sat down in the shadows on one of the chairs formerly my own. From time to time I shouted, 'Hallo! Hallo! Anybody there?'

I must have been there for more than an hour when I heard footsteps; soft, slow footsteps coming from I knew not where. I nearly ran away but, bracing myself, I called out once more and noticed a gleam of light coming from the next room.

'Who's there?' called a voice.

'A customer,' I replied.

'Don't you think it's a bit late to just wander into somebody's shop like this?'

'I've been waiting over an hour to see you,' I went on.

'You could have come back tomorrow.'

'I shall have left Rouen tomorrow.'

I dared not go forward and he showed no sign of coming to me. I could still see the gleam of light shining on a tapestry which showed two angels flying over a battlefield. That was mine also.

'Well? Are you coming or not?' I said.

'I'm waiting for you,' he replied.

I rose and went in his direction.

Standing in the middle of a large room was a very small man, phenomenally fat, and extremely ugly. He had a meagre, ill-trimmed, yellowing beard and not a hair on his head. Not one! As he held up a candle in his outstretched hand to look me over, his skull seemed to me like a little moon in this enormous room filled with old furniture. In his puffy face there were deep furrows into which the eyes disappeared. I haggled over three of my own chairs and, giving my room number at the hotel, paid a vast sum of money for them. They were to be delivered the following morning at nine o'clock. I then left the room and with much ceremony he saw me to the door.

I made straight for the house of the central commissioner of police whom I told about the theft of my furniture and my recent rediscovery of it. He wired forthwith, requesting information from the office of the public prosecutor who originally investigated the theft, and asked me to wait till the reply came. An hour later, to my great satisfaction, he was in possession of the necessary information.

'I intend to arrest this man,' he said. 'His suspicions may have been aroused and he may try to spirit away your property. Would you like to go and have your dinner, then come back to me in two hours' time? I shall have him here by then and will question him further in your presence.'

'Most willingly, Monsieur. I'm very grateful indeed to you.'

I went and dined at my hotel, eating more heartily than I could have imagined possible, very largely I suppose because I was so glad at the prospect of the man soon being under arrest. Two hours later I returned to the police officer's house where he was waiting for me.

'Well, Monsieur,' he said, as soon as he saw me, 'we didn't manage to find your man. My officers have been unable to get hold of him.'

Oh no! I felt faint.

'But . . . you found the house, didn't you?'

'Easily. It will be under surveillance and guarded till he returns. As for the man himself, he's disappeared.'

'Disappeared?'

'Disappeared. Normally he spends the evening with his neighbour, another dealer, a real old witch, the widow Bidouin. She hasn't seen him tonight and can give us no information concerning his whereabouts. We shall have to wait until morning.'

I left him. How sinister and how haunted did the streets of Rouen seem to me then. I hardly slept all night. Each time I nodded off it was into one nightmare after another. I did not wish to appear too anxious or impatient, so waited until ten o'clock the following morning before making my way to the police. The dealer had not reappeared. His shop remained closed. The commissioner said to me: 'I've gone through all the necessary procedures. The public prosecutor's office is aware of these developments. We shall make our way together to the store and have it opened up. You will show me all the items of property which are yours.'

We were whisked away in a coupé. Police officers with a locksmith in attendance were stationed at the shop entrance door which was now open. Upon entering I saw no sign of my cupboard, my armchairs, my tables, or any single one of the objects with which my house had been furnished, nothing at all – whereas the previous evening I had been unable to take a step without bumping into one or other of my former possessions.

The commissioner was surprised. At first he looked at me with suspicion.

'My God, Monsieur!' I said to him, 'isn't it a bit of a coincidence that my property should disappear at precisely the same time as the dealer?'

He smiled.

'True enough! It was a mistake to buy your own things yesterday and pay for them. It's obviously tipped him off.'

I went on: 'What I simply cannot understand is that all the space taken up by my furniture is now filled completely with other stuff.'

'Oh!' replied the commissioner, 'he's had all night . . . and used accomplices, no doubt. This house is bound to lead in some way into the one next door. But don't worry, Monsieur, leave it all to me. The devil won't escape us for long, not while we're sitting on top of his lair, at least.'

Oh my heart, my poor heart! How wildly it was beating!

I stayed for about two weeks in Rouen. The man never returned. My God! My God! Who in the world would ever be able to get in *his* way? Take *him* by surprise? On the morning of my sixteenth day there I received from my gardener, whom I had left in charge of the looted and still deserted house, the following strange letter:

Monsieur,

May I inform Monsieur that last night something occurred here that no one, not even the police, can account for. All the furniture has come back; all, without exception and down to the smallest article. The house is now exactly as it was on the day before the robbery. We cannot get our heads around it. It happened between Friday night and the early hours of Saturday morning. The paths are all trampled over as though everything had been dragged from the gate to the front door. It was the same in reverse on the day we found them to have disappeared.

We await instructions from Monsieur whose humble servant I remain, Raudin, Philippe.

Oh no! No! No! No! I will not go back!

I took the letter to the commissioner of Rouen.

'A clever little restitution,' he said. 'Let's play dead. We'll pick him up one of these days.'

But he's never been picked up. No, they've never managed to pick him up and now I'm as terrified of him as if I had a wild beast on my tracks. Nowhere to be found! He is nowhere to be found, that monster with the moon-skull! They'll never catch him!

He'll never go back to that place of his! What does he care about it? *I'm* the only one who can catch him and I won't do it!

I won't! I won't! I won't!

And even if he does go back, even if he does return to his shop, who could prove that my furniture was there? There's only my word to go on and I can tell that's not being seen as entirely reliable these days. Oh, no! I could no longer go on living that way. I could no longer keep secret what I had seen. I could not carry on living as normal with the fear at the back of my mind that something like that could start up again. I came to see the director of this clinic and told him everything. After a lengthy consultation, he said: 'Would you be willing, Monsieur, to come and live with us here for a while?'

'More than willing, Monsieur.'

'Do you have money?'

'Yes, Monsieur.'

'Would you like a private room?'

'Yes, Monsieur.'

'Would you like to have friends come and see you?'

'No, Monsieur, no one. The man in Rouen might want to get his own back and follow me here.'

And so I have been alone, quite alone, for three months now. I'm more or less happy. Only one thing worries me: what if the dealer went mad? What if he were brought to this clinic? You see? Even in prison you're never absolutely safe you know!

LAID TO REST[1]

Five friends had been dining together. They were all rich, middle-aged men of the world, two of them bachelors, three married men. These monthly meetings of theirs were some of the happiest evenings of their lives. They had all known each other since their youth, remained close friends, enjoyed one another's company and often stayed talking till two o'clock in the morning. The conversation was about anything and everything that might interest or amuse a Parisian and, as in most drawing rooms, it was a kind of verbal version of the news in the morning papers.

One of the most footloose and fancy-free among them was Joseph de Bardon, a bachelor who exploited to the full all the attractions Paris has to offer. Though not exactly decadent or debauched in his habits, he managed to satisfy all the natural curiosity of a fun-loving man in his late thirties. A man of the world in the best and widest sense of the word, he was witty rather than profound, knowledgeable rather than wise and possessed a quick rather than a deep understanding of human nature. His experiences and encounters provided him with a fund of anecdotes, some edifying, some frankly hilarious. He had a reputation in society as a bright fellow with a good sense of humour – everyone's favourite after-dinner speaker whose tales were always the ones most looked forward to. He never needed any urging to begin, as he did on this occasion.

Certain creatures at certain times and places look absolutely in their element, let's say a goldfish in its bowl, a nun in church, or what have you. Sitting there smoking a cigar, with his elbows on the table, a half-filled glass of liqueur brandy to hand and relaxing in a warm haze of coffee and tobacco, he looked like a man in his ideal milieu. Between a couple of puffs he spoke.

'The funniest thing happened to me not so long ago . . .'

A near-instantaneous chorus replied, 'Go on, do!'

And he was off.

'Thank you, I shall. You know I get around Paris a fair amount. As other people window-shop, I watch what's going on. I watch the world and his brother pass by, I watch what's going on around me.[2] Well, some time towards the middle of last September, I left the house one afternoon with no clear idea of where I was going. You know how you always have a vague yen to go and see some pretty woman or other . . . you riffle through your little black book, you do a few mental comparisons, you weigh up the possible delights and you decide more or less on the spur of the moment. But when the sun's shining and it's warm outside you don't always want to be cooped up indoors. On this particular day, it was warm and sunny and I lit a cigar before starting to stroll along the outer boulevard. As I was sauntering along I decided to make for the cemetery in Montmartre and have a little wander about there. I like cemeteries, you know. They sadden and they soothe me and I find I need that from time to time. And of course some of one's chums are there, people nobody goes to see any more. I drop by every so often still. And as it happens, an old flame of mine is buried in Montmarte Cemetery, a lovely little lady I was very keen on at one point in my life, very attached to. So although it's painful, I find it does me good. I mean all kinds of memories come flooding back while I'm there, letting my thoughts drift beside her grave. It's all over for her of course . . .

The other reason I like cemeteries is because they're like cities in themselves, densely populated at that. Just think how many generations of Parisians are packed in there forever; so many people stuck in their caves, their little holes just covered with a stone or marked with a cross, while the living take up so much room and make such a stupid racket.

Then of course you've got all the monuments, some of them much more interesting than in a museum. Though I wouldn't put them in the same league, Cavaignac's grave reminded me so much of that masterpiece by Jean Goujon, the statue of Louis de Brézé in the underground chapel at Rouen cathedral.[3] That's actually the root of all so-called modern, realist art, you know. That statue of the dead Louis de Brézé is more convincing, more terrible and more suggestive of inanimate flesh still convulsed in the death-agony than any of the tortured corpses you see sculpted these days on people's tombs.

But in Montmartre Cemetery you can still admire the impressive monument to Baudin, the one to Gautier, and that to Murger,[4] on which incidentally, only the other day I spotted one poor solitary wreath of helichrysums. I wonder who put that there. Perhaps the last of the *grisettes*[5], now a very old woman and possibly one of the local concierges. It's a pretty little statue by Millet,[6] suffering badly from neglect and all the accumulated dirt of the years. Oh for the joys of youth, eh, Murger?

Anyway there I was, stepping into Montmartre Cemetery, suddenly filled with sadness of a not entirely disagreeable kind, the sort that makes a healthy fellow think "Not the most cheerful of spots, but thank God I'm not stuck in here just yet." The feeling of autumn, the warm dampness of dead leaves in pale, weak sunshine heightened and romanticized the sense of solitude and finality surrounding this place of the dead.

I wandered slowly along the streets of graves where neighbours no longer call, no longer sleep together and never hear the news. Then I started reading the epitaphs. I tell you gentlemen, they are absolutely killing. Not even Labiche or Meilhac[7] can give me more of a laugh than the language of the headstone. When you read what the nearest and dearest have put on the marble slabs and crosses, pouring out their grief and their best wishes for the happiness of the departed in the next world, and their hopes – the liars! – for a speedy reunion, it's hilarious! Better than a Paul de Kock any day![8]

But what I love most in that cemetery is the deserted, lonely part planted with all those tall yews and cypresses, the old district where those who died long ago now lie. Soon it will become the new part of town; the green trees nourished by human corpses will be felled to make room for the recently departed to be lined up in turn under their own little marble slabs.

After I had wandered about long enough to refresh my mind, I realized I was now getting a little bored and that it was time to go to the last resting place of my old love and pay her my ever-faithful respects. By the time I reached her graveside I was feeling quite upset. Poor darling, she was so sweet, so loving, so fair and rosy . . . and now . . . if this spot were ever opened up . . . Leaning on the iron railings I whispered to her a few sad words which I dare say she is unlikely to have heard. I was just about to leave when I saw a woman in deep mourning on her knees at the next graveside. She had lifted her crêpe veil and under it could be seen a pretty head of fair hair, a crown of bright dawn under the dark night of her head-dress. I lingered. In what was obviously deep distress she had buried her face in her hands and, stiff as a statue, was deep in meditation. Absorbed by her grief and telling the painful beads of memory behind closed and hidden eyes, she seemed herself dead to the world in her loss. Suddenly I saw that she was about to break down. I could tell from the slight movement her back made, like a willow stirring in the wind. She wept gently at first then more and more violently with her neck and shoulders shaking hard and rapidly. All of a sudden she uncovered her eyes. Full of tears they were lovely. She looked wildly about her as if waking from a nightmare. She saw me looking at her, seemed ashamed and buried her whole face once more in her hands. Then she burst into convulsive sobs and her head bent slowly down towards the marble slab. She rested her forehead on it and her veil, spreading about her, covered the white corners of her beloved sepulchre like a new mourning-cloth. I heard her moan before she collapsed with her cheek against the tombstone and lay there motionless and unconscious.

I rushed over to her, slapped her hands and breathed on her eyelids while reading the simple epitaph beyond:

HERE LIES LOUIS-THEODORE CARREL
Captain of Marines
Killed by the enemy at Tonkin

PRAY FOR HIS SOUL

The date of death was some months earlier. I was moved to
tears and redoubled my efforts to revive her. Finally they succeeded and she came to. I'm not bad-looking, not yet forty,
remember, and at that moment I must have been looking
extremely solicitous. At any rate, from her first glance I realized
she would be both polite and grateful to me. I was not dis-
appointed. Between further tears and sobs she told me about
the officer who had been killed at Tonkin[9] after they had been
married for just one year. He had married her for love. She had
been an orphan and possessed nothing but the smallest dowry.

I comforted her, consoled her, lifted her up, then helped her
to her feet.

"You can't stay here like this," I said, "come on . . ."

"I'm not sure I can manage to walk . . ."

"I'll help you, don't worry."

"Thank you, Monsieur, you're very kind. Did you have someone here yourself you wanted to mourn?"

"Yes, Madame."

"A lady?"

"Yes, Madame."

"Your wife?"

"A . . . friend."

"One can love a friend as much as a wife. Passion has its own
laws."

"Indeed so, Madame."

We walked away together, she leaning on me so heavily that
I was almost carrying her along the paths of the cemetery. As
we were leaving it, she said: "I think I'm going to faint."

"Would you like to go in and sit down somewhere? Let me
get you something to . . ."

"Yes thank you, I would."

I noticed a place nearby, one of those restaurants where the friends of the recently buried go when they have completed their grim duties. We went in and I made her drink a cup of hot tea which seemed to restore her strength somewhat. A faint smile came to her lips and she began to tell me a little about herself. How sad, how very sad it was to be all alone in the world, to be alone at home day and night, to have no one with whom to share love, trust and intimacy.

It all seemed sincere and so genuine the way she told it. I felt my heart softening. She was very young, twenty at most. I flattered her a little and she responded gracefully. Then, as time was getting on, I offered to take her home by cab. She accepted. In the cab we were so close to each other, shoulder to shoulder, that we could feel the warmth of each other's bodies through our clothing – one of the most disturbing feelings in the world, as you know. When the cab drew up in front of her house she murmured: "I really don't think I can get up the stairs on my own. I live on the fourth floor. You've been so kind . . '. could you possibly give me your arm again, please?"

I said of course I could, and she went up slowly, breathing hard all the time. Then at her door she added: "Do come in for a few moments so that I can thank you."

In I went, naturally.

It was a modest, not to say poor little apartment furnished in simple but good taste. We sat side by side on a little sofa where she started talking again about how lonely she was. She rang for her maid to bring me something to drink. No one appeared. I was delighted about this and imagined that this maid must work mornings only, in other words, she only had a cleaner. She had taken off her hat. She really was quite a charmer. Her lovely, limpid eyes were fixed on me with such a clear, direct gaze that I suddenly felt an irresistible urge. I succumbed on the spot and clasped her in my arms. On her eyelids, which had instantly closed, I rained kiss after kiss after kiss. She struggled, pushing me away and repeating: "Please . . . please . . . please . . . have done!"

What exactly did she mean? In the circumstances there were two ways of interpreting the words. To silence her I moved down from the eyes to the mouth and, putting my preferred interpretation on her request to please have done, complied with it. She put up little resistance and when later we looked at each other again after an insult to the memory of the captain killed at Tonkin she wore a languorous expression of tender resignation which dispelled any misgivings of my own.

I showed my gratitude by being gallant and attentive, and after an hour or so's conversation asked: "Where do you normally dine?"

"At a little restaurant nearby."

"All on your own?"

"Yes, of course."

"Will you have dinner with me tonight?"

"Where did you have in mind?"

"Oh, a very good restaurant on the boulevard."

She demurred for a while but I insisted and finally she gave in, reasoning that she would otherwise be terribly lonely again. Then she added, "I'd better change into something less severe," and disappeared into her bedroom. When she emerged she was in half-mourning and wearing a very simple but elegant grey dress in which she looked slender and charming. She obviously had markedly different outfits for the cemetery and for town.

Dinner was very pleasant. She drank champagne, became very animated and excited, after which I went back to her apartment with her. This little liaison begun between the tombstones went on for some three weeks or so. But novelty, particularly with regard to women, eventually palls. I dropped her on the pretext of some unavoidable trip I had to make. I was very generous when we parted and she in turn very grateful. She made me promise, no, swear, to come back on my return and really seemed to care a little for me.

I lost no time in forming other attachments, however, and about a month went by without my having felt any particular desire to resume my funereal fling. But nor did I forget her. The memory of her haunted me like some unsolved mystery, a psychological teaser, one of those nagging little puzzles you can't leave alone. One day, for some inexplicable reason, I wondered whether, if I went back to Montmartre Cemetery again, I might bump into her, and decided to return.

I walked around for a long time but there was no one there apart from the usual sort of people who visit the place, mourners who have not yet severed all ties with their dead. At the grave of the captain killed at Tonkin no one mourned over the marble slab, no flowers lay there, no wreaths. However, as I was walking through another district of the city of the departed I suddenly saw a couple, a man and a woman in deep mourning, coming towards me down a narrow avenue lined with crosses. To my amazement as they approached, I recognized the woman. It was she! Seeing me she blushed. As I brushed past her she gave me a tiny signal, the merest glance, but conveying in the clearest possible way both: "Don't show you know me," and "Come back and see me, darling."

The man with her was about fifty, distinguished-looking and well-dressed, with the rosette of the *Légion d'honneur*[10] in his lapel. He was supporting her just as I had done when we both left the cemetery that day.

I went off, flabbergasted by what I had just seen and trying to imagine what tribe of creatures she belonged to, hunting as she obviously did on this sepulchral terrain. Was she a single prostitute who had struck on the brilliant idea of frequenting graveyards and picking up unhappy men still haunted by the loss of a wife or a mistress and troubled by the memory of past caresses? Was she unique? Or were there more like her? Was it a professional speciality to work the cemetery like the street? The loved ones of those laid to rest! Or was she alone in having conceived the psychologically sound idea of exploiting the feelings of amorous nostalgia awakened in these mournful venues?

I was longing to know whose widow she had chosen to be that day.'

THE NECKLACE

She was one of those charming, pretty young women who seem to have been born by some cruel quirk of fate into quite the wrong social rank: in this instance, the minor bureaucracy. She had no dowry and no expectations, and it was therefore unlikely that any rich or distinguished gentleman would get to know her, understand or love her, still less make her his wife. Under the circumstances she settled, for a husband, on a petty clerk in the Ministry of Education.

Having no finery or ornament to wear, simplicity of style was her hallmark. But she suffered terribly from such ignominy. Women generally are bound neither by race nor caste, and their own beauty, gracefulness or charm are all they possess in terms of birthright and heritage. For them, in principle, a simple street sparrow may vie with the sleekest swan.

Nevertheless she suffered all the time. She had been destined, or so she believed, for a delicate life of luxury. She suffered when she looked at the poverty of their accommodation; the peeling walls, the worn upholstery and the hideousness of the soft furnishings. Everything any other woman of her class might scarcely have noticed tortured and consumed her soul. The mere sight of the little Breton girl who saw to their humble needs plunged her into miserable regret for her own shattered dreams.

In her mind's eye she trod thickly carpeted and silent ante-chambers lined from floor to ceiling with Oriental hangings and illuminated by huge bronze candelabra beneath which, in huge armchairs, tall, liveried footmen sprawled, slumbering in the heat of wonderful new-fangled heaters. Into her enchanted vision swam enormous drawing rooms hung with ancient silks, where exquisite furniture stood laden with priceless objets d'art; more intimate rooms, cosy and sweet-smelling, where towards evening, close friends and of course the most sought-after men of their acquaintance would call in and pay their respects.

Sitting down to supper at their own round table laid with its three-day-old cloth, opposite her husband who would lift up the lid of the tureen with delight, crying, 'Stew! What a treat!' – she dreamed of exquisite dinners, of gleaming silver, of tapestries on the walls depicting illustrious ancestors or extraordinary birds in fairy-tale forests. She imagined the most succulent dishes served in equally splendid vessels; she heard whispered sweet nothings received with a smiling, sphinx-like gaze, as accompaniment to the consumption of pink-fleshed trout or the wings of a delicate hazel grouse.

She had no elegant dresses and no jewellery to wear, or at least nothing in which she could really take pride and nothing in which she felt truly herself. How she wished to please, to be envied, attractive and utterly beguiling. She had a wealthy friend, an old contemporary from the convent where she was educated but whom she now avoided because of what she felt when they met. She wept for days at a time: tears of sorrow, of regret, despair and deep distress.

One night, however, her husband came back from work looking exultant and waving in his hand a large envelope.

'There you are!' he said. 'Here's a little something for you!'

She tore it open and read the card inside:

The Minister of State for Education and Madame Georges Ramponneau take great pleasure in inviting Monsieur and Madame Loisel to honour a Soirée with their presence at the Ministry of Education, to be held on Monday 18th January.

Instead of rhapsodizing as her husband expected, she groaned:

'So what?'

'But, my dear,' he said, 'I thought you'd be *so* pleased! You never go out and this is *such* an occasion, really! I had the devil's own job getting us an invitation. Everybody wants to go. But not everyone is allowed. Specially not clerks! The whole Ministry will be there in all its glory!'

She cast an irritated glance in his direction: 'And what on earth do you imagine I could put on for such an occasion, may I ask?'

He was unprepared for this and stammered: 'Well . . . what you wear for the theatre, I suppose. That always looks good to me . . .'

He stopped in his tracks, distracted not to say dumbfounded by the fact that his wife was now weeping. Two huge tears, welling in her eyes, began to slide slowly down towards the corners of her mouth.

'What?' he stuttered again, 'what on earth is the matter?'

With huge effort she overcame her obviously painful emotion and replied in a calm voice as she wiped away her tears: 'Nothing. It's just that I haven't got anything to wear. I can't go. Give the invitation to somebody who can.'

He was devastated but continued: 'Listen, Mathilde. How much would it cost to get something suitable, d'you think? Something you could maybe get some wear out of later on . . . something fairly classic?'

She thought for a moment, totting up sums in her head and also taking into account how much she could ask for without shocking her careful husband into an immediate refusal.

Eventually, with some hesitation, she replied: 'I'm not sure exactly. I think I might be able to manage with 400 francs.'

He paled a little at this. It was the exact amount he had intended to put aside to buy a rifle and pay for a few days' shooting at Nanterre the following summer. He and some friends were hoping to bag a few larks there on the occasional Sunday outing. Putting this out of his head he said: 'Fine. Four hundred it is. But make sure you get something really special for that, won't you?'

The date was fast approaching. Despite the fact that her new dress was ready and waiting, Madame Loisel seemed anxious, even worried, and more than a little sad.

One evening, her husband cried: 'What on earth's the matter

with you now? You've been out of sorts for three whole days,
for goodness' sake!'

'I'm sorry,' she said, 'but I haven't a single piece of jewellery
to go with the dress. I shall look like a pathetic nobody. I'd
almost prefer not to go at all.'

'What about flowers?' he said, 'especially at this time of the
year! The beauty of nature! For ten francs you could get two or
three quite magnificent roses!'

She was unconvinced: 'No, that wouldn't do at all. These
women are rich. I should look silly.'

'Well, you *are* a silly thing!' cried her husband. 'Go and
see your friend Madame Forestier! Ask her if she'll lend you
something. You know her well enough, don't you?'

'Of course!' she answered joyfully. 'I never thought of that!'

And the next day, she went to her old friend straight away
and explained the situation.

Madame Forestier walked up to her mirrored wardrobe and
drew from it a large jewel casket. Opening it for her friend, she
said: 'There! My dear, choose whatever you like!'

Madame Loisel's glance fell first on some bracelets, then on
strings of pearls, a jewelled cross of Venetian glass, on gold and
all kinds of precious stones, all beautifully set. In front of the
mirror she tried various pieces on, hesitating and unable to
choose what to take and what to put back.

'Oh I don't know!' she said, 'what else is there? Have I seen
everything?'

'No, indeed!' said her friend, 'carry on looking, do!'

Suddenly she came across a black satin-lined case containing
the most superb diamond necklace. Her heart began to race
with wild desire. Her hands shook as she put it on and it settled
just above the neckline of the dress. She was ecstatic as she
looked at her reflection in the glass.

'Could I,' she said hesitantly, and in an agony of hope, 'could
I take just this? Would you be willing?'

'Of course! Certainly I would!'

She flung her arms around her friend, kissed her over and
over, then ran off with the treasure in her hands.

*

The night of the soirée finally arrived. Madame Loisel was the belle of the ball. She was the most elegant and graceful woman there. Hers was the gayest smile and hers the greatest joy. Every man present looked at her admiringly, asked who she was and demanded an introduction. All the attachés lined up to waltz with her and the Minister himself took note.

She danced in a daze of pleasure and enchantment. The triumph of her beauty and her success went straight to her head and she felt enveloped in a haze of total happiness. Intoxicated by all the admiration and acknowledgements she received, all the desires she knew herself to have awakened in others, she experienced everything most dear and sweet to a woman's heart.

At about four in the morning, she was preparing to leave. Her husband, together with three other gentlemen whose wives had also been enjoying themselves hugely, was asleep, as he had been since midnight, in a little-frequented side room.

He threw over her shoulders the outdoor clothing he had brought for going home; ordinary, workaday garments which clashed violently with the sumptuousness of her evening dress. She was only too aware of the contrast and tried to run away so as not to be seen by other women now wrapping themselves up in rich furs.

Loisel held her back: 'Hang on, do! You'll catch your death outside! Let me call a cab.'

But she was no longer listening, already running down the stairs. Out in the street, not a carriage was to be seen. They set off to look for one, shouting out to the drivers of those they could dimly make out in the distance.

Shivering with cold and disappointment, they walked down as far as the Seine. There they found one of those ancient, bone-rattling vehicles which appear in Paris only after dark, as if ashamed to venture out in daylight. It took them to their place in the rue des Martyrs, where they sorrowfully dragged themselves upstairs. For her, it was all over now. As for her husband, he would have to be back at the Ministry for work by ten.

She shook off her outer clothing so as to look in the mirror and catch one final glimpse of herself in all her glory. Suddenly she cried out loud. The necklace was no longer around her neck!

Her husband, already half-undressed, asked: 'Are you all right?'

Turning to him and half out of her mind she said: 'It's . . . it's . . . Madame Forestier's necklace . . . it's gone!'

He stood up, horrified: 'Gone? What d'you mean gone? It can't have!'

They searched in the folds of her dress, of her coat, in the pockets, everywhere. No sign.

'Are you sure,' he asked, 'are you sure you had it when we left the ball?'

'Yes! I remember feeling it in the vestibule at the Ministry!'

'But if you'd dropped it in the street, we'd have heard, wouldn't we? It must have been in the cab.'

'Yes. Most likely. Did you take the number?'

'No. Did you? Did you look?'

'No.'

They stared at each other aghast. Finally Loisel got dressed again.

'Look,' he said, 'I'll go back on foot exactly the way we came and see if I can't find it.'

And out he went. Still in her evening dress, she remained awake, slumped in a chair, with no fire and no energy left to summon a single thought to her mind.

At about seven in the morning her husband returned. He had found nothing.

He went to the police and to the newspapers. He advertised a reward. He went to all the cab companies and to wherever the slightest hope might still remain. All day long, in the same stunned state of shock produced by this catastrophe, she waited.

Loisel returned in the evening, his face pale and his cheeks hollow. Again he had found nothing.

'What you must do now,' he said, 'is write to your friend saying that you have damaged the clasp of the necklace and are having it repaired. This will give us time to think.'

Accordingly and under his dictation, she wrote.

*

By the end of the week, all hope was lost. Loisel, having aged five years in the interim, declared: 'We shall just have to see how we can replace the jewels.'

The next day, they took the case in which the necklace had lain to the jeweller whose name was inscribed on the inside. He consulted his records.

'I'm afraid, madame, that the necklace was not sold by ourselves. We must have merely supplied the case.'

And so they proceeded, from jeweller to jeweller, searching for a necklace exactly like the first, racking their brains and going mad, both of them, with anguish and distress.

At the Palais Royal, however, they found one day what seemed to them a necklace of diamonds exactly like the one they were trying to replace. It was priced at 40,000 francs. It might be theirs for 36,000.

They asked the jeweller to reserve it for them for three days. He further agreed to a proviso that if, after they had bought it, the original was found, he would repurchase the article for 34,000 francs.

Loisel had in his possession 18,000 francs left to him by his father. He would have to borrow the remainder.

And so he did: 1,000 francs here, 500 there, five louis from this friend, three from the other. He took out promissory notes, incurred ruinous debts, dealt with shady moneylenders and sharks of every type and description. In effect he was compromising the rest of his entire life by giving his signature to a plethora of highly risky commitments. Terrified by the prospect of future destitution and all the accompanying physical and moral sacrifices necessary, he went to collect the replacement necklace and put on the counter 36,000 francs.

When Madame Loisel returned the necklace to Madame Forestier the latter was a little frosty, remarking: 'You really should have returned it to me sooner than this, you know. I might well have needed it myself.'

She did not, however, open the case, which was what her friend had most feared. What if she noticed the substitution? What would she have thought? What would she have said? Madame Loisel would most certainly have been taken for a thief.

She now spiralled down into a life of deep penury. She met it head on with great courage, knowing it was the only thing to do. This enormous debt would have to be paid one way or another and pay it they would. The maid was instantly dismissed. They moved to cheaper lodgings in a garret.

She took on heavy housework and all the menial tasks necessary. Her rosy pink nails grated against rough saucepan bottoms and coarse crockery. She scrubbed dirty linen, shirts and kitchen cloths which she hung out herself on the line to dry; every morning she took filthy garbage out into the street for collection and carried every drop of water up by hand; dressed in humble worker clothes, she haggled with the fruiterer, the butcher and the grocer. With her basket over her arm she traded insults as she marketed, watching with care every miserable sou in her purse.

Every month there were bills to be paid, and promissory notes to renew so as to gain a little time.

Her husband worked in the evenings now, on the accounts of a businessman of his acquaintance, and at night worked on copying at five sous a page.

This régime continued for ten years.

At the end of ten years they had paid everything they owed; everything, including exorbitant interest and the accumulated debts involved.

Madame Loisel now looked old. She had coarsened and become the tough, hard woman which poverty often breeds. With dishevelled hair, her skirts in a twist and reddened, work-worn hands, she yelled with the best of them as she swilled the flagstone floors far below. From time to time, however, when her husband was away at work, she would sit near the window and remember fondly that now long-distant night when she had been so beautiful and so thoroughly fêted.

What might have ensued, she wondered, if she had not lost the necklace? Who could tell? What indeed? How strange life is, how unpredictable! What a little thing it takes to ruin or raise you to heaven!

One Sunday, when she had gone for a stroll along the Champs Élysées as a break from the tedium of the weekly routine, she suddenly noticed a woman walking and holding a child by the hand. It was Madame Forestier, as youthful-looking, beautiful and attractive as ever.

Madame Loisel felt a pang. Should she go and speak to her old friend? Well, of course she should! Why not? Now that everything was paid off, she could tell her the whole story.

She approached: 'Hello there, Jeanne.'

The other woman failed to recognize her and was somewhat taken aback at being addressed so familiarly by this matronly stranger. She stammered: 'I'm sorry, madame . . . I'm not sure . . . I think you might be mistaking me for . . .'

'No, it's me, Mathilde Loisel.'

Her friend cried out: 'Oh! My dear Mathilde! What a change . . . !'

'Yes indeed. Hard times, I can tell you, since we last met. We've been through a lot. Much to do with you, I might add!'

'What on earth d'you mean . . . to do with me?'

'Well . . . you remember that diamond necklace you lent me to go to the Ministry of Education ball?'

'Yes, of course. What about it?'

'Well . . . I lost it.'

'You can't have! You gave it back to me!'

'You're right but what I gave back to you was a replica. Exactly the same. But it's taken us ten years to pay for it. Not an easy thing to do, given our finances. However, thank goodness, it's all paid for now and I can't tell you how glad I am.'

Madame Forestier stopped in her tracks: 'Are you telling me you bought a diamond necklace to replace mine?'

'Yes, of course. And you didn't spot the difference, did you? It was a perfect match, wasn't it?'

She was smiling with innocent pride.

Madame Forestier, clearly appalled, took her friend's two hands in her own: 'Oh my poor Mathilde!' she said. 'Mine wasn't real! It was worth 500 francs at the most! . . .'

Notes

BOULE DE SUIF

First published in 1880 as 'Boule de Suif'.

1. *Boule de Suif*: 'Dumpling', 'Dimples', 'Butterball', 'Lardycake', etc. Literally a ball of fat, suet or tallow.

2. *routed army*: Following the disastrous defeat of the French at the battle of Sedan in September 1870 when Napoleon III himself was captured, the Prussian army continued to make huge gains and moved inexorably westwards. Rouen was captured without a fight and used by the occupying forces as their winter quarters.

3. *francs-tireurs*: Literally 'free-lance', or in this case 'free-shots'. Irregular troops. First formed in 1792 in the Vosges, detachments of these guerrilla fighters sprang up in many of the main cities of France in 1867. Marginal to the army proper, they were particularly feared by the enemy.

4. *National Guard*: The *Garde Nationale* was an ill-prepared body of local recruits mustered for the defence of their individual towns and cities.

5. *Uhlans*: A German name with Tartar roots signifying a lancer in the German, Russian or Austrian armies.

6. *Such an attitude . . . honour and glory*: Maupassant is writing ironically here. Rouen was the city of William the Conqueror and in earlier times a symbol of a free and independent France. Its once brave citizens, traditionally renowned for their stout defence of the town against depredations by the English over the centuries, have turned soft and compliant in the face of the present enemy forces. The suggestion is that commercialism has sapped the former proud spirit of the inhabitants and turned them into followers of expediency.

7. *Croisset*: One of the first places downstream of Rouen and famous for being the spot where Flaubert had his little writing pavilion, which exists to this day.

8. *a fall of cotton-wool*: Rouen in the mid-nineteenth century was one of the most prosperous cities of France and renowned for the manufacture, import and export of textile material, particularly cotton.

9. *L'oiseau vole*: A pun on the name of the wine merchant Loiseau (the bird). '*L'oiseau vole*' can mean in French both 'the bird flies' and 'the bird steals'. In suggesting this game, Monsieur Tournel is hinting broadly that Loiseau is a man who feathers his own nest.

10. *Throughout the Empire*: The Second Empire (1852–70) under Napoleon III, formerly Louis Napoleon, who died in exile at Chislehurst in England.

11. *Orleanists*: After the February revolution of 1848, the monarchist party was divided into *légitimistes* and *Orléanistes*. The latter, supporters of the younger, Orleanist branch of the royal family, hoped to place on the throne the Comte de Paris, grandson of Louis-Philippe.

12. *half a million francs*: Considering that the average salary of a Ministry employee like Maupassant was between 1,800 and 2,400 francs per annum, these people are extremely wealthy, even by Rouennais standards.

13. *Fourth of September*: 4 September 1870, the founding of the Third Republic.

14. *Tôtes*: The village some fifty kilometres from Rouen where Flaubert sets the first part of *Madame Bovary*.

15. *Badinguet*: The workman who lent his clothes to disguise and effect the escape of Louis-Napoleon Bonaparte when the latter was a prisoner at the fortress of Ham in 1846. It thereafter became a nickname for Napoleon III himself.

16. *du Guesclin*: Fourteenth-century warrior-hero and famous scourge of the English to whose raids he finally put a stop by using guerrilla tactics.

17. *the Imperial Prince*: Napoleon III's fourteen-year-old son, Eugène Louis.

18. *trente-et-un*: Card game in which first player to get exactly thirty-one wins.

19. *écarté*: Another card game combining elements of both rummy and canasta.

20. *Judith and Holophernes ... Lucretia and Sextus*: The Jewish heroine Judith, in order to save the city of Bethulia, seduced Holophernes, one of Nebuchadnezzar's generals, who was laying siege to it. First seeking him out in his tent and making him drunk,

she seduced him and cut off his head while he lay sleeping. Lucretia and Sextus seem to have no real relevance to the situation and are possibly a means of indicating the ignorance of the company. According to Livy, Sextus Tarquin's rape of Lucretia led to the dethronement of Tarquinius Superbus and the establishment of a republic.

A PARISIAN AFFAIR

First published in 1881 as 'Une aventure parisienne'.

1. *Chaussée d'Antin*: Then, as now, a popular area and site of the *grands magasins* or department stores such as *Galeries Lafayette* and *Au Printemps*, in their infancy during this period.
2. *bibelots*: Curios or knick-knacks. For a fascinating examination of the issues of collecting, consuming and classifying, and a description of the curiosities, antiques and objets d'art which proliferated in French literary texts during the last decade of the nineteenth century, see Janell Watson: *Literature and Material Culture from Balzac to Proust*, cited in Further Reading.
3. *Busnach*: William Busnach (1832–1907) was a popular playwright famous for his theatrical adaptations of some of Zola's novels such as *Nana* and *L'Assommoir* (*The Drinking Den*).
4. *Dumas*: Alexandre Dumas, *fils* (1824–95). One of the most successful dramatists of the Second Empire and author of *La Dame aux camélias*, which was an overnight success. His father (1801–70), known as Dumas *père*, was the author of *Le Comte de Monte Cristo* and *Les Trois Mousquetaires*.
5. *Zola*: Emile Zola (1840–1902), novelist and founder of the naturalist school of French literature. His cycle of twenty novels, *Les Rougon-Macquart*, includes *Germinal*, *L'Assommoir*, *Nana*, etc. In 1898, in a letter published as 'J'accuse', he campaigned vigorously and in the end successfully for a reversal of the notorious anti-Semitic Dreyfus verdict.
6. *fiacre*: A closed, horse-drawn carriage for hire, named after the inn, the Saint-Fiacre, which was the early depot of those vehicles in the mid-seventeenth century. Readers of *Madame Bovary* will remember it as being the vehicle involved in what Nabokov describes as the most erotic of all literary carriage-rides. Sex on the move, in carriages and later on trains is a theme to which Maupassant often returns.
7. *To the Bois!*: The Bois de Boulogne, then, as now, a favourite Parisian forest park popular for both walking and riding.

8. *absinthe*: A green liqueur made by the maceration and distillation of wormwood (*Artemisia absinthium*) with the addition of other bitter or aromatic plants such as fennel and Chinese or star anise. Consumed in French literary and artistic circles during the late nineteenth and early twentieth centuries. First popularized by being prescribed as a febrifuge to French troops during the 1830–47 Algerian war. Later the drink was proscribed by law in France and its consumption in other countries today is limited if not by law, at least by custom.

9. *Café Bignon*: Smart Parisian restaurant frequented by writers, artists and journalists of the time.

10. *Vaudeville*: A theatre very close to the Café Bignon on the boulevard des Capucines. Later used as a term for popular variety entertainment.

A WOMAN'S CONFESSION

First published in 1882 as 'Confessions d'une femme'.

1. *that chemist*: A reference to a particularly lurid murder which hit the headlines in 1882. A married woman, Gabrielle Fenayrou, was having an affair with a chemist. When her husband and father-in-law discovered this, the two men set a trap for her lover. Luring him to a house they had rented for that purpose, they murdered him and threw his body into the Seine.

COCKCROW

First published in 1882 as 'Un coq chanta' and dedicated to René Billotte (1846–1914), a landscape painter, an old friend of Maupassant and a member of his rowing set.

MOONLIGHT

First published in 1882 as 'Claire de lune'.

1. *his illustrious name*: Marignan (Melegnano), a town to the southeast of Milan and scene of two well-known French victories: first that of François I over the Swiss in 1515, and later that of the wonderfully named Achille Barcguay d'Hilliers in 1859 over the Austrians.

2. *'Woman, what have I to do with thee?'*: John 2:4. Christ's reply to his mother's announcement during the wedding at Cana that the wine had run out. Adding 'Mine hour is not yet come', he

proceeded to perform his first miracle. The abbé Marignan is expressing a popular male isegesis, or biased interpretation, whereby these words are construed to signify some kind of basic antipathy to women on the part of Christ, instead of his revolutionary shift away from contemporary family values.

3. *of whom the poet speaks*: The poet is Alfred de Vigny (1797–1863) in line 100 of his 'La Colère de Samson' ('The Wrath of Samson') in which woman, described as both infantile and treacherous, is 'toujours Dalila!'

4. *Ruth and Boaz . . . holy writ*: Ruth, in the Biblical story, though a Moabite foreigner, comes to represent the epitome of filial piety by her devotion to her mother-in-law Naomi. Since Boaz, a much older and more powerful distant relative, marries her, she enjoys his protection and becomes eventually the great-grandmother of David. The abbé Marignan is clearly casting himself here in the role of similar protector to his niece.

AT SEA

First published in 1883 as 'En mer'.
1. *'Looks like the black to me'*: The fisherman's term for gangrene.

A MILLION

First published in 1882 as 'Un million'.
1. *to separate the Church from the State*: Though total separation between the two did not become law until 1905, since 1880 a number of measures had been taken to limit the role and importance of the clergy in State affairs.

2. *Dieudonné*: The Bonnins named their child 'Dieudonné' meaning 'God-given'. The name Theodore, the Greek equivalent, is part of the papal as well as the royal tradition, being the name of two seventh-century popes, the first of whom was later canonized.

FEMME FATALE

First published in 1881 as 'La femme de Paul'.
1. *Le Grillon*: In reality the Maison Fournaise, a riverside restaurant well known to Maupassant and situated just below the Chatou bridge over the Seine.

2. *The owner . . . red-bearded man of legendary strength*: Alphonse Fournaise, proprietor of the above and nicknamed Hercule.

3. *La Grenouillère*: Literally 'the frog-pond'. Suburban bathing spot on the Seine near Chatou. Immortalized by Renoir whose roughly contemporary painting of the place bears the same name. Another popular Parisian leisure spot.
4. *fiacres*: See p. 307, note 6.
5. *Saint-Lazare*: A prison on the rue de Clichy used mainly for the detention of women.
6. *the can-can*: Initially banned in public places, the can-can became one of the most popular dances at Parisian *caf'-concs* or concert cafés. Its most spectacular performances were at the Moulin Rouge where it was danced by La Goulue and painted by Toulouse-Lautrec.

MONSIEUR JOCASTE

First published in 1883. The disturbing nature of this story may account for the fact that, although it was published in *Gil Blas* in January 1883, Maupassant never included it in any collections of his work.

TWO FRIENDS

First published in 1883 as 'Deux amis'.
1. *Paris . . . breathing her last*: Like 'Boule de suif' and many others, this story is set during the Franco-Prussian war when the population of Paris was reduced to eating cats, rats and any other form of animal life they could lay their hands on.
2. *uniform*: Of the *Garde Nationale*.
3. *Marante*: The Ile de Colombes, setting of the present tale.
4. *rue de Lorette*: A street near the Gare Saint-Lazare leading from the Place Blanche to the church of Notre-Dame de Lorette. It was a street well known to Maupassant who, when he first went to Paris as a young man, lived a few hundred yards away, in the rue Moncey.

AWAKENING

First published in 1883 as 'Réveil'.
1. *coupé*: In this context, a closed, four-wheeled carriage generally used for carrying two passengers.

THE JEWELS

First published in 1883 as 'Les bijoux'.

1. *rue de la Paix*: Then, as now, one of the most elegant and fashionable streets in Paris. It leads from the Place de l'Opéra to the Place Vendôme.

2. *rue des Martyrs*: Monsieur Lantin lives in what was then the bohemian *quartier* of the city, up near Pigalle and Montmartre, the latter a corruption of 'Mont des Martyrs'. As the Haussmannization of Paris drove the working class further outward towards the city limits, it became well known for its cabarets and brothels and for being the home not only of artists but also of pimps, prostitutes and pickpockets.

3. *colonne de Vendôme*: The massive column dedicated to Napoleon's *grande armée*. Forty-four metres high, it is cast from the bronze of 1,200 captured enemy cannon.

4. *Voisin's*: A few steps from the Place Vendôme, on the corner of the rue Cambon and the rue Saint-Honoré.

5. *Café Anglais*: On the boulevard des Italiens, this restaurant, like Voisin's, at the end of the Second Empire boasted a superb cellar.

TRAIN STORY

First published in 1883 as 'En voyage'.

1. *Tarascon*: The Bouches du Rhône area south of Avignon.

2. *murderer who . . . passenger on this line*: A large number of murders on trains had taken place in the Tarascon region between 1882 and 1883. In France generally, sufficiently alarming incidences of the crime gave rise to a largely ineffective commission into railway security at this time.

3. *how beautiful . . . at least to us*: Maupassant was highly susceptible to this kind of beauty and may well have heard the story told in the cosmopolitan milieux he was frequenting at the time *chez* the Comtesse Potocka and others. Later, he himself was to fall deeply under the spell of the Russian Marie Barshkitseff.

REGRET

First published in 1883.

1. *Mantes*: The delightfully named Mantes-la-Jolie lies on the Seine and is the administrative centre of the Seine-et-Oise.

2. *écarté*: See p. 306, note 19.

MINOR TRAGEDY

First published in 1883 as 'Humble drâme'.

1. *Sancy*: Puy de Sancy, at 1886 metres the highest peak of the Massif du Mont-Dore in the Auvergne and the Massif Central.
2. *Notre-Dame-de-Vassivière*: A small chapel and place of pilgrimage west of Besse-en-Chandesse.
3. *Lake Pavin*: A crater-type lake some four kilometres from Besse-en-Chandesse.
4. *Château de Murol*: Surrounded by spectacular Auvergnat scenery, the ruins of this château from the thirteenth to fourteenth century stand dramatically on a cliff and form a fitting analogy to the emotionally bruised and battered old lady.
5. *Lake Chambon*: A barrage lake created by a stream of volcanic lava interrupting the flow of the river Couze.

THE CHRISTENING

First published in 1884 as 'Le baptême'.

This story was dedicated to Antoine Guillemet (1842–1918) a painter, disciple of Monet and of Corot. He was admired by Manet for his still-lifes. He initially used the Normandy coast as the inspiration for his studies of landscape and was considered by Maupassant to be a master.

1. *sugared almonds*: Known as *dragées*, from the Greek *tragemata*, meaning desserts, these sweetmeats have been known since earliest times. In 177 B.C. the illustrious Fabiani distributed them to the populace in celebration of special occasions within the family. Some are made with windfall almonds, some with hazelnuts or pistachios. Others contain a few drops of liqueur and a chocolate, almond or filbert paste. Coloured pale pink, pale blue or white, in France they are still offered in little presentation cornets at weddings, christenings and first communions.

COWARD

First published in 1884 as 'Un lâche'.

1. *a duel*: Duels and duelling were topics dear to Maupassant's literary heart and used by him as the subject of another short story ('Un duel') published the previous year. This was also the year he wrote the preface to a work on pistol-shooting (*Les tireurs au pistolet*) by a well-known *boulevardier*, the Baron Ludovic de

Vaux. An excellent swordsman and crack shot himself, Maupassant's own opinion of the custom is far from approving. Though illegal, duels were still fairly common and Maupassant narrowly escaped having to fight one with the symbolist poet and novelist Jean Lorrain, whom he accused of plagiarizing his own novel *Bel-Ami*.

2. *Tortoni's*: One of the grander of the Parisian cafés the development of which during the nineteenth century as influential social and political venues it is difficult to overestimate. Founded in 1798 and situated on the corner of the boulevard des Italiens and the rue Taitbout, Tortoni's had begun by catering to the needs of stockbrokers and businessmen. By Maupassant's time, it had lost some of its lustre but remained popular with sportsmen. Famous for the delicacy of its ice cream.

3. *Châteauvaillard's duelling code*: The Comte de Châteauvaillard published in 1836 his *Essai sur le duel*, translated into English in 1840 as 'The Code of Duelling'.

4. *Baron de Vaux's book of marksmen*: See note 1 above.

5. *Gastine-Renette*: To this day one of the best gunsmiths in Paris.

ROSE

First published in 1884.

1. *landau*: Designed to carry four passengers, this horse-drawn carriage has two hoods which may be raised or lowered as desired.

2. *Cannes*: This resort and its flower festival, as important in Maupassant's time as now (when it stages the International Film Festival), are associated with several local festivals at Nice, Menton, Grasse, etc., centred on the perfume industry and including battles of flowers.

IDYLL

First published in 1884 as 'Idylle'.

1. *'I'm from Casale'*: Before the unification of Italy, Asti and Casale were part of the kingdom of Piedmont and Sardinia.

MOTHER SAUVAGE

First published in 1884 as 'La mère Sauvage'.

1. *This was in 1869*: In other words, two years before the outbreak of the Franco-Prussian war.

MADAME HUSSON'S ROSE KING

First published in 1887, as 'Le rosier de Madame Husson'.

1. This *conte* has been the subject of many adaptations including a film version by Marcel Pagnol in 1950. Eric Crozier used it to form the basis of his libretto for Benjamin Britten's opera, *Albert Herring*.

2. *the poor crippled iron beast*: Accidents were a relatively common occurrence in the early days of the railway. Maupassant's comparison of the locomotive to a fallen horse anticipates the famously harrowing derailment scene in Zola's *La Bête humaine*, published three years later.

3. *what Lucullus was to Cicero*: Lucullus was a Roman consul in 74 B.C. and conqueror of Mithridates. Having retired from military affairs, he devoted himself to a life of indolence and luxury, living in a style of extraordinary magnificence.

4. *a Crassane pear from a Duchesse*: A Crassane is a very soft, sweet and juicy pear which comes into season late in the year, around November to December. The Duchesse is also soft and renowned for its extremely delicate flavour.

5. *between Balzac and Eugène Sue*: Honoré de Balzac (1799–1850) was a powerful and prolific novelist and author of *La Comédie humaine*, a series of novels remarkable for the scope of their social realism. Balzac's interest in the theories of Mesmer, Gall, Lavater and Swedenborg are reflected in the work, which categorizes its large number of characters as representatives of all types and classes in French society during the Consulate, the Empire, the Restoration and the July Monarchy. Some of the better known titles include: *Le Père Goriot, Gobseck, Eugénie Grandet, Les Illusions perdues, La Cousine Bette, Le Cousin Pons, Les Chouans* and many more.

   Eugène Sue (1804–57) was an immensely popular writer of sensational novels depicting Parisian low-life.

6. *between the Apollo of Belvedere and the statue of General Blanmont*: The Apollo of Belvedere (Museum of the Vatican) is an ancient statue of the Greek god of light, reputed to represent in sculpture the ideal male form. General Blanmont lived from 1770–1846. A marble statue of this son of Gisors stands beneath the castle there.

7. *Baron Davillier . . . Hispano-Arabic pottery*: Jean-Charles, Baron Davillier (1823–83), great patron of the arts who donated his collection to the Louvre.

8. *Charles Brainne ... Charles Lapierre*: These two witty and powerful newspapermen married the two extremely sought-after daughters of H. Rivoire, former editor of the *Mémorial de Rouen*. The paper later became the *Nouvelliste de Rouen* to which Maupassant was a frequent contributor.

9. *Rose King*: The tradition of choosing a Rose Queen, like the English May Queen, dates from very early times and the most famous celebrations of this event in France were traditionally those held at Nanterre. These celebrations endured well into the 1960s in many places, including Saint-Denis, Hay-les-Roses, etc. The irony lost on Madame Husson, not to mention the abbé, is that they are clearly pagan in origin.

10. *Madame Husson*: In real life the name of a friend of Flaubert.

11. *Fête Dieu*: (Corpus Christi) Feast of the Holy Sacrament instituted in 1264 by Pope Urban IV and celebrated on the Thursday following the Whitsun octave.

12. *grande armée*: The army of Napoleon.

13. *Henry Monnier*: Henri Monnier (1805–77), writer and caricaturist, creator of Joseph Prudhomme, the prosperous, self-satisfied and pompous exemplar of the petty bourgeoisie under the July Monarchy.

14. *Bouffé, the stained-glass artist*: The important Gisors figures that Marambot is shocked to find his old schoolfriend has not heard of become increasingly obscure as Maupassant develops his parody of provincial pride.

ENCOUNTER

First published in 1884 as 'Rencontre' and dedicated to Edouard Rod, a Swiss critic and novelist linked with the naturalist movement.

1. *coupé*: In this context, a first-class railway carriage usually unconnected by corridor to the rest of the train.

2. *'How triumphant are the mornings of the young!', as the poet has it*: A line by Oliver Goldsmith which appears to approximate 'Quand on est jeune on a des matins triomphants,' a quotation from Victor Hugo's *Booz endormi*, part of his collection of epic poems, *La légende des siècles*, and cited more than once in Maupassant's work.

HAPPINESS

First published in 1885 as 'Le bonheur'.

A BIT OF THE OTHER

First published in 1885 as 'Imprudence'.

1. *cabaret*: In expressing her desire to go to a real cabaret, Henriette, like many a bourgeois wife in Maupassant's fiction, hopes to experience the thrill of *s'encanailler* – slumming or mixing with raffish Bohemia. In Montmartre particularly, a number of these establishments were in full swing.

2. *a massive mirror ... its clear glass*: The place to which her husband in fact takes her is based on the Café Riche in one of whose rooms there was just such a mirror the surface of which was crazed with names, dates and messages scratched by the diamonds of the many women once reflected in it.

LOVE

First published in 1886 as 'Amour'.

HAUTOT & SON

First published in 1889 as 'Hautot père et fils'.

1. *tilbury*: A light, two-wheeled open carriage for two passengers.

2. *Paris Exhibition*: This would have been the Paris Exhibition of 1878. The Great International or Universal Exhibition of 1889 was to open five months after the publication of this tale. Maupassant was fiercely opposed to the construction of the Eiffel Tower which was one of the latter's main attractions.

NEW YEAR'S GIFT

First published in 1887 as 'Les étrennes'.

1. In this story Maupassant is subtly suggesting the degree of calculation involved in male–female relationships of the time as well as the futility of attempting to assess emotional capital. There is a tradition in France, similar to that of the Christmas box or bonus, of offering gifts of money at the beginning of the year to various individuals who may have called at the house to perform certain services during the past year. This cross-cultural tradition express-

ing a mixture of gratitude and propitiation dates from earliest times and is connected with the notion of looking both ways, forward into the future and backwards into the past, as well as socially both up and down. The gifts themselves are known in French as *étrennes*. In Roman times, as a mark of deference, magistrates were sent branches cut from a wood sacred to Strena or Strenia. Later the offering changed to dates or honey, and later still, to money. Similarly, *étrenner* means to use something for the first time. In children's culture, this survived until some years ago in the practice of being pinched for luck on wearing something new.

THE HORLA

This is the first version, published in 1886 as 'Le horla', of a tale to which Maupassant returned the following year and whose theme reflects his growing fear of madness.

1. *Horla*: A Maupassant amalgam of the French *hors*, meaning 'out of' as in *hors de combat*, and '*là*' meaning 'there'. It suggests the idea of something out of or beyond oneself, and possibly a kind of double. Here Maupassant is close to examining his own state of mind during one of the hallucinatory periods which by this time were becoming more and more frequent and disturbing. Some critics have also connected the word with the cholera which swept through the south of France in 1884.

2. *Musset*: Alfred de Musset (1810–57). With Victor Hugo, Alfred de Vigny and Alphonse de Lamartine, one of the four great figures of the Romantic movement in French literature and one of Maupassant's favourite poets.

3. *Nuit de Mai*: Part of de Musset's series of lyrics *Les nuits* in which he dwells on the anguish suffered through disappointment in love. He was for a time one of George Sand's many lovers.

4. *An epidemic ... or occasionally milk*: Transposed to a distant and exotic culture, the newspaper report reflects a modish contemporary preoccupation in France and elsewhere with vampirism.

DUCHOUX

First published in 1887.

1. *landau*: See p. 313, note 1.

2. *Duchoux*: Literally 'of the cabbage'. A euphemism for illegitimacy reminiscent of the English 'found under a gooseberry bush'.

3. *Duchouxe*: Highlights the southern character of her speech in which the final 'x' is pronounced as in 'books', whereas in received pronunciation it is silent as in 'shoe'.

4. *fichu*: A shawl worn around the shoulders, crossed over the chest and tied at the back.

THE *LULL-A-BYE*

First published in 1889 as '*L'endormeuse*'.

1. *had taken their own lives*: Maupassant's correspondence at this time reveals him to be in the lowest of spirits, anxious about his own poor health, repelled by the contemporary political scene and increasingly worried about the deterioration in the mental health of his brother, Hervé, now institutionalized in Lyon. Several other stories of this period take suicide as their theme and he is clearly now contemplating putting an end to his own unhappy life.

2. *gentleman's club*: Maupassant uses the word *cercle*. It has been described by Richard Burton (see Further Reading) as 'the bourgeois form of sociability *par excellence*, a matrix of political, social and intellectual consciousness as fundamental for the middle classes as the *salon* had been for the old aristocracy.' See p. 313, note 2 on the rise of cafés in 'Coward'.

3. *the Great Exhibition of 1889*: As well as marking the centenary of the Revolution, the Exhibition was a celebration of the fruits of both French colonialism and scientific discovery. Maupassant's attitude to it fluctuated. He saw it as an excellent place to take a woman for a day or for an evening out, but it also represented to him something vulgar and showy which he often deplored.

4. *General Boulanger*: Georges Boulanger (1837–91) was Minister for War in 1886. Having attempted a coup d'état which failed, he fled to Brussels and, ironically, two years after the publication of this tale, committed suicide at the graveside of his mistress.

5. *Sarah Bernhardt ... and Paulus*: Sarah Bernhardt (1844–1923) was one of the most famous of all actresses, said to have 'a golden voice of indescribable beauty'. Judic was a French actress at the height of her success during 1888. Théo (Louise Piccolo) was a contemporary singer of operetta, and Granier an interpreter of Offenbach.

Monsieur de Reszké was one of two Polish brothers who became well-known singers in France. They gave their name to a cigarette sold in England until the 1950s. Coquelin was another contemporary duo of actor brothers, Mounet-Sully (Jean Sully Mounet) a great tragic actor of the period, and Paulus a *caf'-conc'* singer of the time.

6. *Dumas, Meilhac, Halévy and Sardou*: For Dumas see p. 307, note 4. Henri Meilhac (1831–97) was a contemporary playwright who, in conjunction with Halévy, wrote the libretto of *La Belle Hélène*, one of the most brilliant successes of the period. Ludovic Halévy (1834–1908) was the librettist of, among others, Offenbach's *La Vie parisienne*, and writer of drawing-room comedies such as *Frou-frou* and *La petite marquise*, plays which were a mixture of farce, irony and pathos. Victorien Sardou (1831–1908) wrote comedies and historical dramas characterized by complicated plots and highly skilful construction. Most notable were *Les Pattes de mouche*, *Divorçons* and *Fédora* in which Bernhardt played the title role. His melodrama *Tosca* was used by Puccini as the basis of his opera of the same name.

7. *Monsieur Becque*: Henri Becque (1837–99) was highly influential in the development of modern French theatre. In his work, plot is of minor importance in comparison to the faithful representation of life. The play referred to here is probably *Les Corbeaux* ('The Crows'), one of the first naturalist dramas to appear on the French stage.

8. *Comédie Française*: The first state theatre of France, officially named the Théâtre Français and known also after its founder as the Maison de Molière. Its nucleus was the company of actors established by him in 1658. Still in operation to this day.

9. *Figaro*: Then, as now, one of the leading French dailies.

10. *Revue des Deux Mondes*: Founded in 1829 as a review largely devoted to home and foreign affairs. Acquired in 1831 by François Buloz who developed its literary and philosophical interests and made it one of the foremost journals of its kind in Europe. Contributors included Balzac, Hugo, de Musset, George Sand, Alfred de Vigny and Sainte-Beuve. It is still one of the best-known French literary reviews and appears fortnightly.

11. *Vichy pastilles*: Little pastilles which dissolve on the tongue and, taken after meals, act as an aid to digestion.

12. *garde-champêtre*: An authorized agent of the State via the local *commune* and responsible for reporting breaches of law and order in rural hunting and fishing areas and for maintaining public order there. In this case something akin to a water-bailiff.

320 NOTES

MOTHER OF INVENTION

First published in 1890 as 'Inutile beauté'.

1. *victoria*: A four-wheeled open carriage drawn by two horses.
2. *Montmorency*: Forest in the Seine-et-Oise where a house in which Jean-Jacques Rousseau once lived still stands. With its wooded parkland it is a popular weekend retreat and a favourite place to take children for pony and donkey rides.
3. *coupé*: See p. 310, note 1 ('Awakening').

WHO KNOWS?

First published in 1890 as 'Qui sait?'

Maupassant is clearly demonstrating in this tale his increasing terror of madness and, as in *The Horla*, a growing paranoia and fear of inevitability itself. Paul Dukas, twenty-five years earlier, had used the mysterious and threatening proliferation of avenging objects in *The Sorcerer's Apprentice*, as in the 1990s the protagonist of Bret Easton Ellis' *American Psycho* is followed home for ten blocks by a park bench.

1. *Sigurd*: A highly popular and fantastical opera written after the Wagnerian style by Ernest Reyer (1823–1909).
2. *Nevers pottery*: The manufacture of Nevers-type pottery in Rouen was a huge commercial success and, after the substitution of china for silver tableware, became highly sought after.
3. *Moustiers ware*: Moustiers-Sainte-Marie (Basses-Alpes). Famous for its greyish-blue-toned pottery frequently depicting mountain scenes as well as grotesques. Highly valuable.

LAID TO REST

First published in 1891 as 'Les tombales'.

1. *'Tombales'*: A play on words, connected with the tomb and *tomber* (to fall) as well as *horizontale* which was a common euphemism for prostitute or fallen woman.
2. *I watch what's going on around me*: There is a whole literature on this activity known in French as '*flâner*'. One of the better known *flâneurs* of Paris was the poet Charles Baudelaire. Some, such as Walter Benjamin (see Further Reading), have seen it as one of the highest expressions of modern civilization and its intelligent deciphering of the city as a system of signs the beginnings of semiology.

3. *Cavaignac's grave ... Jean Goujon ... Louis de Brézé ... Rouen Cathedral*: Eugène Cavaignac (1802–57), President of the Republic in 1848, was a general and one-time governor of Algeria. Referred to here is a statue of him by François Rude, a sculptor of the Romantic school. Jean Goujon was a fellow Norman and sixteenth-century sculptor, famous in particular for his stunning bas-reliefs. Louis de Brézé, Seneschal of Normandy, was married to Diane of Poitiers, and died in 1531. The de Brézé family was one of the oldest in France.

4. *Baudin ... Gautier ... Murger*: Jean-Baptiste Victor Baudin, doctor and politician as well as deputy to the Assemblée Nationale from 1849, was killed on the barricades on 3 December 1851. Théophile Gautier (1811–72), poet, novelist and journalist, was a Romantic and one of the most vociferous of those supporting Victor Hugo (for example at the *bataille d'Hernani*), in an effort to revolutionize French poetic and dramatic conventions. Later became leader of the Parnassian school. Henri Murger (1822–61) was a writer whose talent was for poeticized, sentimental descriptions of humble life or the rackety and precarious existence led by the artists and writers who people his best remembered work, *Scènes de la vie de Bohème*, upon which Puccini's opera, *La Bohème*, is based.

5. *grisettes*: The name given in the first half of the nineteenth century for the young seamstresses, milliners' assistants, laundresses, etc., of the Latin Quarter. They were popularly seen as hard-working, underfed, of easy virtue and always loyal to their lovers.

6. *a pretty little statue by Millet*: Aimé Millet (1819–81), sculptor, not to be confused with Jean-François, painter of *Les Glâneurs*, *L'Angélus*, etc.

7. *not even Labiche or Meilhac*: Eugène Labiche (1815–88) was a playwright whose well-known comedies include *Un chapeau de paille d'Italie* and scores of others. Henri de Meilhac (1831–97) was a French playwright who produced a long series of light comedies, including the best known, *Frou-Frou*.

8. *Paul de Kock*: Paul de Kock (1793–1871), novelist and prolific chronicler of petty bourgeois and student life.

9. *Tonkin*: Region in north-eastern Indo-China or North Vietnam. Scene of major conflict and lengthy war between France and China.

10. *Légion d'honneur*: National distinction instituted by Napoleon in 1802, of which there are five classes: the *Grand-Croix*, *Grand Officier*, *Commandeur*, *Officier*, and *Chevalier*.

THE NECKLACE

First published in 1884 as 'Le Parure'.